Abbie Eaton lives in Derbyshire, England, and is an emerging fantasy author who writes stories about magic, love, and dragons. When not writing or reading all things fantasy, she can be found with her horses (who often resemble dragons themselves!).

📷 instagram.com/abbieeatonauthor
♪ tiktok.com/@abbieeaton

Also by Abbie Eaton

Dragonhart

Shadowhart

Fyrehart

SHADOWHART

ABBIE EATON

One More Chapter
a division of HarperCollins*Publishers* Ltd
1 London Bridge Street
London SE1 9GF
www.harpercollins.co.uk
HarperCollins*Publishers*
Macken House, 39/40 Mayor Street Upper,
Dublin 1, D01 C9W8
This paperback edition 2026

1

First published in Great Britain in ebook format
by HarperCollins*Publishers* 2026
Copyright © Abbie Eaton 2026
Map illustration © Laura Hall

Abbie Eaton asserts the moral right to be identified
as the author of this work

A catalogue record of this book is available from the British Library
ISBN: 978-0-00-871016-3

This novel is entirely a work of fiction. The names, characters and incidents
portrayed in it are the work of the author's imagination. Any resemblance to
actual persons, living or dead, events or localities is entirely coincidental.

Printed and bound in the UK using 100% Renewable Electricity
by CPI Group (UK) Ltd

All rights reserved. No part of this publication may be reproduced, stored in a
retrieval system, or transmitted, in any form or by any means, electronic,
mechanical, photocopying, recording or otherwise, without the prior
permission of the publishers.

Without limiting the exclusive rights of any author, contributor or the publisher
of this publication, any unauthorised use of this publication to train generative
artificial intelligence (AI) technologies is expressly prohibited. HarperCollins
also exercise their rights under Article 4(3) of the Digital Single Market Directive
2019/790 and expressly reserve this publication from the text and data mining
exception.

For the eldest daughters.

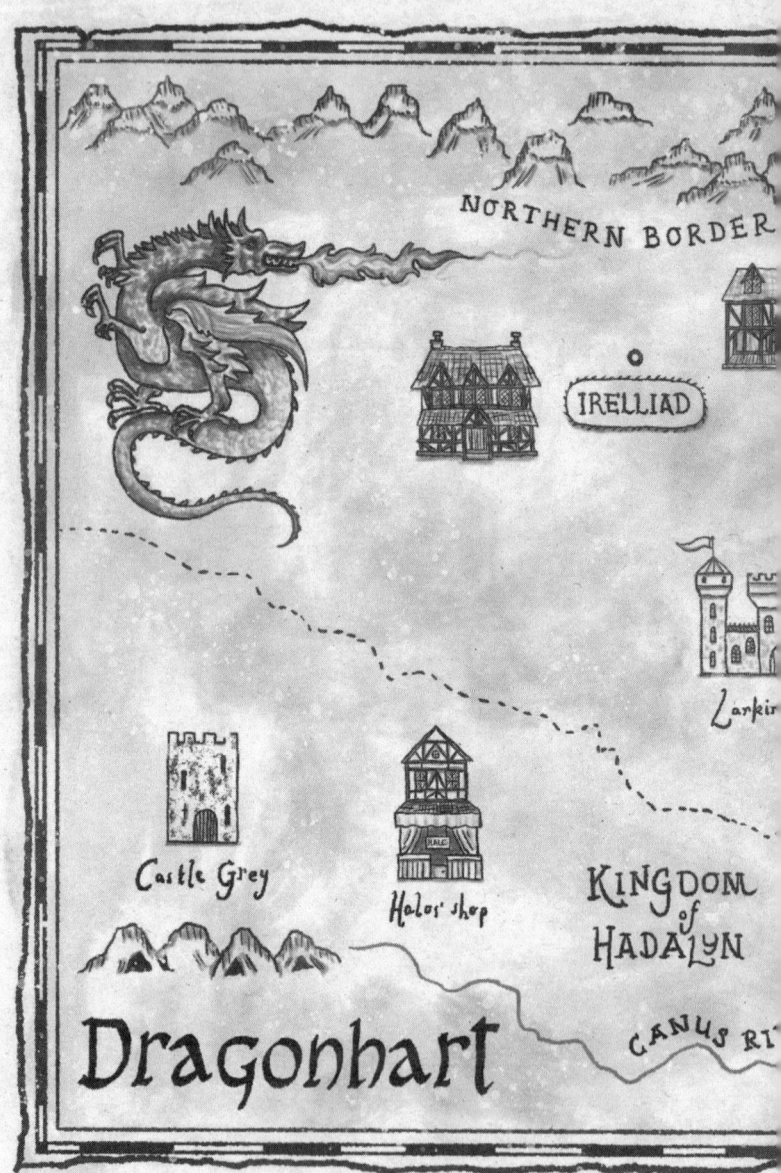

CHAPTER 1

Beyond the Northern Border, nestled in a valley between the mountains, a dragon watches over the kingdom of Flambriar.

Arla Dragonhart had heard the whispers of it, and she'd have to be blind not to notice the dozens of eyes that trailed her as she walked through the city. She only wished she'd brought nicer clothes befitting of the dragon with which she had bonded.

Thara was resting today. She had taken Arla flying for the last three nights. and for wings that hadn't seen the light of day in ... well, Arla didn't know how long actually, she was surprised the dragon hadn't retreated into sleep sooner. She'd have to find somewhere else to be in the middle of the night when the rest of the new kingdom was sleeping. Hark's bed perhaps, if she thought he might actually be in it.

Weeks had passed since the night she had almost bled to death and woken up in this frozen place, and once she had explored the entirety of Claret Hall, she had ventured out into the city. Winding streets were lined by buildings that looked as though they had been carved from the mountains themselves, and smoke rose from their chimneys, clinging to Arla's hair with what she thought might be the loveliest scent of all because this was Flambriar's smoke. It wasn't Kastonia's or Hadalyn's, it belonged to this new kingdom, hidden away from them all.

The people were wary of her – not that she could blame them – and it was an effort to school her face into something that might be construed as neutral when she couldn't manage a pleasant expression. Her reputation as the King's Assassin would follow her across continents, she thought, but that was exactly how it was supposed to be. She'd worked too hard for it not to.

A small head of red ringlets ran towards her, the girl's cheeks pink against the cold. 'Would you like some gloves?'

'Mina—'

The father of the little girl tugged her back before she could get close enough to Arla for her to see the gloves that had been offered. He passed her into the arms of a woman whom Arla presumed was the girl's mother, standing in the doorway of a shop.

She met the man's gaze, careful not to bare her teeth or do something feral as they likely suspected she would. When he only stared at her, she took a slow step forward, careful not to jolt into view the blade sheathed at her waist.

The girl, Mina, watched her, eyes bright and twinkling like the frost that coated everything.

Arla smiled. 'I'd like some gloves very much. What colours do you have?'

Mina's lips parted slightly before widening into a grin that was enough to warm even Arla's battered soul. 'We have red, and black, and purple, and—'

'Purple.' Like a king. Or queen.

'Wait here. I'll get some,' Mina said, ducking out of her mother's arms and rushing back into the little shop.

Arla took half a step back – a surrendering, perhaps, in the face of the girl's parents. They eyed her with a wariness she knew all too well, a wariness she had worked for years to cultivate. She wondered what Cyrus would think of her now, backing down for the sake of some gloves, showing that she did indeed have a heart and wasn't a threat to these people.

The very thought of him filled her blood with fire.

Her king, Cyrus, had known for years that King Elrod of Kastonia was enslaving magic wielders – magics, Hark called them – and sacrificing them in an attempt to harvest their magic for himself. Cyrus had known all the way back in Hadalyn that their sworn enemy was breaking a treaty against the possession of slaves and had done *nothing*.

Mina bounded through the doorway, slipping on the icy ground outside the shop before her father could catch her. The little girl clambered to her feet, hands out in front of her to present Arla with gloves the colour of royalty.

She took them gently, her cool fingers brushing over Mina's own gloved ones. 'They're beautiful.'

'I helped make them.'

Arla met the girl's gaze and saw the bright fire of youth burning there, its innocence enough to tug at Arla's heart.

'Well, you've done a beautiful job,' Arla said, slipping her fingers inside the soft wool. 'How much are they?'

Not that she knew how she was going to pay for them because all of the clothes and books and jewellery she had purchased in the last few days had been billed directly to Claret Hall. She had no idea what currency was even in place in Flambriar and how Hark had managed to set it up.

When Mina didn't reply, Arla lifted her eyes to find the girl had retreated back into her father's hold, her tiny hand held tightly in his.

'Consider them a gift,' he said. 'From her.'

Her heart stuttered only a second before Arla nodded once at the man and leaned down to thank his daughter. 'Thank you very much, Mina, but take this as a thank-you.'

It was a lovely bracelet. Solid gold and tiny enough that it wouldn't look out of place on the child's wrist. It was one from a collection she had at Castle Grey back in Hadalyn – it had been a gift, actually, from Cyrus for her sixteenth birthday.

'Thank you, Lady Reinhart,' Mina's mother said, stepping forwards, her hand outstretched as if she would grasp Arla's before thinking better of it.

'It's Arla, please.' She offered them half a smile before turning back towards the main road that wound through the city, and though she was used to having eyes on her at all times, this was different. The people stopped and stared as she passed, eyes flickering between the purple gloves on her hands and the shop she had just visited. She didn't dare to hope that the people were beginning to trust her; but tolerating her was a start.

The streets on her route back to Claret Hall had already started to freeze again despite the sun still being high enough in the sky that Arla reckoned they had around three hours left of light. She almost looked forward to it – how the sun would dip beyond the mountains and leave the valley that Flambriar rested in doused in dark night. But the city in the daylight was still beautiful. The magics – she really needed to speak to Hark and ask if they could be named something less ... obvious – had carved the city into a labyrinth of markets and shops and restaurants, the number of people here higher than Arla could have ever dreamed. It was sickening, really, that Elrod had been enslaving these people in such numbers. And for so many years ...

Frost glittered as she walked, but her hands were warm in her new gloves whilst she surveyed every corner of Flambriar. It was the same routine she did every day. It was her job to keep these people safe. She had been an assassin for a king who betrayed her; she wouldn't let these people down ever again. Water gurgled in the river and streams that flowed through the city, the stone bridges arching over them so intricately that it was clear there was no way they had been created without magic. It would snow tonight – the scent of it hung in the air, mingling with the sweet spices and woodsmoke that travelled through the sky. Laughter still chased her on the winding path up to Claret Hall and it reminded her too keenly of the two children she had left behind in Hadalyn. Halos's children.

Halos hadn't replied to any of Arla's letters.

The barracks perched halfway up the mountain, slumbering beneath Claret Hall and were its first line of defence should the enemy come knocking. Not that the barracks housed an army yet, just a group of men that had stayed loyal to Hark when his father had ruined Kastonia and begun the enslavement of magics.

But it was better than nothing. All armies had to begin somewhere, she knew that. And even if their accommodation and training ring were lacking the elegance and solidity with which the rest of Flambriar had been built, it would come with time. She was no queen – and didn't want to be – but she had been inside Castle Grey long enough, had spied on council meetings for too many years not to understand the work that went into running a kingdom. Especially one that was on the brink of war.

She shrugged off the thought of armour and the sharp pain in her side that reared up like a phantom to remind her she had almost been killed, and climbed the winding steps up the side of the mountain. The courtyard was bustling with Hark's newly appointed army, some of them running through drills she had mastered at the age of thirteen, whilst others unbuckled the straps holding swords and blades like the ones she kept sheathed beneath her cloak. It was easy to slip through the chaos of the courtyard. Her feet were almost through the door to the castle before Vetta spotted her and whinnied.

Arla owed her life to that horse. For years, the mare had carried her into kingdoms and jobs that had put both their lives at risk, and Vetta had never faltered. It was more than Arla could say for herself.

'I'll be back later,' she murmured under her breath, certain the mare had heard her as she tossed her head and retreated to the back of the stable.

Her boots were certainly too dirty to be walking the pale stone floors of the castle ... hall, whatever this place was, but it had never stopped her in Hadalyn, and she wasn't about to change now. The corridors at this low level of Claret Hall, though not glass-roofed and open to the sky like the rest of the building, were well lit and airy, punctuated by a series of solid wooden doors that she had explored on her second night here. She stopped outside one of those doors, the voices inside reaching her before she had turned the doorknob.

Inside, the scent of ink and parchment hit her as the six people within stood, each of them raising their fists over their hearts in a show of respect she was still certain she didn't deserve.

'Welcome, Dragonhart,' a short man with soft grey hair said.

Arla strode across the room, flicking through the pile of envelopes and sealed scrolls on a desk the colour of cherries.

'I've told you to stop doing that, Noah. Same goes for the rest of you.' She struggled to keep the bite out of her voice, though it wasn't directed at them. It was because there wasn't a single item on this desk with her name on it.

'I'm sorry, milady, we still haven't received word from Hadalyn.'

The same words. Every day.

The urge to palm the blade at her waist was probably not normal, but she couldn't help brushing her fingers over the hilt anyway.

'I can send another letter, if you like? Perhaps they aren't reaching Hadalyn. The mountains are difficult to navigate, even for our birds.'

There wasn't a doubt in Arla's mind that Halos was receiving her letters. Arla had seen the falcons kept in Flambriar, and she was certain they could make it across these mountains and into Hadalyn blindfolded. Halos simply didn't want to talk to her.

And could Arla blame her? After the story Elrod had spun to Cyrus and the rest of Hadalyn – that Arla had corrupted Hark and died at Larkire Palace during her attempted escape – it was no wonder the letters were going unanswered. They likely believed someone was impersonating the King's Assassin, and the letters were a ruse to launch the kingdoms into war.

None of it was Noah's fault.

'Send another letter and send this with it.' It was an effort to dig the small wooden horse out of her training leathers, and even harder to hand it over to Noah. 'If Halos doesn't believe us after this, there's no hope of bringing her to Flambriar.'

Noah was silent as he drafted the letter, sealing the wooden horse inside a bundle of parchments and tying it together with rough string that the falcons would be able to hook with their talons.

'Thank you, Noah. Let me know—'

'The moment we receive a reply I will find you personally, Dragonhart.'

CHAPTER 2

The top floors of Claret Hall were filled with gauzy curtains and the scent of cinnamon, the whole building a vision of glass and wood and stone. Sunlight streamed through the panes of glass that made up the ceilings of the castle, and the flawless hallways spoke of the most ethereal place Arla had ever seen.

Hark had to be around here somewhere. His scouting group was back, and the soldiers in the courtyard were heading back to the barracks.

'Arla Dragonhart.' Two huge arms enveloped her, lifting her off the ground and spinning her so quickly she was surprised she didn't vomit.

The second her feet returned to the floor she whirled on Sebastian. 'You ever lay a hand on me again, I'll cut your arms off.'

Sebastian exploded into laughter, his hair a rich brown in this light which only brought out the green of his eyes. He was handsome, really. There was a kinship developing between the two of them, something that was brotherly, almost. Gods, she was becoming soft!

'What have you been up to today? Scaring the villagers?'

She elbowed him. Hard. 'One, this place is far too big to be called a village. It rivals Hadalyn's capital. And two, who says they aren't the ones scaring *me*?'

Sebastian snorted, earning the pair of them a startled glance from one of the new maids Hark had recently employed. 'I don't believe you're scared of anything. The people probably think you're about to bite them.'

'Good.' She smiled sweetly.

'Care for a drink?' Sebastian said. She hadn't meant to head in the direction of the sitting room they had all been frequenting each night, but it seemed it was where she would end up, anyway.

'It's three o'clock.'

'Your point, Reinhart?'

Hark's crew and her own maids were still adjusting to her new moniker, often fluttering between using her old surname and the name of the ancient bloodline from which she had descended. *Dragonhart*. It felt right.

Seb fell into step beside her, the swords sheathed at his waist knocking her legs as they walked. It was the calmest she'd felt in days.

'Noah said you were after someone to train with. I'd be up for that. Might do me some good to train against Hadalyn's famed assassin.'

'Noah needs to keep his mouth shut.' She didn't know why she had started telling the man in the office downstairs these things. Like how she was desperate for a response from Halos and how she could feel a tornado brewing inside her because she hadn't trained in ... gods, it was *weeks*!

'He just wants to impress you, you know.'

'The gods know why. Everyone else is scared to be within ten feet of me.' Which was the way she liked it.

'Yeah, well, you aren't exactly approachable, Arla.'

'Where's Hark?' She'd had enough of searching what felt like this entire city for him. He'd promised to have dinner with her.

'With the scouting group. I think he's briefing them on tomorrow's events.'

Of course he was.

Hark's fear had been a palpable thing, staining everything in sight ever since Arla had taken a sword to the side for him during his rescue from Larkire Palace. He worried constantly that his father would send Kastonia's army after them, or that Arla wasn't properly healed and might keel over at a moment's notice. But once the fear of Arla collapsing every time she stood up had eased, and the group had taken the time to digest everything that had happened, the subject of Elrod and his army had sparked an argument in Claret Hall that had resulted in a vase being smashed and Thara landing on the balcony railings believing that Arla was in danger.

Hark had been adamant his father would send an army after them, that he would seek revenge for Arla's actions at Larkire Palace and the way Hark and his crew had managed to free every man, woman, and child that bore magical blood from Elrod's prison camp on the northern border. Arla had argued that the people needed stability now, that they needed to feel safe and free from fear of Kastonia's king. Hark had told her it would never happen.

And so he had taken to scouting the neighbouring mountains with a group of his soldiers every spare hour they had. Watching, waiting. Looking for anything that might signal

Kastonia were coming to attack Flambriar. Arla hadn't seen him properly in days.

'So why aren't you down there with him?'

Sebastian opened the door to the sitting room. Decorated in creams and wood, with soft settees, it was always a welcome sight when Arla was still getting her strength back.

'Because it's boring. We know the drill. We go out, we see nothing, we freeze our balls off, and we come back. Same shit every day.'

Seb opened the drinks cabinet and poured each of them a drink, a whiskey so strong it burned her throat seconds after she had swallowed it. She was about to ask after his offer to train with her when Kase floated through the door.

'Drinking in the day, Reinhart? I'd have thought you were above that.'

Arla rolled her tongue over her teeth, setting the glass down beside her as she leant back in the settee. 'Well, I knew you'd be here and not even the gods could persuade me to sit through your company sober. And it's 'Dragonhart' to you.'

Kase's eyes flashed as she crossed the room to look out of the arched windows, but Arla didn't miss the smirk that Kase bit between her lips. There was definitely a respect between the two women. Kase had fussed around Arla in the days after her waking, but the second Arla had been strong enough not to risk dying, the pair had settled back into that prickly understanding that had been formed the moment they'd set eyes on one another.

'Another day of scaring the townsfolk?'

Oh, how she'd missed this.

'Too late, Seb already asked—'

'Enough, please. As much as I enjoy watching you two go claw to claw with one another, it's been a long day,' Seb said, striding over to Kase and grabbing her face between his large hands. 'Play nice, Kasey.'

The speed with which she drew her blade was enough to rival Arla's skill. 'You ever call me that again, Sebastian, I'll tell the dockmaster's son in Vorstrum that you're sleeping with one of the sailors.'

'You wound me,' he said, collapsing beside Arla as if Kase had struck him.

'Not crying over the man at the docks again, is he?' Jack's voice pierced the laughter as he entered the sitting room, cane in one hand, his limp still there despite the hours Arla knew he spent with the healers. She wondered, often, if he would ever recover from the magical injury he'd sustained trying to free the magics from one of Elrod's camps.

'Not yet, but he will be,' Kase said sweetly, and Arla had to swallow the laugh that rose in her throat. She couldn't tell exactly when she had become a part of this ... family, but it warmed her ice-cold heart.

Jack inched closer to Kase by the window, despite the effort standing was clearly inflicting on his leg. Kase's shoulders tensed, her chest rising and falling more noticeably than it had before. At least Arla had that over her.

'Another letter came today,' Jack said with a sigh, his eyes fixed on something in the distance. 'Wasting sickness is spreading through Kastonia again. They can't get on top of it quickly enough and Hadalyn is struggling under the weight of those who are fleeing there.'

The letters Jack received from contacts in Hadalyn and Kastonia always managed to add a layer of solemnity to everything. The kingdoms were still suffering under the wrath of the gods as a consequence of Elrod angering them with his persecution of magics. It was all the worse because, well, it should have all stopped by now.

There was a prophecy that spoke of Arla uniting the kingdoms. It said that she would be the one to put an end to the poverty and sickness that was spreading. She thought she'd managed it by freeing the magics and putting an end to Elrod's schemes. She'd thought that would be enough to appease the gods.

Clearly, it wasn't.

And she didn't have a gods-damned clue what she was supposed to do next.

She swallowed the worry, eager to be rid of Jack's depressing news. 'You're all boring me. I'll see you later,' she said, rising from the settee with the slick surety of an assassin ... and plucked the blade that came flying at her out of the air without blinking.

'You know,' she began, turning to face Jack who had the common sense to look impressed. 'You really shouldn't commit murder on this carpet. Blood is awfully difficult to remove.'

'You know, I still think you should have been a princess.'

Her knees threatened to buckle under her and her heart was thrashing in her chest as that lovely voice filled her ears. Hark Stappen filled the room, even as he leant against the doorframe, a single brow arched as he ran a hand through his tousled hair.

Arla's mouth was dry and her tongue was tied as he met her gaze across the room and *winked* at her.

Gods!

'Princesses don't kill people,' she managed to say, twisting Jack's blade between her fingers.

'Mine does.'

Okay, she really needed to go and stand outside for a moment.

'Ugh. Do we really have to listen to this?' Kase complained, pouring herself a glass of that burning whiskey.

'Feel free to leave,' Arla hissed, but she couldn't summon malice into her voice, not when Hark was looking at her like that.

'Gladly,' Kase said, tossing her silver braid over her shoulder and sauntering out of the room, her arm brushing Hark's in a way that made Arla want to bury the blade right between her shoulders.

Hark crossed the distance between them and lifted his hand to her face. She let him touch her cheek. Allowed the gentle scrape of calloused hands over her skin. 'How are you?'

'Hungry. Ready to kill Kase.' She didn't miss the choked sound Jack tried to mask as he swallowed his drink. 'Oh, and I got some new gloves today.' She pulled the purple gloves from inside her jacket, savouring the feel of the wool between her fingers.

'The people are beginning to like you,' Hark said, moving around her to retrieve the bottle from Sebastian's hands and gulp directly from it.

'They don't trust me. You haven't told them I'm not a threat.' Hark looked at her, the dark rings beneath his eyes more pronounced than they had been yesterday when she'd caught sight of him in the hallway. He was working too hard. And she wasn't working hard enough. Her fingers drifted to the golden brooch pinned to her jacket – a flame encased in a heart. A *dragonhart*.

She was sure the brooch heated at her touch.

'I'm not their king. I don't tell them who they can and can't trust. You almost dying for them should be enough to earn it.' There was a command in his voice she wasn't used to hearing, and truly, she didn't like it at all. He could deny being their king all he liked, but when he slept in a castle that looked over the valley like a dragon protecting a nest, it was hard to deny.

'Were the mountains clear today?' she asked, keen to move the conversation away from Hark's reluctance to step up as ruler.

'Yeah, we'll check the other side again tomorrow.'

Seb opened his mouth to say something and then thought better of it. He caught Arla's eye though, and it seemed to her like a warning not to say what she was about to.

She'd never listened to warnings anyway.

'No one will attack us here, Hark.'

He whirled to face her, and it was so reminiscent of how things had been only months before; how they had spent their whole lives hating one another and sending each other those looks filled with hatred.

She stepped closer to him. Not a chance would she back down.

He looked her dead in the eyes, his own the same icy shade as his father's. 'You are naïve if you think they won't. You made my father look a fool and Hadalyn thinks you betrayed them by being with me. Arla, don't be stupid.'

She settled into that calm place and let the fire within her rise to the surface. Just a taste of it. Just to remind him who she was.

In a lethally soft voice she said, 'I am not naïve, and I am not stupid, *Stappen*. You're forgetting who I am and the things I have done. Nothing will threaten this kingdom.'

His eyes flickered slightly, a yielding she took more delight in than she should have. She didn't know when she would be able to leave that side of her behind – perhaps never. It had served her well for nine years. It had made her the best. It was ingrained on her soul.

'I'll see you at dinner.' Her arm brushed his on the way out of the room and she ignored the electricity that flooded through her body at the contact.

∽

Her feet smacked loudly against the floors of the hall as she made her way to her rooms. Her mind spun with the argument with Hark.

How had it managed to send her heart racing and bring forth a twisting feeling in her stomach?

Why had it rattled her so much? She was King's Assassin; she was *the* dragonhart. A little disagreement over whether there should be scouts in the mountain shouldn't have her wanting to force Hark into submission, and it shouldn't have made her delight in the way he backed down just then.

She knew why though. She knew she was so flustered because this wasn't an argument with a king or a courtier. This was *Hark*. Hark, who was the other half of her heart. Hark, who was the only person in the world who could leave her powerless in the face of her own emotions.

She hated the vulnerability.

Because that was exactly what she was feeling. That was why she had left the room before her voice could crack in front of their friends. Arguing with Hark exposed those soft parts of her heart she wished to keep concealed – the ones she reserved only for him – and it *scared her*.

She shouldn't have walked away. She shouldn't have brought up the topic of Elrod's army finding them. That wasn't what people who loved each other did. Perhaps she should go back. Perhaps she should go and find him and apologise and tell him—

What is wrong with me?

She closed the doors to her room behind her, inhaling the soft silence of the glass-roofed room. This wasn't her — this wasn't who she thought she had always been. Arla Reinhart had always been hard and unyielding. Had always put her own feelings above other people's.

To give way for someone else, to allow that slither of vulnerability to show itself for Hark...?

She was scared.

And the only place she could fathom going in order to dissolve that fear, was into the arms of the man who had caused it.

CHAPTER 3
HARK

'She could eat you alive, you know,' Jack said, settling in the chair opposite where Hark was slumped in the settee beside Seb.

'I know.' Hark sighed, rubbing his hands across his face. She could do more than eat him alive. She had bewitched him like some sort of sorcerer. He would carve out his own heart if she asked him to, he thought. 'But I won't let the people down again. If I have to go out every day into those mountains for the rest of my life, I'll do it. I owe them that much.'

'You aren't your father, Hark. They know it wasn't you. But you can't keep this up. You're exhausted.' He loved Seb like a brother, but in that moment, he wished he would keep his opinions to his fucking self.

'Elrod was after the magics before. There's nothing to say he won't come for them here too.'

'If that happens, we'll be ready for them. You have the King's Assassin, for gods' sake. She went up against Kastonia and broke you out of your own castle. If anyone can keep the people safe, it's her.'

He'd known Seb had taken a liking to Arla, but for him to defend her as loyally as he would Hark ... it meant more than he had the words to explain.

Hark couldn't stop the laughter that bubbled in his throat. 'She's something else, isn't she?'

'Who'd have thought it?' Jack said, rising to his feet with the help of his cane. It made something in Hark's stomach flip. 'The King's Assassin and the Crown Prince of Kastonia.'

'Ex Crown Prince of Kastonia. There's no way in these gods-damned kingdoms his father will let him stay as heir. Little Reuben is up.'

Little Reuben. His little brother – though there was nothing 'little' about him now. At nineteen, he was as tall as Hark and had enough charm for the both of them. The memory of his brother laughing with Arla over dinner filled his ears with a roaring that threatened to send him jumping off the balcony.

'If he's still alive.' The thought made his heart stutter, but it was a possibility all the same.

'Your father won't kill him. He has to have an heir,' Jack said.

'Reuben freed me. If he's alive, he won't have any of the freedoms he was granted before. My father will be working hard to turn him into a smaller version of himself.'

'What has Arla said?'

Hark hadn't dared mention to her his fear for his brother's life. He couldn't begin to untangle what it meant to care for Reuben when he had spent his whole life being jealous of him; of the way it all came so naturally to him; of how his brother would make the better ruler; and of how Reuben knew it too.

Because if he did mention it to Arla ... he knew the girl would go down fighting to get his brother out of that castle and bring him to the safety of Flambriar. He'd watched her almost die once, and he didn't think his heart was strong enough to watch her do that again. To be so lucky as to find someone willing to do that all for him ... it was a gift from the gods. It was the gift of his life, and he'd do anything to keep her safe, even if it meant freezing his arse off every night in the mountains.

'Enough talk of danger and threatened siblings, we've got a dinner to prepare for.'

Ah, dinner.

They'd made it a rule that they would regularly dine together like a proper court because it would do them good to follow the structure that other kingdoms set out. He'd sat through enough of those court dinners to know that it was no different from any other dinner, aside from the fact that they all wore outfits that were more dazzling than comfortable.

It felt too much like being a king for his liking.

But he'd do it for Arla. He knew it was bothering her – the way Flambriar was entirely different from anything else she'd ever known, and the fact that they weren't following the same structure as other kingdoms *at all* because he didn't fucking want to.

But he might just do it for her.

～

The woman who swept into the dining room that evening stole his breath.

Red silk dripped from every curve, every lean muscle, every delicious, glowing glimpse of skin. Heels clicked against the stone floor, their height as dizzying as the woman strutting towards him. Hair swung in loose waves around her shoulders, and her eyes were such a rich coffee colour that he fought not to devour her in front of his friends.

'I do hope I'm not late,' she purred, a smirk settling on her lips that took him back to the first time he had met her in the throne room at Castle Grey. She had been wild then ... now she was a whirlwind threatening to bring down his entire being.

It was Kase who spoke, Hark's own voice still lodged in his throat at the sight of Arla. 'You're late to everything. It's not something to be proud of, *assassin*.'

Arla's lips parted slightly, and she ran the pink tip of her tongue over her teeth before she said through her smile, 'It's 'Dragonhart' to you.'

The whiskey he had been about to swallow caught in his throat, and he was choking on it before he could stop himself. Jack was there, clapping him on the back, forcing him to breathe as Arla looked at him with a perfectly raised brow.

'I thought we were eating tonight, not watching the pair of you spar over the turkey,' Jaz said, his first words all evening. He had been quiet and sullen, almost since Hark had brought Arla here. Hark would have to speak to him soon and tell him to stop holing himself up in the library and avoiding them all when the rest of his crew were working hard to run this kingdom and keep the people whom they had spent years rescuing safe.

And if Hark didn't approach Jaz soon, he could almost guarantee that Arla would. A smirk teased his lips at the thought of it.

'Indeed, I'm starving.' Arla took her seat at the head of the table and began pouring wine into her glass with a vigour by which Hark was almost impressed by.

Dinner passed them by so quickly he couldn't contain the sigh that escaped him when the maids began clearing the table. Arla had charmed them all, of course – even Kase, who had tried her hardest not to smile but had burst into laughter over a story of Arla walking in on the King of Hadalyn with his chief advisor. He had never known Arla to be so ... animated, so intent on actually speaking to them all. He'd known her for almost two and a half years, had seen the masks she often wore and the pretty smiles she could offer men to get them to do her bidding, but this ... he didn't think it was a mask. He didn't think she was playing a game with them that they had no hope of winning.

And when he met her gaze across the table, he felt every piece of himself coming undone.

The others saw it too, he thought, because when Arla rose from the table and left the room as elegantly as she had arrived, he followed her, and his friends didn't say a word.

He was two steps outside the door when a blade came whistling past his ear and planted itself in the wooden beam beside his head.

'Oh dear,' Arla tsked. 'Too slow, Stappen. You'd be dead by now if I had wished it.'

He pulled the blade out of the wall, surprised at how deeply it had struck, before marching towards her. She let him come closer, closer, closer until he had backed her up against the windows, their chests flush against one another as he pressed the blade against her throat.

And she grinned.

'Gods, you will be the end of me.'

She straightened against him, the scent of jasmine intoxicating as she lifted her chin higher. 'Oh, I will be the end of many things, Hark, but you are not one of them.'

He lowered his lips to hers, a brush so featherlight he wasn't sure it existed. To rip himself away from her now would be torture. Her hands roamed his shoulders, arms, torso, the black shirt he wore suddenly too stifling for the heat of Arla Reinhart.

'Arla,' he growled, low in his throat, and she laughed lightly against his lips.

'I've missed you,' she breathed, the words a dagger to his

heart. He hadn't spent nearly enough time with her in the past weeks, and he was going to tear himself away from her any second now.

'Is that a weakness I detect, sweetheart?'

The tiny noise that escaped her lips was enough to send him hurtling off the top of the mountain. Everything everywhere around him screamed *Arla, Arla, Arla!*

And then the moment was shattered with the slamming of a door and the sound of booted feet.

'Why is it always me?' Sebastian groaned, covering his eyes before marching past the two of them. Arla snorted, the sound so foreign to Hark that he couldn't help the laughter that bubbled up against what he was about to do.

'I've got to go. I'll see you tomorrow?'

He watched her face fall. Watched the light in her eyes dim as she looked between him and Seb, and the explanation she didn't need. The red silk that had looked so resplendent only seconds ago seemed to drown her now, as if she were soaked in blood. He hated the way she was looking at him. It was too close to how she had looked at him when she'd walked the halls of Castle Grey – like he was a prick.

It was all gone in a heartbeat, replaced with the mask of Hadalyn's assassin, the girl he had seen do vicious, terrible things.

'Have fun scouting the mountains for imaginary soldiers, Stappen. I'm sure your kingdom will be fine without you. I certainly will be.'

Ice speared through his chest as she shrugged out of his grip then marched down the hallway, heels clicking with a ferocity that would have made him pity whoever it was she was going to kill, had it been a few months ago.

'She's going to be the death of you,' Sebastian muttered.

Wasn't she just.

CHAPTER 4

The clang of steel echoed through the training chambers of Claret Hall with a viciousness that sang in her blood. She'd been up before the sun, forcing herself to run the perimeter of the grounds and biting her tongue against the ache in her side and the breaths that wouldn't come quickly enough.

It had been too long since she had trained so hard, but the idleness of wandering the streets of Flambriar and lounging in the vast rooms of Claret Hall had finally irritated her enough to push her body beyond what it was ready for. She'd done it once – at only nine years old she had begun to push herself to keep up with the royal guard – and so she could do it again. Perhaps she wasn't as fit as she had been a few months ago, but it would take more than a sword to the side to render her incapable of being as good as her reputation promised.

Now, she delighted in the wariness pulsing in the eyes of the soldier with whom she practised. Sebastian had been absent this morning – not surprising given the fact he had likely spent all night following Hark through the mountains – so she had bullied the first soldier she could find into duelling with her. She'd noticed the cocksure glint in his eye when she had asked – likely considering himself more than up to the challenge of taking on a girl with a sword wound – but the quicker she had swung her blade at him, the quicker that arrogance had faded.

She wondered, midway through lunging at her opponent, whether Hark and the guard were back yet. The thought of him ignited something deep within her.

She came at her opponent with a vigour that had long lain dormant, striking and lunging and arching her blade so fast it was a blur of steel between them.

How dare he leave her for days at a time.

How dare he bring her here and find any excuse to be out there.

How dare he create a kingdom and refuse to lead it.

The soldier's blade clattered to the floor, the sound of it dragging her out of the conniption she had wandered into.

'You're as good as they say, milady,' the soldier said, picking up the blade and sheathing it at his waist.

She scoffed, bending to stretch the ache in her side. 'Do you know if they're back from the mountains yet?'

He held the door open for her, and she floated through it with the swagger she had always commanded at Castle Grey. Parts of her were coming back together, she thought. Her whole world had been tilted on its axis and yet she still knew who she was and what she wanted. Whether here or at Hadalyn, she was still the same.

'They will be arriving back in the next hour.'

'Good. Tell Hark I want to see him. Immediately.'

The solider hurried off, his figure growing smaller in the grandness of the hallway. The sun had risen beautifully, a collage of pink and orange as light spilled through the glass panels of Claret Hall. Arla breathed easier than she had for weeks. It was a hand in the darkness, training. Something that could always be relied upon to drag her out of a rut and remind her just who she was.

She probably owed Hark an apology for the way she had acted, but to force those two tiny words out of her mouth? No, he could come grovelling first.

The courtyard was blissfully empty, the frost crunchy beneath her boots as she crossed the cobbles to Vetta's stable. She was saddled, as per her instructions the previous night, and either Jack or another of the grooms had left her bridle hanging just outside the stable, the leather gleaming and soft.

The assassin and her horse were winding down the side of the mountain before anybody could stop them. She'd always loved Vetta's surefootedness – it was one of the qualities she had looked for when Cyrus had told her she could pick a horse from his stables, and even now, on this icy, rocky mountainside, Vetta navigated her way through as if she had been reared by mountain goats.

It was good to be back on a horse again, the movement so much more contained than that of a dragon. Arla hoped Thara would wake today. She knew her dragon had needed the rest after exerting so much energy following a century sleeping beneath Castle Grey, but when the bond between them was quiet, it set her teeth on edge. How had she ever managed before?

There was a spark of unease in her chest that had been growing since her dragon had informed her she was going to be resting. Thara had once told her the dragons had become so weak after a battle between gods that they had gone to ground beneath Castle Grey.

Only, the dragons hadn't woken for almost a century until Arla happened across them.

What if Thara was asleep now, too weak to wake, and Arla was unable to reach her...?

No. She wouldn't let herself dwell on it. Her dragon was fine; she was resting like all creatures did.

The streets began to fill slowly, life resuming a routine she was no longer part of. But they weren't ignoring her like they had done in the weeks when she had been wandering the city. Now, women smiled at her; men nodded ... if not in a friendly way, then at least in a manner that showed respect.

Her interaction with Mina yesterday had clearly changed something amongst the people. As Arla moved between streets, stopping to greet the vendors of shops and stalls, the people approached her, asking after Hark's health and her own, too. She entertained them all, donning the smile and pleasantness she had curated under Cyrus's rule.

The people only grew in confidence the more she was there. They approached her for all manner of things. Could she inquire about importing sheep or goats into the city? Could she ask after the silk Hadalyn shipped in from other continents? Could she do this and this and this?

She tried to meet all of their demands, and if she could not deliver on their requests, then she promised she would ask the appropriate person. Already a hierarchy was forming within the magics, and though she had yet to see any of them wield actual power, she understood things were decided based on the potency of the magic in their blood.

None of it eased the fact that she couldn't feel Thara in her head. She would have to venture up into the mountains and find her dragon tomorrow if Thara did not reach out through their bond.

The dragonhart brooch pinned to her cloak was her only comfort. It was a strange, almost sentient trinket that Arla's fingers brushed more times a day than she could count. It still warmed beneath her touch, as if the brooch were a signifier that her dragon was okay.

She was just purchasing a dress, which even the gods themselves might have been envious of, when a commotion by the river caught her attention. Men argued, their voices carrying, and began to attract a crowd that joined in the fuss.

'Please have this delivered to Claret Hall. I'll make sure you're paid for the trouble,' Arla said to the woman in the dress shop before turning towards the crowd that was steadily growing on the bridge over the river.

'You speak of things you know nothing of!' a male's voice roared, and the way the crowd moved backwards like ripples in a lake, Arla was sure the argument was about to turn violent. It lit something in her blood, blowing on an ember that had always burned within her heart. Her steps fell into that quiet, soft tread she often reserved for her victims as she approached.

'And you defend her like she didn't hunt us down and cut the throats of our brothers!'

Something heavy settled in her stomach. There was no one else they would be speaking of, not when she had flaunted herself through this new city like she had earned this position of power.

There was the sound of flesh on flesh, the dull thud of fist against jaw. The crowd gasped, some of them leaping forwards to pull the two men apart. Static hung in the air – the same feeling she had whenever Thara was close. *Magic.*

The crowd parted around her as if she had branded them, revealing two men double her size restrained by onlookers but still with flailing arms as they tried to reach one another.

'I do hope you're not going to get blood on these cobbles?'

Silence descended on Flambriar, each pair of magics' eyes turning on her as she stepped onto the bridge and came to stand between the two men.

'You have no business here, girl,' one of the men sneered at her, spit landing in a beard of curling, dark hair.

'You speak to her with such disrespect again and I will see to it you are banished from here, Lovell,' the second man said, straining against the grip of those who held him.

'She deserves it. That whore hunted us alongside her king for years. She doesn't have the *right* to walk these streets, to speak to our people—'

Enough.

She stepped forwards, smiling sweetly as she faced the bearded man. 'If we could refrain from such coarse language, I'm sure the parents of the children present would appreciate it.'

A glob of spit landed at her feet.

Before she'd thought about it, her hand was palming the blade at her waist, the silver glint of it catching the sunlight from beneath her cloak, but she didn't see the other male come flying from behind her and land a fist into the bridge of the first man's nose.

'Men and their fucking egos!'

CHAPTER 5

There was half a second during which she contemplated running the pair of them through with a sword. It would stop the noise and the flying fists and feet, at least. But this wasn't Hadalyn, or Kastonia, or a target after which her king had sent her.

So instead of drawing her blade, she dived into the middle of the fighting and for the first time in her life, tried to stop it.

Hands flew at her face, the crack of knuckles a driving force as she attempted to get in between the tangle of men. Her hair caught on something – or perhaps someone pulled it – and yet she couldn't shake the giddiness that came with being involved in something violent. She had missed it in a strange sort of way, and when the bearded man landed a fist against her cheekbone, the sight of her blood on his knuckle sang to the violence inside her.

Arla threw her own fists back, relishing in the splitting of skin beneath her blows. More people joined in, but all she could see was the man who had spat at her – the man who had accused her of hunting the magics and slaughtering them.

She hadn't known.

'I hope you die, you traitorous bitch!' he yelled at her, and Arla had to resist the urge to laugh. She had been called far worse.

'Death tried to take me,' she said between the pull and push of the fight. 'She failed.'

He came at her again, and everything was beginning to quiet, the crowd calming as if they thought the danger might have passed. She was aware that the other man – the one who had been arguing initially – had been pulled away, a group of people branching off to tend to the broken nose she knew he had sustained.

'Stop, now!' she said.

To her surprise, he did, panting as he stood there, eyes tunnelling into her as if he could kill her just from that stare alone.

'I am sorry for the things I have done, but I am here to help you. If you want to blame me, fine, but know that I will protect this kingdom and its people with or without your support.'

He said nothing, only looked at her as if she had crawled out of the depths of hell. She almost liked it. She turned to face the first man who, despite his bloody nose and the blackening of his eyes, raised a fist across his heart. A mark of respect, of support, for her.

She didn't see the elbow that barrelled into her side.

There was blazing white pain, the screaming of the scar where he made contact and the wave of nausea that overtook her as the bearded man stepped back. She couldn't breathe.

The man with the broken nose launched himself forwards again, barely held back by the people tending him. 'You fucking—!'

The pain burned in her side. It was a stark reminder that she wasn't fully healed; that she wasn't ready to thrust herself into a fight she would ordinarily be more than capable of winning.

'Your parents deserved what they got! I only wish you'd had your pretty little throat cut too!'

Less than a breath later, she was running at him, blade outstretched.

He'd die for it. He'd die for bringing her parents into it. He'd die for saying that the people of Hadalyn deserved what had been done to them.

She'd kill him, she'd kill him, she'd kill him—

'No, you don't.'

Arms wrapped around her waist, hauling her backwards with a strength that shouldn't have come from such a slight body.

She didn't care who held her, only that Lovell was in front of her, and she'd carve his fucking eyes out—

'Enough, Arla. It's enough,' a voice said in her ear, pulling her back despite the strength of her attack.

She'd cut his limbs off his body and keep him alive whilst she did it!

'Arla, stop. I've got you.'

She didn't care, didn't care, didn't care—

'Dragonhart.'

The ancient voice in her head was the only warning before a mass of dark green, scaled claws landed on the bridge.

People screamed, some of them collapsing where they stood – Lovell one of them. Bodies scattered, the sight of Thara too much up close despite how many times they'd seen her from afar.

Arla relaxed in the grip of ... Kase. It was Kase who held her back.

'All is well, Dragonhart?'

She held the dragon's eye, magic swirling through her irises as Thara watched her back. Slowly, Arla sheathed the blade at her waist and felt Kase release a breath against her.

'I'll make sure he's dealt with,' Kase said softly, nodding at a pair of soldiers Arla hadn't seen arrive. They hooked Lovell's arms between them and lifted the unconscious man to his feet, dragging him away in the direction of the barracks. She didn't know what would happen to him – didn't care, actually.

'Dragonhart?'

'Sorry, Thara,' Arla thought, running a hand down her quickly unravelling braid. *'All is well. I ... I got carried away.'*

'Matters of the heart often hurt the most, Dragonhart. Next time, I will burn him to nothing.'

She didn't deserve the dragon that had chosen her, that had carried her dying body out of Kastonia and kept her warm as she lost too much blood on the way into Flambriar. Thara's voice was a comfort in her head, a reassurance that the dragon had not abandoned her.

Kase shuffled uneasily beside her, an indicator that she was still uncomfortable around the dragon, no matter how many times she had seen Arla converse with the creature of the gods.

'Why were they fighting?' Kase asked.

'Because of me.'

Kase sighed, scanning the quickly dispersing crowd as if they would give her the answers Arla would likely keep from her.

'You can't fight with them, Arla. They're just beginning to trust you.'

Arla whirled on Kase, and she wasn't sure if Thara's low rumble was just inside her head.

'I won't hesitate to break their trust if they behave like that again. If they want to blame me, fine, but to attack each other is unacceptable.'

'They fight because of who you are. Of who you could be.'

Thara growled in warning, and this time Arla saw Kase's already pale face turn visibly white. Arla knew what Kase was hinting at: how they all wanted her to step into her power as dragonhart and rule these people with magic in their veins.

She wouldn't do it.

She didn't bear a kernel of magic; didn't have any power of the gods; didn't have anything to make her different aside from the dragonhart namesake and a brooch that warmed to her touch. The message the gods had left, that the last dragonhart would unite the kingdoms...

She would unite nothing.

Not when they had each wronged her, not when she couldn't get Flambriar to accept her fully. There would be no unification, no matter what the gods had said. If they wanted it doing, they could do it themselves.

'They don't fight because of me,' Arla said softly, looking out over the winding stretch of water that ran through the centre of the city. 'They fight because they have no leader. They fight because Hark brought them here and spends all his time in the mountains. They're scared and they have no one to rule them.'

Her stomach flipped.

She knew Hark was in the mountains because he wanted to keep the people safe. And she knew, deep down, that there was a reason he wasn't stepping into his role as leader, that the fear of it plagued him. She'd just have to fix that, wouldn't she?

Kase shook her head slowly, straightening the collar of her jacket before heading back towards Claret Hall. 'I'll see you at dinner.'

'To the skies, Dragonhart?'

Arla regarded her dragon and felt the chill that always pebbled her skin whenever she looked at the creature she had found sleeping beneath Castle Grey. A creature that had known her for her entire life, despite never making contact.

'*Yes, to the skies.*'

～

Arla didn't think she would ever get used to the feeling of riding a dragon. The solid, burning mass beneath her, the wind tearing through her hair and her cloak, the *magic* that swirled around her, its static energy a serenade to her blood. They flew for hours, weaving through clouds of thick fog and diving between the mountains.

She could do it forever and never tire of it.

'*Your anger is burning straight through you, Dragonhart.*' Thara's voice in her head was both a relief as well as a scolding. She had missed the dragon and felt the absence of her all too keenly when she wasn't there to comment on every emotional variation in Arla's mind.

'They'll never trust me, and Hark refuses to lead them.' Her voice was lost on the wind, but she had no doubt the dragon had heard her.

'*Yes, the boy does refuse to take responsibility for the kingdom he has carved out. He will learn in time, or he will be forced to.*'

'What does that mean?' Arla suspected the dragon knew more about the fates and future of their world than she shared – she was a servant of the gods, after all – and it bothered Arla that a bond as close as theirs still contained secrets. But, rather than answer her, Thara dived deeply between the mountains, stealing Arla's breath as her stomach was left behind. Her eyes streamed as Thara plummeted towards the valley, her heart pounding wildly in her ears as the ground inched closer.

The dragon banked upwards at the last second, spreading her wings wide and powering up, up, up. The laughter that burst free from Arla's throat was a sound foreign to her own ears. She wished Hark could hear it.

'*Worried, Dragonhart?*' There was an amusement to Thara's voice she hadn't heard before, and through the laughter that kept bubbling free from her lips Arla forced the words out.

'You don't fill me with confidence when you disappear to sleep for days at a time. Forgive me for the lack of confidence as we tumble to the ground.'

Thara made a sound beneath her that was as close to a laugh as she thought a dragon might be able to make before turning back towards Flambriar. Claret Hall was a beacon on the top of the mountain, the lights from within shining against the sunset. She could only imagine how beautiful it was inside the building right now. With the oranges and reds and pinks of the sunset, and the glass ceilings of the palace, it would be like standing inside a rainbow.

'*Then we will grow your confidence along with this kingdom.*'

CHAPTER 6

Arla's mood had been darkening in the hours that had passed since the fight on the bridge this morning, and it chased her down the perfect hallways of Claret Hall, too, until she was sure there must be a rain cloud attached to her by the time she finally entered the dining room.

Dinner passed uneventfully, and when it came time to leave the dining room, she thought Hark might disappear into the mountains again and return just before she woke to push herself to the limits of what her body could handle. As it happened, before she could save her icy little heart from splintering and leave the room first, he caught her elbow.

'Somewhere to be, Reinhart?' She didn't think she'd ever get used to the low smokiness of his voice. How it felt like a blessing and a curse all at once because her mouth was suddenly dry.

'Always. Unless you had another idea?'

She took half a step forwards and looked up at him through her lashes. A cruel smirk wound its way onto her face, and she revelled in the way his eyes darkened.

'Don't do that,' he groaned, reaching out to tuck a stray strand of gold behind her ear.

'Why? Am I too tempting?'

She watched the beginning of his unravelling. The way he closed his eyes and inhaled deeply before running a hand through that dark, dark hair.

'You tempt me even when I hear you nearly killed a man this morning.'

'Haven't I always?' she said sweetly.

'Fuck, Arla,' he said, pulling her closer to him so that their chests brushed for every breath. 'As much as I would have no complaints about spending the rest of the evening under that delightful glass roof in your bedroom, I was going to ask if you wanted to train with me?'

'Train with you?'

'Seb said you've been duelling the soldiers each morning, and he hasn't had time to train with you. I'm not doing anything tonight, so I thought—'

'You thought what better way to spend your evening than getting your ass handed to you by a literal assassin?'

He smirked, the expression so teasing she could feel herself coming apart right there.

'Come on then, let's see what you've got.'

She laughed, hooking an arm through his as they headed in the direction of the training rooms. 'As long as you promise not to dislocate my shoulder again.'

Hark coughed, elbowing her lightly. 'After watching you *relocate* it, I can promise that won't be a move I'll ever be trying again.'

'Good, even easier to beat you then.'

She had missed this.

The challenge presented by a worthy opponent and the skill she had to dig deep to remember. It had been too long since she had duelled with someone as skilled as Hark – perhaps she never had. His skill with a sword had always been whispered about at Castle Grey, but she had only ever experienced it during the short stay at Larkire Palace – his father's palace – before she had found out about the magics.

He had shocked her then – had got the better of her too. But she had learned what it meant to underestimate her opponent, and she'd be damned if she ever did it again.

She met the arc of his sword with a strength that sent a clang echoing through the training rooms. Hark didn't relent for a minute. He fought her as though he wanted her dead, and despite the sweat already carving tracks down her back and sticking to the silk of her dress, she couldn't help the grin that blossomed across her face. She met every swing of his sword just as he met hers. She ignored the tugging in her side; the scar of her sword wound would have to get used to this. This is what she had been born to do.

Her blood sang in her veins, and the whip of silk around her ankles was a welcome challenge against a man equally matched to her in skill. They danced that deadly routine for almost an hour, until they were panting, and Arla finally struck his sword hard enough that Hark dropped it.

'Nice to see you haven't lost the stamina,' he said between breaths.

She sucked in deep lungfuls of air. The fitness had been coming back quicker than she thought it would, and the muscles that had begun to lose their definition in the weeks she had been resting and exploring the city were becoming lean and strong again.

'Nice to see you haven't lost the ambition to kill me, Stappen.'

He shot her a smirk that set thousands of butterflies off in her stomach before his face sobered, and he looked at her with enough wariness that she was glad she still held the sword.

'You're not happy with me.'

She hadn't expected it to come so abruptly. She'd thought they would dance around it like they had done with everything else in their lives. Her stomach flipped. She didn't know if her heart could handle the confrontation with him – it hurt too much. And that was concerning.

She sheathed the blade at her side and bent to relace her boots. He was the one person with whom she could afford to let her guard down.

'I'm glad you noticed.'

'Arla—'

'I'm angry because you disappear whenever I want to see you. I'm angry because you've changed my entire life and spend most of your time in the mountains. I'm angry because these people need a leader, and you won't be one.'

A thunderous silence stretched between them until she finally stood again and looked at him. Hark was staring at her as if she were something exotic and unruly. His lips parted slightly, a crease marring his forehead in a way that made him look so much older than the twenty-two years he carried.

'So that's why you were fighting today,' he said, his tone bitter and filled with something he had never once directed at her. 'To get my attention? You let Lovell sit in our dungeons with nothing to eat or drink because you felt left out?'

Arrogant, selfish, prick—

'I don't know what you expected when I told you I was saving these people, Arla, but for once in your gods-damned life take a step back and realise not everything is about you. This world, this *kingdom*, is not your playground. You are not the single most important thing here, and it's about time you started to realise it.'

Blow after blow after blow. She bit her lip to stop it trembling.

It shouldn't hurt the way it did, not when he had called her far worse in the past – not when he had told her explicitly that no one would ever love her.

But she had thought things had changed.

She steeled herself, rolling back her shoulders and slipping on the mask of King's Assassin. Hark had the common sense to balk as she took a step towards him and said in a lethally soft voice, 'I don't expect to be the single most important thing in this place you call a kingdom,' she seethed. 'But you know what, Stappen? I thought I might be the single most important thing to *you*.'

Her voice cracked on the word and she shoved his chest with a strength she didn't know she had, enjoying the flicker of surprise that spread across his face.

She turned towards the door, biting her lip against the sting of tears.

'Dragonhart?'

'Don't come crawling to me when this place burns to ash.'

CHAPTER 7
HARK

Kase had the sense not to say a word as she bandaged his bleeding knuckles and picked glass out of his skin. There had been one thought conceived in his mind as he'd watched Arla leave the training rooms and slam his fist into the floor-length mirror; he was a prick.

An awful, ignorant, conceited *prick*.

She hadn't deserved a word of it.

But as usual, Arla Reinhart had managed to get beneath his skin and remind him how much of a failure he was. She was right. Every word of what she had told him was true. He was spending every waking moment in the mountains, scouting and following what he thought might be footprints in case an army was hiding out, ready to descend on his kingdom. And yes, he was avoiding spending time with her because he hated to see the lost look in her eyes now that he had brought her here.

It was all his fault.

He had dragged her out of her fucking kingdom and brought her here to blend into his court and behave as if she hadn't spent the last nine years of her life commanding a castle and hunting people down for a living. And now ... now he had forced her to spend her days walking the city and being downright pleasant to people! He could see the boredom, the loss, and the anger at the betrayal her king had inflicted on her.

Truth was, he didn't want to spend time alone with Arla for fear she'd tell him she wanted to leave. He wouldn't survive that.

Dragonhart or not, this place was foreign to her – this *life* was foreign to her.

And it was all his fucking fault.

And the people needing a leader...

Well, of course she was right about that, too, wasn't she?

Of course, they needed a leader. They needed a king. But who was he to take that role? Yes, he had rescued them and overseen the construction of a new kingdom hidden in the mountains, but he bore no magic in his blood. How could he take charge of a kingdom filled with magics? They would never accept it – never respect him.

And he would not rule as his father had done.

He would not rule with an iron fist and bend his people into submission. He had seen the effect of it, seen how Kastonia had been plunged into poverty whilst the royal family kept everything. He had seen and heard how the people hated them for it. He almost felt bad for his brother, inheriting all of that.

The thought of Reuben ... well, there could be no thoughts of Reuben. It would send him spiralling.

'You know, I think I prefer you when she's torn you to pieces. You're quieter – depressive, almost,' Kase said, removing the bowl filled with glass shards and Hark's blood, and pouring them both a drink.

He didn't know how this kingdom had any reserves of whiskey left.

'She'll leave after this. I can see it in her eyes.'

Kase was silent for a moment, picking at the thread on her sweater before she finally spoke. 'I think you underestimate her, Hark. She isn't the sort of person to run a mile just because you fought.'

No, she wasn't. But he could see how much it was hurting her. He knew she pushed her body to the point of exhaustion every time he disagreed with her just so she could outrun the ache of it.

'I didn't fight with her, Kase,' he said with a sigh. The most painful parts were coming out now, the parts he hated himself for. 'I told her she meant nothing. I told her she wasn't important – to this kingdom or to ... me.'

He couldn't meet Kase's eyes as she pinned him with that icy stare. 'You fucking idiot.'

CHAPTER 8

Her feet were numb by the time she'd trekked through the snow to find Thara. Arla tore off the flimsy slippers she had donned for dinner and trudged the rest of the way barefoot, glad when the heat radiating off her dragon sank into her skin.

'The boy forgets you have the ability to kill him, Dragonhart. Perhaps a reminder?'

Thara rose from where she lay against the side of the mountain, the snow surrounding her a shade of red that had Arla feeling sorry for the goats. For all of ten seconds.

Wordlessly, Thara lowered herself closer to the ground so Arla could climb onto her back. The silk of her dress was soaking and wrapped around her ankles, but Thara's fire was already warming her up, and if not the fire, the wind would surely dry her dress.

'The mountains, Thara. Let's see what's so interesting about them that the boy spends half his time up there.'

The dragon tensed beneath her before launching off the ground in a spray of snow and ice.

They moved through the air as though the gods parted the sky for them. Gliding and twisting, higher and higher and higher. Claret Hall was a glowing spec beneath them, and for the first time in days, Arla could breathe again.

'Ask the question, Dragonhart. You humans give too much power to your emotions.'

Arla huffed. There was no keeping secrets from a dragon.

'I don't know what I'm doing. Ever since I was named Dragonhart, I feel as if I've lost myself. You say I'm meant to unite kingdoms, but all I've done is break them.'

Thara was silent for a moment, the only sound the beating of her wings against the night sky. They were so high up that Arla thought she might be able to reach out and touch the stars if she wanted.

'It is not for me to speak the plans of my masters and the fates, but know that everything happens as it needs to. You forget that the strongest things are forged after they are broken.'

Masters and fates. The gods and their plans.

Truly, if she ever made it to the eternal gates, she would have to try very hard not to fight with the gods themselves.

'It will come in time, but you must have patience and know that only you can decide what troubles your heart.'

'Why are you here, Thara?' She didn't mean it to be offensive, and she could sense that Thara knew it wasn't meant that way, but Arla needed answers. Why, after so long would the dragon come to her aid and then sit back and watch her make a mess of things?

'I am here because you are a Dragonhart. You will not know of the times and worlds before this, but the dragons and their harts worked as closely with the gods as you work with your court in that hall. My presence beside you is an oath sworn centuries ago. I will be at your side no matter what. Even if you let your human heart rule

the course of things for now, I will be there when everything falls into place. It is my ancient promise.'

Frustration simmered like poison beneath Arla's skin. 'So, tell me,' she whined. *'Tell me of the harts that came before. Tell me what it is I'm supposed to be doing,* please. *You say there is no bond as close as that between a dragon and their hart, and yet I feel as though I'm floundering. I beg you to tell me something.'*

Thara was silent, though Arla was aware of the dragon's conflict thrashing within the bond. *'I cannot speak of it, Dragonhart. The one who came before you ... he set all this in motion. Gods do not play fair, and in this, the fates are perhaps even crueller.'*

'Please tell me what I need to do,' Arla begged. *'Please, Thara. I need to know how to unite the kingdoms.'*

The sadness felt cool as it washed through the bond. *'I wish I could tell you everything. But for now, all I can do is guide you.'*

Fucking impossible. This was Arla's life. Arla's destiny. To keep it all from her...

'I will risk the wrath of the fates, if you wish it, Dragonhart. I will bear their ire for you.'

'NO!' The word was out of Arla's mouth before Thara had finished speaking through the bond. Arla would not allow the dragon to bear any punishment from the fates just because Arla was too impatient to wait and learn. She wouldn't *ever* ask Thara to bear that sort of pain because of her. If there was one thing that Arla was certain of in Thara's cryptic revelations, it was that the dragon was right; there was nothing like the bond between a dragon and their hart.

'I am with you. I will not let you falter.'

For now, it was enough. Her head hurt after the dreadful day she'd had. Besides, the mountains beneath her were breathtaking.

And hidden between them, as if the snow could keep her eyes from prying, a man watched over Flambriar.

∼

Thara landed as silently as if the world had ceased to create sound.

The man watched the kingdom from an outcrop of rocks that almost blended with the blanket of snow against the night. He wore a band of red silk around his waist, and the blades he kept sheathed at his side spoke nothing of a friendly visitor.

So this was what Hark had been up to, tracking down men in the mountains.

He'd never mentioned actually finding one.

Thara rose as quietly as she had landed, and Arla exhaled softly when the man wasn't startled and nor did he turn to face them. Her fingers drifted to her brooch, and she revelled in the wave of *something* that swept through her. She'd missed the thrill of taking a victim by surprise.

She crept forwards on quiet, bare feet, ignoring the bite of cold already threatening her skin with a wasting disease. Her victim grunted, pulling his cloak tighter around his shoulders as he continued to spy on her kingdom. On her home.

Maybe she should watch him? Maybe she shouldn't harm him at all and instead bring him back to Claret Hall for questioning. The sight of Thara would probably be enough to persuade even the most loyal of soldiers to talk.

'Don't play with my food, Dragonhart.'

Arla tried to block the image out. Yes, death at her hand would be a far kinder fate than whatever Thara would do to him. And besides, Arla had missed the split second of terror that would shine in someone's eyes just before she ran a blade through their heart.

He was so lost in watching a sleeping Flambriar that he didn't even know she was there until her blade was pressed against his throat and she whispered in his ear, 'You know, you really ought to be careful, up in these mountains alone. I've heard they're home to monsters.'

He whirled on her, eyes wide and bright. But she had expected it, and with his own action of turning on her, he ran his throat against the silver blade, spilling rivulets of crimson across the snow and her feet before he had a chance to understand just who had come to kill him.

His body fell the way all dead bodies fall, and as he lay there, beneath her, Arla struggled to summon even a spec of remorse.

Nine years.

That's what it had taken to twist every morsel of humanity out of her. She didn't care as Thara landed beside her and took the body in her mouth, swallowing it so crudely that Arla found it hard to look away. It still shocked her. A dragon. Eating a man she had just killed.

'You smell of blood and anger.'

Arla scoffed and climbed onto the dragon's back.

'Good.'

Dawn wasn't far off when Arla finally arrived back at Claret Hall. And although there was only a handful of soldiers and the odd maid working in the place, she knew they would speak of her arrival for days.

She could only imagine what she looked like, arriving on the back of a dragon, her hair still pristine, a soggy silk dress twisted around her ankles, her bare feet soaked in blood and traipsing red footprints across the stone floor.

And then there was the blood smeared across her face and hands.

Yes, they'd talk about her for days.

Lilith and Rheia hadn't waited for her, as she had requested, and only when she finally closed the door and stood in the quiet safety of her room did Arla allow herself to feel the pain of her argument with Hark. This ... this was why she didn't love. This was why she didn't let herself get close to people, because they only ended up disappointed in her.

Hark had told her she wasn't important.

As if she had ever been anything but. As if she weren't currently the only person left in existence that had the blessing of the gods.

Fine. If Hark wanted to ruin his own kingdom, he could go ahead. But it was Arla who had listened and spied and been privy to everything her king had ever done; she had learnt what it meant to rule people. If Hark wouldn't let them love him, she would make them love her.

There was a reason she'd had Lilith weave a crown into her hair.

CHAPTER 9

There was a heaviness that hung in the air of Flambriar's streets.

The careful trust she had grown between her and the people in the days before her fight with Lovell had all but been erased. They looked at her with wariness again, and there was a clear divide between those magics who hated her and those who were willing to at least be on the same street as her.

Fine. She'd have to work harder than she'd hoped, but this was fine.

She'd bought a pie that smelled of goat and mint from a woman with magic in her eyes.

She hoped it would be enough.

Lovell, she discovered, lived in a quaint little house not far from the bridge where he had attacked her.

When he finally opened the door to her incessant knocking, her palms were sweating beneath the pie she held, and Lovell's eyes looked positively murderous.

'What the fuck are you doing on my doorstep?' he growled

at her, his left eye blue and purple, showing the cost of yesterday's fight.

'Before you slam the door in my face, I want to talk,' Arla said. He looked at her as if she would attack him, which wasn't an unfair judgement to make, but still, the pie was burning her hand. She watched his eyes flicker to it.

'The woman at the shop said it was your favourite?'

He reached out cautiously, prying it from her hands and bringing it closer to his face. He inhaled deeply, and she was sure she saw delight light up his eyes for a handful of seconds.

'You'll have to try harder than asking Elsie for a pie, girl. We don't want you here.'

He was already closing the door. It was slipping away from her, this chance at winning them back.

'Wait.' She wedged her foot in the door. Lovell sighed heavily and put the pie down.

'Five minutes.'

He was committed to leaving her standing on the doorstep, choosing to step out of the house and close the door behind him.

She spoke before he had the chance. 'Why don't you want me here?'

He huffed and then looked at her as if she had gone mad. 'You hunted and killed our people based on an instruction your king gave you – a king who knew about the enslaving of mages. You think that just because you broke Hark Stappen out of prison and aided him and his crew in rescuing the last of our people that were kept in Kastonia's grip, you think we'll forget what you've done? There are people *missing*, girl. People unaccounted for. My wife is dead. My daughter's blood was taken by Elrod. As far as we're concerned, you were complicit in it all.'

Ice was growing inside her. Or maybe it was darkness.

They still blamed her.

People were dead, and some still missing. They were bitter, and there was nothing she could ever do to patch that wound.

'Tell me what you'd have me do. Please, Lovell. I want this kingdom to be safe. I want your people to be safe. Some of the...'—*mages,* he had called them—'some of the mages came from Hadalyn too. Let me fix this in any way I can.'

She hated that she was begging, but she'd be damned if she let this kingdom fall because the trust and care holding it all together came crashing down. Lovell was looking at her with pain in his eyes – raw, rugged pain that slithered inside her and pressed against the ice in her stomach.

'My daughter,' he said quietly, looking down as if it would protect the shard of his heart he was about to share. 'They took some of her blood. We don't know what for. What if he does something to her? What if he can find her by using it?'

It was a question they'd gone over for hours in Claret Hall. Elrod had taken their blood and sacrificed them, and she didn't want to think what else he had done. Thara had told her it was impossible for Elrod to use their blood against them, but...

She was a dragonhart, blessed by the gods, looked up to by the people in ancient times. She should know the answers. She should have knowledge about the magic and how it worked.

'I promise you, Lovell, that they won't find your daughter. Not by using her blood, not by coming here. I will stand in front of this very door and bleed out before I let them have her. Your fight is done. You are all safe here.'

It was a promise she wasn't sure she could keep, but she had made it anyway. And it wasn't a lie – she *wanted* to be able to keep it. She would indeed protect this kingdom with her life. She would die before she'd allow an enemy soldier to breach its borders.

'It will take time,' Lovell said softly. 'Time for them to trust you. We see you down here. We see Hark up in the mountains. But we don't see him holding an audience with us, listening to us, leading us. We need the support. We need stability. The mages have suffered for too long at the hands of men.'

He lifted a hand and extended it to her. It was a strange gesture, but she had seen it done amongst the people here before. She took his hand in hers and shook it, but she feared she would not be able to hold up her end of the deal.

'I will keep her safe. I'll keep you all safe. But there can't be open hostility against me, Lovell. I have lost a family too.'

More than once.

Both times at the hands of Kastonia's king.

'It is done.'

~

She went from door to door. She listened to their stories and their worries. It was always the same: they didn't feel safe; they feared that Elrod would use their blood somehow; they were worried about the mages that were still missing.

With every promise she made, she felt the weight of it settle on her shoulders.

Eventually, she'd pried herself out of the city and headed up the mountain to Claret Hall. Noah looked terrified when she burst into the room and requested any letters from Hadalyn.

No answer.

Halos was ignoring her.

She told Noah to send another falcon.

Spending time with the mages had awakened in her a thirst for knowledge. She wanted to know how their magic worked, their history, and the significance of the dragonharts.

She wanted to know why the gods had once been so involved with society but had now been absent for so long. She wanted answers to all of it, and there was only one place she might find them.

Jaz was standing at a long oak table in the centre of the library, turning between his fingers the yellowed pages of a book that was so old the leather spine was cracking. A cloud of dust hung in the air.

'Took you long enough,' he said without looking up to see who had entered.

The library was a vast room, and the only place inside Claret Hall that hadn't been crafted out of huge panes of glass – in order to preserve the books, she imagined. The floor was polished wood, and row upon row of wooden shelves held leather-bound books that made her ache for the comfort of the library of Castle Grey.

'How did you get so many books here?' she asked, brushing the spines of the books with her fingertips. These were important books – on magic lore and the ancient kingdoms and the gods that had governed it all. To create such a collection should have taken decades – lifetimes.

'How often did you browse Castle Grey's library for anything other than romance novels, Dragonhart?' Jaz said without looking up from the text he was reading.

She wanted to laugh.

Of course.

The library at Castle Grey was extensive – so big she had never explored its entirety in all the years she had called the castle her home. Hark had lived there for two years. He must have been smuggling books out by the dozen, and perhaps from his father's castle too, and wherever else...

It was the first time she had truly felt at home in this hall;

the fact that some of these books had come from Hadalyn too was a comfort she hadn't realised she'd been seeking.

'I need to know—'

'About the gods and your role as a dragonhart?' Jaz said, turning to face her finally. He looked the most rested she'd ever seen him, his eyes sparkling in the sun that streamed through the arched windows on the far wall.

'You've been expecting me, then.'

Jaz snorted and returned the book he had been reading to its place on the shelf. Arla had never felt comfortable around him. There was a subtle animosity that simmered beneath his skin, and it was directed firmly at her. She didn't know what she'd done to offend him, but he wasn't someone around whom she felt she could let her guard down. Despite the flowing plum-coloured cloak and his insistence on spending all of his time in the library, he was deadly with a blade, and Hark had inducted him into his personal crew.

'I suspected you almost immediately after you woke. Dragonharts have long since disappeared from this world and the people no longer know how to act around them because they don't understand their role. Of course, you will have questions too.'

Jaz took a seat at a reading table, pulling a chair out for Arla too which she collapsed into gracelessly.

'Kase told me about the dragonharts,' she began. 'That we were once vessels for the gods and acted according to their will. We kept the mages safe and delivered messages from the gods.'

Jaz stared at her with an intensity that made her feel as though there was something wrong in her soul. Something wrong that only he could see. He narrowed his eyes before he spoke.

'That's true. And dragons such as Thara served the gods and

their dragonharts too. But what now, Reinhart? The gods are angry. The dragons sleep beneath Castle Grey. So how, exactly, are you going to unite everything?'

Wasn't that the question indeed?

The gods were angry because the balance of magic was off, because Elrod had been killing the mages and attempting to use the magic himself. The dragons had fallen asleep after a battle between gods almost a century ago that had left them too weak to do anything other than go to ground. The kingdoms were crumbling beneath the gods' ire ... and she was somehow supposed to fix it.

She'd thought she had. She'd thought that freeing the mages and stopping Elrod would be enough to bring the gods back and help the kingdoms flourish again. Kastonia had been on the verge of falling for years, and Hadalyn was still suffering under the weight of the refugees that poured through from Kastonia. The news came from letters written by spies that Hark had planted across the kingdoms: the kingdoms were still falling. Perhaps it wouldn't be long until Flambriar started to fall, too.

'What do I need to do?' she asked.

'I've been poring over these texts since the moment we got back to Flambriar, and I still don't have an answer yet. Speak to your dragon. Ask her what she knows.' Jaz's face was solemn, and she saw the worry that marred his expression. He understood the urgency.

Speak to your dragon.

Frustration roiled in her blood. She knew Thara couldn't or wouldn't tell her more. The gods and the fates forbade it.

'Thara is cryptic at best, even when she is inclined to actually share information with me. She won't speak of the gods or the fates, no matter how hard I push her.'

Jaz sighed, running a hand across the back of his head.

'Then I will keep looking.'

Arla stood up, biting her lip against the ache in her legs after this morning's climb. She was almost out of the door when Jaz spoke again.

'And Reinhart? Keep an eye on Hark. He's going to drive himself mad if he spends every waking minute hunting an invisible army.'

She could only nod.

She didn't tell him about the man she had killed last night.

CHAPTER 10
HARK

The soldier in the sitting room had not stopped talking for twelve minutes.

He spoke of bloody footprints, a demon girl that had slid off the back of a dragon and stormed through the hall last night, silk dress tangling at her ankles with blood dripping off her hands.

He didn't have it in him to tell the soldier that Arla Dragonhart wasn't, in fact, possessed. It was just the way she always had been: violent and uncompromising when her mind was set. And who was he to tell her she couldn't be that person anymore? She had struggled to adapt to life in Flambriar; it was to be expected that she would lash out eventually. If the rest of them didn't understand her, well ... he didn't give a fuck, really. She was his, and he was hers, and no matter how many times she came back here covered in blood, he'd defend her.

He only hoped no one had seen her kill whoever her victim had been, and that it wouldn't reflect badly on his court.

'I'll have a healer see to her, Stan. You're excused.'

Stan left immediately, and Hark couldn't stop himself from heading in the direction of Arla's rooms, but his fingers wouldn't close around the doorknob no matter how much he willed himself. They'd fought, and he had been cruel to her. It was no wonder she'd expressed her anger the only way she knew how and gutted someone whilst everyone else was asleep.

He could hear the fire roaring in the grate even from behind the door, and he didn't think he was imagining the soft tinkling of china or the faint laughter that reached his ears. Perhaps he should go... If she were speaking with Thara, then all he would achieve would be upsetting the pair of them with his presence.

No.

He'd come here to make amends, to lay an olive branch between them. He had told her he loved her weeks ago, and he'd meant it. Meant it with every ounce of his soul.

The doorknob was cool beneath his fingers.

He found her curled up in an armchair by the fireplace, a blanket across her lap and her hair in loose waves around her shoulders. A book rested between her fingers, and the tinkling sound had been the tea set Kase had procured for her at the market in the city. She wore only a slip of pale pink silk, and he longed to feel it slide over her skin.

'Hello,' she said softly, lifting her gaze to meet his where he hovered just behind the chair.

'Hello.'

'You haven't been here in weeks,' she said, closing the book and pulling her knees up to cross her legs beneath her.

Hark took the seat opposite her, almost groaning as the heat from the fire seeped into him. 'I ... Arla, I...'

'I know.' Her eyes held none of the fire or violence he had come to know, only a gentleness that was foreign and yet so ... right.

'Would you like to come scouting with me tonight? You can bring Thara.'

The way her eyes lit up nearly shattered his fucking soul.

She was beautiful.

And yet he wanted her eyes to light up like that for *him*. He hadn't given room to the jealousy that had begun to fester whenever he caught her away in her own mind, conversing with a creature that knew Arla in a way he never could. He couldn't compete with that sort of bond – he shouldn't try, either. It was a connection that had been forged by the very gods and it was entirely different to what he shared with Arla. And yet, the things he felt for her... The way his heart could barely keep up whenever she glanced at him... That had to be forged by the gods too, didn't it?

Arla leaned forwards, already braiding her hair. 'That depends.'

'On what?'

'On if you can keep your eyes off me long enough to make it up the mountain without breaking your neck.'

He couldn't stop himself reaching for her. She fell into his arms, the jasmine scent of her wrapping around him as he pulled her closer. She was so soft, so perfect, so lovely in his arms that he didn't think he would make it out of this bedroom, let alone up the mountain.

'You know the soldiers and the maids think you're a demon, don't you?' he mumbled into her hair, relishing the way she curled closer into him.

'Good. What did you tell them?'

He chuckled, inhaling the scent of her. 'That you can do no wrong. That you are not, in fact, a demon, and never have been.'

Arla snorted. 'There was a time when you wouldn't have defended me killing people, you know.'

'Hmm,' he said, twisting his fingers in her hair. 'But that was before. Whatever you do, I'll defend you.'

She stiffened slightly, a flash of something flickering in her eyes before she sank into something lovely and soft again. 'I'm corrupting you,' she mused, playing with the collar of his shirt.

He placed a palm on each side of her face and tilted her head upward. Those coffee-coloured eyes were flecked with the gold of the fire, and a teasing smirk tipped up her lips.

'Don't look at me like that,' he groaned.

She only shuffled closer to him, sitting in his lap so she was eye level. Gods, she was a picture of a goddess. The strap of that godsforsaken nightgown had slipped down her shoulder, and her hair curled loosely around her face. She'd ruin him. And he'd fucking let her.

'I'll come scouting with you, Hark,' she purred. 'But I'm not getting dressed.'

Fucking gods.

~

He wished she'd got dressed.

Her cloak kept parting in the wind, teasing him with glimpses of her skin and that pink nightgown. He didn't know how she wasn't freezing, though he supposed the fact that her dragon lurked so close was enough to warm her.

They'd marched up this mountain quicker than he ever had with the soldiers and the scouting group. He was prone to forgetting just how fit and lethal she was. It was hard to remember when she was dressed like that.

Their boots crunched in the ice and days-old snow, and Hark tried not to let the sound grate on his nerves. He wished they were silent. An enemy soldier would hear them coming a mile off and scatter before he had a chance to notice.

'Do you not get bored being up here every night?' Arla asked.

Hark swallowed the wariness at feeling Thara's breath brush the back of his neck before he answered Arla. 'Do you not get bored of running laps of the grounds every morning and pushing your body until you're sick?'

'Point taken.'

They kept walking, as silently as they could manage, scanning the open space around them.

'I'll do anything to keep them safe. I won't lead a kingdom like my father did. I don't want them to fear me.'

It was the whole point of it. The basis for his fight with her. He wouldn't rule as a tyrant, with absolute power.

'They aren't scared of you, Hark,' she said softly, weaving her hand into his. 'They're scared of not having a leader. They're scared that they've been abandoned.'

He squeezed her hand lightly, glad that it was there, glad that she was mature enough to forget their fight and walk with him tonight. He loved her so much it hurt him. He'd do anything for her. Anything.

Which was why he pushed thoughts of his father to the back of his mind and made himself say, 'I know they need a leader, but I don't know how. You know what you're doing. You're far better at this than me. I know I told you I wouldn't force you to be a queen, and I won't. But I need your help if this is going to work. I need you to help me build this kingdom.'

Arla was silent for long seconds, her eyes so piercing in the starlight as she mulled over what he'd said. It was true, every word of it. He knew they needed help, but he didn't know how to give it.

'I'm here,' she said softly, stepping closer to him and placing her right hand on his cheek. Her fingers were startlingly cold. 'I'm always going to be here. I promised you I would stand at your side whilst we helped the mages. I'm not going to run away, Hark. Tell me what you need and I'll do it.'

He didn't think he could love her any more if he tried.

Arla inched closer to him, until her lips were pressed against his and her hands slid to the back of his neck. 'I love you,' she whispered against him, all jasmine and honey and *Arla*.

He kissed her back as if his life depended on it. As if she were the very thing his blood craved. His hands roamed the slight curves of her body, sliding beneath the cloak and tangling in the delicate material of her nightdress.

'You are magic,' he mumbled against her, and he felt the smile spill over her lips as he kissed her harder.

'It's been said before,' she whispered back.

He pulled her even closer as the kiss deepened. He wanted more, more, more—

His blood ran cold as she stiffened against him.

Oh gods, he'd gone too far. She had been with men under the direction of her king and Hark didn't know what they'd done to her. Perhaps she couldn't stand the touch of someone else...

'I'm sorry. I didn't hurt you, did I?'

Her eyes were far away, her head tilted slightly as though she could hear something he couldn't.

'Arla, I'm sorry, I shouldn't have—'

'Something's wrong.'

His heart stopped beating.

'What do you mean something's wrong?' he growled, already unsheathing the sword at his side and spinning in the direction she faced.

There was nothing but open mountains and snow and ice and stars.

'Arla—'

'There's no one here, but something feels off.'

She still hadn't looked at him, her eyes unblinking as her chest heaved and Thara inched closer to her. He'd almost forgotten about the dragon.

Only when Thara's snout nudged the hand hanging slack at Arla's side did she come out of whatever reverie she had disappeared into and she looked up at him, her face grim with the clouds of worry in her eyes.

'Thara can feel it,' she said quietly, rubbing her palm over the dragon's face. Hark tried not to shudder as the dragon breathed out a cloud of hot, sulphur-scented smoke. 'Something doesn't feel right. It's like ... the magic is ... off.'

Hark spun around. If Kastonia was moving against them—

'There's no one here, no one for miles and miles,' she said, reaching for his arm. 'But something isn't right. Thara thinks the gods are unhappy still.' She quietened then. It had been a long time since Hark had seen her look so fragile, so young. Eighteen years had moulded her into something far more mature than she should be, so much so that he often forgot she was still barely an adult, living this life for the first time, just like him. He wanted to keep her safe from it all.

'It's my fault. I was supposed to unite the kingdoms but ... I don't know how.'

He pulled her close to him, ignoring the low rumble in Thara's throat. 'It's not your fault. We'll find a way. Jaz has been searching through the library every day to find something on the dragonharts. It's not your fault, Arla, and whatever storms are coming, we'll weather them together.'

A soft, gentle smile soaked into her lips. She was so lovely like this. So perfect.

'Together, then?'

He pressed a kiss atop her head.

'Together. Come on, we should go to bed.'

He needed to spend time alone with her, with no dragons or kingdoms to distract them. He needed to see that pink nightdress in all its glory.

CHAPTER 11

Thara's presence in the back of her mind was like a slab of marble – cold and unyielding. The dragon had kept her awake all night, even though Hark wrapped her in his arms and whispered lovely things into her ear, and held her while they slept.

'You humans sleep too much,' Thara said as Arla lay tangled in the bedsheets. It was far later than she was used to sleeping in, though she would likely still be the first up and about the hall. The sun had only just risen.

'It's not like you slept beneath a castle for decades, is it?'

A rumble vibrated down the mind bond and Arla chose to interpret it as amusement from the dragon. She didn't dare admit she was still slightly afraid of Thara.

She dragged herself out of bed and onto the balcony before she could regret it. Flambriar was coming to life. There were horses pulling wooden carts laden with wood and food and ... silk. Silk. Her chest hurt to breathe because ... because it meant that one of the trade deals had gone through. Flambriar was actively trading with the continent.

The flutter of hope was quickly smothered by the worry of what it meant. Other kingdoms knew they existed now. They would have to be cautious whilst they were still establishing themselves – a new kingdom was the ideal target for someone more powerful to take over.

'There is nothing more powerful than those with the blessing of the gods.'

Right.

It wouldn't stop an army from attacking though, would it?

A tiredness was settling in her bones already. She was supposed to unite them all. The very thought of it made her want to crawl back beneath the sheets.

But she would begin anyway.

First, she would tackle Flambriar and its lack of leadership, then she would help Jaz in the library. There had to be something to give her an indication of what she was supposed to be doing as a dragonhart, seeing as her actual dragon would give her no clues.

'I have no right to interfere with the fates and their plans. And nor do you.'

'Is everything alright?' She knew Thara was off in the mountains searching for the source of the strange magic she had felt last night. She could feel the physical distance in their bond.

'It is better than before, but the balance is off.'

Arla went to speak and found the bond between them blocked, as if a huge wall stood between them.

Fine. If Thara wanted to be left alone, she'd let her. Perhaps Thara was tired of how often Arla actively sought out the bond between them just so she didn't feel quite so alone in a new kingdom so far from Hadalyn.

Get a grip, Arla.

She chose the warmest clothes Rheia and Lilith had found

for her – knitted sweaters and thick leggings instead of her usual leathers – she couldn't be King's Assassin today. She pulled her cloak around her shoulders and set off for the city.

The people watched her all day. They watched as she helped set up the beginnings of an apothecary where the healers could mix and sell medicine. They watched as she made sure there was somewhere the pregnant women could deliver their babies safely. Flambriar might have been set up nearly two years ago under Hark's instruction, but it had been created as a refuge, not as a prosperous kingdom with an efficiently functioning administration.

By the time she left the city and began the long walk up to the hall, her body ached and her toes were numb right to the bones. She felt like she'd never be warm again.

The sun was setting quickly, as it always did this far north, and she longed for spring so that she might get a glimpse of something green rather than the endless ice and snow that turned everything into various shades of white and grey.

She was so preoccupied with trying to tease Thara along the bond in her mind that she almost walked straight into Jack, who was leaning more heavily on his walking stick than he had been three days ago.

'You're working too hard. Let the grooms sort the horses. Vetta will tolerate them the more time she spends with them.'

Jack smiled softly at her and her stomach clenched uncomfortably at how tired he looked. He was barely older than her, yet he looked more than double the twenty-two years he'd walked the world. She knew he'd been seeing healers to try and reverse the magic that had damaged him, but it was weeks later and if anything, he looked more exhausted than ever. Arla knew it worried Kase – that she spent hours in the library with Jaz when she could, researching the effects of magic on a mortal body.

'I heard you made quite the stir in the town today,' Jack replied, ignoring her lingering gaze as he fell into a shuffling step beside her. 'The people will like that. They need someone to give them direction. We tried when we brought them here two years ago, but ... we were never here for long enough to establish anything solid.'

She didn't blame him. She didn't blame any of Hark's crew or Hark himself for not being able to manage Flambriar and keep it a secret whilst also smuggling Elrod's slaves out from under his nose.

Thara chuffed softly down the bond.

'I haven't seen you much lately,' Arla said, holding the door open for Jack as they stepped into the warmth of Claret Hall.

'I've been trying to sort the trade agreements with Kase. She can be ... harsh on those who are scared to trade with us.'

'I hear we're trading silk,' Arla said, the hope of it still a burning ember in her chest.

Jack grinned up at her. 'We are indeed.'

She tried not to let her eyes stray to Noah's office door as they strolled past it, but she couldn't ignore the pull behind her navel that urged her to break the door down and tear through every scrap of paper on the desks until she found one that bore Hadalyn's seal. Until she found one that bore Halos's name.

'Patience, Dragonhart.'

She said goodbye to Jack then went to her bedroom, trying her best not to allow even a prickle of pity to mar her face. She knew Jack hated it and that he wanted them all to stop looking at him like he was going to break at any moment.

When she opened the door to her rooms and a bony hand gripped her wrist and yanked her inside, it was the first time in her life that Arla was glad she didn't have a blade that was easy to access.

Lilith pulled her into the room, kicking the door closed behind them and ushering Arla further inside. Only when she had Arla backed into a corner did the maid finally speak.

'Do you have any idea how many times I've had to lie for you today?' Her grey eyes burned with urgency, and the scar on her jaw stood out starkly in the dimly lit bedroom. Arla's heart fluttered in her chest and heat rushed through her veins. Lilith had never spoken to her this way – had never laid a hand on Arla unless it was to try and tame her hair.

'I have absolutely no idea what you're talking about, but please don't let me stop you from explaining, Lilith,' Arla said, already pushing her way out of the corner and removing the blade pinning her hair up so it fell in loose tangles below her shoulders.

The maid grabbed her arm again. Arla snatched it back before whirling on her. 'Don't *ever* touch me without my explicit permission,' she growled through her teeth. A flicker of fear passed across Lilith's face as she snatched her hand back to her chest.

'Forgive me, but this is important.'

Arla sighed, unclasping her cloak before collapsing into the seat beside the fire and beginning to unlace her boots. 'Go on, then.'

'You killed someone the other night, didn't you?'

Arla thought her heart might have stopped beating.

Arla kept her eyes concentrated on her boots when she finally spoke. 'Well, I do hear you're all calling me a demon.'

Lilith exhaled loudly, throwing her hands up. 'Arla, we all expect you to come back covered in blood – you are who you are. But no one is missing from the city. I checked today.'

Gods! How had she been stupid enough not to have covered her tracks?

She sat up slowly, meeting Lilith's serious eyes as the maid stepped closer to her. 'The other maids in this hall talk, you know. I had to tell them you got into a fight with Thara. That you fell off her in the mountains. That it was *your* blood you were covered in.'

'Well, if I ever need an alibi, Lilith, I know where to go.'

'It's not funny.' Desperation had crept into her voice, and when Arla really looked at her in the light of the fire, silver lined the bottom of Lilith's eyelids.

'Lilith.'

The maid turned away, raising a hand to her eyes as if she could avoid the inevitable scrutiny of the assassin before her.

Arla reached for her arm and turned her gently. 'Sit down.'

Lilith took the seat opposite her, and Arla tried to fight the blush that crept into her cheeks at the memory of who had sat in that chair the previous night, and how he had looked at her as if she were a goddess.

'If I tell you the blood was mine—'

'She wouldn't believe you,' a voice said, hurrying out of the bathroom with a blue silk dress scrunched in her hands. Rheia looked as flustered as her sister, but with a sharpness to her tone that Lilith had been lacking. 'Arla, we're not stupid. I found your dress shoved beneath a stack of towels.'

Ah. She'd meant to dispose of it earlier.

'Right, seeing as you're both incapable of staying out of my business,' she began, offering her chair to Rheia, who took it gratefully. 'I'll have you know that ... well, obviously I killed someone, but I was nowhere near Flambriar when I did it.'

Both maids' faces paled.

'Don't tell me you flew—'

'To the northern border, yes. I wanted to check out the camp there to see if there was anything important I could learn. There happened to be two Kastonian soldiers posted there. They deserved it.'

Too easy.

It was too gods-damned easy to lie through her teeth to the two women who had cared for and trusted her the moment they had met her.

The worst part was that they actually seemed to believe her.

Rheia visibly relaxed and colour began to return to Lilith's cheeks as they listened to the fabricated story.

'Don't forget your lies, Dragonhart. They will fell you when you least expect it.'

She didn't heed Thara's warning. Mostly because she was so glad the dragon had opened the bond back up again. Not being able to communicate with Thara had eaten away at her all day.

'But you can't tell anyone. Hark would lock me up and throw away the key if he knew I'd done something as dangerous as that.'

'He'd be bloody right!' Lilith scolded.

'Lilith, I'm serious. You tell the maids that it was my blood, that I got hurt falling from Thara. Make it up. But no one can know I left Flambriar.'

It was only after the maids had stoked the fire and left her that she wondered why she hadn't told them the truth – that someone had indeed been spying on Flambriar and she'd done Hark's job for him. She'd sworn them to secrecy anyway.

But no.

Today she had made a difference. She had helped establish the roots of what would grow into a beautiful kingdom. She wouldn't upset them all with this news yet. Hark had enough on his plate without her interfering. He was already so stressed, and her not settling in properly, her arguing with him about stepping up as leader was adding to that stress. He needed to relax, needed to stop worrying before he gave himself a heart attack – the gods knew she'd kill him if he dropped dead on her.

She made herself ignore the shadow in her chest that told her she was being selfish. That she was keeping it from him not only because she didn't want him worrying about a threat she had already neutralised, but because if she told him ... well, it would be real then. They would be at war, and she had hardly made it out of the last one alive. Nine years the battle of Grey Hill had haunted her. She wasn't ready to do it all again...

And besides, Hark was up there every night anyway. If there were still people hiding in the mountains, he'd catch every one of them.

It wasn't her job to worry him.

CHAPTER 12

Over the following days, Arla had spent every spare moment in Flambriar helping establish a proper school, a proper place for the healers to work, and a proper place for the blacksmiths. It filled her with a satisfaction she hadn't felt since she'd left Hadalyn.

Kase came with her to the forests. They met in the courtyard at the hall to find Vetta and Eros already saddled and waiting. Arla had spent a lot of time in service to the king travelling across the kingdoms, and she and Vetta had seen their fair share of forests.

None of them felt as ancient as this.

The loamy, rich scent of centuries-old wood filled her senses as they rode through the trees, the horses' hooves snapping pine needles and leaves and whatever else lay underfoot. There was magic in the trees – she could feel it in the air, feel the pressure of it looping around her as if it recognised her very blood. It was magic, and ancient ... and she had never felt calmer. This place was safe, it was hidden, it was—

'Somewhere the gods watch over, Dragonhart.'

She committed the knowledge to memory. Should they ever be attacked, should they ever need a place to hide, a gods-blessed forest might be the only place in the world that could conceal them.

Grunts filled the air in the distance, and deep voices that even from afar sounded so synchronised that Arla knew these men had perfected the art of harvesting the wood from the forest over years.

'I should leave the hall more often. This is the most relaxed I've been in days,' Kase said beside her, her leg brushing Arla's when their horses walked too closely.

'It's definitely been a lot.' Arla sighed.

'You've been busy. The people have been talking about you, you know.'

Arla laughed quietly. 'I'd be surprised if they hadn't. They likely think I've come and turned their world upside down.'

Kase was silent for a few seconds, reaching an arm above her to feel the branches of a low-hanging oak. 'Sometimes I think you have to turn the world upside down to do good.'

There it was again, those distant, glassy eyes that spoke of a past perhaps as painful as Arla's. She shouldn't ask. She would deserve it if Kase ran her through with a blade for being so nosy.

But she'd never cared about someone threatening her...

'How did you come to work with Hark?' she asked softly, already regretting her words when Kase's shoulders tensed.

'He freed me from his father's prison.'

Arla huffed. 'What did you do, comment on how grey his hair was turning?'

Kase stilled atop Eros, and it was at that point that Arla knew she was treading on ground that was ready to swallow Kase whole. She was quiet. Too quiet. And for long enough that Arla didn't think she'd answer.

'I killed my uncle. Hark was sent to Hadalyn not long after I escaped.'

There were some wounds that were not to be pressed, no matter how much time had passed. Arla knew it herself; she still couldn't stomach the thought of anyone but her speaking of her parents.

'In time, Dragonhart.' A wave of warmth travelled down the bond.

Hark was a better man than she could ever hope to be. He'd gone against his father for longer than she had known. He'd risked everything to save a teenage girl locked beneath a castle.

He'd saved her, too.

The sound of the men was louder now, and she could smell the freshly cut wood, the sap seeping into the air.

'Any joy in the library?' Kase asked.

It was an odd thing, this relationship between them. When they weren't actively trying to kill each other with their words over dinner there was a common ground that they were both content to rest upon. If only until the boys came back.

'Not yet. Jaz is still looking. I know I'm supposed to protect them. I can feel the draw in my blood to keep them safe. But I've found nothing about uniting kingdoms. Nothing about ending this deranged hunt of the mages.'

'You call them mages, now. Hark always said magics.'

'I call them what they wish to be called. It's an honour they've probably never had.'

Kase straightened in the saddle as a clearing came into view. 'I'll make sure everyone keeps it in mind.'

The sight before them stole any words Arla had been contemplating. She had seen magic – and the harm it could do –

but she had seen the gentle beauty of it too – the way the healers could close the most gruesome of wounds.

None of it compared to this.

The men stood at random points in the clearing, their hands stretched upwards, their eyes fixed on the towering trees around them. Magic sang in the air, the static of it lifting the hairs on Arla's neck as she watched the men carry out a task that should have been impossible.

They called to one other, their hands arcing and flicking, and the magic copied the movement in the trees. Huge branches were cut from sequoia and redwoods and pines, the magic slicing through them with ease and also carrying them softly to the ground, manoeuvring the branches onto the back of a cart pulled by six horses.

She felt like she wasn't breathing. The control and manipulation it took to master the magic so artfully was beyond impressive. Beside Arla, Kase exhaled and Eros pranced beneath her.

She turned slowly, scanning the rest of the clearing. She couldn't help but be drawn to the magic. Wherever she turned, she saw the beginnings of new life.

Dozens upon dozens of saplings were sprouting from the earth, the green of their leaves so striking against the dark, muted colours of the forest. Tears filled her eyes. It was beautiful magic.

'Watch your backs, ladies!' one of the men called, and they both managed to nudge their horses forwards in time to avoid a giant branch floating down right where they had been standing. Lovell was there too, across the clearing, helping a younger man master the art of securing the wood to the cart. Arla didn't know how it didn't buckle beneath the weight, but the horses pulling it stood firm, and the cart didn't so much as creak beneath the wood.

The man who had warned them of their imminent impaling strode forwards, wiping a cloth over his forehead as he came to stand beside them. 'What can we do for you?'

Arla felt something in her chest pull. It was an old, primal instinct to protect them, something that had been baked into her very blood.

'We're here to see if there's anything we can do for *you*,' Kase said, snapping Arla out of her haze.

'It appears you are more than equipped,' Arla said lightly.

The man smiled, the corners of his mouth creasing heavily as he wiped the sweat from his forehead again. 'We were the first to get set up in Flambriar. Someone had to build those houses and that fancy hall. We've grown since then.'

Arla could see it in the delicacy and finesse of the magic they wielded. Two years they'd had to perfect the art of it. They'd crafted Claret Hall and the rest of the city, and she didn't think she'd ever see anything as impressive ever again.

'I recall you being rather impressed at the body of a sleeping dragon beneath your castle.'

'I was terrified of you all and you know it,' Arla sent back.

'Well please let us know if there's anything we can do or if there's any extra help you need,' Kase said to the man, nudging Eros forwards as the group called her over and offered to show her the wood they had harvested.

Arla was in awe of it all.

But her assassin's eye never missed a single detail. Which was why, when she saw the threads of red silk tied to the base of one of the saplings a few metres away, she looked into the trees and met the gaze of a girl with auburn hair who held a finger in front of her lips.

She would look back later and wonder why she didn't shout or fire an arrow at the stranger.

She did neither. All she did was offer the subtlest of nods to the stranger and kept her lips sealed.

'Kase, we should go. I offered to help the women in the fabric shop.'

It was a lie, but Kase trotted back over to her, a smile parting her serious face as the men shouted their appreciation at the visit Flambriar's court had made. They rode back in silence, as if the sight of the magic had rendered them mute.

Arla didn't care. She had other things on her mind. Like why a red-haired woman was spying on the mages in the forest, and why she hadn't made a move to attack.

It plagued her all evening – until she could finally slip away and disappear into the forest to find out who exactly was watching them, and why.

CHAPTER 13

Thara dropped Arla near to where she had seen the rogue woman, and Arla relied on the silent feet of her assassin training to track her movements.

'Hark is going to kill me if I end up dead,' she sent Thara's way.

The dragon replied instantly, huffing down the bond, *'The boy keeps his own scouting secrets, Dragonhart. It is time we had ours.'*

Ours. Like they were a team.

Her fingers drifted to the brooch above her left breast, the metal hot beneath her touch as a wave of solidarity washed through her.

The redhead stood between the trees eyeing the clearing from which Arla should have emerged.

She'd never been predictable.

The dragon had grumbled when Arla had requested that Thara fly her to the far side of Flambriar and then loop back, but once she realised that Arla intended to sneak up on the woman undetected, the dragon had gone silent.

Arla palmed the blade at her waist, twisting the one she

held in her hand in a practised move that spoke of hours in dingy alleyways and on the rooftops of brothels. She moved like a wraith, slipping between trees and floating across the ground as if her feet had been gods-blessed.

She lifted an arm into the perfect position to slide her blade down the side of the redhead's neck to rest lightly on her throat...

The girl spun before Arla had the chance to draw a breath.

Their blades met in a clang that rattled the forest and startled the birds.

The blades clashed between them, the strength of the girl enough for Arla to feel her muscles have to work to hold her at bay.

There were not many who could hold her with a blade.

With her left foot she kicked out, swiping the redhead's ankles from beneath her. The girl fell at Arla's feet and the top of Arla's blade puckered the creamy skin at the girl's throat.

'That wasn't very friendly,' Arla drawled.

The girl's eyes flashed, and she swallowed against the steel at her throat before she spoke.

'Neither was sneaking up on me.'

She spoke with an accent that had to have come from the continent. She was beautiful, with round green eyes and a heart-shaped face, and hair that fell as pin-straight as Kase's.

'Don't pretend you haven't been sneaking around *us*. You're lucky I haven't killed you just for merely existing in these woods.'

'Always so violent, Dragonhart. I'm beginning to like it.'

When the girl reached for the blade she had dropped beside her, Arla struck forwards, pinning the girl's wrist beneath her booted foot. The girl hissed, bucking beneath Arla's hold.

All she achieved was a blooming bead of crimson at her throat.

'You know,' Arla tsked, eyeing the girl who had the sense to look up at her with the first inklings of fear, 'most people, when they have a sword to their throat, prefer to remain still.'

'Most people don't survive contact with you by remaining *still*, Arla Reinhart.'

Something flared in Arla's blood. Challenge. Entertainment. It might be fun to go to war against a new female opponent. They always were more entertaining.

'So, you know my name – though I go by Dragonhart now – and you know my reputation, but I don't know yours. It seems I'm on the back foot already.'

The girl looked like she might laugh – for a split second, there was a sparkle in her eyes and the beginning of a widening of her lips. She didn't, though. 'I don't think there are many people that haven't heard of you and the things you've done. You're known even on the continent.'

She'd thought as much.

'Semantics. Now tell me what you want and what the fuck you're doing in my kingdom.'

She pressed the blade harder, relishing in the bead of blood that ran down the column of the girl's neck.

'I don't mean any of you harm—'

Arla pressed harder. 'I don't take kindly to liars.'

'Don't kill her, Dragonhart. I prefer my meat fresh.'

'I promise. We don't mean any of you harm.'

'I'm getting bored, Red. I suggest you start speaking because a very hungry dragon won't stay out of my head and is reminding me that her teeth are even sharper than mine.'

The girl's face paled in the moonlight.

'We're a resistance – the Red Blades. We started it as a way to take down Elrod. Some of the mages he took are with us now.'

Lovell's words echoed in Arla's head – that there were mages still unaccounted for.

Bile rose in her throat as that primal need to protect the mages reared in her blood.

'Settle yourself. We will burn them all to ash if they have harmed them.'

'If you have touched a hair on their heads—'

'They're safe, I promise you they're safe,' Red said.

'Then why do you keep them?' Arla growled.

'They want to fight. What Elrod did to them ... well, you can understand why the mages wish to fight back.'

She thought her heart had stopped beating. Her voice lethally soft, she demanded, 'Explain, now.'

'We're no different than you, I swear it,' the girl choked out. 'We rescued them only to keep them from the king, nothing else. It was only when more and more of them gathered that the idea of the resistance formed – an army to take down Elrod of Kastonia and make him pay for what he did to them.'

Arla blinked slowly. 'You aren't a mage, though.'

The girl smiled. 'Neither are you.'

A frustrated sound growled free of Arla's throat. 'I'm a dragonhart.'

'But you didn't know that before. It didn't stop you rescuing them, did it?'

No. It didn't.

How had this resistance been formed without Hark or his crew's knowledge? Why ... why were they *here*?

She was shaking, the sword digging further into the girl's skin. 'Then why have you been spying on us?'

The girl swallowed, the lump in her throat bobbing against

the tip of Arla's sword. 'Because I want the chance to speak to your people. To see if they wish to join the resistance too.'

Arla scoffed before she could stop herself. 'You aren't getting within a hundred yards of my people. You think I'll let you convince them to join you in what is *suicide*?'

'Don't you think some of them will *want* to?' the girl snapped.

No!' Arla laughed in disbelief. 'No, I do not. And even if they did, it would be foolish to march on a king and his army, especially when they're being led by a pathetic girl who's currently at the end of my sword.'

The girl's eyes narrowed. 'They won't be led by me. I'm just a soldier. Please. Give them the choice. What Elrod did was heinous. He deserves to die for it.'

'I'm not disputing that,' Arla said, her anger already dissolving because she could ... she could understand the motive. Could understand the *anger* and that need for revenge. She'd harboured it within her heart for years after Elrod killed her parents. 'But I won't allow my people to be sent to their deaths.'

The girl sighed. 'We have long despised the kings and their methods. We have always believed in the old religion, in the dragons and the gods and the dragonharts. They are safe, and we will keep them safe whilst they march against the man who wronged them. It would be better with you on side.'

'Never,' Arla said softly. 'Never will I ask them to fight.'

'You won't give them the choice?'

She considered it for all of three seconds. 'No. Not yet. Not whilst they're still afraid. In time, perhaps, but not now. They deserve the peace they had ripped away from them for years.'

'Two months then. Let me come back in two months and speak with them.'

Against her own instinct, Arla let the girl stand, keeping the blade gripped firmly in her hand. She didn't know why she capitulated.

'I will consider it. But you are not to spy on my kingdom again.'

The girl nodded once, a sharp incline of her chin, before she met Arla's gaze again. 'My name is Sylvie.'

Arla tilted her head, studying the girl's face as if it would betray something sinister lurking beneath the surface.

Arla sighed. 'You're a fool. But I understand your need for revenge. Tell your leader not to send you in their place next time. It's cowardly.'

Sylvie nodded again in that sharp, jerky movement before breaking into a run and disappearing into the trees.

'You don't trust her, Dragonhart.'

Arla began the walk through the forest to where she knew Thara was lurking and listening.

'No, I don't, and I won't risk the safety of this kingdom until I do.'
'I knew I picked you for a reason.'

It was as close to a compliment she thought she'd ever get from her dragon.

She hadn't been able to sleep for the remainder of the night.

Which was why, when the sun finally rose and she wandered to the training rooms to practise with Seb, she forced the Red Blade out of her mind. She couldn't trust them, and if she made a decision so soon after they had met, she was at risk of damning Flambriar. She'd push it out of her mind, let herself come to terms with it and decide whether they could trust what the girl had said before she broached the topic with the court.

'You'll have to start sleeping, Dragonhart,' Seb called across the room to her when she finally arrived to train. 'You look like you got into a fight with death.'

It was true – she was pale and her head pounded from the lack of sleep. 'Death wouldn't last five minutes with me,' she grunted, pulling a blade from the rack bolted to the wall. 'She tried, remember?'

'How could we forget,' he said, chuckling lightly, already bracing himself for the attack she would launch on him.

'Indeed,' she said, ignoring how the scar at her side still bothered her. How the tightness of the tissue restricted her movement and how she'd had to learn to adapt around it. Not that it made her any less deadly; she'd happily take on Hark's poorly constructed group of soldiers and have confidence that she'd beat them all.

'Let's go then, dragon girl. Show me what you've got.'

Despite the fire that flared in her blood at the ridiculous name, Arla found herself grinning as she leapt forwards and launched a barrage of lunges and blocks and stabs with the blade she had come to think of as an extension of her. Sebastian whistled low through his teeth, his own grin faltering for the briefest of seconds when he failed to move quickly enough and Arla nicked his cheekbone. The sight of the crimson blooming on his tanned skin was enough to send her into a frenzy.

It had always been a drive – blood. Perhaps when she had time to stop, she might wonder if it had anything to do with the way she'd watched it slowly leak from her parents' bodies for hours until someone had found her. Still, now she had cut him, she wanted even more. It called forth a hateful, wicked ardour she could lose herself in. The sight of blood elicited such a primal response from her that she was often afraid of it.

It never stopped her swinging the blade, though.

She went at Sebastian like he was a threat only she could see. She swung the blade with vicious, controlled strength. Sweat beaded on Seb's skin. Arla wasn't even panting yet.

She tunnelled everything into the arc of the blade, the swiftness of her dodge, the power she had honed in her muscles. She could feel Seb weakening – the way his blade didn't hold her as strongly as it had done before, the slow shuffles he made with his feet where there had been quick steps before.

'I'm out,' Seb said between gritted teeth.

She didn't care.

She kept moving forwards, kept swinging her blade. He didn't try to attack her now, only blocked and defended himself. She was almost through his defence – he'd be dead in seconds.

'Arla, that's enough.'

It was a taunt. One that lit up in her blood. Not long now. He'd drop the sword, and then she'd impale him, straight through the torso.

'I said ENOUGH!' He was shouting now, the desperation in his voice an encouragement to keep moving forwards.

'Dragonhart.'

Almost there, another swing of the blade and—

Strong arms wrapped around her, pulling her against a solid chest as they lifted her off the ground. 'If you're going to kill people, sweetheart, I'd rather you did so outside.'

It took too many heartbeats before she realised what had happened.

Seb was regarding her from across the training room, sweat dripping off his face. Her sword hung loosely in her hand, and ... Hark held her so tightly against him she didn't think she could breathe.

'Steady,' he murmured in her ear, his lips brushing her skin, the scent of whiskey flooding her senses.

She realised then how close she'd come to losing control. Just that single speck of blood on Sebastian's cheek and the lack of sleep had stripped away her control.

'I'm sorry,' she panted, barely catching her breath. Gods, she'd have collapsed if Hark hadn't stopped her. Her legs shook, her breathing coming too quickly.

'Go, Seb. I'll find you later,' Hark said.

Sebastian hung his blade up and offered them a weak smile before limping out of the room.

Gods, she'd fucked up.

'They aren't used to fighting like that. You took him by surprise, is all,' Hark said, turning her to face him.

'I would have killed him,' she mumbled.

'Yes, but you didn't.'

'Why are you defending me?' she snapped, shrugging out of his grip.

It would never leave her, would it? The years she had spent under Cyrus's instruction. To kill and kill and kill... She didn't know how to do anything else when the thoughts in her brain unravelled and she couldn't wind them back in.

Hark stepped up beside her immediately, turning her back to face him.

'I will always defend you,' he swore in a voice so low it sent a chill skittering across her skin. 'I don't care how many men you kill, I don't care what wretched things you do, I will always defend you because you are *mine* and I love you.'

Her chest heaved, the adrenalin from the duel finally beginning to ebb. He shouldn't defend her. She was wicked, and violent, and she had felt herself slipping more and more as each day passed, that well of violence in her filling and filling until she was certain she would overflow with it.

And yet ... she had never been so grateful for him. That he

should defend her, that he should look at her and still see *her* rather than this thing the world had turned her into made everything feel better. To be loved was to be seen, and Hark devoted himself to ensuring it.

She wanted to tell him about Sylvie – wanted to say she'd seen the Red Blade spying on her and had done nothing to stop it.

She wouldn't, though. Hark would refuse outright to have anything to do with *anyone* spying on their kingdom and she needed him to understand. Sylvie and the Red Blades wouldn't be a threat, Arla would make sure of it. And just like the way she'd kept killing the man in the mountains a secret, she would keep this one too, if it prevented a war. If it gave them just a few more months of peace.

She'd seen the lack of sleep that had drawn dark circles beneath his eyes, had seen the frown lines on his forehead because he couldn't switch his brain off. She wouldn't worry him with this, not if she didn't need to.

'Take the day off, Arla,' he said, lifting a stray curl and tucking it behind her ear. 'You've been working hard. The people are starting to trust you and you haven't stopped for a minute. Take the day off, go read, go fly, go and *sleep*. Gods, you look exhausted.'

She felt it then, the bone-deep tiredness she'd shrugged off for weeks now nipping at her heels.

Hark kissed her forehead softly, an action so lovely and so gentle that she fought the lump in her throat. She didn't deserve this kind of love. She didn't deserve someone who wasn't scared of her, who always managed to find a way to bring her back to herself no matter how many times she lost control.

She gripped him tightly. She'd fought for this life. She wouldn't allow anything to take it from her. So if that meant listening to Hark Stappen for once in her life, she would gladly go to her rooms and go to sleep. She'd gladly spend the day lounging around the hall and reading as many of those books as she possibly could if it meant it would help. She had worked too hard to get here, she wouldn't become the undoing of Flambriar and its court now. Thara sent a lick of warmth down the bond.

Besides, she had forever to build a kingdom.

CHAPTER 14

'You know she often bites those who pet her without permission?'

Arla had spotted the child – no older than twelve – stroking Vetta over the stable door. The girl tensed, spinning quickly to face Arla.

Recognition flared in the girl's tawny brown eyes, intrigue rather than fear lighting up her face.

Arla didn't know how to take it.

The girl turned back towards Vetta, pulling her hand gently away from the mare's face before she spoke softly. 'She's bred for war. She would never hurt those that are allied with you.'

Arla huffed out a laugh.

'Try telling that to her grooms. Your horse has the spirit of a firedrake, Dragonhart.'

'And who would they be, exactly?'

'Not from your world.'

She paused for a moment, watching the pair of them. Vetta's attention was fixed on the girl with soft brown hair and gentle eyes beside her.

'What's your name?'

'Elin.'

Arla stepped closer, resting an arm over the stable door and stroking the mare's neck. 'Well, Elin, are you? Allied with me?'

The girl met her gaze, an intensity burning there that made her look older than her face indicated.

'I have been allied with you from the moment we heard you were trying to help us. Even if you weren't the last dragonhart, I think the people would still follow you. They like your hope, and your viciousness. It's the most we've ever seen.'

Arla struggled to swallow around the knot in her throat. What was it about a child speaking of hope that had brought her this close to tears? Perhaps because she had been the same. Perhaps because Arla at nine years old had clung on to the tiniest scrap of hope and turned it into something bigger than she was. She saw it burning in Elin's heart. Saw loyalty there that she didn't feel she deserved because of what she had done.

'Are you a mage?' Arla asked.

'No,' Elin said, her voice so soft and lovely that Arla thought she might be able to listen to it forever. 'My sister might be, but she's too young for us to know yet.'

'And how old is your sister?'

'Two. I'm twelve. Our mother died last year from a wasting sickness. It was in her blood – the healers couldn't do anything.'

It was exactly what Arla had seen in Elin at first glance: a loss great enough to shatter continents. It was why she recognised the fire in the girl's soft eyes – they were like a paradox within tawny irises.

'I lost my parents too.'

Elin smiled. A sad, lovely smile. 'I know. It's why I follow you. You're stronger than I am. I want to be like you.'

An ice-cold spear plunged through her heart. No. Nobody

should be like her. Nobody should ever want to do the things she had done or have to experience all the ways she had betrayed her very soul to get the things she wanted. This girl in front of her ... gods, she should never, ever want to be like Arla. She wasn't strong – the loss of her parents was still a gaping chasm in the centre of her chest.

But she couldn't say any of that, could she?

Arla reached for Elin's slender hand, so small and gentle in her own.

'Sometimes strength has a funny way of finding us. I find it often comes best when you lend yours to someone else who needs it more. Don't wish to be like me, Elin. Wish to be like yourself. Your own strength will always be stronger than mine.'

The girl's eyes filled, but she wouldn't blink. Not a single tear fell as she nodded once at Arla and somehow found it within her to bury those tears and square her shoulders.

'If you ever need help looking after her,' she said with a pointed look at Vetta, 'I know how to, and I've studied the war horses a lot. I know they can be temperamental but ... I'm not scared of them.'

When she left, Arla felt a little less alone than before.

CHAPTER 15
HARK

She never failed to quicken the pace of his pulse and force his hands to flex.

'You look like the beginning of spring,' he murmured as Arla sashayed into his embrace. She smelled like honey and fire and jasmine, and he knew that under the gauzy, flowing, sage-green fabric her skin was as soft as velvet.

'I didn't know we were spouting poetry over dinner this evening, but if we are, at least give me time to fucking hang myself,' Kase said, stabbing the duck on the table so viciously Hark was surprised she didn't shock it back to life.

Arla chuckled against his neck and ... gods that sound! It was like falling stars.

Fuck, the poetry really did need to stop.

'How angry will you all be if I steal Hark away?' Arla said, though she was clearly going to do it anyway.

'Have him! We might get a chance to talk about something other than how much he loves the colour of your hair,' Seb said, swallowing whiskey like it was water.

Jack laughed, leaning back to rest an arm across the back of Kase's chair. 'He's all yours, Dragonhart.'

Hark thought he felt her tense slightly, but she was soft in his arms again in less than a heartbeat.

'Jaz?' she asked.

His friend looked at Arla so intensely it was enough to make him want to disappear, but Jaz dismissed the steely look Hark sent him and nodded once. 'Have fun.'

He followed her through the winding corridors and she ... she looked as though the very earth had bent to her will and gifted her its beauty. She led him into the oval room, where he had first found her awake at Flambriar and practically fallen to his knees and begged the gods not to let him lose her. She settled into the settee, her lithe body almost swallowed up by the plump cushions and blankets the colour of snow.

'I'm not going back for dinner, am I?' he asked, failing to hide the smirk that pulled the corners of his lips.

She smiled softly, a smile that was still so rare it stole his breath each time she deigned to grace him with it. A smile he could have had for two years already if he had only told her how he felt.

'I won't keep you long, but I doubt dinner will be as carefree as before.'

He knew what was coming. She didn't need to say any more...

'Arla—'

'Let me speak.' There it was. The authority she had always wielded. The ability to dig deep and pull forth the voice of a person who had been born to lead. A voice that had been forged by the fates.

He didn't think she would ever understand.

'I know you don't want to rule them, Hark, I do. And it's not something I want to get into again – at least not tonight – but something needs to happen. Something needs to change. The people are worried again. I had a woman come to me today and tell me that the lot of them are convinced that Elrod is going to find them and hurt them and use their blood to create something evil—'

'He can't. Thara said he couldn't—'

Her eyes flashed, and he could have sworn he saw embers burning within them.

'I know that and you know that, but they don't believe it. Hark, they see you up in the mountains every day for the gods' sake! They don't believe they're safe because they see you giving them a reason to believe they're not. Every. Fucking. Day. I had to lie to them, you know. I had to stand there in the middle of a kingdom *you* built and tell them you aren't scouting for enemies but rather spies that *we* have planted in other courts. We don't even have the numbers here to *have* spies.'

There was a desperation to her voice, a near hysteria he hadn't seen from her before. There was a crack in her careful control. He should be grateful, really, that she cared so much for a kingdom he had created and hidden from her. He should be grateful that she was allowing him to see this loss of composure.

He pushed away the thought that it was only because she was a dragonhart that the fates and the gods had *made* her care this much.

Still, he loved her. Would lay down his life for her. So why couldn't he give her this? He sighed, dragging a hand through his hair in the way he knew she had come to like.

'I'll stand in front of them and promise that we will keep them safe, Arla, but it won't be enough. They need to hear it from more than just me and you.'

'Thara,' she whispered.

'Thara.'

Silence opened up between them, a chasm he hated more than anything. How had he managed to fuck everything up so quickly after he finally had her?

He'd patch it up. He had to. Because fighting with her ... well, it wasn't an option. Not at all. He could only do this with her at his side, and if she wasn't, he didn't want any of it. He'd let the gods burn it all before it came between him and Arla.

'I know how badly you want this to go well,' he said, reaching for her. 'I know you feel all of this pressure because they gave you a new name, but this isn't all on you, Arla. We're in this together and you don't have to take all of this on by yourself, not anymore.'

He'd seen it. Seen her trying to manage the kingdom, trying to make everything just *perfect*, since she'd been declared dragonhart, and though she was trying to hide how she was struggling to settle in here, Hark had seen straight through it all. Seen her floundering beneath it all because she didn't want it all to fail.

'I prefer our old fights. The ones where Cyrus would have to split us up,' she said, a wry grin twisting onto her lips.

He had found himself looking back on his time at Castle Grey with a surprising fondness. Despite the constant, agonising stress of what his crew was up to and how he was trying to build a new kingdom whilst being stationed in an enemy one, everything had been simpler.

He missed fighting with her too.

'Come and fight me over here, assassin.'

She was upon him before he had finished blinking.

He didn't think he would ever get used to the feel of her body being so close to his. How she was suddenly straddling him, a blade pulled from the gods knew where resting against his throat.

'Aren't you wicked?' he purred and tried to bite down on a smile as he watched her eyes narrow and she leant forwards. Her lips were a breath away, the scent of her all-consuming, those tangles of blonde curls already claiming him for her own. The skirt of her dress parted at the slit she had cut to access her blade and revealed a beautifully soft leg.

'Eyes up, Stappen,' she murmured, the soft flesh of her lips brushing his as she spoke.

It was the beginning of the end.

The blade disappeared from his throat and fell clattering to the floor. He tugged her closer, until there was not an inch between them. Their lips met and fire erupted.

He kissed her as if his very life depended on it, and she kissed him back as if it would save the world. It wasn't the careful featherlight touches they had come to learn, this was urgent. Desperate. A cacophony of teeth and tongues and wandering fingers. She tugged at his shirt, tearing through the buttons as if they were a personal insult intended solely for her.

'You owe me a new shirt,' he said against her lips, tugging her even closer.

He felt the smile break across her lips as she pressed them against him. 'The only thing I like more than you in a black shirt is you without any shirt at all.'

Gods, she was ruination personified.

It was like daring to touch lightning.

He stood up, clutching her close to him as her legs snaked around his waist. He carried her through the winding hallways, ignoring the darting stares of maids that caught sight of them.

He made it to his own rooms, crashing through the door and laying her across the midnight sheets of the bed. Every part of him screamed her name, her scent, her taste. He could lie with her forever, tangled beneath the stars and let everything else burn around them.

The world fell away, and then there was only him and the blonde whirlwind that had stolen his heart.

CHAPTER 16

Hark arrived in the courtyard looking as regal as Arla had ever seen him. He'd arrived in full dress uniform, as befitted a king. There was an air of authority that attached itself to him, and Arla bit down on the kernel of hope that bloomed in her chest. He had it in him. He'd had it all along. He could be a king if he wanted – he was capable of it.

'Are we ready?' Arla asked, twisting the pommel of her blade in her hand. Today they had a kingdom to address.

'Let's go, Dragonhart,' Jack said, and as a group – as a *court* – they began the descent down the mountain, finally arranging themselves in the cobbled square that lay at the heart of Flambriar.

A calloused hand wrapped around her wrist and tugged her backwards, away from the others, and she turned into a cloud of whiskey and leather.

Hark's eyes were searching, curious, as if he were trying to find a secret that had been buried beneath her skin. 'I wanted to make sure you were all right before we do this,' he said softly.

Gods, she hadn't realised how much she'd needed him until now. Her lips parted, her tongue thick in her mouth. 'I just need this to go okay. I need them to trust us.'

Hark threaded his fingers with hers, and the quiet confidence he exuded was both new and old. This was the Hark she had fallen in love with – the man who had orchestrated the sabotaging of his father's camp on the border. She trusted this man, was devoted to him.

'It's okay to be nervous, but it's going to be fine,' he said, not an ounce of hesitation or uncertainty in his tone. 'And even if it's not, we will have each other, and that is the only thing that matters.'

She might have cried had she not been afraid of having puffy eyes when she addressed the people. But he was right; they had each other, and even if the world and the fates and the gods were against them, she could do it as long as he was beside her.

'Okay,' she said softly.

Hark nodded, a charming smile spreading across his lips. 'Okay.'

It didn't take long for the people to gather.

Murmurs spread through the crowd, eyes settling on the court that had gathered as one, with Hark at the forefront. Arla could see the apprehension in the way his throat bobbed and the way his fingers flexed at his side. And then, when silence settled like a blanket over the people, Arla watched him swallow that nervousness, roll back his shoulders, and step forwards to address his kingdom.

'I will start by offering you all an apology.' Hark's voice

echoed through the square, every bit a commander. A king. 'I have been absent since my return to Flambriar, and I understand the concern.' A ripple spread through the crowd. Every man, woman, and child kept their eyes fixed on him, awe and wonder and ... loyalty shining brightly in their eyes.

'You have spoken to your dragonhart of worries about Kastonia and its king. I am here to tell you that your fears are unwarranted.' A shudder ran its fingers down Arla's spine.

Your dragonhart. As if it were the most natural statement in the world. Not a single mage had balked at Hark's words, and he hadn't faltered either.

The world seemed to grow before Hark, lying down at his feet as he stepped into his role. For the first time she could see it happening, could see the confidence he bled when speaking with his people.

'I know you are worried. I know you see me and my court up in those mountains, but I would be failing you if I didn't track what the other kingdoms are doing. We are new, but we are strong, and nothing Elrod, or Kastonia, or any kingdom beyond can do will harm you here. I know you might think it is easy for me to say, but I hope you will believe your dragonhart, and the one who serves the gods.'

Arla's breath snatched in her throat, her fingers trembling gently against the hilt of the sword. She could do this. She'd addressed people more times than she could count, back in Hadalyn – had reworked Castle Grey's entire staff around her. This should be easy.

She couldn't help the wave of nausea that rose in her throat.

'Steady yourself.' Thara's voice was an anchor, drawing her back to herself. To her place as the protector of these people. She knew Thara had landed behind her before she felt the dragon's breath at the base of her neck or heard the worried shouts

of the mages. She stepped forwards as Hark inched back, so that Arla stood before the people, her dragon at her side as they stared at her with expressions she couldn't read.

Rolling her shoulders back she said, 'Unlike Stappen, I will not apologise for my actions or the decisions that have led me to stand before you today. Many of you don't trust me – perhaps you hate me?' Thara rumbled low in her throat. 'But I am the last dragonhart, and the gods tasked me with protecting you, so although I did not know it before, I know it now. And you have my oath that I will lay my life before yours to keep you safe. It doesn't answer your fears, no, but I am not the one to do that. If you won't believe me, believe the dragon that stands beside me. A creature of the gods, a blessing of the fates.'

Hark's fingers brushed hers, a bolstering, a reassurance that he was *right here* with her. She hoped it would be enough. That the sceptical looks on their faces would change.

'You do your dragonhart an injustice by failing to believe her. I hope you will extend more courtesy to me.'

Arla was just as shocked as those around her when she understood that it wasn't just her hearing Thara's voice in her head. The fear was written on their faces. She thought she saw a woman faint, and there was a distinct cry from someone a little further back. The children looked at their parents with round eyes and tilted heads, the most innocent of Flambriar's people spared the presence of such a creature in their minds.

She could have sworn Thara sent something resembling a laugh down the bond, and when the crowd didn't react, Arla was certain the dragon kept their bond separate from the one with which she spoke to the people.

'Show off.'

Warmth heated Arla's neck before Thara addressed Flambriar again. *'You fear that which you do not know. You are content to worry yourselves over courses that have yet to come to light. Hear me, when I say this, and from now on you will listen to the one who is blessed with guarding you. Elrod of Kastonia does not have the power to harm you with the blood of those who fell before. You fear your own magic without having truly used it. There will be worse things than fear of magic, blessed ones. Remember, you are descendants of gods, and I have yet to meet a god who has ever bowed before a king.'*

There was a pause. A deafening silence. Hark's hand brushing hers.

And then ... and then, one by one, the people of Flambriar dropped to their knees and bowed before Thara, and Hark, and Arla. They were willing to try to trust the court.

Arla felt Hark tense for the briefest of seconds, and before he could let a single doubt blossom in his mind, she threaded her fingers through his.

'Together?' he whispered.

'Together.'

She raised their hands high, her throat tightening as the people began to cheer, and clap, and in that moment she knew they could do it. Hark might lack the confidence to rule, but she never had, and together they would do it. Together they would keep a kingdom.

CHAPTER 17

The rest of the day was spent in the city. The members of the court mingled with their people, helping any who needed it, talking with the mages and allowing them the chance to get to know the people who lived in Claret Hall.

Arla couldn't help the knot of emotion that stuck at the base of her throat.

'Because they are yours, Dragonhart.'

They weren't hers to rule, but they were hers to protect. Hers to lay her life down for. It was a strange sensation – the tugging in her core that drew her to the mages – but she supposed this new life was going to be filled with new things – the bond with Thara, for one.

A whisper of air at her side was the only indication Kase gave as she sat beside Arla on the snow-packed hill where Arla had come to rest.

'It's a good view,' Kase said softly.

It was. Below them, the people still laughed and congregated in the streets around the men, Jack seemingly becoming the expert on livestock and growing crops. Jaz had disappeared into the schools to come up with a plan for what the children should be learning, and Seb was on the roof of a pretty cottage helping the mages construct a roof that looked as if it could take a thousand storms. She ignored the fact that the people still weren't using magic, guessing it would come in time, just as it had for the men in the forests.

And then there was Hark. He had spotted her on the hill a short while back, and even from this distance, Arla's heart had clenched when she saw the brilliant smile split his face. People tugged at his sleeves, and he listened to them each in turn, that steady smile never faltering, not even for a second. This was what he had been born to do. And though he could no longer claim Kastonia's throne, he had Flambriar.

'About time he stepped up, don't you think,' Kase said.

Arla turned her head slightly to face the girl – they weren't friends yet, still too many sharp edges to soften first – and found Kase's steely eyes staring back. There was a softness in the corners of her lips and the angle of her jaw, one that had been missing for some time – or perhaps hadn't ever been there at all. Arla had felt it too, the slow unravelling of that coiled, wicked thing inside her. Was this what safety felt like? Did it mean she could allow herself to relax and not sleep with a blade under her pillow every night?

She cleared her throat slightly. 'I don't know why he fears ruling like his father when he is everything that bastard isn't.'

Kase let out a low laugh, though no amusement lingered there. 'His father is the worst man alive. There is no scenario in this world in which Hark would ever become like him. I don't think the fates would allow it.'

Something twisted in Arla's stomach. She had never heard Kase talk of the fates before, of those whose wishes swayed even the gods and their plans. And something about the way she spoke about Hark? It wasn't jealousy that bloomed in Arla's chest, but there was something she didn't like. Something she felt she was missing and was being shielded from. She could take a guess at what it was, but really, did she want to ruin what had been a perfect day?

'First we deal with kingdoms, and then we deal with the heart.'

'When did you become so wise?' Arla threw back to Thara.

'Since I had to listen to your endless, ridiculous human thoughts all day.'

'What do you plan to do next?' Kase asked, drawing Arla's attention away from the dragon in the back of her consciousness.

'What do you mean?'

Kase leant back on her elbows, the ice crunching beneath her weight before she spoke again. 'You're restless already, and you haven't heard from your friend. So what's next, Reinhart? I'm not as stupid as you might think.'

Her heart clenched at the mention of Halos. Her first ever friend. One she had worried over constantly. One she had thought of as a sister.

One who hadn't replied to a single one of Arla's letters.

'Nothing. For now,' Arla whispered. It was barely a breath and yet she knew Kase had heard her, and she didn't try to decipher what the quick nod of Kase's head meant. She could see so much of herself in Kase and it made her nervous. Not that the girl would betray her, no. But that she would be an accomplice in whatever Arla had planned, regardless of whether it endangered the kingdom and irrespective of the fact that they couldn't stand each other half the time.

She wondered if that was friendship.

'Tired, ladies?' Sebastian called to them. Arla and Kase clam-

SHADOWHART

bered to their feet, both women already smiling. It was beginning to feel more like a family each day she spent in their company and Arla couldn't help but begin to love them as they began the trek up the mountain to the hall.

She hung back, sliding her hand into Hark's as the pair of them trailed behind the rest of their court. The sky was dimming to a soft lavender, the deeper shades of night already pushing the boundaries of daylight as they strolled hand in hand. His calluses rubbed against her own and it felt like a reminder of who they were. Of what they had gone through. They were more a comfort than anything.

'You did it,' she said, failing to keep the grin from parting her lips. Hark looked down at her, and ... gods, she often forgot how tall he was. How he towered over her like this. Perhaps she had become so used to him she no longer saw the differences between them at all.

'*We* did it,' he said. And that *we* ... it was a promise they had made to each other. That they would lead *together*. 'You know, I think you rather enjoyed scaring them all half to death with that dragon of yours.'

She laughed, a proper laugh. 'I think you enjoyed the looks the women were giving you – some of the men, too.'

It was Hark's turn to laugh then, and if she could capture the brilliance of the sun, she thought his laugh might be close to it. He did it so rarely, and when he did ... gods, when he did it was like a ray of light in darkest night. How had she never noticed it before?

'I enjoy the looks *you* give me more,' he purred in her ear, eliciting a sinful number of goosebumps across her skin.

'Well,' she said, jutting her chin out and revelling in the slight shake of his head he tried to hide, 'perhaps if you come back to my side of the hall tonight you can learn just how many of those looks I have.'

He pulled her to him, and he smelled like leather and woodsmoke. 'You're going to be the death of me, Arla Dragonhart.'

'I do try my best.'

His lips brushed hers gently in the fading light. 'You do, you wicked, violent little whirlwind.'

Oh gods! She thought she might melt right there on the ice.

'But there won't be time for that.'

Her breaths came quickly. He was standing far too close for her not to take advantage right on top of this mountain where the entirety of Flambriar could see them—

'I think the sound of goats dying would be preferable to your adolescent pining.'

Fucking dragons.

'I told Marianne we would all visit her restaurant tonight. She's been open a few weeks now and I think it would be good for us to visit, no?' Hark said.

Right, of course.

The people. Mages.

Flambriar.

She cleared her throat, turning away from him if only to hide the flush she was certain was creeping over her cheeks.

'That sounds great, really great.'

There were cool fingers caressing her cheek, and then he was turning her chin gently to face him.

'If there's one thing I can't stand more than you being hurt,' he whispered, 'it's you thinking you have to hide from me. I want to see every blush, every smile, every gods-damned tear. And just because I said we don't have time to go to your rooms before dinner doesn't mean we won't have time after, does it?'

Gods, she really was falling in love with him.

'Well, that sounds like a plan,' she managed to say, and when he smiled at her she thought the world would never be more perfect.

He walked all the way to her rooms with her and promised that he would find her after dinner, and he would see that blush spread across her cheeks like ink blotting silk.

Her reply had been positively scandalous, and as she bathed and brushed her hair and asked Lilith to braid it into something regal, those words Hark had teased her with played on a loop in her brain.

There was no way in this gods-damned kingdom she'd be able to concentrate on anything other than him over dinner.

They emerged from their own rooms bedecked in the finest garments and jewels their kingdom had to offer. Arla was aware she had managed to amass far more exquisite diamonds and jewels than the rest of her court and from the narrowed eyes Kase sent her way and the small shake of the head Jaz tried to hide, they knew it too.

All of her belongings were beautiful but this dress ... if she had been born into a different life, one where she was a queen, this was the dress she would have picked. It floated around her as though she controlled it with her mind.

'That's going to get ruined the second you get on a horse,' Kase said bitterly.

Arla smirked, running her tongue over her teeth before she split off from the court and made for the gates across the courtyard. 'Who said I was travelling by horse?'

Thara chuckled through the bond, and it seemed the dragon

even approved of the exaggerated beauty of Arla's outfit, lowering herself as close to the ground as she could to aid Arla in mounting.

'The boy looked a heartbeat away from fainting, Dragonhart.'

He had. Hark's lips had parted, and he had been unable to form words when she had strutted through the hallways of Claret Hall. His eyes had darkened, a wild, primal urge brewing there that she was sure she had incited earlier in the day. If there was one thing she loved more than fighting with females, it was seeing what her words could do to men. Specifically, Hark Stappen.

There was a rightness to flying a dragon, something inside her that approved and craved the bond between them. Like she had been born with it in her blood. Arla hadn't ever given much thought to the fates – had vehemently denied the existence of the gods and their dragons until a handful of months ago. Her fingers drifted to the brooch pinned to her cloak.

Arla had always felt watched inside Castle Grey, had always felt a presence drawing her to the tunnels beneath the palace, no matter how often she was scolded for wandering down there. And for her to even end up inside Castle Grey... For her to have become the King's Assassin...

There was no way the fates hadn't planned it all. Hadn't written it in the sands and the stars.

And she'd never been more grateful for it.

Thara landed softly in the cobbled square and Arla hopped from the dragon's back as easily as if she had been doing so her entire life. Her friends waited as their horses were led away by grooms that appeared out of stone buildings with softly glowing lights in their windows. Her boots, hidden beneath the flowing length of her dress, clipped across the cobbles, and Arla took comfort in the weight of the dagger strapped to her thigh.

Hark would tell her off for it. He would tell her it was unnecessary and that it made it seem as if they didn't trust their own people.

Arla knew better.

She had seen trust and the complacency it bred; she would not become it.

'Where's Sebastian?' she asked as a firm hand snaked around her waist, wrapping her in an embrace of woodsmoke and whiskey.

'Here,' a voice called from behind them. Arla turned to face her friend and ... the two children that were with him.

A girl with soft brown hair and eyes the colour of owls walked at his side. 'Elin?' Arla said.

'Hello,' the girl answered, a sheepish smile breaking across her face. Arla looked back at Seb who winked at her and carried a child no older than two years old. She had tumbling curls a shade darker than Elin's that fell down her back as she nestled her face into the crook of Sebastian's shoulder, a teddy clutched in a fierce grip even as the hand lay slack at the child's side.

'Your sister, I take it?' Arla asked Elin, who was looking at her as if she couldn't understand what she was seeing.

Arla felt the same, actually.

'Don't look as though you wish to stab me, Dragonhart.' Seb chuckled, making his way closer. Arla could just make out the tanned skin of the sleeping child he carried, and she struggled to piece it all together.

'I might not wish to stab you if you had told me you were a father.'

The court erupted into laughter.

'The day that prick becomes a father is the day I walk straight,' Jack laughed, leaning heavily on his cane. Even Elin laughed.

'I'm glad you all find it so amusing,' she growled, failing to tamper the annoyance rising with every echo of laughter that came from her court. Hark laughed too, and she shrugged out of his grip, suddenly finding that sound the most annoying thing she'd ever heard.

As if she'd ever compared it to fucking sunlight.

'They're not mine,' Sebastian finally said, shifting the sleeping girl's weight in his arms. She didn't so much as stir. 'My nieces – Elin, I believe you've met, because she's often in places she shouldn't be.' The girl narrowed her eyes slightly, and Arla shot her a quick wink. She knew all too well the lure of places you weren't supposed to be.

'And Vivianne – Vivi, we call her. They're my sister's girls but...'

'I'm sorry,' Arla said softly, recalling what Elin had told her about their mother and the wasting sickness.

Sebastian said nothing, only inclining his head and offering her a smile that was too sad to belong on his face. She wished she'd known. She'd have made sure the girls had places in the hall, had been offered anything they could have wanted—

Seb seemed to know what Arla was thinking before she could say anything. 'They split their time between me and my sister's friend. Cardia looks after them when I'm busy. Makes sure Elin goes to school instead of sneaking off to visit other people's horses.'

Arla swallowed thickly. She hadn't known... 'Yes, well, I'd rather be at the stables than school too, so I guess we have that in common.'

Elin's face lit up, and Arla thought she might be one of the prettiest girls she had ever seen. Vivi stretched in Seb's grip, nestling closer to him.

'Can we eat? I'm starving,' Kase finally interrupted, and truly, Arla was hungry, too.

They didn't have to answer because a lady with wiry black hair emerged through the restaurant's doors, the scent of spices and roasted meat reaching Arla almost immediately.

'Had I known you were intending on eating out here, Mr Stappen, I would have set some tables.'

The woman winked at Hark, and Arla had the unnerving feeling she'd seen this woman before. Perhaps she had come from Hadalyn and Arla had passed her in the streets. Maybe she had been one of the slaves she had helped free from the camp at the Northern Border.

'Shall we?' Hark said, linking Arla's arm in his own and leading his court through the double doors of the restaurant.

CHAPTER 18

They followed Marianne to the back of the restaurant, through glass-paned wooden doors that parted before she had laid a single finger on them. It was simple magic, but it captured Arla's attention all the same. She wished the mages would all use it more.

The room was made of oak beams and glass panels that distinctly reminded Arla of Claret Hall's sitting rooms. A table had been laid with cutlery that had been polished so it shone, and down the centre of the table lay twisted foliage, like the eucalyptus she had seen growing in glass houses across the river and evergreens harvested from the forests. Softly glowing lights had been wrapped around the oak frames of the windows, and beyond the glass lay a pristine night and millions of twinkling stars.

'I hope this will be satisfactory for you. We didn't have long to prepare, you see,' Marianne said, pulling a seat out for Arla.

'It is perfect,' she said, her voice faraway even to her own ears. It *was* perfect. And as the rest of the court took their seats and Arla looked at each of them, she swallowed the lump in her throat and poured from the bottle of wine already waiting for them. Hark took the seat to her left, and Elin slid in to her right, looking up at Arla through thick eyelashes as though she might disappear if she tore her gaze away for any longer than a second.

Food arrived quickly – an array of fish and venison and vegetables that had been cooked in spices that set her taste buds alight. They laughed over dinner, and even though Arla couldn't tear her attention away from the court and the conversations about Seb's love life or the way Jaz had once charmed his way into a private dinner with Hark's mother after hand-delivering books on rare flowers that came from continents too far away to ever visit, she had still noticed the faces that appeared from time to time in the doorway to their private dining room – the faces of mages that couldn't quite believe their leaders had ventured down from the hall at the top of the mountain.

Kase's hand gripped Jack's under the table, his eyes growing wearier as the night wore on, but he smiled and laughed and chatted with them all the same.

'You still look like you want to kill someone, Dragonhart,' Jaz said across the table.

Arla leant back in the chair, trailing her fingers over Hark's where it rested on her bare thigh at the slit in her dress. Just a little higher and he'd find the dagger she had hidden. She smiled at the thought. 'I always want to kill someone. Tonight I'm struggling to decide who.'

'Who are the choices?' Kase asked.

'You're top of my list, obviously.'

'Well of course,' Kase said, but there was no malice in her voice.

'And then I don't know. I—'

'Am bored,' Jaz interrupted. Each set of eyes turned to him, and Hark's fingers halted their tracing along Arla's thigh.

'Excuse me?'

'You're bored, Reinhart. Don't deny it. You haven't had to sit still for a second since you were nine years old. I don't blame you for feeling restless. There isn't anyone to kill.'

Ice formed in her stomach, her heart fluttering slightly. She wouldn't admit that. She wasn't bored. Yes, she pined after Halos and her unanswered letters, and she longed for someone to tell her what to do or give her instructions to hunt someone down.

'No one tells you what to do.'

But she couldn't allow herself to slip into that feeling of uselessness. She had felt it in the past and knew that it wouldn't just linger there, it would confine her to her rooms and leave her unable to fathom the motivation needed to get up and do anything.

'Just because I'm bored, Jaz, does not mean I don't want to be here. Just because I'm altering my sense of purpose doesn't mean I don't care about these people or this kingdom. Perhaps I should come and hound you in the library more often. Perhaps then we would find the answers I seek.'

There was a collective silence. Even Sebastian didn't chip in with a ridiculous comment that would send the table into roiling laughter. Because now they all knew.

They knew how out-of-place she felt. How she struggled to know her purpose, even as a dragonhart, and derive a sense of her own worth.

'You are worth more than the skies and seas. You are worth everything this world has to offer.'

She'd have to speak with Thara about flattery and how it had never worked on her.

Just when she thought the silence might last forever and the night was ruined, a tiny voice pierced the fraught silence.

'Dragon.' Vivianne finally lifted her head from where she'd slept against Seb's chest for the entirety of dinner and looked directly at Arla. She had the biggest blue eyes Arla had ever seen, and with a heart-shaped face and peach-coloured lips, she looked almost nothing like her sister.

'Hello, Vivi.'

The child's eyes widened further than what should have been physically possible. 'Dragon,' she whispered.

Sebastian chuckled, lifting Vivianne to sit properly on his lap. 'She might resemble one, Vivi,' he said, 'but Arla isn't a dragon.'

'Dragon.' Her arms reached for Arla who couldn't help the twang of pain in her chest as the little girl blinked at her. She reminded Arla so desperately of Ettie – Halos's daughter – that Arla couldn't help herself reaching over and holding Vivi's hand in her own.

'I'm Arla.'

Vivi clambered forwards so that her knees rested against the table. Seb grunted, and Arla heard Jack laugh under his breath.

'Arla dragon,' Vivi said, reaching with her other hand to touch Arla's face.

The child's fingers against her skin were electric – a static spark in the connection of flesh that stirred something in Arla's chest. Magic, perhaps. Vivi was a mage and would likely start presenting with magic soon, Arla thought.

'Arla dragon,' Vivi said again.

'That's right,' Arla replied softly. Vivi ran her hand over the diamonds pinned through Arla's ears and then the brooch at her throat.

'She likes you,' Elin said at Arla's side.

'Well, I like you too, Vivi.'

'I'm surprised she's awake,' Sebastian said, standing and lifting the child from the table. Vivi let out a cry of surprise as Seb lifted her, the tunic she wore so long it covered her toes as she wriggled between the fabric and Seb's hold. 'Hasn't slept for two nights Cardia told me.'

'It feels like longer, that's for sure,' Elin said with a sigh.

'I wish you'd told me about the girls sooner, Sebastian,' Arla said, rising from the table in a curtain of diamonds and shimmering fabric. 'And the rest of you are equally awful for not telling me either. Perhaps Elin and I should make you sleep outside tonight?' she said, winking at the girl. Elin grinned widely, which was the strongest expression of emotion Arla had ever seen her make.

'Try it, Reinhart, and I'll personally burn every one of those books you had delivered this week,' Kase said.

Arla bit her lip against the laughter rising in her throat. Gods, the wine had been good indeed. 'Is that a declaration of war, Kasey?'

She did laugh then. Sebastian roared, and Hark choked on his wine. And then they all collapsed into tear-inducing laughter, even Kase, who shook her head at Arla in a way that promised revenge.

The evening had been perfect, and warmth lit her chest as the court filed out of the restaurant, stopping to say hello to the mages who reached for them. Just as she was about to leave, Marianne beckoned Arla over. Arla urged Hark and the others to go on, saying that she'd meet them back at the hall, and sat across from Marianne at a table almost hidden from the rest of the restaurant.

'You have enjoyed tonight, I hope?'

'It has been beautiful, Marianne. Truly.' Arla shocked herself sometimes – how easily she slipped back into her role as courtier.

'You've settled here well, Arla,' Marianne said, and again Arla couldn't shake the feeling that she'd spoken to this woman before. 'You've been spending time in the library with Jaz, I hear?'

Arla was silent for a moment, waiting for whatever it was she thought Marianne was digging for.

When the woman didn't continue, Arla finally spoke. 'I have. I want to learn more about the dragonharts.'

Marianne's brow twitched slightly, and she rocked back in her seat.

'That's good. You know there were many of you once. You're supposed to unite the kingdoms, I hear.'

Bile rose in Arla's throat, and she twisted the skirt of her dress tight between her fingers. Not this again. It kept her up at night, the wondering and worrying about what it all meant and what in the gods' names she was supposed to do.

Marianne seemed to read the worry on Arla's face because her eyes softened and she reached across to hold one of Arla's hands. She could have sworn a spark of energy passed between them, and Thara rumbled softly through the bond.

'Keep reading, Dragonhart. You'll find the answers you seek.' Marianne smiled before rising to her feet and walking away, leaving Arla with only her diamonds to keep her company as she mulled the words over in her mind.

She'd keep reading, but she didn't think it would ever be enough.

Hark was waiting for her in her rooms when she returned to the hall. She opened the doors to find him lounging on her bed, feet crossed at the ankles and the top three buttons of his shirt undone. She couldn't help the shiver that teased her skin.

'Don't look so surprised, Dragonhart,' he purred. She would let it all go to hell if he kept looking at her like that. Forget the kingdoms and the gods and the fates, she would let it all burn for Hark Stappen.

'What surprises me,' she began, prowling towards him, 'is that you still insist on separate bedrooms when you come here looking like that and staring at me as though I'm not wearing anything at all.'

'*Fuck*, Arla,' he hissed. She loved it, the careful undoing of him she had become so proficient in over the last few months. There had been a time when she had struggled to get beneath his skin at all. Now she lived there, burrowing into the deepest parts of him so that she could have him between her teeth and relish the way they had both changed.

'Thank you,' she said softly. 'For tonight – for everything. I know you don't want to be like your father, Hark, but believe me when I say I don't think you could be like him even if you tried.'

She stroked a hand down his arm, and gods, he was looking at her as if she had fallen from the stars. 'I know I've been difficult, and I don't adapt to change very well—'

'Hey,' he interrupted, sitting up straight, his hands settling on her elbows as she stood in front of him. There was a seriousness in his face that made her throat tighten. 'Don't apologise to me for being who you are. I know, and I *see* every part of you, Arla. I knew it two years ago, and I know it now. You don't have to apologise or feel out of place. And if you're struggling, if you're going into that dark place, you tell me, okay? You aren't alone anymore; we go through this together. And today?

Standing up there? That was all for you. *Anything* to make you feel like you belong here, it's yours.'

Gods, she could hardly breathe around the lump in her throat, and she knew her eyes were filling with useless tears, and she didn't *care*. She loved him. So, so much.

'You looked radiant tonight,' he murmured as she climbed onto the bed, crawling towards him so that the rest of the world melted away and there was only Hark Stappen and a star-covered ceiling. He reached for her, tugging her close so that she straddled his lap, drowning them both in that magnificent dress and the diamonds she had worn like armour.

'And you looked like a king.'

His lips came crashing onto hers.

Afterwards, when her body felt soft and her heart beat a lazy, contented rhythm, Arla lay her head on Hark's chest and relaxed into his fingers running through the golden waves of her hair enough to send her into the throes of sleep.

'This might be my favourite thing in the world,' she uttered softly, her own fingers drumming a rhythm against his muscled forearms.

Hark chuckled, pressing his lips against her temple. 'Imagine when there's no prophecy hanging over us, I might not let you leave this bed for days.'

She'd like that.

Arla snuggled closer, pushing all thoughts of the prophecy to the back of her mind. The gods knew it had taken up enough of her worries in recent months. 'We could live in a little house by the water.'

'You wouldn't stay here?' Hark asked, though there was no

annoyance in his voice that she might leave Claret Hall, only a soft curiosity that made her smile.

'I'd have both.'

Hark laughed then, a lovely sound she wished to bottle and get drunk on.

'Of course you would.'

He was silent for a few seconds before he continued. 'What else would you want – besides a pretty cottage by the river?'

Sleep was tugging at her, and yet Arla couldn't help the swelling of her chest, the smile that split her lips as Hark continued stroking her hair.

'I'd want to have a garden, where I might grow lilies in the spring. And I'd want a hound, too, and I'd name him Treasure, and he'd pretend to hate you.'

It was a beautiful dream. One she had wished for since her very first days in Flambriar.

Hark shifted beneath her, tilting her chin up so that she stared into eyes of icy blue.

'You will have it all,' he vowed, brushing her cheek with the pads of his fingers. 'You will have a garden, and a hound, and we will camp in the mountains and watch the stars once all the ice has melted.'

She didn't think it was possible for her pathetic heart to pine for something more, and it scared her deeply.

But that future? The one where their lives were peaceful?

She'd solve a hundred prophecies for that.

CHAPTER 19

There was something in the air at Claret Hall over the next two weeks – in Flambriar, too.

Arla's steps felt featherlight as she wandered the corridors of the hall, and when she trained with Seb or Hark or any guard that would risk it, gone was the angry, dangerous streak that slightly terrified her, and in its place was a skill that she had honed and perfected over the years. Her moves came easily, and the pain in her side was just a memory. She spent evenings flying with Thara over the mountains, pushing Sylvie's request to the back of her mind. Everything here was too good – too *happy* – for her to ruin it by bringing it up with the court.

Besides, she still had more than a month before she had to meet with the Red Blade again. There was nothing to say she must make a decision by then, no matter what she had told Sylvie. She didn't know why she still kept it from Hark and the rest of their court, only that it felt too late now. She should have said something weeks ago. Perhaps, if she were lucky, Sylvie would disappear and never come back, and Arla wouldn't have to make any difficult decisions regarding letting the redhead converse with Flambriar's people and convince them to go to war.

The rest of the court had been filled with a joyful energy too, and Arla wished it could stay like this forever, that she could be allowed to live in this suspended peace far away from the other kingdoms.

But she couldn't, could she? Because whilst the mages and the court might be the most relaxed they'd been since Flambriar had been founded, Jaz had been holed up in the library, and Arla knew she couldn't avoid it forever.

It was why she found herself heading there following a particularly hard duel with one of the guards after Noah's falcons had returned to Flambriar without a single scroll bearing Hadalyn's crest. She entered quietly, careful not to scuff her boots on the wooden floor as she wandered between the shelves to find Jaz sitting beside the window with a pile of books resting on the floor beside him.

'Nice of you to join me,' he said without looking up.

'Stop being so miserable,' she huffed, collapsing into the chair opposite him and earning herself a scathing look. 'If the gods want me to unite the kingdoms, they should make it a little easier. I can't read every single book in this library.'

'Who said the book is in this library?'

She stilled. 'You don't think it's here, do you?'

Jaz sighed heavily, closing the book he held and leaning back in his chair. He looked tired – as if he had spent every second available in this room looking for anything on the gods and the dragonharts. 'I think the only way you're going to find out anything about the dragonharts is by reading the ancient texts, many of which we have here. But there's nothing to say there aren't still books hidden in Kastonia and Hadalyn. And there's nothing to say there aren't books that have been lost to time. It's been a century since the dragonharts walked the land, Arla. If your dragon won't give us the answers you seek, then the books have to.'

'Tell him I will scorch his skin and rip the flesh from his bones—'

'Thara is bound by the gods and the fates. She cannot speak of what she is commanded to keep silent. I may be a dragonhart, but Thara's loyalty lies first and foremost with her masters.' The venom that dripped from her words was enough to have Jaz looking sufficiently wary, and Arla didn't know if it was Thara's anger or her own that simmered in her voice. She had begged the dragon so many times to help her, to tell her what she needed to do, but even the news that entire streets of Kastonia were succumbing to wasting sickness and there was no medicine left to help did not change Thara's mind. Thara's turmoil had been a wild, thrashing thing down the bond, begging Arla not to force her to speak of such things. Arla wouldn't blame Thara for not speaking of it, and she wouldn't allow anyone else to either.

'We keep looking. There will be answers somewhere,' she muttered.

'Why?'

Arla looked up at him. Jaz's arms were crossed over his chest and he was looking at her as if she were the most boring thing he had ever seen. 'Excuse me?'

'Why are you still looking? The people are safe here, you said so yourself. You're the happiest I think I've ever seen you, and so are the rest of this court. So why unite the kingdoms?'

It was a question she'd been asking herself for days now.

'Because I won't let Hadalyn fall to the same poverty and ruin that is taking over Kastonia. Cyrus may have betrayed me, but Hadalyn is still my home, and they are still my people. They don't deserve for the kingdoms to fall, and who's to say it stops there? The gods are angry that the balance is off, Jaz. They won't stop once Kastonia and Hadalyn have fallen. The people will flee, and they will end up here and then Flambriar will be punished too. Gods, the continents themselves will fall if we don't find a way to right what Elrod did!'

'That's my point,' Jaz said. 'This was Elrod's doing, not yours. Why should it be up to you to fix it?'

Had there not been animosity between the two of them from the very moment they had met, Arla might think Jaz was defending her — that he was trying to find a way to keep her from having to be the one to unite it all. But she could see straight through him. He was intrigued by her. He still didn't believe that her loyalty lay anywhere other than to herself. It made her want to stab him.

'Because I'm a dragonhart. Like it or not, the gods chose me, and I have to restore the balance that bastard upset by sacrificing the mages. I don't think the gods are going to accept me asking them not to kill us all, even if I say please.'

It all sounded ridiculous when she said it like that. Even more so considering the fact she hadn't believed in any of it mere months ago.

Save the kingdoms...

She was close to watching them all burn.

'Then I suggest you pick up a book and start reading, *Dragonhart*.'

∼

Her eyes had to be bleeding, surely.

As the clock signalled the fifth hour of her being curled up in the library with only Jaz's relentless sighing for company, she was ready to stab herself with her own blade.

That was when she found it.

Hidden at the bottom of a torn page stained yellow with age, sharp handwriting gave her the first promising piece of information she'd found in weeks.

'You'll want to read this,' she said, surprised how dry her mouth was and how heavy her tongue felt. Jaz came around the wooden table to peer over her shoulder and read the words on the torn parchment.

> ...*magic they are gifted is enough to break and make worlds. The gods have gifted them well, and the harts are a gift to us...*

'Do you think this is about the dragonharts?' Arla breathed.

Jaz nodded, turning the page to see if the passage continued. It didn't, the book too damaged and old to offer anything else on the history of the dragonharts. 'I think it speaks of them having had gods' magic once. That they were gifted it in order to protect the mages,' he said.

'But I don't have magic,' Arla said, and all too quickly her chest was tight. What if she'd done something wrong? What if she was supposed to have magic and keep them all safe? What if—

'I think this speaks of a time before even the dragons were here,' Jaz said, his eyes fixed somewhere far away. 'It says the harts were a gift to the people, but it doesn't mention the dragons.'

'But the dragons were here when the gods left the earth centuries ago. They became the only way the dragonharts could contact the gods.'

'I think things were very different from what we have been taught,' Jaz said solemnly, rubbing a hand across his brow.

'So what then?' There was a storm brewing inside of her, threatening to topple this entire hall if she couldn't work it out. She had come to the library for answers on how she was supposed to unite kingdoms. Now ... now she had more questions than when she started.

'I don't know,' Jaz said with a sigh. 'I don't know in what order the dragons and the gods and the harts came, but I think you all had magic once – gods' magic, strong enough to shatter worlds. I don't know what happened or where that magic went, but wherever it disappeared to the gods followed. And now it's only the dragons and you left.'

The dragonhart brooch felt hot through the fabric of her shirt, as if it was teasing her, goading her into finding something *more*...

The doors to the library swung open, but the click of feet across the wooden floor belonged to an unfamiliar person. When Noah's head peered around the bookcase, a scroll clutched tightly in his right hand, it took everything she had within her not to vomit.

'Forgive the intrusion, Dragonhart. This came for you. The falcon landed a little less than half an hour ago.' Noah held out the scroll to Arla and she snatched it so violently it was embarrassing. But she had been waiting for this, hadn't she? This was going to be the last piece of her that would feel whole again, and Halos would be the one to fix her.

Later, when she had calmed down and considered the fact that Halos would never seal a scroll with wax, Arla would realise that the crest melted into the seal was not that of Hadalyn, but of a kingdom she had visited only once before.

Her eyes scanned the letter quickly, skipping over words as

if she could absorb them just by glancing. She couldn't help the way her heart sank the more she read, nor the feeling that the knot in her stomach was going to suffocate her when she finally read who the letter was from.

Her voice was small when she looked up at Jaz and said, 'It's from the Princess of Malarye. They want me to visit them.'

~

No one was particularly keen on her travelling to Malarye, and they were vehemently against her going alone.

She stormed out of the sitting room and away from the five concerned faces blinking at her and decided to dissolve her anger the only way she knew how: by punishing her body until she collapsed.

She recalled what Jaz had said in the library: *'Only the dragons and you left.'*

Right, because it was too much to ask that she be given some sort of explanation, wasn't it?

'Patience, Dragonhart. You humans are too quick to resort to anger.'

'I'm angry because I've been left flailing in the dark by gods and fates who obviously find this all very amusing.'

A rumble rattled down the bond, raising the hair on Arla's neck as she climbed the highest point of Claret Hall. Her arms were burning; she needed to train harder.

'I assure you no one, least of all the gods, finds this amusing. The fates have tied the gods' hands. They cannot help you, Dragonhart, and I am even blinder than they are.'

One day, if she ever got to meet the fates, she'd stab them one by one. Into tiny little pieces. And scatter the pieces across the kingdoms. Maybe set fire to them.

She tried to summon the anger in the bond, but that too was failing her. Now she was just confused and tired and desperate.

'What do you think I should do?'

Thara didn't answer her until she'd made it to the highest window ledge of the hall and her limbs trembled with the effort as she pulled herself through it. Arla thought, for a brief moment, that Thara had shut down the bond, and the plummeting, sharp feeling in her stomach was utterly embarrassing.

She'd come to find the bond too much of a comfort.

'You will go to Malarye and learn what it is they wish to tell you. Queens and princesses don't invite guests to their shores for pleasantries, Dragonhart, as you well know. There will be knowledge worth gaining on the continent. The gods are reluctant to tell me anything anymore, but they speak of patience, and they speak of your strength especially. I hope in time it will all become clear.'

Arla could hear the sorrow in Thara's voice, the sting of betrayal that gods who had once cherished their dragons were now keeping secrets. It made her angry. Not just for her but for Thara too. Thara, who had woken and left the rest of her kind sleeping in Hadalyn in order to help a girl who didn't have a clue how to do anything.

'I chose you for a reason. Don't ever doubt my belief in you, Dragonhart. Know that I do not.'

She blinked the tears from her eyes before they could fall.

Patience. Strength. She could do that – she had *always* done that.

But time...

Time she did not have.

'Do you think I'll ever meet the gods – or the fates? I'd love to have a word with them.'

Thara huffed a laugh down the bond. Having worked out her anger, it didn't seem too bad. She could do this. Hark had stepped up and addressed his people, and now it was her turn. She could step up and be patient and *strong* and whatever else the gods wanted whilst she waited for everything to play out.

'I think if the gods ever meet you, they will have met their match.'

She hoped so. She hoped that all of this had made her strong, but that it hadn't turned her into something sharp and unforgiving. She still felt those bursts of anger, the almost primal urge to kill and hurt anything that stood in her way or threatened the people she loved. She hoped she wasn't too far gone. She hoped there was a way back for someone who had done horrible, wicked things.

She hoped she hadn't ruined herself.

CHAPTER 20
HARK

Anticipation buzzed in his veins, hounding him as he buttoned his suit jacket and downed the glass of whiskey he'd requested be brought to him whilst he readied himself for that evening. He'd been looking forward to it in a strange sort of way. Yes, it was a celebration in honour of the mages that had lost their lives under Kastonia's persecution, but he'd heard about the planning that had gone into tonight, and it was going to be spectacular.

'Do hope you're dressing up tonight, Stappen, I've just seen your girlfriend and she's the picture of regal,' an amused voice drawled from the doorway. Sebastian leaned against the doorway with one arm above his head, his fighting leathers replaced with a suit worthy of drawing the most modest of Flambriar's citizens into bed with him.

'Don't you have children to be looking after?' Hark said, the smile on his face foreign as he looked at himself in the mirror. Flambriar had aged him. Physically, but he also felt it like a weight on his soul. He just wanted them all to be safe.

'Said children are currently clinging to Miss Reinhart like she's the most exciting thing they've ever seen,' Seb laughed.

He was not surprised. He'd seen the awe in Elin's eyes, and Vivi clearly wasn't far behind.

He smoothed his jacket and shot a grin at his friend before donning the mask of Flambriar's ruler. 'Then I guess we'd better get going.'

~

They'd agreed to meet in the sitting room, the one with a huge fireplace and a dining table already pocked with dagger marks – the one with brown leather armchairs and chaises in which Arla Dragonhart was already lounging, her fingers curled around the stem of a glass containing that delicious sparkling wine. The other hand hung loosely at her side where a two-year-old with unruly dark curls played with the silver rings adorning the assassin's fingers.

Regal was too tame a word for the way Arla looked.

If the world still turned, it was her at its core. She was starlight, and fire, and magic.

Emerald fabric clung to her like a second skin, the skirt fanning out around her as if she commanded every scrap of silk and tulle and whatever else the gown had been made of. Hark didn't think he had ever seen something so exquisite.

'You're drooling, Stappen,' Kase remarked, shooting him a grin that lit him from within. His friend was a picture of lethal beauty. Silk, black as night, slid across her skin, pooling at her feet like a waterfall of obsidian.

'I don't know, I quite like him like that.' Her voice was thick as honey and lit with the spice of the wine she sipped. The trousers of his suit felt far too tight.

Seb handed him a glass of something cold and bitter. He swallowed it in one. 'You certainly have a way of bending palaces around your finger, Dragonhart.'

She blinked once, soft, dark lashes brushing the skin beneath her eyes before she turned her head to assess the entire court that had gravitated around her.

Arla had always had a certain pull, a way of becoming the centre of any room no matter whether it contained kings, or nobles, or the merchants that brought produce from the other kingdoms.

He tried not to think of Malarye and the fact he wouldn't be joining her.

But if Arla was worried about her impending trip out of Flambriar, it didn't show on her face as she stood, her dress fanning around her as the assassin moved toward him. She had always possessed a unique brand of movement. All fluidity and lethal grace. It was far more arousing than he cared to admit.

She stood so close he could smell the very scent of her. Could almost feel her skin beneath his hands.

She looked up at him, her hands coming to the bowtie at the base of his throat. For every brush of her fingers against his skin he was sure he would combust.

'I have no interest in bending palaces to my whims, Stappen. That particular skill is reserved for you alone.'

Fucking *gods*! The things he would do to have her out of that dress and splayed before him right now.

Judging by the look in her eyes, he guessed she was thinking something very similar indeed.

She shot him the coyest smirk he imagined possible before turning back to face the court. He was glad to have shared this moment with the goddess who stood before him.

'It's time,' she said softly.

And though Hark knew she didn't understand what tonight meant yet, he knew she would be right at the front of it. She had lost the people that made up her soul, and if there was anyone to lead them down the mountain to honour the dead, he could think of no one better than the girl with a heart forged of fire.

CHAPTER 21

The valley was awash with starlight and flickering torches as Arla led the court down the mountain and into the city of Flambriar. There was music somewhere in the distance, and she could just about see the roaring flames of a bonfire beyond the peaks of lovingly constructed houses. There was magic in the air – a floating, gilded thing that injected giddiness into the court despite what tonight represented.

This night might have been a chance to honour the dead, but Flambriar had come alive.

Claret Hall's court trailed behind Arla, their footsteps soft against a ground finally clear of snow. She hadn't thought the frost would ever fully thaw this far north, but it was as though the gods had saved this night for them and allowed bare arms not to feel the biting wind of the mountains.

Hark's fingers wound through her own, and Arla held them tight. Oh, the singing, it sank into her bones! Something ancient and fervent and magic. She knew it ran in her veins, this song of old. A song perhaps crafted by the gods themselves to honour those who had fallen.

And then Flambriar's square stole her breath clean away.

She had expected mourning black. She had herself chosen to wear green because those who had fallen at Kastonian hands deserved something bright to hold onto.

But no.

Flambriar had come together in a cacophony of colour and gems and soft flame that burned in the palms of every mage. They sang a haunting melody, every note hauling a lump into her throat. It was a song for them all. For the mages who had been held captive. For those who had lost their lives during the imprisonment. For those who had been slaughtered on Grey Hill all those years ago.

It was a promise.

That it would not happen again. They would not allow it.

The court filtered in behind her and Hark, positioning themselves in the circle that had formed in the cobbled square, a blazing bonfire at its heart. No one paid them any attention; tonight they were all there to honour those who had given their lives to keep this secluded corner of the world safe.

Arla gripped Hark's hand tighter, as if his solemn strength could keep her upright. She knew how much this meant to him, too. They may not have fallen at the end of a sword, but he had lost a brother. A mother. A ... father.

Because she failed to believe that the same man who wore the Kastonian crown had ever truly been this evil. She wanted to believe that he had loved Hark once upon a time. That he had been a king and a ruler and a father before his greed had turned him into something the gods condemned. She squeezed Hark's hand. *I'm here.*

The final lingering note wound through the crowd, the

flames in their palms flickering out as Flambriar was enveloped in silence.

There was nothing for long minutes, only bowed heads and linked hands and a prayer that the souls of the dead had found their way home.

It was like an oath, and Arla didn't think she had ever been prouder.

'They are yours. Your pride is well placed.' A shadow passed over them, the tug in the bond stronger than ever as Thara looked down on her.

'Are you ready for tomorrow?' Arla replied, her eyes still trapped in the flames of the roaring fire.

'Enough talk of tomorrow's journey, Dragonhart. Tonight is about remembering the past.'

Her dragon always knew how to make her feel minutely small.

'But yes. As if my capability was ever in doubt.'

A smile crept onto her lips.

As though they moved as one, the people of Flambriar bowed before the bonfire, reciting words of an ancient language Arla knew she would find in those books at Larkire with the strange symbols etched on their spines. It shocked her sometimes, the weight the old religion still carried and the continuation of it amongst a people that had been ruthlessly hunted.

There would be no speech from Hark, or from her, or from any of them. Tonight, every being that stood in the square was equal. There were no kings or queens, no leaders or rulers, no dragonharts and no gods-blessed. Tonight was not about them.

One by one, the crowd began to disperse, smaller groups branching off to speak quietly whilst a quartet of musicians began to play soft music on stringed instruments. There was food being brought out and laid on huge slabs of wood that had to have come from the men that worked the forests, and Marianne tended to it all, handing out hot breads and cheeses to children, pouring glasses of warm, spiced wine that reminded Arla so vividly of the market festival in Vorstrum.

Gods, it felt so long ago. Like years had passed when it had only been ... could it really only have been three months ago?

A hand snaked across her waist. 'Come and sit by the fire. You'll catch a chill.'

Hark looked ... entirely delicious tonight. He was freshly shaven, and the way that black suit hugged every inch of his body? There was no way he wasn't spending the night with her once they returned to the privacy of Claret Hall.

'Stop looking at me like that or else I'll show the entire mountainside the wicked things I want to do to you,' he purred in her ear, and that sound, those *words*, dragged warmth to her core. He was enough to reduce her to ashes.

'I'd light him up before he ever got the chance.'

Arla disguised a laugh, and from the way Hark rolled his eyes before gifting her with a wide grin that showed off those secret dimples, she knew he was aware there was a secret conversation going on with Thara.

She followed him closer to the fire anyway, where their court mingled with the people, sharing stories and listening to the ways in which the mages had been expanding the kingdom. It was fascinating, truly, the ease with which they were beginning to wield their magic, as if all they'd ever needed was permission to tap into the gift they had been forced to hide their entire lives.

Food and drinks were handed out and dancing began around the fire, the people moving so gracefully and meaningfully that it pricked Arla's eyes with salty tears. There was a tug on the bond then, a reassuring arm that leant its way across her shoulders.

'I am with you.'

She didn't know why those four words almost had her choking back a sob. Perhaps because as she looked around at the court and their people, at the *family* that had been formed, it was the first time in almost a decade she had not felt so alone.

She knew the girl had crept beside her despite the silent way in which Elin always moved.

'Hello, Elin.'

If the girl was surprised Arla had noticed her, she didn't show it. 'Hello.'

Silence hung between them, and Arla had spent enough time watching townsfolk stutter at the feet of her king to know the girl wished to ask her something she was perhaps too scared of the answer to voice.

'I don't bite. You can ask me whatever question is burning a hole in your mind.'

The girl laughed. 'Will you train me?'

Something heavy swung in the pit of Arla's stomach.

'Train you to do what?' She already knew what was coming next, her mind scrambling for a way to get out of this situation.

'I want to be like you. I want to be as strong and quick as you are.'

Unlike some of the other children, Elin had never been scared of her. She didn't know if it was a good or bad thing that Elin had no qualms about looking her dead in the eyes and never once flinching.

'Elin, I—'

'Don't tell me I'm too young. Don't tell me it's not something I want to do. You were younger than me when you were allowed into Castle Grey.'

Elin was twelve. Three years older than Arla had been when she'd first felt the blooming of an idea in her heart: to be the best assassin the world had ever seen; to work herself to the bone so that no one could ever take something precious from her again.

Elin had lost her mother, too. Who was Arla to tell her she didn't have the right to channel her pain into the solid swing of a blade or the burning tear of muscle?

Arla looked at the girl. Really looked at her. She took in the soft eyes and angled face, and Arla could see the resolve there. The need for an outlet to release the things that had hurt her. It was like a call to something she recognised in her own blood.

'Do not look at the child and deny her the very things you were gifted, Dragonhart.'

'Her uncle will kill me if she gets hurt.' It had been Arla's first thought. Seb had already lost his sister; Arla didn't know how he would react if his niece got hurt in what she could feel was a looming battle. Elrod hadn't made a move yet, but there was an unease that pricked her skin each time she thought of Larkire and the man inside its palace. Something was coming, she was sure of it.

And who was she to deny a child the ability to be able to defend herself if that battle came?

'Her uncle won't dare to draw the blood of my hart.'

A chill snaked down her spine.

Elin shifted her weight from one foot to the other, and that single action persuaded Arla to look the girl dead in the eyes and say, 'First lesson, stop shuffling. Your body is strong enough. It can stay where you put it.'

The ghost of a smile brushed Elin's lips before disappearing. She stood straighter, stiller, before inclining her chin so slightly it was as though she hadn't moved at all.

'Come find me when I'm back from Malarye and maybe we can both learn how to fire a bow properly.'

The girl did smile then, a stunning, delicate thing that Arla found herself reciprocating. Maybe they could learn something from each other.

'What's going on over here?' a rumbling voice said, and they both whirled to find Sebastian marching towards them, a wide grin parting his lips and a toddler hanging off his hip. Vivianne reached for Arla the moment she was close enough.

'Girl talk. Not for the ears of brutes like you.' Arla beamed.

Sebastian gripped her, smirking as he pulled her closer and wrapped her in a hug. She laughed, and so did he, and so did the two little girls.

'One day, Dragonhart, that mouth of yours is going to get you into trouble.'

Over Seb's shoulder, she could see Hark walking towards them, Jack and Jaz and Kase in tow.

Hark's arm snaked around her waist, prying her from Seb's grip. He laid the softest of kisses on her lips. She had always loved perfect things; this easily made the list. 'I distinctly remember you dancing to music like this. With ribbons in your hair.'

How could she forget it?

That festival at Vorstrum had been one of the first times she'd truly let Hark see the real her. Had been one of the first times she could remove the cloak of the King's Assassin. She had danced, and laughed, and got delightfully drunk.

'I distinctly remember you cracking a smile back then,' she shot back, collapsing into laughter as he spun her in his arms.

She didn't think she'd ever seen Hark so happy. It filled her with an emotion she didn't know how to name.

'I still smile remembering how lovely you were that

evening,' he purred in her ear. Her cheeks heated, and though she was never one for embarrassment, she hid her face in the crook of his neck.

'Come and dance with me, Arla,' Jack said, a wide smile so heartbreakingly beautiful piercing his tired face. She grinned back, swallowing the wave of worry that Jack still wasn't better. He still used that awful cane to walk, and Arla had heard Kase speaking with the guards about adapting his saddle so he could ride the horses for longer without being in pain.

No, she wouldn't think of that tonight.

She twirled out of Hark's grip, ducking when he reached for her again. 'How could I say no to you?' she teased.

Her cheeks ached from laughing and she thought her heart might burst. She had danced with them all – with some of the mages too, an understanding and more importantly *trust* blossoming between them.

Huge branches had been cut from the trees in the forest and laid on the ground to provide seating that still hummed with magic as Arla touched her hands to them. It was where she found herself long after she'd finished dancing, Kase, strangely, at her side as they watched Flambriar's people through the flames of the bonfire.

'Do you think you'll find your answers in Malarye?' There was an edge to Kase's voice, something that skittered between intrigue and wariness.

Arla shifted, mulling over the question in her head. She didn't know what she would find in Malarye. She'd only stayed there for a night when Cyrus had taken her to visit the kingdoms on the continent four years ago. She remembered mountains and strange temples and women who trained with arrows. She had been impressed back then, jealous even of their prowess with a bow.

And then of course, there were the libraries.

'I don't think their princess would have invited me if Malarye didn't have something I want.'

Kase turned to face her, blue eyes sparkling in the heat of the fire. 'Be careful, Arla. Malarye will want something in return. I don't think you should be travelling there alone.'

'I won't be travelling alone. I have a dragon, Kase.'

'That you do. Do get enough rest, Dragonhart. It would be a shame if you fell off my back into the ocean.'

'Worry about yourself,' Arla shot back.

Thara huffed a laugh, and her amusement was followed with a lick of warmth down the bond.

'Never.'

'Perhaps. But there are some things Thara can't protect you from. Malarye has extensive underground tunnels – far more intricate than those in Kastonia. Thara won't be able to reach you down there if something happens. Malarye has never given us a reason to be wary of them, but they can be vicious when provoked.'

'What—?'

'My uncle was from there. I wouldn't wish the things he did on my worst enemy.'

Arla wanted to ask her more, but storm clouds hovered in Kase's eyes and Arla wouldn't force her to tell a story that still caused her so much pain. The gods knew she was familiar with those feelings herself.

'I'll be careful,' she said softly, glad when the shadows hounding Kase's face relented slightly. The girl's widening eyes were the only warning before a hand gripped Arla's shoulder, and it took everything in her not to spin and snap the person's slender wrist.

When she did turn, she was met with the smiling face of a woman with jet-black hair and eyes the colour of sand.

'I didn't have you down as stupid, Cardia,' Kase drawled from her position beside Arla.

Cardia snatched her hand back from Arla's shoulder in an instant.

'I'm sorry, Dragonhart. I didn't mean to startle you.' Cardia's voice was bright, like the sun. She had deep brown skin and wore a beautiful cloak Arla coveted immediately.

She liked her right away.

'Nice to meet you, Cardia. Sebastian has told me all about you.'

The woman's eyes turned wary for half a second before she blinked it away. 'All good things, I hope.'

'Of course.' Arla smiled gently, hoping the action would breathe ease into the woman, who looked as if she feared Arla might bite her. 'You were a friend of his sisters?'

Cardia's eyes filled with tears and Arla wanted to curse herself for how stupid she was. This woman had lost a friend. Arla had felt the pain of going all these months without contact with Halos; she couldn't imagine the irreparable damage it would do to her if her friend had died.

'Lexi was a fierce friend. I hope I can help raise her children to be as strong as their mother.'

Gods, Arla's own eyes were filling, and she was struggling to swallow. What was *wrong* with her?

'It is not a weakness to have empathy for others, Dragonhart. Pity those whose hearts are made of stone.'

Arla took Cardia's hands in hers, glad they were soft and had not known the roughness of handling a sword. 'From what I've seen of those girls, you're doing an excellent job.'

Cardia's smile was enough to rival the stars.

'Tonight we honour Lexi and the other souls that have gone to the eternal gates. She won't ever be forgotten.'

A lone tear rolled down Cardia's cheek, but she smiled through it, bending to kiss Arla's hands. 'Thank you, Dragonhart. It means more than you know.'

Arla watched the woman walk away towards the group of mages who tended to the children. Hark was there too, a young boy gripping his hand as he spoke with the adults around him.

'It should be you,' Kase muttered quietly. 'You live and breathe this role better than any of us could have predicted.'

Arla bit down the nasty things she suddenly wanted to say. This was Hark's kingdom. She had told him she didn't want to be a queen.

'Sometimes the best things aren't the right thing.'

Kase was already answering Hark's beckoning call, but Arla didn't miss the word that escaped her lips.

'Exactly.'

Arla had thought Hark was calling her over to mingle with the people, so she wasn't prepared when he handed her a lantern made of parchment, a flame flickering inside it. The hundreds of others around her all held similar lanterns.

'What is it?' she asked.

Hark smiled, lacing her free hand in his. 'Tonight is about honouring those who have fallen. A lantern for each of them. It's an old practice, only kept alive by those who follow the old religions. The Letting of the Lanterns predates even the dragonharts, I've heard.'

All around them mages held lanterns, creating a sea of softly glowing flame across the square. They began to walk, a procession for the dead made of brilliant, beautiful light, the people solemn and silent and remembering.

They climbed the hills in silence, stopping only when the mages did. Arla looked around her, at the people she would risk her life for. She still couldn't explain it, that tugging, gnawing sensation in her very blood that these people were her purpose, that the gods had demanded it of her. There was still so much she couldn't explain.

And then, as if a veil had been lifted and the souls of the dead themselves lit the sky, lanterns began to float towards the stars. One by one they were released, a prayer for each soul, a promise that it would never happen again. Lanterns floated higher, higher, higher, until they were so far away she could only make out the tiniest pinpricks of light.

She thought it was the most beautiful thing she had ever seen.

'It has always been known to take the breath of those who witness it. It is a sacred practice, one the gods will be sure to bless.'

Arla didn't have the words to reply. Not when there was a sea of glowing flames above her, mingling with the stars and the very blackest of nights. Thara was right, its beauty did take her breath away, and the tears that pricked her eyes reminded her too keenly of the lump in her throat she had been trying to swallow all evening.

Magic hung in the air, a static, *alive* thing to which she was growing accustomed. The dragonhart brooch burned in solidarity.

She hadn't dare tell any of them that an ache was growing inside her, that there seemed to be a part of her missing, like a hole that magic might slot comfortably into. She couldn't, could she? Not after she had been so disgusted by the thought of it not so long ago. She hadn't believed in magic because it had never helped her, never saved her.

'We didn't help you either. Yet you have never not cared for us.'

Her heart stuttered in her chest. No, from the moment she had realised the dragons slumbered beneath Castle Grey, she had cared desperately for them, like a calling in her blood that answered the call in theirs. Gods' magic.

Magic was different. And besides, it was not for her anyway.

I don't know what order the dragons and the gods and the harts came, but I think you all had magic once...

She shook off the echo of Jaz's words and refocused her gaze on the sky above her, a million lights twinkling as if the gods had placed diamonds and jewels amongst the stars. That haunting melody from earlier had begun again too and the song was threaded through her veins, sending chills across her skin. It was a beautiful sound – an ethereal night of magic and love and loss.

She wished it could stay like that forever.

It was a silly wish. She would be leaving for Malarye in a few hours, and she wanted to be well rested for whatever awaited her in the kingdom on the continent. Hark seemed to understand it when he met her gaze, tucking a stray strand of soft gold behind her ear.

'Let's go,' he murmured, laying a kiss softly on her head as they turned from the wonders of the lanterns.

She let him lead her back up the mountain, his fingers twisted in hers as she stared out over the valley, the lanterns peppering the darkness. Perhaps this was what she had waited for all her life. Perhaps this secret corner of the world would be enough to chase away the shadows that haunted her. Perhaps this was enough to show her that she wasn't broken beyond fixing. Perhaps it was enough to show her that she wasn't broken at all.

'You are not broken.'

A peacefulness floated to her through the bond, the final words of her dragon before Thara rested, like Arla should be.

But Hark had been looking at her all night with fire in his eyes, and where their skin touched now, she was sure she would be set alight.

Claret Hall was silent as they entered through the courtyard, its people and soldiers and maids all enjoying tonight down in the valley as equals. The mountains stood tall around them, steadfast protectors against any who would try to breach the walls of their kingdom.

Arla didn't let her mind drift to Sylvie and the Red Blades.

They wandered the halls without speaking, too content to bask in each other's company. They made it to the lovely oval room with the tall windows, and Arla was reluctant to let her hand leave his as Hark poured them both a drink.

'Are you ready for tomorrow?' he asked, collapsing into the cushions beside her. Arla sidled up to him, resting a cheek against his shoulder as if the act of not being able to touch him was an affront to the gods.

'I'm always ready, Stappen. You know that.'

Truthfully, she hadn't let her mind stray too far towards what she would find in Malarye or the people that awaited her there. She preferred it that way. Cyrus had sent her on so many jobs and to so many different locations over the years that she would never get anything done if she took the time to worry over what would await her in each location.

'I wish you'd let me come with you,' he said with a sigh, bringing the whiskey to his lips.

Arla could feel the tension in the hard ridges of his body, the clipped tone he used only when she knew he truly cared about something.

She smiled softly, her finger swirling the rim of the glass she held.

'You have Flambriar to look after. The people need you here, Hark. And I won't be going alone, I have Thara.'

The words that left his lips next had her heart racing. 'You've been keeping secrets. I know you've been up to something. That there's something on your mind.'

Her mind immediately went to Sylvie and the secret of the Red Blades. 'I... I haven't kept anything a secret.'

A low whistle forced its way through Hark's teeth. 'You're a terrible liar, Arla. Always have been. I want to know who it was you killed. Why there isn't a body, and why you haven't spoken of it since.'

Oh, she'd been such a fool. He'd figured it out. That she'd seen someone spying on Flambriar and hadn't told him. *Why* hadn't she told him?

'Hark, I...'

He cut her off before she could make an excuse. 'You're reckless, you know?' he began, his body so preternaturally still as he pinned her with an icy gaze. 'I found out from the maids that you'd killed men at the northern border. That you *left* Flambriar to do so,'

Her heart steadied at the lie. He hadn't found out she'd kept spying soldiers from him, only the lie she had told Lilith and Rheia. 'Hark, they deserved it,' she began.

'I'm not saying they don't deserve it,' he snapped, wringing his hands in his lap. 'But that was dangerous, and you *didn't tell me*. What would have happened had you got hurt?'

Too many lies, and she'd made them all up to protect her

own fragile heart. To pretend that things were okay and Flambriar wasn't being tracked down, just as she'd told Hark.

'I'm sorry,' she whispered, her eyes meeting his. 'I didn't want you to worry. I was with Thara and I was so *angry* when I saw those men, that...'

The words did nothing to ease the grim set of his mouth.

'I can't lose you again. Not like before. We barely made it out last time and there were both of us, Arla. You going to Malarye alone ... I won't bear it if something happens to you.' His hand reached for her knee, the contact firm as if it would anchor him and the worry he couldn't tamp down.

'Listen to me,' she said, placing the glass on the table and turning to face him. 'I will be fine. I am an assassin, you know, and this time I won't have you to distract me. There will be no sword wounds. I promise.'

At the ease in her voice, he seemed to relax slightly, though if the clouds gathering in his eyes were anything to go by, she doubted Hark would have the luxury of sleep whilst she was gone.

Fine. She'd have to get rid of those storms herself.

Her hand trailed lightly up his arm, and within seconds she saw the shift in him, the way his eyes turned to such a dark blue, like waves crashing against cliffs. The way a smirk teased the corner of his mouth. The way his hand tightened on her knee.

'You know, I could have fallen at your feet tonight,' he said, his voice rough and lovely.

'Well, why didn't you?'

His eyes flared and she revelled in the game she played. Like a mountain cat toying with its prey.

'Because,' he murmured, sprinkling kisses across the bare

skin of her shoulder, 'the things I would do to you require no audience, Dragonhart.'

Her blood heated at the title, her skin suddenly too tight, too much.

'And what things would they be?' she whispered, her heart stuttering in her chest as his hand brushed across every inch of her bare skin.

He chuckled low in his throat, something wicked and sinful in the sound that had her arching closer to him.

'As delightful as you are right now,' he said in a guttural voice that had her legs tightening around him, 'you are mine and I won't risk any of the others finding us in here when I show you just how much I've been waiting to worship you.'

Mine.

Her blood heated, molten and throbbing between her legs.

'Then by all means, don't keep me waiting.'

A dark laugh escaped him, and then they were racing through Claret Hall, laughter and kisses and sinful touches scattered behind them as they crashed through the doors to Arla's rooms, the stars the only witnesses as he laid her on the bed and devoured every inch of her.

CHAPTER 22

The water was the warmest it had been in months. She had turned sixteen yesterday, on the longest day of the year, and Cyrus had finally let her have the afternoon to herself. They'd returned from the continent only a week ago, stopping briefly in Glacit and then on to Velor to renew trade deals. She didn't know why he hadn't just sent the ambassador; there was nothing interesting about trade talks that should require the king and her of all people.

But it was done, and they were home, and Halos had promised to swim with her today. Her friend had been strange lately. Quiet. As if she held a secret she couldn't bear for the world to know. Arla had her suspicions, but Halos was two years older than her and what she got up to in her spare time was none of Arla's business, no matter how friendly they were.

Besides, Halos wouldn't be able to keep it a secret for long, if what Arla suspected was true.

Her friend took her time easing into the water. The Canus River was so calm today that they would be able to see the silver fish lurking beneath them if they looked carefully.

'Happy birthday. I missed you whilst you were gone,' Halos said, *beaming a smile as she swam towards Arla.*

'I missed you, too. You won't believe how dull Cyrus can be when he's discussing the price of fish.'

Her friend laughed, and any worry she had held before seemed to disappear into the water, long forgotten.

'Maybe we could watch a play tonight? The tickets for the theatre are all sold, I believe, but...'

Arla's heart leapt. Halos knew her so well.

They had become practised at sneaking into the theatre and hiding on the floor where the boxes reserved for nobles were. It had happened so often now that the adrenalin that had filled them the first dozen times no longer had the same effect. Now they just enjoyed watching the plays.

Of course, Arla could have fluttered her eyelashes at Cyrus and asked nicely for the royal box – the gods knew he'd never been able to say no to her – but to have this between her and Halos was too precious to ruin it with rules and propriety. She loved Halos as if they shared the same blood. They'd both lost families in the battle of Grey Hill seven years ago and there were still raw, aching cracks in them both that they had tried to fill for one another. In the end, it was easier just to have someone who understood. Who didn't need you to speak of it to understand why some days there were tear tracks on cheeks, and the idea of getting out of bed was an impossible concept.

Halos was the reason she hadn't stepped off her balcony the day after she'd made it into the royal guard by enduring the test of torture and strength to prove herself. She'd let them hurt her and she'd come out of it feeling nothing. She hadn't jumped because she didn't think Halos would know what to do if she lost the one remaining person in her life. Her friend had struggled to adapt to running her mother's shop on Main Street, and Arla wouldn't leave her to cope alone.

She was swimming, and then she ... wasn't.

She was inside Castle Grey, inside the throne room, sitting on the throne. Cyrus was standing before her on the steps in a reversal of their usual positions. He was shouting, she thought. He must be. His mouth moved, wider and wider, quicker, spittle collecting on the corners of his lips, his brow pinched and angry. Perry lingered by the doors, panic blurring the edges of the man's face as Cyrus edged towards the assassin on his throne.

He was close enough to touch her, close enough that when he raised his fist Arla flinched.

The blow didn't land.

There was a splatter of something warm and wet on her cheeks, and then the King of Hadalyn sank to his knees, the tip of a sword sticking out of his throat.

'No, no no, no no—!'

She lunged for him, her hands flapping because there was so much blood. The light left the king's eyes, and the sight of it painted a glazed, painful picture that would haunt her for eternity.

She dared to look up then, to see who had managed to sneak in and kill him.

Halos only looked triumphant as she tore the sword out of his throat.

∽

She woke with a sheen of sweat coating her skin.

'*Dragonhart?*'

Dawn was barely peeking through the glass ceiling.

She was late.

It went against everything in her blood to untangle herself from Hark's hold, to leave him sleeping peacefully as she donned her leather assassin's uniform and slipped quietly out of Claret Hall.

Thara waited for her in the courtyard, her scales such a polished emerald they were almost obsidian when the first rays of sun hit the dragon.

'You're late,' Thara huffed as Arla climbed aboard with an affinity that still managed to surprise her. The blood in her veins ... gods, she didn't think she would ever feel as though she deserved it.

'I know,' she replied out loud, the concentration needed to speak through the bond too strenuous when the fingers of her dream were still lingering on the edge of her mind.

Get a grip, Arla.

'Has the boy upset you, Dragonhart?'

Arla laughed then, a meek, pathetic thing that made her feel better all the same.

'No, Hark hasn't done anything wrong, and the sooner you start accepting him the better.'

The hulking body beneath her rumbled. *'Never.'*

Arla had a heartbeat to grip the horned spikes on Thara's back before the dragon was lifting from the ground, flapping the magnificent span of her wings as the ground swayed beneath them.

She loved it every time. Now she had it, she never wanted to give it up.

Flying offered her an escape she seemed to have been looking for her entire life. A distance from the things that plagued her. Even the terrible dream of Halos and Cyrus seemed far away now, insignificant against the sprawling mass of mountains and the ocean in the distance.

She wanted to know why the princess had sent her a letter, and indeed how she had managed to *find* her in the hidden kingdom of Flambriar. The trade merchants were not as trustworthy as they had promised, clearly.

One thing was clear though, the kingdoms were still suffering, and the gods were still upset with them. But how was she supposed to unite them?

It was a stupid prophecy, one that the fates had made to mess with her, she imagined.

As if the fates hadn't done an excellent job of pissing her off already.

'Careful, Dragonhart, your thoughts are obnoxiously loud.'

'Stay out of them, then,' she called over the wind, flexing her fingers.

'What's scalded your scales this morning? I preferred you bleeding out compared to this incessant sulking.'

Thara was right, she was sulking.

Arla made the effort to pull at the bond and speak to her dragon, a closeness she knew Thara would appreciate despite her dreadful mood.

'I'm nervous, I think. It's not a feeling I am well versed in.'

A flurry of warmth was sent through the bond, and it calmed something in her mind.

'It is good to be nervous, Dragonhart. It means what you are about to do is important. It means you care. You may be nervous, but you will not be afraid.'

Sometimes she wished Thara had been with her nine years ago. The ancient wisdom that the dragon possessed often brought her to the brink of emotion and offered a clarity that felt like clouds parting after a storm.

'Malarye can be violent, Kase warned. Though it is known for its priestesses, I don't think they are as godly as they would have us believe.'

Thara huffed, the amusement evident in the bond. *'Well, I didn't pick you for your meekness, did I?'*

Arla laughed, properly this time. What was wrong with her?

Of course she could take on Malarye. She was an assassin. *The* assassin. If Malarye wished for violence, she would deliver it to them on a silver platter.

'*Better,*' her dragon rumbled.

~

By the end of her fourth day flying, Arla thought her muscles might give out on her entirely.

Thara had taken the strain well, though Arla didn't miss the way her dragon slept deeply when they landed on rocky outcrops in the ocean each evening. Now, with the distant view of land finally gracing the landscape, Arla could feel the fatigue her dragon tried to hide.

'Not long now,' Arla murmured, the dark bruise of a kingdom appearing closer and closer. Thara didn't answer her, and that was enough for Arla to know the dragon was tired. She had denied it vehemently the entire way, sending a flick of irritation down the bond each time Arla accused her of needing rest.

Arla could almost make out the structures of buildings and the mass of people waiting on a rocky beach when the first arrow struck Thara's hide.

The world halted, and then a swooping feeling fell through Arla's stomach as Thara faltered, her wings beating furiously to right them. The dragon rumbled, and then, when a second arrow struck her shoulder, she roared loudly enough to break the sky. Arrows and crossbolts rained down around them, long silver tips shooting by her as Thara tried to dodge them.

Fear was a foreign thing, but when Arla felt them drop another foot, it seemed to claw up her throat and swallow her. They'd die, then.

Archers on the beach continued to fire at them, and through her exertion Thara let slip the pain and anger and it rushed through the bond, devouring Arla in a blinding white rage of pain and wrath.

She screamed then, and it was like a summoning, a calling for everything to *stop*.

It made no difference – arrows showered them, another sticking in the spot behind where Arla sat. Thara barely managed to dodge the ones that came blazing with flames.

The dragon roared again, that pain so all-consuming it threatened to swallow Arla whole through the bond. Her head was on fire, her arms and legs and *everything* screamed.

And they had to keep moving forward. Had to keep going towards that beach because Thara was beyond exhausted, and there was nowhere else to land.

'*Keep going,*' she managed to choke out, her tears burning her skin as she gripped tighter. She couldn't fall here.

And yet Thara fell another foot, the thrashing waves of the sea even closer than they had seemed before. Arla could see the people on the rocks now, dressed in white, firing and firing and firing from crossbows that shouldn't have been able to reach them so far away.

More bolts left those crossbows, and as Thara dropped again, she let out another roar, dousing the air in front of them with fire that burnt the arrows to ash. Thara really did struggle then, the fatigue washing over Arla through the bond enough for her to contemplate letting go and falling to a watery death.

She choked a sob through clenched teeth, gripping tighter and tighter with hands that were cramping. '*Keep going, we're nearly there.*'

'*They will burn for what they have done.*'

Arla didn't doubt it, not when another crossbolt landed in

Thara's chest. Arla looked down, saw the tip of the bolt dangerously close to the dragon's heart, and she was filled with a centuries-old rage.

It bloomed within her, from ashes into a roaring flame, burning, burning, burning through her blood, filling her with something old and dangerous. Thara was there too, somewhere in the bond, watching, still beating her wings through the pain as that power filled Arla's blood. Her mind was faraway, her body not hers either as she felt her fingers fumble around the Dragonhart brooch pinned to her cloak.

At the touch of her fingers on the metal the entire sea erupted.

Waves as tall as palaces rose from the ocean and devoured the round of arrows coming right at them. There was a roaring in her head, and she wasn't sure if it was her or the dragon that made the sound, only that her blood felt alive, and when her fingers fell from the brooch, the waves fell back into the sea...

Leaving a smiling priestess on the shore of a wet beach, archers arranged around her as Thara crashed onto the sand and sent Arla sprawling.

CHAPTER 23

Arla's feet were under her in an instant and she was marching towards the priestess with the fury of a thousand burning suns.

'I do hope you're not expecting I leave you alive after that?' she snapped, forcing herself not to turn and check her dragon was okay.

The priestess smiled softly. 'If you make a move towards me, these men will cut your guts from your body and leave them strewn over these rocks for the crows to peck at.'

It was enough to make Arla pause and take her in.

The priestess wore a gown of white that hugged her frame as though it had been stitched to her skin. A cape of pearls decorated her shoulders, her tanned skin in such contrast against the netted pearl garment. Arla dragged her eyes down the woman's body, noting the pearlescent hair and the deep green of her eyes. She reminded Arla too much of Kase, though after the revelation that Kase's uncle was from here, she could only assume the rest of her family was too; that Kase herself bore the blood of Malarye.

The priestess smiled again, the action so irking that Arla ran her fingers over the hilt of the blade at her side, delighting in the way the archers cocked their bows towards her. The priestess lifted a hand to steady them, and then Arla remembered just who she was.

'Attempting to shoot me out of the sky is an act of war.'

The priestess had the decency to look wary before she straightened her spine and took half a step towards Arla.

'The magic of your people does not scare us, Dragonhart. Not yet, at least.'

Arla didn't let herself dwell on the knowledge this woman had somehow collected about Flambriar or her dragonhart status. Instead, she focused on Thara as she heard the shuffling of rocks behind her and the scuff of stone against claw.

'*Are you all right?*' she sent down the bond, not turning her back on the threat in front of her.

'*I will be better for the bolts being removed. My flesh cannot heal around solid objects.*'

Despite the worry that nipped at her with the thought of those bolts still piercing Thara's skin, Arla was glad the dragon was talking.

She felt even better at the huff of hot breath at the back of her neck and the way the eyes of the archers widened in response.

She steeled herself. 'So you know who I am, and the magic I have at my disposal,' she said, her voice lethally soft. 'I would love to know why you thought firing at us was a good way to begin our relations?'

Arla watched the priestess swallow, it was not fear in her face. No, it was certainty. A decision had been made behind those brilliant green eyes.

'Because only one born of ancient bloodlines would have survived it.'

Thara huffed down the bond, her voice filling Arla's head before she could speak. *'A test. To prove we are what we claim.'*

'I should think arriving on a fucking dragon would be proof enough,' Arla shot back.

'Breathe. We need their alliance.'

Thara was right. As usual.

So she took a breath. And another one. And another one until she was looking past the priestess and out over Malarye.

There were cliffs beyond the shoreline, and huge sand training rings that contained targets both on the ground and suspended in the air. *Archers indeed.*

Further still, there were forests – great, ancient things – that spanned as far as Arla could see. She had no doubt the tunnels Kase had spoken of would be concealed in there. Houses peppered the landscape too, no order or pattern between them, which made Arla think they had been built wherever someone had stood still long enough. They were harsh stone structures, like juts of rock sticking up to mimic the mountain behind them.

None of it captured her attention like the palace did, though.

It perched on the side of a cliff like a limb. Mild in its complexity, the castle could have been overlooked had her eyes not been trained to look for these sorts of things. She remembered it too, from years ago, a castle high up, overlooking the sea.

But nothing about Malarye's castle was remarkable. A structure of stone and small turrets that she doubted would be well protected if someone happened to conduct an aerial attack.

A wave of warm amusement crashed through the bond and tugged a smile at the corner of Arla's mouth.

'What is it that you are finding amusing, Dragonhart? It seems to me you have threatened us with an army,' the priestess said.

The urge to snap the woman's neck was growing by the minute.

'Indeed. That is usually the expected response to shooting someone out of the sky, is it not?'

'I wouldn't know,' the priestess hissed, 'seeing as you're the first to ever be *in* the sky.'

Arla's jaw ached with the strain of clenching her teeth. 'I suggest—'

'I do hope we are granting our guests an amicable welcoming, Crea. I'd hate for them to return home and speak of Malarye's lack of hospitality.'

Arla hadn't seen the woman approach. Though now she looked upon her, there was no doubting a queen stood before them.

Jet-black hair framed a face as white as snow with lips the colour of blood. Her smile, Arla was certain, had been practised for long hours in a mirror from the moment she had been old enough to understand the weight of the golden crown on her head. She wore a simple dress that reminded Arla of the forest, all pines and oaks and secrets. There was a warmth that emanated from her, a breath of fresh air amongst the hostility with which they had been greeted.

Arla didn't doubt the queen had commanded it.

Still, she bowed before the queen of Malarye. 'Your Majesty. It is a pleasure.'

When Arla rose, she found the queen watching her, her head tilted as if Arla were an exotic thing found in the underground markets of Kastonia. There was a crinkling of the eyes and then she was smiling softly again, locking the mask of a ruler back into place.

'Mara, please. And the pleasure is mine, Arla Reinhart, though I do believe it is Arla Dragonhart, now, is it not?'

'My court would laugh at me for insisting so, but yes, it is Dragonhart.' A tightness flew down the bond, gripping her chest in something that felt a little like pride.

Queen Mara took a step towards her. 'Then I hope you will forgive our ... eccentric welcome. We have long worshipped the gods; it is not in our nature to accept heretics on our shores.'

The hairs on Arla's neck bristled, as if the gods themselves were opposed to their own mention. Or perhaps she was fed up of the doubt that the gods had chosen her.

She ignored the fact that she too had doubted until a few months ago.

Heretic. She had arrived on the back of a creature blessed by the gods themselves. If she was opposed to the beliefs, then Thara would have snapped her neck.

A fog hung over Malarye, though the air was balmy, and Arla was already too warm in her uniform. She would need to remove the sheepskin lining soon, or she would seriously overheat.

'Your ... *welcome,*' Arla said slowly, 'has resulted in my dragon being pierced with crossbolts and arrows longer than my arm. We have travelled for four days to your shores at the request of your princess. From where I stand, the only heretics are those wishing to shoot a creature of the gods out of the sky.'

Silence seeped across the beach, so deafening Arla wondered if anyone had heard her at all.

'I can only apologise that it was necessary,' Mara said, hardness creeping into the edge of her voice. 'Though you will understand when I say that the security of a kingdom outweighs anyone or anything. My people will not be placed in the way of harm unnecessarily.'

There was a glint in the queen's eye, a goading thing pushing Arla to snap. But not here. Not in front of so many people. Arla didn't know how Mara had come to know of Flambriar, or how much she knew, and Arla would not reveal any of her hidden kingdom's secrets before she had worked the queen out.

'Crea, please arrange for Lady Re—Lady *Dragonhart* to be shown to the castle once she is content her dragon is well tended. And send a healer, too. I do not remember instructing quite so *many* arrows to be fired.'

The queen was already walking away, booted feet crunching rock beneath them as she began to walk back up the cliff.

Walk back up the cliff.

As if she were no better than the rest of her people.

Arla hated that she was already beginning to like this queen.

Crea cleared her throat, and just the movement of her in Arla's eyeline was enough to ignite a rage within her. Her fingers twitched on the blade still sheathed at her wrist.

The priestess only grinned at her. 'I'll send someone to show you to your rooms. A healer will be along shortly to tend to your dragon.'

'I do not require the help of traitors.'

'They are not traitors. They have no allegiance to us. And I do not know how to remove arrows from your skin, so let them help,' Arla shot back, glad to feel Thara's presence in her mind. It had been too similar to death when she had felt the strain through the bond.

The archers dispersed, some following Crea who gradually worked her way up the cliff following the queen whilst others found their places at watch towers carved into the rocky outcroppings overlooking the beach. Arla turned her attention to Thara then, whom, despite the arrows sticking out from between her scales, looked remarkably bright.

'There is no use for worry – it is a useless emotion. Let us take things as they come.'

Arla didn't know why tears pricked her eyes. How did her dragon manage to rouse emotion from even the most secure vaults in her heart? She suddenly wished for Hark. He had always commanded the same effect – the siphoning away of worry.

'You are strong enough to do this. You wouldn't be facing it if you weren't.'

Arla swallowed the lump in her throat. Thara was right. She could do this. Whatever *this* was.

'Excuse me, Dragonhart. Mistress Crea sent me to aid you.'

Arla had watched the healer approach them from the direction of the palace, their long brown hair in braids that hung low past their shoulders. The healer had a kind face, and though Thara eyed them at first, Arla felt the dragon relax as soon as the healer was close enough to touch them.

'I am Diath. I will remove the arrows so you may heal, great one,' they addressed Thara directly, and it was in that moment Arla knew they were a mage.

'You have magic?' The words were out of her mouth in a splutter, her tongue tripping over her teeth as Arla inched closer to where Diath made to lay their hands against Thara's scales.

'Many of us fled when King Elrod began his purge, though mages had travelled here for centuries before. We have been around longer than Kastonia's king's persecution, Dragonhart.'

Diath's hands roamed carefully over Thara's body, leeching

away pain. Arla watched the strain in her dragon's eyes dissipate.

'Be still, I will be as gentle as I can,' Diath murmured, their voice raspy but low enough that it was soothing. The whole beach was, despite the archers hidden amongst the rocks, and despite the sea's relentless crashing against the shore, like a balm to the worry that had swamped her on their arrival. The sun would be setting soon, and though it was warmer here than back in Flambriar, once the sun dipped below the horizon there would be a chill in the air.

Diath's hands moved with expert precision, gently teasing the arrows from between Thara's scales. If the dragon felt any pain, she did not show it, not even to Arla who couldn't take her eyes away from the barbed ends of metal as they were delicately extracted from Thara's skin.

'It is an abhorrent test and I am sorry you had to endure it,' Diath spoke lowly, their lip caught between their teeth as they struggled with the splintered end of an arrow in Thara's shoulder.

'Did you?' Arla asked. 'Have to endure it, I mean.'

'Malarye is particular about who is allowed into their queendom and even more so about those who profess to carry the magic of the gods. All who claim they are blessed are tried this way. Only those who possess the magic can hope to make it across the border.'

Queendom.

'Do they not have a king?'

Diath laughed, shooting a hand quickly to rest against Thara's side as a groan rumbled up the dragon's throat. It subsided immediately.

'Once. Until Queen Mara killed her husband.'

A chill flitted through the muscles at Arla's shoulders. 'Brutal indeed. How did you make it here?'

'I healed every hole those arrows made in my body as I lay dying on these very rocks while they watched. I was welcomed once I had proved I could lose my body weight in blood and still stand.'

Kase had been right. Malarye, despite its devotion to the gods, was a barbaric place prone to violence. Crea had ignited a ferocity in the pit of Arla's stomach that had her itching to draw a blade and mar that perfect white gown with the blood of the priestess.

Her hands clenched at her sides.

'Your body will heal quickly, great one,' Diath said, gliding their hands over Thara's scales once more before clasping them in front of their body.

The healer was already departing before Arla could snap herself out of her thoughts of this violent *queendom* and how she could manipulate it to her advantage.

'Thank you,' she called, offering a smile when Diath turned back to face her and nodded once. 'Know you will always have a place in Flambriar, should you seek it, Diath.'

They offered the ghost of a smile in return. 'Perhaps I will take you up on the offer one day, Dragonhart. I suspect there will be a need for healers in the coming months.'

Arla didn't let herself dwell on the words or what they meant. She had spent too many hours thinking of it herself.

'Go and rest in those rooms your hosts spoke of Dragonhart, I will be there in the morning. We will put the world to rights then.'

Arla didn't have it in her to argue.

CHAPTER 24
HARK

His muscles tore beneath his fighting leathers as he swung the blade again and again. He had long cherished the burn that wielding a sword curated, the salty drip, drip, drip off his forehead as his body moved with a lethal grace. Steel clanged around him, a private cacophony of promised violence as his lungs ached with the strain of the practised movement.

None of it was enough to drown out the ever-circling thoughts of where *she* was.

'Steady, Stappen, you're going to hurt yourself,' Seb panted as he met the arc of Hark's blade.

Hark grunted, tossing the hair plastered with sweat to his forehead. 'Then it will be my own fault.'

Seb hissed as Hark's blade nicked the side of his arm, a line of crimson already welling between the cut fabric of his tunic.

The sight of it was enough to send Hark's blade clattering to the ground. 'Sorry,' he mumbled, raking a hand through his hair.

'I know you miss her – we all do,' Seb said, sheathing the

blade at his waist and clapping an arm around Hark's shoulders. Hark leant into it, the solidity a bolstering thing that steeled the aching part inside of him. He did miss Arla. More than anything. More than he would have thought possible. She had taken the most necessary parts of him and kept them for herself. She had wriggled her way beneath his skin and fused her soul to his.

Truly, he felt lost without her.

He'd seen it in his friends too, the impact Arla had made on them – on the entirety of Claret Hall and Flambriar itself – in such a short space of time. As if she had been a part of them from the very beginning. Without her here now it was as though Flambriar's heart was missing, like something was irrevocably gone from this place of magic. A fluttering had begun in his stomach from the moment she'd left, like the wings of a hummingbird taking flight.

'She'll be back soon,' Hark said, bolstering himself against the ache in his heart. 'And with the answers she needs so the kingdoms will stand strong again. Flambriar will be strong.'

'I know. And she'll probably be giving Malarye hell as we speak.'

Laughter burst from Hark's throat. 'We'll be lucky not to have a new enemy once she returns.' But even through the laughter, he couldn't muster amusement – not really. Not without her.

And with that anger still festering in her heart? He knew he would defend that to the ends of the earth, too. To him she was perfect, and he'd spend his life making sure she knew that.

Even if she sparked war with Malarye.

∽

Hark spent the rest of the day in the city, mingling with the people, offering aid where he could, just as Arla wanted him to. Now that he was beginning to know these people, to get used to the smiles and the way they congregated around him upon his arrival in the town, it was becoming easier to lead them. Just as she'd said it would be.

He wanted nothing more than for Arla to rule at his side. To be a queen. To claim her birthright and lead these people as the gods had wanted. It was all wishful bullshit.

Arla didn't want to be in charge of this kingdom any more than she wanted to be caged inside Claret Hall. He'd seen her impatience on the days when her routine suffocated her, and he had noted the instant decision to go to Malarye. She hadn't mulled it over, hadn't discussed it with him. Arla had seen the chance to escape for a little while and clung onto it as if it were a wild beast ready to flee if she took too long to slay it.

'If you can start thinking of ways to boost the number of soldiers we employ rather than what Arla Dragonhart looks like beneath the leather of her uniform, we might be able to make it to dinner before Kase guts us,' Jaz groaned, slamming an armful of parchment onto the mahogany table beside Hark.

Hark tried to ignore the heat in his cheeks as he met Jaz's gaze and was relieved to find his friend's eyes glittering with shadows of amusement. Yes, Arla Dragonhart had made her mark.

'Sorry,' Hark said as he sighed. He seemed to be saying it a lot recently, but he couldn't take his gods-damned mind off her and—'The soldiers, right. We need to boost their numbers.'

Jaz shot him an incredulous look, rolling his eyes before drawling, 'We have enough for one flank of an army, but the rest of the mages are too young or too old or we need them to run the city.'

Of course. Hark had thought they might run into this little problem.

They had created a new kingdom and filled it with people who had been persecuted for years. There simply weren't enough of them to build an army. And they would need one if Hark knew his father – and fuck, did he know him.

Despite Arla's insistence that Elrod wouldn't dare touch the mages again and wouldn't approach them here, Hark shared his father's determined, unyielding streak. He knew his father was planning something while Hark and these people hid away here in the mountains.

There would be war. He didn't know when or how or where, but Elrod would come for what had been taken from him, and Flambriar needed to be ready when he did.

'We can only do what we can, Jaz,' he said. 'Our numbers will grow the longer we're here, and you're forgetting we have another army still sleeping beneath Castle Grey.'

Jaz frowned, frustration inking itself into the lines of his face. 'We can't rely on dragons that Arla says will come. They haven't so far, what's to say they can still fly? They've been there almost a century, Hark. We need numbers, *non-flying* numbers.'

Hark loved Jaz like a brother, had always found him to possess a unique combination of being constantly pissed off with him and finding amusement in him at the same time, but fucking gods he was insistent.

'Jaz, the numbers will grow, I know they will. In the meantime, we make sure the soldiers we have are fit and ready to fight.'

'That's all well and good, but—'

The sound that echoed through the corridors chilled his very blood.

He was out the door in an instant, Jaz on his heels, cloak flapping around him as Hark took in the picture before him.

He noticed the blood first. Or rather, the trail of it that was smeared all across the vast stone floor.

Then he took in the colour of the uniform worn by the man held between two of his own soldiers, and physically recoiled.

He would have preferred to see the scarlet of his father's army, not a uniform as black as night that had been seared into his memory months ago.

The soldier now crumpled at his feet wore the uniform of the camp at the northern border. A man who had been complicit in his father's scheme to capture and sacrifice the mages.

He groaned at Hark's feet, earning himself a solid kick to the side from one of Flambriar's soldiers. Hark wanted him to do it again. Again. Again.

Arla would have revelled in it.

But he had vowed not to rule as his father had done, and that meant he wouldn't use violence as a tool. So, going against every gut instinct, he raised a hand to halt the soldier currently breaking the guard's ribs.

'Where did you find him?' His voice was a faraway thing, an echo through his mind as he struggled to keep a lid on the anger that begged to erupt from him.

A group of soldiers had followed the procession into Claret Hall – the entire team Hark had sent scouting this evening. It was one of them who stepped forwards, a woman with deep brown skin and a scar running through her brow.

'He was at the top of the valley, watching the city. A spy, no doubt.'

Hark had thought as much. 'Take him to the dungeons, I'll deal with him there. For now I want you to return to scout the mountains. Every inch of them. If anyone is found they're to be killed on sight.'

At that, the man at his feet cried out. Hark didn't have it in him to tell his soldiers not to further injure the soldier as they hauled him down to the lower levels of the hall, deep within the mountain.

Hark was already following, the clip of his boots on the flagstones drowned out by the shuffling of soldiers making their way back out into the mountains.

'No one in the city is to know of this. I will not worry them over what we don't yet know. If anyone asks, it was a training exercise.'

He was met with solemn eyes and the sharp jerk of chins.

'Gods fucking help us.'

～

There was a small shard of his heart that felt sorry for the man in the dungeons when he finally made his way down there.

That small shard was quickly shattered when the man spat at Hark's feet. Blood swirled into the glob of saliva that reflected the light of the torches. He should have asked Seb to do this – the gods knew he might have more control.

'This will be simple,' he began, his voice accented with the authority of a king. 'You will tell me why you were in those mountains, where the rest of your unit is, and what your king has planned.'

'And if I don't?' the man hacked, his face contorting as the shackles bolted into the wall chafed his wrists.

Flambriar had not been built to keep its enemies alive for long.

The dungeon itself was well lit and clean; dry and warm,

though not uncomfortably so. It was magic that filled these chambers, the weight of it heavy beneath thousands of tonnes of rock. It kept clean air winding through the place despite its location within a literal mountain. Hark suspected it was the most well-guarded prison, should anyone ever try to escape. He half wanted the man to try it when he lunged at Hark, spitting the foulest names the gods had created. Arla would be impressed.

Hark laughed then – a dark, twisted sound – as he crouched to the man's level. He thought he recognised him. He'd spent so many years living in Larkire Palace he'd have been a fool not to notice the most loyal of his father's soldiers. The name Bain was familiar.

'If you don't, death will be a kinder fate than what we can do to you. Don't forget, you imprisoned and tortured the very mages who reside here. I don't imagine there is a limit on the pain their magic can inflict.'

Bain had the sense to gulp before attempting to steel himself. Hark admired it in a way, though the man's stubbornness was going to get him killed quicker.

'My soldiers are in the mountains scouting your unit, and they will kill every single one of them. Do not mistake me when I say I will do terrible things to keep this kingdom safe. Maybe I should start with you.'

Hark didn't let himself think as he stuck a thin-bladed dagger into Bain's left pectoral. He didn't let himself process the anguished scream that reverberated through the dungeon. He thought he heard his guards laugh.

'Fuck you, *prince*. And fuck that blonde whore. You should hear the things men say about her... The things they want to do to that jumped-up bitch—'

There was a clatter as two of Bain's teeth hit the rock wall and fell to the floor.

Hark looked down at his fist, as if it had moved without him being aware of it.

As it happened, it was actually Sebastian who flexed his knuckles, his eyes wide and his face twisted into something capable of a violence Bain had no business withstanding.

Hark hadn't even heard Seb approach.

'Speak of her again and I'll force those teeth down your fucking throat.'

'Come to protect your master like the dog you are?' Bain spat blood through his remaining teeth and Hark grabbed his friend's sleeve to stop his fist reacquainting itself with the prisoner's jaw.

'You'd know all about dogs, Bain. Loyal as one till the minute of your death.'

Ah.

There was a personal hatred between Seb and the man before them. It was all coming back to Hark now. It was something that went back to when Seb's sister had been alive. Bain had driven her out of Larkire and spread such malicious lies that Lexi had been scared to speak to a man again. That was the thing about Bain, his ego had always been too large, and when a woman had the nerve to deny him something ... he had always been a vicious male.

'Laugh while you can. He'll burn this place to the ground. Your precious whore with it and those kids of your sister's—'

The blade was deep inside Bain's heart before he could finish speaking, the gush of blood spilling over Hark's hand a welcome warmth as he twisted the blade and watched the life blink out of the soldier's eye.

'Fucking prick,' Seb said with a growl, and when Hark

turned to face him he wasn't surprised to see those familiar shadows had returned to Seb's eyes. His sister had meant more to him than anything ever could, and he disappeared into himself often when he was reminded of the pain of her death.

Hark had no time to dwell on what he'd just done.

'Let's join the others. I want the whole mountain range scouted before sunrise.'

Seb nodded silently, anger and pain etched on his face.

CHAPTER 25

Dinner had been a quiet affair. A bowl of steaming venison stew and fried potatoes delivered by a male servant who looked at her with an apt keenness. The rooms she had been appointed were dark and warm, and not a single window to satisfy the assassin within her. Though she supposed the palace was indeed built into the side of a cliff and had anyone decided to give themselves chronic blisters by carving windows, she would only be looking into a wall of rock anyway.

There was a fireplace, at least, and even though Malarye was certainly warmer than Flambriar, Arla was glad of the flames in this shadowy, hidden-away room. The bed was grand and piled with furs and woollen blankets that had seen better days, but for once, she didn't mind the simplicity of it all. Arla had grown accustomed to the luxury at Castle Grey, and she was treated like a queen in Flambriar, too. Malarye's simplicity presented a change, and it put her in the perfect mindset for spying.

No one had come to speak with her last night after she left Thara resting in a clearing of the forest just beyond the cliffs, and for that she was glad. She had fallen asleep holding tightly to her bond with Thara, refusing to let go of it for fear that Thara was hurt and hiding it from her. She was certain her dragon had lulled her to sleep through their connection, breathing soft clouds through the bond that filled Arla's mind and lured her into sweet oblivion.

The bond was the first thing Arla reached for when she woke up.

'You've become awfully clingy, Dragonhart. Perhaps a blunt force to the head might knock some independence back into you.'

Arla yawned, stretching her limbs then braiding her mane of hair into something that looked a little less like a bird's nest.

'Perhaps answers to why on earth they've called me here might have a better effect.'

'Then may I suggest you get up and start demanding answers like we both know you're capable of doing?'

Arla smiled to herself, already reacquainting herself with Arla Reinhart, King's Assassin. She was more than capable of demanding answers, and if she could just forget what her blood represented – what *kingdom* she represented – she would have no qualms about manipulating and lying to get the answers she needed. And if not, there was always sheer force.

'Better.'

The hallways inside Malarye's palace were as gloomy as Arla's rooms. Low torchlight gave the passageways an eerie feel, and it was not at all what Arla had expected. The palace was clean, and she could smell food somewhere, but nothing about the place screamed royalty or luxury.

Perhaps Queen Mara liked it that way. She certainly was not as straight forward as Arla had first thought, and to kill her husband? Well, there was definitely more to the queen than her soft smile and welcoming demeanour.

It didn't take long for Arla to find a hall with high windows that looked out over the sea. The space was as big as the entire ground floor of Castle Grey, and dotted throughout the space were small desks carved from rock with dozens of palace staff and advisors scurrying through the place like mice. At one end of the room, behind a desk of similar plainness, sat Mara, wearing a very ordinary pale blue shirt with the sleeves rolled up to the elbows.

The queen spoke to any and all who approached her, signing parchment after parchment and scribbling down notes from advisors who whispered in her ear.

This was a working queen. One who had foregone everything royal life had to offer and had jumped headfirst into what it meant to rule. Her people orbited round her like she was their own personal sun with a pull to her stronger than any other force, and the people all smiled and laughed as they worked. A pang of jealousy tarnished the back of Arla's throat. Flambriar would never work like this. Its people were too wary, and Hark was too stubborn to realise he needed to be a leader and shape the role according to his values.

But he'd been trying, hadn't he? He'd promised to step up and look after the people whilst Arla was gone.

'You know the answer. We should have killed him when we had the chance.'

Ire threatened to drown Arla, and it took every ounce of restraint not to scream back down the bond.

'The goal was to rescue Hark. I swore it on my sword that I would go back and kill his father.'

She had sworn it, but she wasn't naïve enough to think she would ever be able to sneak into Larkire again, let alone kill the king who sat on its throne. She wondered, briefly, what Orson was up to. Was Hadalyn's ambassador still smoothing things over between Hadalyn and Kastonia or had the scheming rat truly betrayed his king and switched sides?

'Ah, Arla, good morning.' Mara's voice echoed through the vast space, capturing the attention of everyone in the room before they quickly averted their eyes and continued with what they had been doing before.

Arla moved as if her legs were stuck in treacle, a wariness in her blood that thought better of bringing out the swagger of King's Assassin. Her boots made soft thuds on the flagstones as she told herself to get a grip.

'Your Majesty,' she said, nodding her head in a practised movement. She wouldn't bow, not now she was a dragonhart. She would bow to no king – or queen.

'I trust you slept well?' Mara asked, hastily scrawling her signature on a formal-looking document an advisor swiped across the table.

'Well enough, thank you.'

The queen beamed, the light of her smile brightening her eyes in this lowly lit place. 'I'm glad to hear it. I thought you might like to have a tour of the city. You've travelled all this way and it would be a shame not to explore, no?'

Arla's tongue felt heavy. She was missing something. Though she hadn't seen the queen on her first visit to Malarye with Cyrus, she would have expected Mara to at least acknowledge Arla's time here, even though she spent it in a small inn close to that rocky beach. Mara was keeping something back, playing Arla with sweet smiles and the pretence that her queendom was open for Arla to discover its secrets.

She highly doubted that.

'I'd love to see more. My last visit was fleeting, to say the least.'

It wasn't surprise that flickered in Mara's eyes at Arla's

words, but understanding: that there was no game Arla would not partake in; that Mara was evenly matched in the young opponent who had arrived on the back of a dragon. Something thrilled in Arla's blood at the prospect.

'Indeed. I'll have my daughter show you around. She was especially disappointed to have missed your arrival,' Mara said, her eyes boldly meeting Arla's.

Arla ran her tongue over her teeth. 'I was surprised, Your Majesty, not to have met the princess already. It is her invite I have taken up, after all.'

Arla didn't believe for one moment that the princess would have written that letter herself, but if the queen wished to share only half-truths and keep cryptic her motivations for inviting Arla to her country then so be it. She would play the game. For now.

Mara offered no explanation for why the princess couldn't meet with Arla until the afternoon, but it gave Arla the opportunity to find Thara in the sprawling forest beyond the cliffs. She looked a darn sight better than she had when Arla had left her yesterday evening. Where her scales had begun to dull on their arduous journey to the continent, after a night of rest the dragon almost shone beneath the shafts of sunlight poking through the boughs of branches above them.

'You scared me yesterday,' Arla said slowly, a hand tracing the sleekness of Thara's scales as the pair of them wandered through the trees. It was a testament to how vast the forest was that Thara walked beside Arla, only occasionally having to duck her enormous head.

'You forget I have lived many lives before this one. I was around

when the gods were warring, Dragonhart. I tell you I have had worse things pierce my skin.'

Arla forgot sometimes exactly how old Thara was – and the life and world and people that the dragon had known before her. Gods, she'd spent nearly a hundred years asleep!

'I often forget that they warred. What started it?' Arla said, forgoing the bond. Thara was right, she *was* relying on it too much, craving it like a soft blanket. She shouldn't forget that she had a voice. But a war between gods...? The impact must have been catastrophic. It had been enough to send the dragons to sleep after all...

'The gods have warred many times – over fates and lovers and the one who fell.'

'What do you mean?'

Thara was silent for a moment, the only sound the combined crunch of leaves and fallen branches beneath their feet. When the dragon's voice finally filled Arla's mind, there was a sombreness that sent a chill skittering down her spine.

'Not all gods are good, Dragonhart. Power can be a fickle thing, never enough once you have tasted it. There is one who always wanted more, one who would use dark, forbidden magic to achieve it. There is a reason the gods look down upon the Kastonian king and the blood magic he has tried to conduct. It damned one who ruled before him. They won't suffer a repeat of it.'

Arla's chest felt too tight. There was so much she didn't know. So much history that should have been inked in her blood but ... she had spent her life denying it. Spent her life denying the existence of gods and magic, and she had never taken the time to learn.

'You won't find any of this in your books. Dark magic and its consequences are not documented for a reason, and the fallen one has been erased from the minds of any who ever knew of his deeds.'

'Whose side did you fight on? In the wars, I mean.' Arla didn't know if she was expecting names – didn't know if the gods even had them, but Thara's answer raised goosebumps on her arms as if she had given Arla the very identities of those responsible for the world.

'Whomever was right.'

There was a snap of branches that had Arla whirling, blade drawn, her feet planted squarely on the uneven ground.

'My mother said I might find you here.'

A petite frame dropped from the trees. She had a pretty face too similar to her mother's for Arla not to know her immediately. She was perhaps the most beautiful woman Arla had ever seen.

'Princess Hyacinth.'

The princess smiled. 'Just Hyacinth, please. It's a pleasure to finally meet you.'

Hyacinth offered a hand to Arla, and she shook it slowly.

'You were following in the trees?' Arla questioned, her gaze lifting to the dense growth above them.

'Oh, no, forgive me, I wasn't spying. I've been training all morning, and the trees were the quickest way to find you.'

Thara rumbled softly, and a sprinkling of unease flowed through the bond. Arla shut it down immediately.

'Your mother lets you train?'

Hyacinth's grin grew wider. 'What use is a princess if she can't defend her lands and her people?'

'Indeed,' Arla said, twisting her lips to avoid the approval flooding her body. Hyacinth would be a valuable ally.

There was a girlish glow to the princess that betrayed her age. Arla knew Hyacinth was in her early twenties – around Halos's age, she thought, as a pang of longing stabbed her deep in the gut – though the softness in the princess's eyes made her look younger than even Arla.

The princess had been kept sheltered, obviously, though the confidence of the way she held her head and her eagerness to train told Arla that the girl dreamed of greater things than a castle carved into a cliff.

'What would you like to see first?' Hyacinth asked, but her voice was distracted and her eyes … gods, her eyes were focused on Thara and—

'Don't hurt her!'

Arla barely had time to form the thought she sent through the bond before the princess had reached up to run her slender fingers across the scales of Thara's chest.

Arla thought her heart might stop as Thara shifted beneath the touch, a warning growl spilling from her throat.

Hyacinth, however, didn't balk beneath the dragon or snatch her hand away. Instead, her eyes widened with something like awe. The innocence in her parted lips tugged something in Arla's core. Would Arla have been so gentle if she had been protected by her king rather than sent out to kill in his name?

'Forgive me,' Hyacinth murmured softly as she removed her hand, clutching it to her chest as if it had been burned.

'You better not have—'

Thara growled, *'Of course I did not harm her.'*

The princess shifted on her feet, pine needles crunching beneath the movement. 'I have long studied the gods and their dragons, but for you to be here now … it is not a prophecy I expected to be fulfilled within my lifetime.'

The word sunk into Arla's chest and pierced her with a hundred tiny needles. 'What do you mean prophecy?'

Hyacinth stared at her with round, doe-like eyes that were so green against the tawny brown of her hair. 'Walk with me.'

Arla didn't miss a step, falling into line next to the princess, so close that the floral scent of her washed over Arla. Peonies.

'You have heard that you will be the one to unite the kingdoms, no? It is why you have come here, isn't it? The gods have never been clear in their intentions nor have the fates who wrote them. But people often forget the second part of that prophecy spoken whilst the last dragonhart lay dying on his own blade.'

Arla's heart pounded furiously against her ribcage, her blood rushing in her ears. There was a rush of air behind the two women, the flap of leathery wings and the creak of breaking branches as Thara took to the sky. Damn the fates and their secrets.

Arla cleared her throat. 'What second part?'

Hyacinth was quiet for a moment, her fingers reaching to pluck a wild rose that she twisted into her hair as she walked.

'That when the risen takes flight to seek an ally, the clock will begin its duel. You have come here for help, Dragonhart, but you have set in motion plans laid down almost a century ago. If you don't find a way to unite the kingdoms soon, all that will be left is ash.'

Another secret her dragon had kept from her...

A pit opened up in the centre of Arla's chest. A writhing, black thing that swallowed every hope she had once had. It was all too much, the fates tying this prophecy around her neck like a noose. She hadn't asked for any of it. She hadn't wanted to be a dragonhart or unite kingdoms. All she had wanted to do was survive.

But she couldn't say any of that now.

She swallowed, her mouth sour and coated with a panic

that made her heart race faster. 'Tell me of the last dragonhart. What happened to him?'

She hadn't realised they'd reached the edge of the forest. When she looked up, there were the training rings and the temples and the beach beyond that.

Hyacinth laid a gentle hand against the crook of Arla's arm. 'Another time. You must come and watch the training. It's really rather special.'

Arla didn't want to watch archers or sword fights or any of the things that sang to the violence in her blood. She wanted answers and information and for her dragon to stop keeping things from her. This was *her* life. *Her* destiny. That she should be kept in the dark was fucking *cruel*!

'I cannot speak of what the fates prohibit—'

A roaring ripped through Arla's chest as she followed Princess Hyacinth through the forest, her eyes fixed on the girl's back as her mind sent pulses of agonised fury through the bond.

'Fuck the fates. You told me this bond runs deeper than anything, that it is as old as time. You keep secrets from me knowing how desperately I seek the knowledge, and how dangerous it is to blunder about in the dark. You're as cruel as they are.'

Arla slammed the bond shut before Thara could reply.

CHAPTER 26

The princess of Malarye had been right.

The training rings really were something. The priests and priestesses, still in those long white robes, moved with such fluid motions that it looked more like dancing than combat. There was a synchronicity between opponents, the barbs of their curved blades hooking together as the swords clashed. The training was conducted in silence, only the shifting of bare feet in sand and the clash of steel indicated there was anything happening at all.

Arla stood at the side of the ring, resting her elbows on wooden rails that had been worn smooth – perhaps by observers that couldn't keep their hands still, either.

'They practise for eight hours a day and spend another four in the temples. It is the way of our army,' Hyacinth said softly from her place beside Arla. The princess's fingers drummed restlessly against the rails, as if she knew too well the feel of the cutlass in her palm and longed to stand in the sand, too.

Arla had the overwhelming urge to want to duel with her.

The men and women in the training rings continued as

though she wasn't watching, as if a foreign assassin stood with their princess at the side of the ring every day. The snap of a bowstring didn't so much as stir their concentration as they moved through complex drills that made Arla's muscles ache just watching. She loved the weapon, and had often wished she had spent more time training with a bow than her sword. There was a subtle elegance to it that suited her perfectly and made her fingers twitch.

The arrows soaring overhead did nothing to ease her restlessness.

She turned slowly, as if the lack of speed would prevent an arrow being shot straight through her heart. There was a single line of archers, their eyes pinned firmly on the targets buried into the rockface beyond the training rings. Thirty of them fired at once, the whistle of arrows followed by the solid thud was the only signal that every single arrow had met its mark. Crea was amongst them, her pearl cape reflecting the sun so Arla had to squint to make out the head priestess's face in the line-up.

'Impressive,' she murmured.

The royal guard in Hadalyn had trained ruthlessly, often working through drills for hours on end to make sure they were fit enough to march should anyone ever threaten the borders of Hadalyn again.

But gods, it had never been as well organised as this. Each member of this ... *army* had a job to do, as though they were a vital cog in a larger machine. Hadalyn had never used their archers separately from their groundsmen; they required every soldier to be proficient in using both a bow and a sword. But in Malarye, they treated each soldier as an individual and adapted their ranks accordingly.

Hadalyn could learn something from this.

Flambriar certainly would.

The thought of her new kingdom and her people wrenched something deep in her stomach, almost tugging her forwards. An ancient tug to go to them, go to them, go to them—

'Control it. That urge will grow until you are incapable of being away from them if you do not learn to tamp it down.'

Ah. She'd wondered when her dragon would make a reappearance.

'I'm still angry with you for keeping secrets.'

Thara huffed through the bond. *'That is a human emotion, Dragonhart. Always the strongest.'*

Hyacinth's hand was a gentle tug at Arla's elbow again, and it made her realise how much Arla had changed.

Three months ago, she might have cut the girl's throat for daring to lay a hand on her, but that was before she had begun to unlearn the ruthlessness Cyrus had coaxed out of her. That had been before she had felt the primal need to protect her people.

Hyacinth could touch her. It was fine.

The princess, however, seemed to read whatever was in Arla's eyes – danger, perhaps? – and pulled her hand away slowly, as if Arla might bite her if she moved too fast.

'Sorry. I shouldn't have,' Hyacinth said, her voice suddenly lower than before. 'The touch of another is not always a welcome thing. I have known it too; I will keep my hands to myself.'

Curiosity was tart on Arla's tongue. 'I'm sorry you've known unwelcome hands. Might I suggest cutting them off next time?'

The princess raised her eyes to meet Arla's gaze, laughter spilling over her lips and brightening the beauty of her face. 'I find the throat to be a more effective deterrent.'

This time it was Arla who couldn't contain her laughter.

Gods, she was beginning to like the princess too much and too quickly.

'Your troops are well trained, and they wear the disguise of priests well, too.'

'Oh, they are not disguises,' Hyacinth said. 'They really are priests. They worship the gods devotedly. They train only to keep our borders safe. We have known peace for almost five hundred years. We intend to keep it that way.'

A hollow feeling opened up in the bottom of Arla's stomach. She wished such a peace for Flambriar too, though she had a feeling war would be unavoidable if she couldn't stop whatever Elrod was doing. Malarye would not be an easy ally, if one at all. And if she had set the prophecy into motion by coming here... If she was on a countdown to uniting the kingdoms... Would Malarye be on her side or against her? Nothing *felt* different. Surely if a prophecy had been triggered, she would feel something change inside her?

'What about the rest of your people?' Arla asked as Hyacinth began to stroll between the rows of training rings, careful not to drift too close to where the archers fired wave after wave of arrows at their targets in the cliff.

'They are perhaps the most important thing in my life.' Hyacinth paused, and when Arla looked at her Arla could see there was an oath inked there. She would protect her people at all costs and with her life. Arla felt the same way.

'Since my birth, they have blessed me with a kindness I cannot possibly deserve. They helped my mother raise me when the winters were harsh and she was occupied with court duties. My people raised me as their own. I intend to return the honour when I am queen.'

There were shadows in the princess's eyes, haunted, dark things that hid secrets they could plague only her with. Arla longed to know what they were. What secrets was Malarye hiding and why had their queen killed its king. Had those unkind hands Hyacinth had spoken of belonged to him?

'Where are they ... your people, I mean?' Arla asked, stepping into place beside Hyacinth as they continued their perusal of the training grounds.

'Beyond the forest. We wanted them safe, landlocked in the middle of the queendom should our borders ever come under attack. They will start to drift over here when the sun begins to set. The temples are lively places at night, and you've arrived just in time for a wedding.'

She didn't have time for weddings. She needed answers. She needed to know what Malarye wanted because she had not been invited here to make small talk.

She'd spent too many hours achieving nothing already. Enough was enough.

'Hyacinth—'

'Ah, here we are,' the princess interrupted. 'We so hope you allow us to watch you train. Your skill is spoken of even here, Dragonhart, and it would be beneficial to our army to see new ways of combat.

Beneficial indeed! So they could learn her skills – and her weak points – in order to work out how to take her down should it ever come to that.

'You don't believe that. Stop sulking.'

She choked on the laugh in her throat. No. No one could ever hope to master the way she moved. The years of practice had made her unpredictable and entirely wild when it came to wielding a blade. No one would be able to learn her tells; she doubted she truly knew them herself.

She rolled her shoulders, her blood already calling for the violence, her mind aching to slip into that calm space where nothing and no one could touch her. It had been both a blessing and a curse when Cyrus had sent her on jobs for days at a time. She had come back filthy and bloodstained and entirely feral. It had taken him and Perry too many hours to haul her back out of that place in her own head.

Now she wished to feel it again.

'Am I to have an opponent or would you like me to cut myself down?' she said smartly, stepping into the ring and unsheathing the sword at her side. It was a short blade, not one she would wish to carry into battle, but it would be fine for the purposes of this demonstration. Especially if she were to go against those curved blades.

But Hyacinth was looking at her, head tilted, a wary expression on her face.

Thara chuckled through the bond.

'It was a joke, Your Highness. I will duel whomever you see fit.'

The princess's eyes softened, her lovely smile returning as she tapped the shoulder of a priest beside her. 'Laurence will be your opponent.'

'No. I will.' A thunderous voice reached them from the far side of the training ground. It was Crea, and she marched towards them, her bow discarded.

Arla's own grin widened. She could think of no better opponent to knock on their ass than the woman who had ordered her dragon be impaled with arrows.

'Crea, that really isn't necessary. Laurence will be—'

'No bother, Your Highness. I'd be more than happy to duel the infamous King's Assassin,' Crea said, striding into the ring.

Hyacinth looked between the priestess and Arla, the control she'd wielded only moments ago already lost to a strong-willed woman dressed in white. The princess looked tiny now, her beauty not enough to command those beneath her. Crea knew it too.

'You know,' Arla said, the blade in her hand a familiar friend, 'where I come from, I'd have had your head for disrespecting a member of the royal bloodline.'

Crea scoffed, unsheathing a hooked blade from somewhere beneath that bloody gown. What a shame it would be to see it marred with the priestess's own blood. 'Then it is lucky we aren't in Hadalyn and I have offended no one.'

She lunged then – a sneaky, bitch thing to do.

But Arla had expected it from the second Crea had stepped into the ring. Besides, Arla was capable of sneaky, bitch things too. Loved them, actually.

She ducked Crea's strike, sweeping back up to drive her blade into the open gap Crea had left at her right hip.

The priestess spun with expert grace, leaving Arla stumbling forwards onto her left foot. No matter, if she was finally to have an opponent worthy of her skill, she would open that locked box inside her mind and let them all see what it meant to take on the King's Assassin.

There was a cold, unfeeling place in the centre of Arla's chest as she swung her blade and danced around Crea like a nymph. It beckoned to her, an urge to descend deeper, deeper into that violent shred of soul that had been trained to hurt.

She spun and swung and lunged without feeling. The world disappeared, only the white robed woman in front of her mattered as she swung her sword again. Again. Again.

Red, like summer berries bloomed in a devastatingly straight line across the arm of the priestess.

Something in Arla's chest liked that.

She launched herself forwards, ignoring the hissing and snapping of her opponent. All that mattered was that they needed to die. She hoisted her blade again. Spinning, striking, blocking, and all as naturally as breathing. She was fire and ice and darkness. She was wrath and fury and danger. No one would beat her.

'That will do.'

The voice in her head hauled her back to herself, wrenching something in her stomach that almost had her heaving. She looked down. Down to where Crea lay in the sand, the tip of Arla's blade pressed gently into the column of her throat, the skin splitting beneath its weight. The priestess was blinking at her, as if the fog that had smothered Arla's consciousness was seeping into her too.

She'd done it again.

She'd lost control. Lost who she was in the dance of sword fighting. She'd have killed Crea had Thara not intervened. She ripped the blade away quickly and offered a hand to her opponent.

Crea took it hesitantly, her eyes round and wary as she clambered to her feet, laying a hand over the now red fabric covering her arm.

'Apologies. I didn't mean to draw blood, Crea.'

The priestess hesitated, but then Arla watched the hardness creep back in, a mask slotting into place as the woman rolled back her shoulders and tilted that sharp chin upwards. 'You apologise for something I willingly stepped into. You are weak if you feel the need to cover your skill with false words.'

Hyacinth sucked in a breath. Arla had forgotten the princess was watching, that *all* of the army was watching.

'You'd rather I killed you before your people, then?' Arla said, her voice dangerously soft.

Crea blinked lazily at her, a smirk turning up the corners of her mouth. To her credit, the priestess hadn't so much as winced at the slice in her arm. 'Yes. But it is true what they say. You don't know when to stop. You lose control so thoroughly it is hypnotising to watch.'

Before Arla could respond and say it was a lie, Crea was turning away, sheathing the curved blade beneath her robe and bellowing orders to the soldiers to go back to training.

'Perhaps you would like to bathe before dinner? The wedding I spoke of is happening tonight. You might want to rest before then?' Hyacinth's voice was a lovely, soothing thing, and it let Arla fall into herself and be led like a lamb back up the cliff to the stone palace. The princess spoke quietly the whole way, pointing out the small pink flowers that grew between the clefts in the cliffs and talking about their ability to heal some of the harshest of wounds. She spoke of those strange curved blades called *serabti* and explained that these blades were thought to have been used by one of the gods when they walked the world a millennia ago.

But despite the history and the facts she should be remembering about this kingdom, Arla couldn't forget what Crea had said. She had lost control and did not know when to stop. Was it true? Had she truly gone so far under Cyrus' rule that she couldn't stop herself from becoming death incarnate? The tugging in her mind, the urge to push and push when she saw the bright bloom of blood on her victims... There was no way she was in control then. No way she could claw herself back from it without the interference of others. It had happened just now and she had almost gutted Seb in training back at Claret Hall, but she had felt herself slipping long before that...

Had she always been like this?

For longer than you could ever know.

She didn't know who had spoken – her, or the dragon that had chosen her.

CHAPTER 27

Salt fish and boiled vegetables were delivered to her door the second she finished bathing.

Here, so close to the sea, fish could be caught and eaten the same day. To make it across the mountains to Flambriar, fish had to be frozen or dried to stop it going bad.

Queen Mara had been absent when Arla arrived back at the palace, her desk empty and the entourage of advisors and courtiers missing from the hall, too. It looked even larger without so many people to fill it, the space like the maw of a great cat ready to swallow anything that wandered into its jaws. Would the princess ever be able to wield such a bite, or would her people only see a pretty face and kind eyes and decide her too meek before her reign even began?

It didn't matter. This was Malarye and Arla had no allegiance to it or its princess ... yet.

She picked out the simplest gown she had packed – a plain thing that was the colour of green only found in lilies just before they bloomed. She would have liked to wear something lovely and bejewelled, to show off the power that came with her position in Flambriar, but for a wedding? No, not even she could upstage a bride.

She had washed and combed her hair, glad there were no maids to do it for her. Glad, because she didn't think she could stand to have anyone near her whilst her mind tried to make sense of the last twenty-four hours.

This kingdom clearly had knowledge beyond what lay in Hadalyn and Kastonia and *definitely* Flambriar. No one had seemed shocked to see her arrive riding Thara, and the healer? Mages had been coming here long before they had sought shelter in Flambriar. But what was Malarye concealing that she didn't yet know? Hyacinth had mentioned the last dragonhart dying on his own sword and how the prophecy had been set in motion for a second time. It lit a hope in her chest that maybe she could find answers here. That maybe these people would help her if she could figure out what they wanted in return.

And then there was the case of the magic that had flowed in her own blood. She'd felt it before. When she was fleeing Larkire Palace after rescuing Hark, she had felt the surge through the bond before it exploded through her hands. And yesterday ... when she was certain they were going to kill her and Thara, there had been that burst of power through the bond and she had used it to create a great wave that could not possibly have formed naturally...

This magic ... it scared her almost as much as losing control did. Damn the fates and the gods and whoever else had prohibited Thara from speaking of what it all meant. She hadn't asked to be the last dragonhart. She hadn't asked for this blood in her veins. Why shouldn't she demand the truth?

Gods, she missed Hark. He'd know exactly what to say and exactly what to do with his hands to distract her for long enough that nothing seemed so dark and lonely.

Her skin heated at the thought.

When she finally emerged from her rooms, the halls were still empty and only the distant rumble of voices informed her that someone had bothered to wait for her at all. Her dress whispered at her ankles, the blade she'd strapped to her thigh catching slightly on the thin material. She wore boots beneath the silk, laced tightly for the walk to the temples beyond the cliffs. She wondered if the gods cared about marriages between people. Did they bless those who entwine their lives together in the temples or did they hate that the buildings could be used for something other than worshipping them?

The thought was bitter in her mouth. She had gone from not believing at all, to believing so hard that she was dedicating her life to the service of the gods and their wishes.

And now she was beginning to despise them.

'They listen, you know.'

'Clearly so do you,' Arla replied down the bond, the chortle of what could be mistaken for nothing other than laughter echoing back at her.

She needed to apologise to Thara. Her dragon was bound by the fates and the gods. Who knew what would happen to her if she tried to tell Arla the things she was supposed to keep hidden.

None of this was Thara's fault. It wasn't Arla's, either.

Queen Mara and her court were gathered at the base of the cliff. They had only waited so long for their guest, it seemed. She bit back a smirk as she sauntered down the hill, her arms peppering with goosebumps as the wind nipped at her.

'Good evening, Dragonhart. Is all well?' the queen asked, her voice harder than her daughter's but lovely all the same.

'Of course. I was admiring the castle is all. I didn't get to see it when I was here last.'

Arla thought the queen's chest hitched slightly, but if she felt any discomfort, it ran away from her in smooth rivulets, barely there at all as she brightened that courtly smile.

'It is not often our buildings are admired. They are built for safety and practicality. I don't doubt you have seen palaces far grander.'

The courtiers were whispering to each other, though when Arla shifted her gaze over them, she didn't feel the surge of irritation that often came when she knew others were talking about her. Because ... it turned out they weren't.

They clearly had far better things to discuss as they swapped scrolls of parchment and spoke of training and temples and trade as the procession began to make its way to a temple with tall bronze spires just beyond the training rings.

Queen Mara didn't linger near Arla like she had expected – like any ruler she had ever met did when a foreign dignitary came to stay. She walked instead with her own people, still working even on the way to a wedding. Crea was thankfully missing, but so was the princess, whom Arla was beginning to suspect kept very much out of the way of her mother's court, so she walked alone at the back of the procession, eyes scanning every inch of the kingdom before her.

The temple where the wedding was to be held was a magnificent structure. Arla was certainly too wicked to stand before such a place. It was a hulking, beautiful building of carved stone and bronze fixtures. It reached with tall spires high enough that she was sure a person could pluck the stars from the top of them. Stained glass windows filled with glorious torchlight sat delicately near the top of the temple, wrapping around the building like an embrace of rainbows and starlight. Warmth seeped out from a huge archway with pillars taller than Thara to guard the doorway, and there was music, too, drifting out into the night. Not far away, the sea crashed against the rocks on which the temple had been built, the scent of brine and salt and freedom weaving its way through the air. This was a godly place. She could feel it in the way her heart quickened, in the way the air felt alive like it did when she was surrounded by magic in Flambriar. It was a blessed place, built for the gods – and perhaps by them. The golden brooch she'd pinned above her left breast felt impossibly hot to the touch.

Arla followed the court without missing a step, sucking in a breath so deep her lungs ached as she passed beneath the archway into the temple and felt the weight of a thousand worlds press on her chest.

The feeling disappeared as quickly as it came, but from the way Diath was looking at her from their position in the fourth pew on the left of the temple, she knew the healer had noticed Arla's reaction.

Crea stood at the head of the temple before an altar of dazzling jewel-encrusted cups and daggers, her robes as white as alabaster, the pearls shimmering beneath the torchlight. She looked ... regal. Which, in Arla's opinion, was a problem. Because the princess who did in fact carry royal blood stood to the right of the priestess, her beauty breathtaking but entirely lacking the power she should exude.

Queen Mara had ushered in a wave of silence, the quiet following her down the aisle as she took a seat at the very front of the temple. Hyacinth's panicked stare told Arla everything she needed to know: that where she stood was usually the queen's place. Perhaps Mara was doing her best to push her daughter to take on more responsibility, to establish herself amongst the people and step into the role she had been born to. Arla could relate but she felt for the princess too – out of her depth beside a priestess who carried the dignity of her role far better than she.

The court began to take their seats, filling the front rows of pews. Arla took a seat next to Diath, their kind smile a reassurance amongst practices with which she was not familiar. Already she couldn't wait for it to be over.

She had attended only three weddings in her life: her parents', when she was too small to understand any of it; the daughter of a lady her mother had been friends with, who had died during the storming of Grey Hill; and the third wedding was when she had only just been inducted into the royal guard and was training for King's Assassin. Hark had been at Castle Grey for less than a month at that point and they had bickered so loudly that Perry had been made to sit between them for the wedding of a nobleman from Grey Hill to a girl no older than Arla. She'd protested so loudly against it on their return to the palace that Cyrus had stopped inviting the man for dinner whenever Arla was at the castle.

She felt like she was trespassing at this wedding, inside this astonishing temple filled with soft torchlight.

Half a dozen women dressed in plain white gowns had been playing violins softly at the back of the temple, and when the notes changed and the music found its way deep inside Arla's skin, she turned to face the musicians. A gasp fell through her lips as two women began the walk down the aisle.

Their fingers entwined, the women walked to the altar, their veils as long as the temple and dazzling white. The pillars that lined the altar seemed to shrink beneath their very presence, the temple suddenly too small to contain whatever power the women possessed.

She didn't know she'd moved until Diath's fingers closed

around her wrist. Arla looked up and met Diath's eyes as every member of the congregation took their seats.

'Their pull is strong, but you will get used to it,' Diath whispered softly, their eyes fixed on the two women. Crea touched their heads, her mouth forming words Arla couldn't hear. The tug in her core pulled again.

She hadn't expected it to be so strong – for the need to protect the mages to overwhelm every sense. Had the feeling been growing since she had first discovered her true bloodline?

'Be still, Dragonhart. They are not yours to protect.'

Of course they were. She had felt the magic they possessed before she had truly had a chance to look upon them. They were mages, and that meant it was her duty to keep them safe. Her duty to stand between them should any try to—

'*Enough!*' The command shattered through the bond, so loudly she jerked back in the pew, her body going taut as she snapped out of whatever daze she had lost herself in. There it was again. The lack of control.

'They have great magic and it speaks to your blood. But you will learn to control it soon enough,' Diath murmured softly, their fingers still tight round Arla's wrist to ... what? Anchor her? Stop her storming down the aisle to interrupt a wedding for ... *what?* What did she think she was going to do when she came within touching distance?

The Dragonhart brooch felt hot through the fabric of her dress.

The service began, Crea's voice lilting through the temple to conduct the marriage ceremony. Arla escaped into her own mind, replaying memories from her time at Castle Grey, reciting training drills and moves she would know even if she were dead. At some point during the ceremony, Princess Hyacinth handed over the wedding bands and took a seat next to her mother.

Arla paid none of it any attention. Her blood ached. There was an urge growing within her, something telling her to get the mages out of the temple – out of this country – and hide them in Flambriar where they would be safe.

They're safe here.

She shook her head. Of course they were. Malarye didn't discriminate against those with magic in their blood; the queendom had opened its doors for them, actually, and the place was so committed to the gods and their wishes that Arla knew with certainty that they would never lay a hand on a mage.

So why did that ancient thing in her bloodline want nothing more than to run to the front of the altar and drag the two women back to Flambriar where they would be safe? Where they would be hers.

Diath's fingers tightened around her wrist again.

'Tell me of Hadalyn, Dragonhart. What is it like since my kind fell asleep?'

Thara's voice was a comfort and a distraction, and Arla leant into it as Crea continued with the droning nonsense of the wedding ceremony.

'It has beautiful places, like the river and Grey Hill – once it was rebuilt after the battle. But it is beginning to fall to sickness and poverty like Kastonia already has. You can see it in the slums, how they're growing each month and starting to encroach on noble land. I wonder if it would already have fallen had it not been for your presence.'

Thara rumbled softly in her head. *'I think you are right. The gods are angry with what Kastonia's king is doing. They are confused and panicked. I believe they see no other way to stop him than to condemn the kingdoms and hope something better emerges from the chaos. They have begged and bargained with the fates about how to stop the corruption of magical blood.'*

'What have they bargained?' Arla asked.

'Gods' bargains are not taken lightly. And if broken, the consequences are borne by those of us who serve. Some have taken a vow of silence in exchange for answers. All it has achieved is broken promises and dragons too weak to fly.'

There was a solemnity in Thara's voice that curdled in Arla's stomach. The fates had harmed the dragons because the gods had broken their vows...

She didn't know who she hated most.

'Have they ... have they harmed you?' She didn't know if she wished to hear the answer. Didn't know if she would be able to contain the rage that simmered beneath her skin if she found out Thara had been hurt. It was a strange thing, the bond. Somehow a mark against her dragon felt like a mark on Arla's soul.

'No. My god did not make a bargain to break.'

Intrigue picked at the corners of Arla's mind, but she wouldn't push Thara to give her more, not when this was the most her dragon had ever told her of the gods and how the fates were intervening. What had changed? Why now?

'Why would they break their bargains? If the fates delivered answers, surely the gods could be content with that?'

Thara sighed. *'Know that the gods did not take these vows lightly. They care for us more deeply than any bond. It has, I believe, devastated them that their dragons have been harmed for their mistake.'*

'What mistake?'

'When the fates granted them an answer to their question, the gods did not like it. Did not understand it. The outrage it caused was

enough for even the most steadfast of them to speak and break their vows.'

Arla knew what Thara would say. She could taste the bile in her throat because the fates had fooled them all. She asked the question anyway.

'What answer did the fates give?'

'Two words. Two words that broke gods' bargains: Arla Reinhart.'

CHAPTER 28

Her chest was too tight.

So not even the gods knew how she was supposed to fix things! She was beginning to think she existed only for the amusement of the fates.

But why now? Why, when the gods had left so long ago, was it *her* that had to be the one to save the kingdoms? Why had almost a hundred years passed before this fucking prophecy had to come to fruition? What did the fates have against her?

Crea concluded the wedding ceremony and the two women kissed, an action so tender it felt impolite to be in the same vicinity as them. The music began again, a rendition of violins at the back of the temple. Thara was still there in the back of her mind, still pressing gently on the bond as if begging Arla to ask the question burning on her tongue.

'How are you able to tell me this now?'

Thara was silent for too long. So long that the congregation had risen to their feet, Arla's wrist still tightly in Diath's grip as the two brides began the walk back down the aisle. But eventually Thara's voice filled her head, so ancient and wise and trilling with magic.

'Because you are finally asking the right questions.'

The bond snapped shut almost immediately, and Arla cursed the dragon whom she was sure sent a rumble of laughter before disappearing from her head. How was she only just asking the right questions when she had been asking the same things for *months*?

Diath's fingers finally relaxed their grip and Arla brought her wrist to her chest, rubbing the smooth spot of skin where the healer's hold had been. The brides had come to a halt at the entryway to the temple, a cheer greeting them from outside as the musicians reached a crescendo that made Arla's heart pound.

The temple had come alive in a sea of colour and laughter and wide smiles that were so infectious she found her lips breaking into a grin that for once didn't feel at all faked. She forced Thara's words from her mind. She could untangle them later when she visited her dragon for an aerial survey of this queendom. If she was beginning to ask the right questions, then Hyacinth's solemn warning that a faraway clock was ticking wasn't so terrifying. She would find out what the fates wanted and stop whatever it was Elrod was doing. That would be enough to unite the kingdoms and fulfil the prophecy. She just needed to know where to start. The people were cheering again, and this time she joined in too, laughing as fireworks were set off outside and the brides were ushered out under a multitude of garlands of tiny blue flowers. Diath called for Arla to follow, their eyes bright as they offered a hand to Arla.

But it wasn't Diath's gaze that sent a shiver down her spine as they left the temple and made their way to the palace in the cliff. It was the queen's. She met Arla's gaze over the heads of dozens of Malarye's citizens and in those eyes, there was a knowing that set hummingbirds fluttering in Arla's stomach.

It was time to find out exactly why Malarye had invited the king's assassin to its shores.

∽

The procession to the palace was a lively affair. Banners of coloured silk were tied to wooden poles that twirled in the wind and garlands of wildflowers were placed around the necks of every person who had come out to see the marriage union. Arla barely noticed the trek up the cliff – wouldn't have noted the incline at all had it not been for the burning in the back of her calves.

The palace was still as colourless and practical as ever, though someone – or several *someones* – had laid out huge oak tables bearing platters of food large enough to feed an army. There were meats wrapped in pastry, fruits carved into fancy shapes, cheeses that made her stomach growl and a dozen other things she wanted to stuff into her mouth and savour with delight.

'I thought you could use a drink. You looked awfully hot in the temple,' a soft voice said beside her, and Arla turned to find Hyacinth pushing a goblet of what looked like pink wine into her hands. The princess looked radiant in a gown of periwinkle chiffon, her skin pinked and glowing in the soft lights of the hall. Gone was the panic in her eyes that Arla had spotted in the temple. Now she was at ease and she seemed so very soft and lovely.

'It was … uncomfortably hot in there,' Arla said, to distract from the fact that she had been about to abduct the two brides and take them back to Flambriar before she had disappeared into her head to converse with a dragon.

Gods, if someone had told her this four months ago...

'Weddings in Malarye have always been a grand occasion,' Hyacinth said, swiping a canape of fish and green vegetables from a man holding a bronze platter. 'Two hearts being bound together should be celebrated, should it not? The gods have always blessed those who love so strongly.'

Arla wondered where the old religion had come from. Who had made the rules. Who had decided what the gods blessed and what they didn't. Perhaps the gods all found it rather amusing.

'It was a lovely ceremony,' was what Arla settled on, snatching one of those canapes for herself and trying not to moan at the taste of it. 'I was surprised to see that they were mages. You certainly have more of them here than I thought possible.'

She struggled to keep the bite out of her voice, that protective need flaring up inside her like an inextinguishable flame. Hyacinth's eyes widened and when she spoke Arla could have sworn there was a hardness to the princess's voice she hadn't heard before.

'The mages have not advertised the fact that they have safe passage into Malarye for fear of what Kastonia's king may do if he finds out. It is his border from which they must procure a boat, after all.'

Of course. If Elrod had known the mages were fleeing, he'd have captured any who attempted to charter a boat to the continent. She couldn't blame the mages for wanting to keep this sanctuary a secret. She couldn't blame Malarye, either.

'Apologies,' Arla said. 'It was a shock is all. There's much about your queendom I don't know, and it seems you have information that may be useful to me.'

The princess tilted her head. 'Such as?'

'Tell me of the man you spoke of earlier – the last dragonhart. You said he died on his own blade?'

Hyacinth's features softened, the perfect bow of her lips widening slightly as she offered Arla a simple smile. 'Yes, but it is a sad story, not one for a wedding celebration. But I am more than happy to share it with you, if you come find me tomorrow? Perhaps we could have lunch and I could show you the main town. I'm sure our people would be interested to meet you.'

Irritation was a slimy thing that coated Arla's skin. She wanted answers *now*. She'd come here at the invitation of this princess and had yet to be shown anything of interest. And Hyacinth was still *smiling* at her.

There was a shard of her that wanted to snap the beautiful woman's neck.

'I do enjoy your violence, Dragonhart.'

It was enough to break the spell and shatter the image of slowly strangling the princess of Malarye.

'Lunch would be nice.'

Hyacinth nodded, her gaze lingering on the simple dress Arla had donned. 'You look very pretty. I'm sure Hark is missing you.'

The princess had turned and was making her way over to a group of finely dressed women before Arla could ask what the princess knew of Hark. The thought of him started an ache in her chest.

No. She couldn't let herself think too much of him because she was already a heartbeat away from leaving Malarye and flying home. If she thought of Hark for too long, she doubted she'd make it to the end of the night before escaping the queendom's shores.

Instead, she hovered at the edge of conversations. A polite smile here, a brief introduction there. It was all too ... courtly for her taste. This was the job of a king. Hark should be here to introduce himself as Flambriar's ruler. Arla should be outside, stalking thieves or killing spies.

The briefest of touches to her elbow and then Arla was enveloped with the scent of honeysuckle. Queen Mara nursed a drink the same colour as Arla's own, and though the queen looked pleasant enough, there were storm clouds in her eyes. Finally, they might get down to the business of why Arla had been invited here and what exactly it was the queen wanted from her. And, more importantly, what Arla was going to ask for in return.

'I hope you enjoyed the wedding, Dragonhart. Bria and Vyne were honoured to have you there. It means a lot that a dragonhart should be present to witness the union between two of magical blood.' Mara was blinking lazily at her, as if she knew Arla could see straight through the niceties.

'I haven't seen Bria or Vyne since the wedding. Clearly I am not as important as you would have me believe ... Your Majesty.'

The queen's eyes flashed, and then the corners of her lips curled slowly into a wolfish grin.

'Arla Reinhart, I was wondering when your temper might make an appearance.'

There was a predatory sharpness to the queen's face as she ushered Arla to the side of the hall where they were partly hidden by long, ash-coloured curtains. This woman had killed her husband. Her king. And she had not lost her head or her title for it. Mara knew manipulation and how to wield it with a viper's accuracy. She had kept the support of her people, after all.

Arla curled her fingers, inspecting the nails on her left hand as she answered the queen. 'My temper is nowhere near as dangerous as my wit, Your Majesty. And right now, I have almost had enough of the games and the things I am not being told. So, let's start again, shall we?'

The queen had the sense to look wary as Arla's voice lowered into that lethal softness she reserved for the likes of those who were moments away from finding themselves impaled on the end of her blade.

'Why did you invite me here?'

Mara ran her tongue over her brilliant white teeth, and then it was like a weight had been lifted from the queen's shoulders. The façade dropped, that impenetrable royal act plunging like a rock as she let the words tumble out of her mouth.

'I want you to train with my soldiers. You have skills they could only dream of possessing, and though I refuse to send my army to war with Kastonia, I think it is inevitable we will be caught up in it somehow. I want them ready to march, trained by someone lethal. Perhaps in return they can teach you something of archery. I hear it is not a skill in which you are as adept as you would have the world believe.'

What?

She was certain disbelief danced in every line of her face ... and then she was laughing. So hard her stomach ached with it.

'You want me to train your army?' She couldn't stop the words that burst from her lips ensconced in laughter. Surely the rest of the wedding party were looking now, stretching their necks to see who had the audacity to laugh in the queen's face.

She didn't care.

'I only speak truths, Miss Reinhart.' Though the situation

was entirely laughable there was not an ounce of amusement on the queen's face. She didn't jest, didn't use the words as a cover for something else, as a guise to manipulate Arla into something she couldn't yet see. Arla didn't miss the fact the queen had used her old name.

'You couldn't have put any of this in a letter?' Arla asked, a brow arched as ire flashed in Mara's green eyes.

The queen squared her shoulders. 'Would you have come?'

Clever.

'No,' Arla said. 'No, I wouldn't.'

'Precisely.'

Now the words had settled, she was beginning to think them through. Perhaps training with a new army wouldn't be a bad thing. Mara was right, she was poor at archery. She had laughed with Hark about it that night in the tavern before the world had descended into shit. And to train again, properly, with her favourite weapon – with an army no less ... it was too tempting. No one at Flambriar would be able to blame her for it. They'd seen the way she spent hours pushing herself or duelling anyone who dared to lift a sword against her. They knew she was bored.

And *gods*, she'd missed the structure of training with the royal guard at Castle Grey.

'I will train with your army,' she said, eyes watching for any twitch of movement in Mara's face that would indicate she had been tricked. 'But I want an alliance for Flambriar. If I give my skills and time to your soldiers, they had better not be used against me. Ever. And if we go to war, I want your vow that you will come to our aid.'

Mara's skin blanched, her lips trembling slightly before she seemed to remember who she was.

'Perhaps we can discuss this somewhere private?'

'No,' Arla said. 'You wanted this conversation in the middle of a wedding, in a hall filled with people because you wanted them to see you win against the famed King's Assassin. Don't give in now, *Mara*. I'm sure you can twist them into supporting you, whatever answer you're about to give me, and I suggest you make it one I want to hear.'

Here she was. Arla had missed her machiavellian side that took delight in the panic of her opponents. It had been too long since she had allowed herself to become the girl Hadalyn had groomed her to be.

The queen took a deep breath, perhaps to steady herself, and looked Arla square in the eyes. 'I will not send my people to war, not when Elrod is rumoured to have men that are twisted and cursed. But you have my assurance that Malarye will not march against Flambriar. Ever. We may not come to your aid, Miss Reinhart, but we will not be your enemy, either.'

'Coward.'

Arla was inclined to agree with her dragon.

Half of her wanted to scream at the queen. To tell her how pathetic it was. How ridiculous it had been to invite Arla here to train her army, only to refuse aid should it ever come to that.

But the other half, the half that knew how important it was to have a friend, even if they said they would not fight, was roaring on behalf of Flambriar. Malarye might not send soldiers, but if Arla could learn something from them, it was worth it, wasn't it? If she could learn skills to take back to her own people, to build her own army, surely that would count for something if Kastonia ever came for them?

And ... well Arla was clever. Had learnt from the very best when it came to making deals between kingdoms. This arrangement was weighed in Mara's favour, so much so that Arla was tempted to mount her dragon and fly back home for the insult.

But Cyrus wouldn't have done that. Cyrus would have sipped his wine and made a show of pondering Mara's proposition. If Arla could win the queen's trust by agreeing to a deal that Arla held the poorer end of, there would be room to manoeuvre later...

She steeled herself, mirroring the strength of the queen before her.

'You have a deal.'

CHAPTER 29
HARK

Jack's leg shook against Hark's as they waited outside the healer's office. This was the sixth time they'd come here, and though it had given Jack a modicum of improvement, Hark didn't think he would ever forget the screams that came from his friend's mouth. He certainly wasn't looking forward to hearing them again. The healer – Nia – had tried countless methods to cure Jack from whatever magic had struck him one night when they had been trying to rescue mages from the border. None of these methods had worked until a week ago when she had finally felt comfortable enough in her own magic to try and draw it out of Jack. He had bellowed and screamed loudly enough that the citizens of Flambriar had frozen in the streets.

But it had been the only thing that had given him a shred of comfort. For two days afterwards he had managed to walk straighter, and the cloudiness of his eyes had cleared slightly. Kase had been at his side through all of it, just as she was now, her knees as jittery as Jack's.

'You know, I half wish Reinhart were here. She'd have some

wisecrack that would make me less nervous about feeling my blood boil,' Jack said with a grim laugh. His blood boiling – that's what he'd told them it felt like. Nia's magic attached itself to the magic inside Jack and siphoned it into Nia. The healer, although she hadn't screamed out in pain like Jack had, had been slick with sweat the last time, her lip bleeding where she'd bitten it from the strain. Both of them had told Nia they would find another way, but she'd brushed them off and said she owed it to them. For saving her. For the accidental strike of magic Jack had sustained when all he had been doing was trying to rescue the mages from the camp on the northern border.

'Wisecrack? Try completely insulting and not fit for the ears of anyone under the age of eighteen or above the age of fifty,' Kase snorted.

Hark smothered a laugh. Gods, he loved his friends. Loved that despite their differences they'd all accepted Arla into the fold. Fuck, he missed her. She was a bolstering strength that he wished was here right now. When she was with him, well, everything seemed a little easier. A little more doable. Like the world actually might *not* end.

He sighed, running a hand through his hair. Arla loved when he did that. Had told him so multiple times. Especially when his hands were on her and she was soft and lovely and—*Fuck* he needed to get it together. 'Are you sure you want to do this down here? Nia could come up to the hall. It—'

'Shut up, Stappen,' Jack said. 'I come here just like any other patient. I don't want special treatment just because I'm part of your court.'

Your court.

Like he was a king or something.

It wasn't Hark's court. They'd all started saying it and he despised it. He wasn't in charge of them; they shouldn't have to answer to him and yet ... they did. Without question. They followed Arla's whims too – that, he could understand. She was born of a bloodline so ancient and worshipped that it would be utter blasphemy to go against what she said.

It hadn't stopped them all bickering endlessly though, had it?

He was about to say so when the door swung open before he could voice any of it.

'Jack, hello.' Nia's cheery face appeared in the doorway, her tanned skin looking far healthier than it had done when they had left her last week. 'Are you all ready?'

Were they *all* ready? Because it wasn't just Jack who would be inside that room. Hark and Kase would be there too, holding Jack to the bed as Nia sent her magic through him.

'Let's get this over with,' Kase said with a sigh, wringing her hands together as she followed Jack and Nia through the door. Hark reached for her elbow, leaning down to whisper in her ear.

'You don't have to be here if you don't want to. Seb said he would come.'

Kase turned to face him, those dazzling blue eyes as hard as ice chips. 'I won't leave him.'

There was nothing else to say. Jack was already lying down on the infirmary bed. The room was bright, airy. It smelt fresh, and the walls had been painted a soft shade of beige. It was soothing, almost, in contrast to what was about to happen.

Nia was quiet as she plaited her dark hair into short braids that barely touched her shoulders. She was a kind woman, with soft curves and an appetite for the cheeses Hark had made sure to deliver last week as a thank-you. She always spoke softly, with an accent Hark couldn't quite place – originally from Gravidum, perhaps. Her voice was a balm to the pain she was about to inflict.

Jack's legs were restless again.

'I hear you found some relief in the days that followed our last session,' Nia said, moving to stand by the side of the bed. 'That means we're heading in the right direction. We've touched the magic inside you. Now we need to tug.'

Jack swallowed, nodding his head curtly. Hark was sure Kase's hands trembled where she wrung them on the front of her sweater. He'd seen Arla do it when she was nervous, too.

'Just keep going,' Jack said gruffly. 'The sooner we get it out the sooner we can forget this ever happened.'

Nia lowered her eyes, the tilt of her chin the only acknowledgement. There was no warning as she brought her hands to rest over Jack's body.

And then he began screaming.

～

'Enough, please...'

Jack had been screaming the words for the past half hour. Kase wasn't trying to hide the tears now as they ran silently down her cheeks, her grip on Jack's wrists never wavering as he bucked and thrashed beneath her hold. Hark held onto his friend's ankles, pinning him to the bed as Nia continued to chant and roam her hands across the surface of Jack's broken body. A thick sheen of sweat coated the healer, and Hark was sure her legs would buckle at any moment, but she didn't relent.

The air felt alive, as if the corruption of magic in Jack's blood was being siphoned off into the room and cursing him for ever possessing it.

Sweat was slick on Hark's skin too, the strain of holding his friend down burning through every part of him. Screams tore through them all, a sound so visceral Hark didn't think he would ever be able to unhear it. Kase shook as she held Jack's wrists, but not for a single moment did she stop murmuring to him.

Nia moved her hands again, and the sound that left Jack's throat was enough to shatter worlds.

'It's okay, you're okay,' Kase sobbed, lowering her head to his as if whatever remained of her strength could be passed onto Jack. She flinched as he screamed again. 'It's all right, we're here.'

Fuck, this was breaking his heart.

This was all his fucking fault.

He had told his friends to start extracting mages from the border whilst he was still stationed in Hadalyn. *He* had been the one to demand they keep going, even though his father's soldiers were becoming wise to the raids and had started fighting back.

He was the reason Jack had been hurt and was having to go through this. He didn't know how he'd ever look Kase in the eyes again. Jack was strong, he ... well, he knew his friend would take this in his stride just as he did with everything that had ever been thrown at him.

But Kase ... Kase had been through too much already. Kase had been at the mercy of her uncle's unkind hands after she'd watched her mother die of a wasting sickness. Hark couldn't imagine how fucked-up this was for her.

Wet, rasping noises came from Nia's lips, almost drowned out by the hoarse howls from Jack. Kase didn't try to hide the way she was breaking as heaving sobs wracked her body. She still didn't let go, not while Jack still undulated on the bed.

He couldn't take much more of this. None of them could.

But then, as quickly as blinking, Jack relaxed into the bed, his eyes closing, the bulging veins on his head smoothing out as he became ... peaceful.

Nia stumbled backwards, sending jars of herbs and medicines crashing to the floor as she struggled to catch herself on the table behind them. Hark reached for her, steadying the woman who looked as though she were mere seconds away from collapsing.

'I'll be right as rain soon. Just need to sit down,' she panted as he helped her to the leather armchair in the corner of the room. He moved as though his body wasn't his own, collecting the healer a jug of water and pouring it into a glass for her. She drank it greedily.

'Thank you,' Hark said lowly. 'For what you're doing for him. I know it can't be easy.'

Nia waved a wand. 'It is the least I can do to repay what you all did to rescue us. My pain won't be half as bad as his.'

They both turned to look at Jack's unconscious body, the rise and fall of his chest the only indication he was still alive. Kase had draped herself over him, her head rising with the movement of his chest as she held onto his poor body. Fuck, he hated to see her like this – to see any of his friends like this.

'Look after them both,' Nia said. 'Magic is often the hardest ailment to pull from the body. It isn't pleasant for any who are involved in it.'

Kase looked up at them then, her face as pale as her hair, eyes bloodshot and lined with silver as she pried herself from Jack.

She was silent as she left the room and Hark knew the ghosts of everything that had come before hounded her out of the healer's office. Perhaps they were all destined to be broken.

~

Hark found Kase sitting on the balcony of the sitting room, her legs dangling over the side of the railing as she perched precariously on top. She looked so small, so insignificant against the sprawling city beneath them, steadily growing each day. Perhaps the vastness of the world would be enough to drown out the thoughts in her head.

'If you're thinking of jumping, could you wait until Arla's back? Arranging funerals seems more her forte.'

Kase grunted, turning to face him. He couldn't hide the relief when she lowered herself back onto his side of the railings. 'It would be a grand affair, I'm sure.'

Hark smiled. It would indeed if Arla Dragonhart had anything to do with it.

Kase lowered herself onto one of the carved wooden benches on the balcony, close to the doors so the warmth from the hall still reached them. He took a seat next to her, nudging her with a knee if only to evoke a smile. Something she didn't do enough.

'How are you holding up?' he asked tentatively. Push too far with Kase and she'd shut him out for a long, long time.

'Better now I'm outside.' Her voice was too quiet. Too not like herself. He'd seen it in Arla when she'd first awoken here. She'd felt faraway from herself for days as she tried to build the strength she had lost after almost dying. 'I just want him to be okay. I know I don't ... that I'm not...'

'I know,' he murmured, taking her hand in his, surprised by the warmth as they watched the sun set below the mountains and shower Flambriar in gold and orange and pink.

'Do you think he does? Know, I mean?' There was no need to ask her of what or of whom she spoke. It had been as obvious as breathing from the moment Jack had first joined their crew.

'He knows, Kase. Don't think he doesn't watch you every

moment of every day. The prick hasn't known a day's peace since he met you.'

She laughed, a bright, twinkling sound that never failed to make him smile. He loved Kase. Desperately. She was the sister he'd never had, a sibling that had meant more to him than his brother ever could.

'I want what you and Arla have,' she said quietly, her gaze fixed on the sunset. 'I've never seen someone look at a person the way she looks at you. Like you're her entire world.'

Gods he couldn't do this. Couldn't think of her. He swallowed the lump in his throat.

'I have loved her for longer than she ever knew. Sad, isn't it, that I used to wish for her to fight with me just so I could see fire in her eyes and pretend it burned for me.'

'Maybe. But look what you have now.'

Oh, he knew. He knew how fucking lucky he was to call her his, for him to be able to touch Arla without risk of having his throat cut. He wished she were here now. She'd know exactly what to say to cheer everyone up – or how to change the subject, at the very least. Was she okay in Malarye? Had she managed to piss its royal family off within five minutes like he knew she was entirely capable of doing? Gods, he hoped she made it back safe. He'd tear the world apart if she didn't.

Kase seemed to read his mind. 'She'll enjoy Malarye. They're violent enough to give her a bit of competition. If she manages to make it onto the shore without dying.'

His blood stopped flowing.

'What do you mean *if* she manages to make it onto the shore?'

Kase sighed as if she couldn't believe she was having to explain this to him. 'Malarye doesn't take kindly to guests, especially those who claim to have magic. Arla's been sheltered in

Hadalyn and has spent years denying the existence of magic or the gods; she won't have expected the welcome they likely gave her.'

He was going to fucking kill Kase. 'What welcome?' he ground out.

'They'll have tried to kill her.'

It was an effort not to strangle the silver-haired girl next to him.

'And you didn't think to mention this to anyone? Let alone Arla?'

Kase turned to look at him, her eyes clearer than they had been in hours. 'She was bored here, Hark. No one is equally matched to duel with her, not even you. She's been wanting to stay on top of her training, and I think she'll appreciate nearly being killed. It will keep her on her toes.'

In the name of the *fucking gods*—

'Not a good enough reason,' he growled. Kase had the sense to shift beside him.

'Relax. If Arla Dragonhart was dead, don't you think we'd have heard about it by now? News like that would have reached the darkest corners of the kingdoms quicker than you can say dragon – which, by the way, she is paired with, if you recall.'

Hark had never been so glad of Thara's existence. His heart had beat too hard in his chest for every second that Arla had been gone, for the regret that he hadn't gone with her, and that he wasn't there to protect her should anything happen.

And yet ... he believed in her. He *knew* she was more than capable of handling Malarye by herself and that lit a glow of pride within him that burned far brighter than the regret eating away at him.

Silence stretched between him and Kase, the night getting

darker for every moment that passed until he found the courage to speak again. 'You never talk about Malarye.'

Kase's shoulders went rigid like a wall building between them to protect her from the things she didn't want to say. 'There's nothing much to say. My parents died and I was left with my uncle. I was sixteen when he moved us here and...'

She didn't need to say the rest. She'd already revealed as much about her past as he suspected she was going to. Her uncle ... that man had deserved everything she had delivered him.

Kase cleared her throat, straightening as she pulled a blanket from the far end of the bench and placed it over them. 'Don't tell Arla. She'd ... how did she put it the first time we met? Ram those jewels in my ears down my throat? If she knew we were huddled beneath a blanket watching the sun set together.'

There was no malice in Kase's voice, not when it came to Hark and Arla. She knew they loved each other, and Hark was pretty certain she looked at him in the same brotherly way he looked at her. But yes, Arla would do something violent if she could see them now, and so Hark shuffled, putting a larger gap between him and Kase. He loved Arla too much to ever make her wonder if there was something in his heart for anyone else.

'Where are the others?' Kase asked.

'Seb is scouting tonight, and Jaz hasn't left that damn library all day.'

Kase sighed. 'He hasn't stopped since we got here.'

It was true. Ever since they had settled in Flambriar, Jaz had combed through every book they'd smuggled into that library, trying to figure out how Arla was supposed to unite the kingdoms. Hark hadn't thought it mattered at first. He'd imagined that rescuing the slaves would put an end to it and the kingdoms would begin to flourish again.

That was before merchants and traders started arriving in Flambriar every day telling of how there were food shortages and sickness spreading not only through Kastonia and Hadalyn but on the continent too.

Jaz had barely slept since then.

'I think something bad is happening in Kastonia,' Kase murmured softly. 'Arla said she spoke to someone in the markets back when she was in Kastonia who seemed to believe there were strange things happening at Larkire Palace. What if Elrod is up to something we aren't expecting? What if it isn't enough to just save the mages?'

'Let's wait and see what she comes up with in Malarye. They've invited her there for *something*. And if they're as devoutly religious as you say, hopefully they will have some answers.'

Kase scoffed. 'That or she'll torture it out of them.'

Hark couldn't stop the smile that broke out over his face as the night sky finally winked into existence. It was always cold here at night, and he didn't think when summer finally came it would make it much warmer.

He was about to say so when the balcony doors crashed open, the glass rattling in the panes and Sebastian appeared, hair ruffled with sweat and a mad panic in his eyes.

Dread pooled in Hark's gut immediately.

'Soldiers, three of them,' Seb panted, bracing an arm against the railings. 'In the mountains. We can't kill 'em.'

Hark snatched his sword without thinking. Kase too carried blades that slotted into leather braces on her arms and another set hung loosely at her hips. Seb only stood still long enough to rally the remaining guards stationed at Flambriar, and then they were all running.

Hark had seen enough of these mountains to last him a fucking lifetime. He'd spent months scouting them every day for any sign of Elrod's men or threats to Flambriar and just when he'd started to become comfortable, they'd been fucking found.

Dozens of Flambriar's soldiers were dotted across the mountain above Claret Hall, their focus fixed somewhere in the distance. Some held bows and fired arrows seemingly at random. Others stood and watched whatever was playing out in front of them, a mixture of shock and dread marring their faces.

Kase fidgeted at his side. Already he could sense her eagerness to jump into whatever was unfolding ahead of them. He gripped her wrist just as she went to take off. 'Be bloody careful. Whatever's up there has even Seb spooked.'

There was challenge in Kase's eyes when she blinked back at him, a resolve there that whatever he tried to keep her from she wouldn't listen. Flambriar was her home too and he'd be damned if he tried to stop her from defending it. He released her arm and watched her go, long legs striding up the mountain beside the other soldiers that had been called up from the hall. He saw her hesitate for the briefest of seconds as she reached the outcrop of rocks obscuring everything from view, and then she disappeared out of sight.

'Here we fucking go,' he muttered, and then his own feet were marching, loose rocks shifting underneath his weight as he reached the rocks.

What was unfurling before him defied any sense of logic.

Six of Elrod's men dressed in those fucking black uniforms stood before nearly thirty of Flambriar's soldiers, arrows sticking out from shoulders and torsos like they were pincushions. Even from this distance, Hark could feel the wrongness seeping off them and tarnishing the mountainside.

Sebastian was at the front, directing men to swing heavy blades at the Kastonians ... only for the blades not to cut them down at all.

With every strike of a sword, blood leeched from them, a thick, oozing mess that didn't look *normal*. And of course it wasn't, because no matter how many times Flambriar's soldiers struck them, they didn't fall.

And with every swing of their own swords, Elrod's men managed to wound Hark's own soldiers enough to send them retreating back to the rock where Hark stood transfixed.

There was a heartbeat during which he wished there was a blonde-haired, wicked-mouthed assassin at his side. She wouldn't have balked, wouldn't have cared that whatever stood before them wasn't anything they had ever encountered before.

He wondered if the gods were laughing.

And then that heartbeat passed and Hark was drawing his sword, his legs thundering across the rock as he ran straight at those *things* threatening his kingdom.

Whatever confidence he looked to have possessed must have bolstered his own soldiers, because as Hark breached the line, they began running too, swords raised, determination thundering in every footfall.

And then there was madness.

Kase was at his side and then there was Seb, swinging blades against the six bodies that wouldn't fall. They hacked at the men, their blades cleaving through flesh that split and bled a liquid too dark, too thick, to be anything other than evil. Whatever Elrod had done to create them...

'What the fuck are they?' he growled, spitting blood through his teeth as one of the men sent an elbow into the side of his jaw.

'Something that needs to fucking die,' Seb panted between swings of his blade. Flambriar's own soldiers fought behind them, dragging those too injured to keep swinging blades back towards that outcrop of rocks.

Still Elrod's men didn't fall.

Perhaps this was what Thara and Arla had felt in the mountains that night they'd come scouting with him, and why they had said something felt *off*...

'I'll have your father's head for this myself, Stappen,' Kase snapped as her blade struck deep above the heart of one of the men. He didn't so much as flinch.

Of course...

Hark lifted his blade above his head, hoping to all the gods that listened that Seb would cover him long enough not to have his torso run through ... and then he cleaved the head straight from the shoulders of one of Elrod's men.

The world halted, and then, as slowly as the sun sets, the soldier's body crumpled to the earth and did not rise.

Hark met the blood-splattered faces of Seb and Kase, a mixture of shock and relief passing in their eyes as they turned towards the five remaining soldiers still battling Flambriar's own.

'Their heads,' Sebastian bellowed. 'Take their gods-damned heads!'

The bodies fell pretty quickly after that, but his mind felt entirely too far away as he trudged back down to Claret Hall, Kase and Seb not far behind.

'The men will bring the bodies back to see if we can figure out what the fuck your father's done, Stappen.' Sebastian sounded tired. Too tired. Hark was trying not to feel anything at all, especially the knot of dread tightening in his stomach.

His father had found them. And worse than that, he was sending soldiers into Flambriar that couldn't be killed. Thara had said it was impossible for Elrod to use the mages' blood for anything, but after tonight...

Fuck, he needed Arla to come home.

The hall was a hive of activity, maids rushing about gathering spare bandages and cleaning liquids to take down to the barracks for those who had been injured, soldiers filling Claret Hall's corridors with noise and fear and blood.

Hark had expected it. He knew the noise they had made in the mountains couldn't have been missed and that Flambriar's citizens were likely barricaded inside their homes. What he had not expected though, not in a million years, was to see Jack hobbling down the hallway towards them, leather armour strapped over his chest and a sword that looked too heavy grasped in his hand.

A small, squeaky sound escaped Kase when Jack raised his other hand in greeting. And then she was running, the clatter of her blades hitting the floor and drawing the attention of everyone in the corridor. She flung her arms around Jack's shoulders, burying her face in the crook between his neck and shoulder.

'You stupid idiot,' she said against his skin, and Hark could hear the relief in her voice that Jack was actually *standing* after the way they had left him in the healer's office that afternoon.

'Let's leave 'em to it. I reckon Jaz will want to hear about this,' Seb muttered in Hark's ear.

That knot of terror squirmed in his stomach again, but he had to do this. He had to keep these people safe, and that meant tackling whatever the fuck his father was up to.

He sighed, dragging a hand through his hair. 'I'll meet you in the study.'

CHAPTER 30

It didn't matter how many times she felt the wind in her hair or the locked plates of scales beneath her thighs; Arla didn't think she would ever get used to the feeling of flying. Malarye stretched out beneath her like a map of bruises and spilt ink, all cliffs and dark green forests. The queen's words had kept her from sleep for too long as she turned them over in her head. She was to train here, with Malarye's army, in return for them not marching against Flambriar if the world descended to war...

She was beginning to think she'd made a bad deal.

'Not all bargains are meant to benefit you, Dragonhart. Be glad that they have vowed not to stand against you.'

Thara was right, of course, but Arla still needed answers. Her dragon's revelations yesterday, though surprising, had not told her enough.

'It would be easy to leave, you know. We could keep flying west and not look back.' Her voice was almost lost on the wind, but from the rumble of the dragon beneath her, she didn't doubt Thara had heard her.

'I do not have answers as to what it is the fates have planned for you, Dragonhart, and neither do you. Patience is not a quality you have been gifted in abundance but as I have flown you thus far, perhaps you might learn some.'

A grin tugged the corners of her lips. *'You wish for us to stay here?'*

A wave of warmth pulsed down the bond. *'For now.'*

'Did the other dragonharts have to deal with all this nonsense? And fates that plotted against them?' It was a risk to ask the question – she didn't wish to spark another argument with her dragon.

But instead of the silence Arla had expected, Thara's voice was steady in her mind.

'The ones that came before were strong of heart, but they were not like you. The fates left them alone, for the most part. They did their jobs well, communicated between dragons and mages, kept the mages safe. Until Damon, the fates were content to leave the dragonharts alone. And after Damon, there is you. It seems the fates enjoyed their meddling too much to give it up just yet.'

'What makes me and Damon so special?'

There was a pulse of silence, a warring through the bond, as if Thara battled with what she could and could not speak of.

That furious spark in Arla's chest revolted at it.

'I don't know why they chose you and Damon. But know that I will not allow what happened to the one that came before happen to you.'

Damon...

'What happened, Thara?'

Only silence rippled in the bond. *'Thara, please.'*

It was like waves crashing against sharp, jagged rocks. The bond thrashed, Thara's fight against what was forbidden to be spoken of, a wild, tumultuous thing.

The world split open.

Flashes of a boy with dark hair. Fire. Gods with faces she couldn't quite make out, battling with magic that was powerful enough to shatter the stars.

It all came, quick, unrelenting. Images of the past – memories that Thara had lived through. *'He used—'*

Pain shattered through the bond, and the dragon fell ten feet through the clouds, Arla's hands flailing for grip as Thara fought the prohibition the fates had created. *'He used too much. It was never enough, and he wanted more.'*

Another billow of blinding pain through the bond and this time Thara screeched a sound so hideous Arla wished to never hear it again for as long as she lived.

Still her dragon fought to get the words out. To tell Arla what had transpired a century ago despite the pain the fates flooded her body with.

'Damon wasn't himself. The things he did ... it broke him.'

This time, when the whip of pain came slicing through the bond, Thara unable to shield Arla from it, they fell so quickly she was certain they'd end up a pile of ash and scales upon Malarye's shores.

'Stop,' Arla panted. 'Don't tell me anything else. If this is the price, I won't let you pay it.'

The fact that Thara didn't answer spoke enough of the dragon's pain that Arla instantly hated herself. The pain through the bond ... it was a fraction of what Thara must have felt. This punishment from the fates, the way they'd banned them from speaking of the past ...

It wasn't worth her dragon's pain.

Thara flew in silence for long, long minutes, an unspoken agreement that Arla wasn't to mention what had just occurred.

Good. She didn't want that to happen *ever* again.

Arla coughed, clearing her throat as the wind ripped through her hair, her dragon's scales hard beneath her thighs as Thara finally regained the altitude they'd had before.

'If we're going to be training with Malarye's army, maybe we should start learning how to ... well, fight together. They nearly shot us out of the sky. If we have to fight against Kastonia, who says they won't do the same?'

Thara chuckled, though rivulets of pain still tricked through the bond.

'I thought you'd never ask.'

'For the gods' sake,' Arla snapped, dropping the bloodied bandage at her elbow as someone tapped on the wooden door to her room. She'd spent the morning with Thara, flying high above the forest, practising not vomiting as Thara dived whilst Arla tried to keep a sword in her grip. She had made the mistake of not paying attention – despite Thara's many warnings – and had failed to duck her body close to Thara's in time for a branch to take skin off her arm. She was damn lucky she hadn't fallen.

'As if I'd have let you.'

Someone was tapping on the door again.

'Ugh, fine, come in.'

'Sorry to disturb, it's just we said we would have lunch— Oh, gods, let me do that for you.' Hyacinth entered the room, bending to pick up the unravelled bandage and reach for Arla's elbow.

She stopped herself before her fingers could so much as brush the bloodied skin.

'I can do it myself,' Arla protested, spinning away from the princess who was looking at her with scrunched brows.

Hyacinth moved around Arla, the scent of peonies making her nose itch in the cramped room. 'Let me, please. That's what friends are for, right?'

She wouldn't know, would she? The one friend she'd had wasn't answering any of her letters.

Arla cleared her throat. 'And are we? Friends?'

Hyacinth smiled in a lovely, girlish way, and Arla hated how something in her was beginning to soften towards the princess.

'Of course. If we aren't friends, then we are enemies, no? Someone who is willing to train with our army doesn't sound like an enemy.'

Arla hissed as the princess pulled the bandage tightly around her elbow. 'Enemies no, but I can't help but feel like I've been coerced into something I did not agree to. Tell me, Hyacinth, why your mother refuses to send troops to my aid should I call for it but expects my skill in return?'

The princess chewed her lip as she finished knotting the strip of fabric. Arla didn't expect Hyacinth to answer, but when she did speak, there was confidence and certainty in her voice that lifted the hairs on Arla's arms.

'Know that you have our support against any and all that come for Flambriar. We recognise the blood that runs in your veins and the title bestowed upon you by the gods, Arla Dragonhart. That is why you have our support. But know that this fight is bigger than us all – bigger than you and your new kingdom. We will not send our people into a war between gods – because it *will* come to war, you know that. Elrod has twisted and bent the rules of magic, and the gods are displeased. You can't believe he isn't still offending the gods – the kingdoms are still falling, after all. *You* are the one the gods have chosen, so if there is to be a war it is to be between the two of you.'

She knew that.

Had known it for weeks now, since the first letters had started arriving saying that sickness and poverty were still spreading.

She couldn't ask anyone to go to war for her, especially not those from the continent who had stayed their blades in the battle of Grey Hill. They had remained neutral then; she couldn't ask them to fight now.

Hyacinth was at the door now, bright-eyed and ready for the lunch Arla had promised to take with her. It didn't matter that it felt like there was a shadow spreading within Arla's chest, that although she had known for a while now that Elrod was still up to something, that she had been named Dragonhart for a *reason*, it still felt like drowning to hear the words come from someone else's lips.

'I do hope you have good wine here,' Arla said lightly, ignoring that gaping feeling in her chest. 'If I am to train within a hundred meters of Crea this afternoon, I'll need to be at least three glasses deep.'

Hyacinth laughed, holding the door for her. 'She has that effect on people.'

Malarye's main town was exactly the coastal, quiet place Arla had expected when she had last been in the queendom with Cyrus – not that she had ever got to see it, mind. Lunch was a peaceful affair, a selection of seafood laid out on a platter between Arla and Hyacinth as they sat outside a restaurant owned by a frail-looking man. The sun had basked everything in bright hues, and it was the first time in nearly a year that Arla had felt the warmth of its rays on her face. The sea crashed against the rocky shore in the distance, the air salty with its proximity. People shopped at stalls and markets with pale blue awnings, and children traded shells wherever she looked. Here, away from the palace and the border, it was hard to believe that Malarye was anything other than this quaint little town hidden beyond a forest. Arla couldn't help but admire the defences in place to keep the people safe. Any enemy would have to endure the archers on the cliffs and manage to cross through the forest before Malarye's people were subjected to fighting. The shoreline that Arla could see from the restaurant was so treacherous and littered with deadly, hidden rocks that no ship would be able to get anywhere close.

People stopped to say hello to the princess or to offer her a smile, and though it was kind, she could see it was a nicety. Not one person here believed the gentle princess sitting across from her was capable of leading them once her mother passed – Arla could see it in their eyes. It was tolerance, not respect. The princess would likely have her throat cut before she ever made it to sit upon the throne – Kase had said Malarye's people were violent, after all.

'It is quiet this afternoon as most of the men are out catching fish,' Hyacinth said, sipping from the glass of pink wine.

Arla couldn't help the wave of irritation that washed over her. 'Why not the women too? They are just as capable.'

Hyacinth beamed at her, and it took Arla a moment to replay the words she'd spoken and decipher that she hadn't said *anything* that was amusing.

'Do not think I am joking, Your Highness. Why should the women not have the same opportunities as men?'

'No, no, I don't find it funny at all,' the princess said. 'But I have waited a long time for someone to think the way I do. I too find it backward that we send the men out up to their waists in the sea every day when the women are to stay at home with the children. It is wrong, and I have pushed the issue with my mother so often that she will not hear me speak of the sea any longer.'

Gods, if Hyacinth could just harden up that meek shell of hers, she would make a good queen.

'I am pushing for it in Flambriar too,' Arla sighed, twisting the brooch on her uniform. 'But people are stuck in their ways – especially those who have come from Kastonia's rule. I try to introduce the women to helping with the cutting of firewood because their magic is just as adept as the men but many are too afraid of what others will think of them.' It was ridiculous when Arla herself had never cared one jot about what people thought of her.

'Then maybe together we can start to change the way our people think.'

In another life in which she wasn't some pawn for the fates, she might have come to know the Princess of Malarye sooner, might have befriended her. Now it just felt that getting too friendly with someone was a cause for the fates to intervene. She still couldn't believe they hadn't tried to separate her from Hark.

Hyacinth paid the man at the restaurant but there was a tightness in both their smiles that suggested Malarye's funds were dwindling. This queendom was succumbing to the gods' wrath just as Hadalyn and Kastonia had.

The princess hummed softly as they made their way back through the town and then the forest, the looming thought of training with Malarye's soldiers enough to keep Arla from snapping that she stop with the mindless noise. Eventually though, as the training rings came back into view, Arla couldn't help but ask the question that had been bothering her since yesterday.

'Tell me of the last dragonhart. You mentioned him yesterday. Will you tell me why he died?'

Hyacinth stopped her humming immediately, her fingers playing with weeds and the spindly branches of trees as they walked closer to the edge of the forest.

'Damon was said to be magnificent,' Hyacinth began, her voice wary. Strained. 'He loved the mages with every part of his soul. He took their queries to the gods and delivered answers with a devotion only found in the blood of dragonharts. But...'

Arla's jaw ached with the strain of clenching it. 'But what?'

'But he ... he began to change the older he got. He grew hungry for power, wanted greater magic. In the end, it turned him wicked, and the gods became concerned. It is said that the obsession with power drove him to madness, and he impaled himself on his own sword. You have heard the stories of what happened next – how mages were hunted for their magic and the old religion began to die out. The other dragonharts were already dead by then, and the dragons disappeared not long after that.'

Her heart fluttered in her chest. There was so much she didn't know – too much. Jaz had mentioned something before ... that he thought the dragonharts had once possessed magic.

'Enough talk of death and wicked things,' Hyacinth exclaimed, her cheerfulness a tonic to the wrongness Arla felt in her blood. 'We have training – well, you do, at least. But I would like to watch.'

Arla didn't think she had a choice about being *watched*. Not when there was a crowd big enough to be a small army clustered around the training rings. Thara was there too, her enormous spiked tail shifting slowly from side to side in the sand. None of the soldiers dared take their eyes off her.

'Who can blame them?'

Arla snorted. *'And you say I'm vain.'*

Someone must have noticed Arla's approach because suddenly there were dozens of eyes focused solely on her as she marched closer to the rings. It was like stepping back into the courtyard at Castle Grey ready for training with the royal guard. It was like meeting an old friend.

'I don't know about you,' she called, 'but standing around gawping at a creature that could break your necks doesn't constitute warming up, does it?'

There was a breath of silence, and then a murmur spread through the crowd, a nervous energy charging the air that had Thara huffing hot air in the direction of the soldiers.

Arla was sure someone screamed.

In the next breath, the soldiers began warming up – lunging, jogging, stretching, lest the dragon and the sharp-tongued assassin have their heads.

It was easy to spot which of the men and women before her would have the skill to keep up with the exercises she would put them through, and all too easy to see which ones wouldn't. Those she could use to her advantage and get them to teach her how to handle a bow and arrow effectively.

Arla edged closer to Thara, her entire body relaxing as the dragon's snout nudged her shoulder. She wondered if Thara found the same level of calmness when Arla was near.

'I have told you before that the bond ties your soul to mine. To be apart is to ache for the other half of you.'

She didn't know why the dragon's words made her eyes sting, but she blinked the tears away quickly. She focused on the soldiers and assessed their fitness. They were sweating far too soon, but it was nothing she couldn't fix in a week or so.

Arla raised a hand for them to stop, delighting in the feel of command as every set of eyes focused on her – even Crea who, still dressed in those ridiculous robes, watched from the side of the ring with morbid curiosity. Good. Arla hadn't decided yet whether she would kill someone or not.

'Always so violent, Dragonhart.'

'It makes a point.'

Thara nudged her almost playfully and Arla couldn't help the grin that lifted her mouth.

'We are not here to make points. Leave them alive.'

Arla looked out at the dozens of faces watching her. This wasn't the entirety of Malarye's army, she was sure of it. But if they wanted to keep troops hidden and do themselves a disservice by not allowing all members to attend these sessions, so be it.

That flame still burned brightly in the centre of her chest, a calling that this was something she could do, something she was good at.

She grinned again.

'Let's begin.'

CHAPTER 31

They weren't entirely useless.

She kept telling herself that, as she climbed the steps up the cliff to the palace, cursing the ache in her joints from too many rounds of duelling.

She must have gone against almost thirty opponents in the hours they had trained, coaching each of them how to use their blades effectively in close combat. It had taken her longer than she would have liked to master using those strange, curved blades Malarye's soldiers wielded.

They were definitely unfit – too used to standing and firing arrows rather than practising hand-to-hand fighting – but right now, legs aching as she finally entered the castle, Arla felt that way too. It would be an effort to drag herself back down the cliff tonight to train with Thara, and only the memory of that feeling of the wind in her hair and the weightlessness as her dragon dived, kept her upright. She wouldn't be as stupid as to get hurt tonight.

Tomorrow, she would do it all over again, making sure she also improved her skill with a bow, too. The thought of allowing someone to teach her ... anything, irritated her. She hated not being good at something immediately. Hated the feeling that someone else had the upper hand while she tried to better her skills.

But for Flambriar she would subject herself to it.

A cavern opened up inside her chest as she thought of Claret Hall and the people inside it. People she loved. Desperately. Gods, she was even missing the sharp snips Kase would send her way. But more importantly, she didn't yet have her answer.

She knew there were libraries deep beneath the ground in Malarye, that the priestesses guarded them and there was no way that Arla was gaining access without permission. There was a gnawing though, deep in her bones, that told her she needed to get inside those libraries. She needed answers from those libraries, and if it meant she had to train and play the part with the army, then she would do it. Let them like her, let them trust her. Anything to help her figure out how to unite the kingdoms.

Food was delivered to her door whilst she changed into something that might protect her arms more should she not be paying close enough attention ... again. She ate and didn't give herself time to think about how exhausted she was before returning back outside. The wind tore at her immediately, and for a split second she imagined she was home at Flambriar, standing on the balcony looking out over their new kingdom.

Instead, there were almost a hundred steps she needed to descend to reach the bottom of the cliff and find her dragon.

'Not if you jump.' Thara's voice in her head had her reeling backwards.

'You want me to jump? Some of us don't have wings you know.'

Thara chuckled. *'And some of us do. Trust me.'*

No. No way. Absolutely no way would she jump from the side of this cliff.

'It didn't stop you at Larkire, did it?'

No, but... 'Larkire was completely different,' she heard herself say out loud. 'We were about to die. This is just madness.'

'Why do you not trust I will be there to catch you?'

'No, I-I know you will, I just...' Was about to jump off a *cliff*.

'Then what's stopping you, Dragonhart, if not fear that you will fall?'

She knew the answer, could feel it burning on her tongue. Had known it for so long it felt like a betrayal to attempt to voice the words.

So she sent them down the bond instead.

'Because before I didn't care if I died. I became King's Assassin because I didn't care if I got killed on the jobs I was sent on.'

'And now?'

'Now I want to live.'

Thara's voice was soft, soothing. *'So live.'*

Arla stepped over the edge.

Falling was a foreign feeling, one that even infants recognised as being wrong – or so Halos had told her when the twins were small. It silenced the world, shut everything out so the only thing she knew was the weightlessness of falling through cold, dark air.

It lasted for only a second because the next thing she knew there was the familiar warmth of Thara beneath her, rows and rows of scales digging into her legs as Arla scrabbled for purchase on the dragon's back. The dragon soared, higher, higher, higher until the castle looked like a blot on the landscape of the cliff. The clouds dampened her golden hair and she laughed into the wind, twisting her hands around the spikes of

Thara's shoulders. This ... this was *magic*. Or as close to it as she thought she could ever get.

'Is this living enough for you?' Thara mused.

'Yes, a million times yes!' Arla cried out into the night, laughing as Thara swooped low and her stomach dipped too. It fed her soul, lit her within so that she was sure she radiated enough to light the entire continent. And dragonhart or not, she knew she had been born for this, felt the thrill in her blood as Thara glided between cliffs, twisting sideways so Arla had to grip with every muscle in her body so as not to go plummeting to the earth.

If Kastonia ever came for them, this would be enough. If she could master a bow too, she would be unstoppable. Nothing would ever threaten her or her people again.

Thara twisted and ducked and soared between the cliffs, dropping lower and lower until Arla could reach out and touch the tops of the trees in that sprawling forest if she wanted. She kept her body tight against Thara's, learning every movement of the dragon's body so she could match it with her own.

By the time Thara landed at the base of the cliff, the weight that had settled in Arla's chest had all but dissipated, leaving an elation that she was sure she would never be rid of. She had improved again tonight, had kept up with the way Thara's body moved beneath her and managed to avoid injuring any part of herself. Gods, she loved flying.

'Tomorrow you will learn to dismount before we hit the ground. Make sure there is a healer available tomorrow night, Dragonhart.'

Thara didn't give her the chance to protest before the dragon flapped those enormous emerald wings and launched herself into the sky.

Arla began climbing the steps immediately, a smile so wide her cheeks ached as she marched.

The morning had passed by quicker than blinking. The soldiers had already improved since yesterday, their blades coming quicker, their feet surer.

Arla only hoped she would be just as quick to find her skill with a bow. One of the men had volunteered to train with her for the afternoon, a man who didn't look at her like she was incapable, but like there was fine-tuning to be done.

Good. She didn't think she could bear it if any of them looked at her like she was entirely useless.

Hyacinth had arrived at some point, her hair loose around her shoulders as she sat on the ground beside Arla after the soldiers had gone, opening a basket filled with herbed bread and jams made of vegetables. The princess had brought a carafe of wine, too, and Arla gulped it as they basked in the spring sun, watching as Malarye's army set to work with whatever occupied them in their afternoons.

'I've not seen them in such good spirits in, well, forever.' Hyacinth laughed, handing Arla another piece of bread. 'They're enjoying the training already. Crea will be livid.'

At that, Arla snorted, unable to contain her delight at the prospect of pissing off the priestess.

'Good, she tried to kill me.'

Hyacinth laughed, the sound twinkling and lovely. 'You know it wasn't personal.'

'Perhaps. But I've been known to hold a grudge.'

The princess burst into laughter again, and, right there, on the floor of a training ring in a foreign queendom, Arla knew she had made a friend.

'Suppose I turn out to be rubbish at archery...'

'Oh, don't be stupid,' Hyacinth said, smiling as she sipped

the remaining wine. 'You're Arla Dragonhart! I don't think there's a single thing you're rubbish at. No one in this queendom has ever dared to upset Hadalyn for fear its king would send you after them. Your reputation is flawless, even out here. You'll be a better archer than my own army in no time at all.'

My own army.

A small smile settled on Arla's lips. Finally, the princess was beginning to think of this country, these *people*, as hers. It was a small, almost imperceptible change, but it was there, nonetheless. And it would be needed if she had any hope of ruling after her mother.

'Looks like it's time for your lesson,' the princess said, rising and shaking the sand from her skirts as a man with deep brown skin approached them.

~

Arla was embarrassingly poor at firing arrows.

In his defence, Mason had been patient with her, even when her elbow had slipped and she'd caught the edge of his jaw. He had been careful not to put his hands on her when she held the bow at the wrong angle, and he had stayed calm whilst she cursed every god under the sun and spewed words that would make a king blush. He hadn't been shy or scared of her, and because of that she knew he was the right man to teach her. He'd been handsome, too, which had helped. His skin gleamed under the sun and the long black hair that ended at the base of his back was the shiniest hair she had ever seen. Truthfully, she hadn't thought there was much to firing an arrow – she'd fired enough of them in her eighteen years – but through Mason's careful teaching, she had begun to understand the subtle art of it.

Perhaps there was a skill to it she simply hadn't had the time to master.

She'd never admit it, of course.

Hyacinth was never far away, tending to the small flowers that grew along the cliffside or petting the goats kept in pens that were far too friendly to consider eating. The princess had opted for a soft life, one that spoke of beauty and kindness. It would be a shame to see the role of monarch batter it out of her.

Arla knew Hyacinth was keeping a close eye on her, but she, too, was observing the princess. It was unexpected to find that the princess's presence didn't bother her. In fact, it was almost … nice, to have a friend.

Gods she was getting too soft.

'There is strength in softness, Dragonhart. Even the hardest of hearts can feel it.'

Hyacinth was at Arla's side the moment she handed the bow back to Mason. He shook her hand in that odd way, his grip tight and reassuring.

'It was nice to meet you properly, Dragonhart. You will improve in no time at all.'

She couldn't help the warmth in her cheeks as Mason walked away.

'He is handsome, Arla. Perhaps Hark wouldn't mind sharing you.'

She didn't know what possessed her to elbow the princess lightly, biting down on the laughter in her throat as Hyacinth erupted into a delighted giggle.

'Hark would kill him before I got the chance to ask,' Arla laughed, surprised at the way Hyacinth linked their arms and … Arla let her.

'Come on, I'll walk you back to the palace. I have some time before I'm due to help Crea in the libraries.'

Now *that* was an interesting piece of information indeed.

'Perhaps we could go back via the libraries? I've heard they're something to behold.'

She expected the princess to tell her it was not possible, or ignore the question completely.

As it was, Hyacinth squeezed their arms together and smiled.

'Of course, though don't expect anything special. You can hardly see anything from the outside and you are, regrettably, forbidden from entering.'

'Why?'

Hyacinth's smile faltered for only a second. 'Because the books in those libraries are said to date back to the time of the gods themselves. My mother is ... protective of them, to say the very least.'

'Even against a Dragonhart?'

Hyacinth sighed. 'Even against a Dragonhart.'

She let the conversation drop. For now that was enough; she had the information she needed.

The underground libraries in Malarye did indeed include texts on the gods and nothing would stop her from getting into those chambers.

CHAPTER 32

There was hardly time for her to think as she shed her training leathers and pulled a loose-fitting shirt over her head. It would be easier to manoeuvre whilst she trained with Thara. The leggings she'd packed were black and tight and perfect for concealing blood should she fall from a great height and impale herself on a rock.

'You will not because you will concentrate.'

Arla sniggered as she braided her hair into a crown on top of her head. There wasn't much time to think of anything, let alone the libraries they had passed which had stone steps descending into tunnels below ground, all lit with soft, golden light. Crea had scowled when Hyacinth had led Arla to the entrance of the tunnels.

There wasn't much time because she needed to be on Thara's back before the sun set – it would be harder for her to judge distance in the dark – and she had asked Diath and Hyacinth to be there too in case she really did hurt herself. The princess had lit up from within, a beaming smile spilling across her perfect face as she promised to be there the second Crea was done with her.

Arla didn't want to ask why Crea had such a hold over the princess.

Diath would be waiting though, their eagerness obvious the moment Arla had asked.

Dinner was a hasty affair, her teeth tearing into bread and cheese as she jogged through the castle, ignoring the disapproving stares from maids and courtiers alike. The queen was nowhere to be seen.

Diath would be waiting for her at the edge of the forest where there was sufficient clear ground for her to practice dismounting in motion, and enough coverage from the trees that they couldn't be spied upon from the palace.

This time, when the power in the bond grew stronger, signalling Thara's proximity, Arla didn't hesitate as she jumped from the ledge of the cliff. She landed more gracefully this time, her body already adapting to the way her dragon would swoop beneath her and send them high into the clouds. Again, a peal of laughter burst from her lips, the sheer joy of it sending waves through her blood. This time, she didn't grip with her hands, instead opening her arms out like her own personal wings. The wind tore at her, the sunset in the distance bathing everything in soft, colourful light. And for a moment, for just a tiny moment, she forgot that she was missing Hark and her people and Flambriar. Because up here, in the clouds where no one could touch her, she was completely free.

All too soon they were careening towards the edge of the forest. Thara weaved between the cliffs, forcing Arla to keep her body tight against the dragon's as she twisted and turned and pulled on every ounce of strength Arla had to keep herself upright. It was ... exhilarating. There was no other word for it.

She was panting by the time Thara landed by the trees, her brow slick with sweat from the strain of holding on. Her hair was matted, and her legs ached like nothing else, but the grin she knew was lighting up her face was reflected back to her in Diath's face.

'That was impressive! No one alive has seen anything like that,' they said, handing Arla a canteen of cool water as she slid from Thara's back.

'I fear what comes next won't be half as elegant,' she said, laughing and stretching out her muscles.

Diath eyed her, their hands twitching at their sides as if they were resisting the urge to place them on Arla's weary muscles and heal her.

Arla wouldn't allow it; this pain meant she was getting stronger.

'Forgive me, Dragonhart,' they said, 'but why is it you are almost risking your neck to train this way?'

The response came out of Arla's mouth before she had time to think.

'Because whatever is happening in Kastonia is enough to upset the gods. I don't believe for one second that there isn't magic involved, and if I can protect my kingdom from the skies as well as I can protect it from the ground, then at least I can die knowing I did everything to help.'

Thara rumbled down the bond. *'You will not die.'*

She couldn't know that – the fates didn't divulge their plans.

'I don't imagine you've called me here to simply watch. I assume there is a significant risk of broken bones?' Diath asked, raising a dark brow.

Arla was already hauling herself back onto Thara's back.

'If I get through this with only a broken bone, I'll consider it a success.' Her words were lost on the wind as Thara launched into the air, stealing the breath from her lungs as the ghost of a gasp left Diath's lips.

The speed with which her dragon darted between treetops and cliff edges meant all Arla could do was hold on and rely on instinct. Her body ducked and weaved with the solid mass beneath her, but she grazed her cheeks and elbows on branches whenever she became careless enough not to keep herself tight against Thara's body. Her lungs burned, her fingers were numb with the chill of the wind rushing by and yet her body felt *alive*. Laughter burst from her at every dive, every twist, every time she narrowly avoided slamming herself into the side of a rockface.

'You laugh now, but if you do not concentrate, Diath will be scraping you off the ground,' Thara warned.

The thought was sobering enough for Arla to grip the dragon a little tighter.

'As we approach the ground, look for an opening and jump. I take it I do not need to instruct you on the execution of landing without snapping your human legs?'

At that, she could smile again.

'No,' her voice felt small against the sky. 'That, I can do.'

'Might I remind you that you have not attempted such a thing from the back of a dragon before?'

Indeed.

But there was no time to think about that or how indeed she would land, because the edge of the forest was in view again, the ground growing larger as Thara descended. There were two figures watching her now, Diath and the slight frame of Hyacinth, who was *waving* at her.

The ground was rushing at them now so fast that a flicker of panic flared in Arla's chest. She tamped it down in a heartbeat.

She was good at these things; she had jumped off buildings and honed her body to work for her. It would be fine.

But the speed at which they were swooping toward the ground...

There was barely a second before Thara pulled up from the earth, her wings flapping backwards quickly as Arla jumped...

And then she was falling.

The ground came hard and fast, a solid smack of loam-scented earth as her feet connected and her knees bent. Everything else came as second nature.

Her body rolled without her thinking about it, her head tucked in so she wouldn't break her neck. Twigs snapped, a sound frighteningly similar to bone, and rotting leaves and brambles pulled at her hair as she rolled through the dirt. The momentum of the roll kept her tumbling, her body so used to the movement that she wasn't expecting the wave of sickening pain that burst through her spine.

She tried to get to her feet as her body came to an abrupt stop, gasping as sharp pain flooded her senses. She opened her eyes – hadn't realised she'd closed them, actually – and reached a hand out for something to indicate she was still alive.

Her fingers brushed over the rough surface of rock and entangled tree roots. She didn't have it in her to cry out. She could only breathe through the waves of pain that rippled through her spine where she had rolled directly into the rock.

She didn't think it was broken because she could move her feet, but fucking *gods* it had been a long time since she had felt pain so acutely!

So she kept breathing. Deeply. In and out, in and out, as the rustle of movement sounded around her. A whisper of concern flared through the bond, but she couldn't focus on it as Hyacinth's face peered down at her, the princess's worried gaze unnerving enough that she wondered if she had indeed broken her back.

Diath's hands were like lightning as they touched her skin, and within seconds that pain began to ebb, leaving only a dull throb at the base of her back. She tried to stand, glad when the movement didn't render her a squirming mess on the floor.

'Are you all right?' The panic in Hyacinth's voice was ... embarrassing.

'I'm fine,' Arla replied, stretching her limbs and ignoring the pain. At least this was bearable. When she had broken her ankle in training at Castle Grey, she had been unable to stand the constant pain of it as she kept working through the training of the king's guard and had resorted to taking those strange powders they sold down in the slums.

'It was unlucky,' Diath said, their eyes scanning Arla's body. 'But impressive, nonetheless.'

It was sad, really, the burst of pride that erupted in her chest at the words of a healer. *Impressive*. She had worked her entire life to be just that.

'Impressive, yes, but you could have died. Hopefully tomorrow should prove less lethal,' Hyacinth said softly, her voice like melted butter.

'You would hope,' Arla said, straightening her shirt and brushing off the remnants of forest that clung to it. 'This should be second nature by tomorrow.'

Diath and Hyacinth met each other's eyes before they looked at her with an exhausted understanding.

The healer's voice was tired when they finally spoke. 'And why would that be?'

Arla felt Thara drifting closer, the surge in the bond more powerful as her dragon circled back around. 'Because we're doing that again.'

Diath and Hyacinth didn't have the time to protest before Thara swept in from above them, her wings scattering the loose earth and whipping the loose strands of Arla's hair around her face.

She'd treasure the look on the healer and the princess's faces for the rest of her life as she jumped and reached for the spikes on Thara's back, using the momentum of Thara's upward surge to fling herself onto the dragon's back.

She'd treasure the yelp of laughter that followed her, too.

They practised the manoeuvre a further eight times, each one better than the last. She only broke three fingers during the course of the evening, which, all things considered, was a triumph.

Diath set the fingers almost immediately, and though they ached on the walk up the cliff to the palace, they were certainly no longer broken. Hyacinth watched her the entire time, picking leaves and sticks and mud out of Arla's hair each time Diath had to heal her. She left before Arla's final attempt – which had been by far the most successful – to carry out whatever princess duties she had been assigned.

Arla had never been so grateful for a hot bath. She let the bubbles and the lavender oils soak away the ache in her muscles, resisting the urge to close her eyes in the low light of the room. The bed was too inviting, calling to her to climb beneath the soft blankets and fall into a dreamless sleep.

She'd only been in bed for five minutes when there was a knock at the door and Hyacinth's cheery face peered round the doorway.

'I brought you a gift.'

Now that was a welcome surprise.

The princess entered the room smelling of spring and looking like a rose. Her hair was still slightly damp from having washed it, and it lay loosely around her shoulders. But the gift she carried?

Gods, it had been too long since Arla had had the pleasure of eating chocolate cake in her rooms at Castle Grey. Just the sight of it... She didn't know why a lump rose in her throat.

'Well, usually people look happier than that when they receive cake as a surprise,' Hyacinth said.

'I think it might just be the best surprise anyone has ever brought me,' Arla said, snapping out of the nostalgia that rendered her motionless. Her time at Castle Grey was over. The sooner she learned to accept it the better.

~

Arla didn't know at what point her relationship with the Princess of Malarye had deepened so that she was now comfortable for them both to be sitting on her bed, the chocolate cake long since devoured, laughing over trivial matters such as why Crea always looked like she would bring the wrath of the gods down upon them, or why it was so damned dark in this palace. But that shift between them? Arla cherished it. It was a lonely existence not having Halos as her friend anymore and though Hark was the other half of her heart and she would die for the Flambriar's court, it wasn't the same as having a friend that was just hers.

The night slipped by until Arla was sure it must be nearly dawn. Hyacinth's eyes had turned soft and droopy, her head resting against the headboard next to Arla's as an easy silence fell between them.

The question came from nowhere, but it was a subject she had pondered repeatedly and yet she was still none the wiser.

'Did the dragonharts have magic before?' She knew the answer because Jaz had researched it, but it didn't explain that strange power she had felt surge through the bond with Thara when her life had been in danger twice before.

Hyacinth turned to look at her, a curious frown creasing the skin on her forehead. 'I'm sure they used to, yes. But ... you don't have magic, do you?'

It scalded her like a brand in the centre of her chest. The words felt bitter and stinging on her tongue. 'No, but something happened and ... for a moment I think I did.'

Hyacinth sat upright, the tiredness vanishing from her eyes like the gods had erased it themselves. 'What do you mean?'

'Back at Larkire, when Hark and I were surrounded and there was no way we could have made it out alive, something happened. It was like the bond between Thara and me opened up and I could access her magic too. The same thing happened when we first came here and the archers tried to shoot us out of the sky.'

'The wave...' Hyacinth murmured. 'But we all thought Thara was responsible for that.'

'No ... at least, I don't think so. Her magic doesn't work that way. But I felt her magic in the bond and could use it, I think.'

'I can't say I've ever heard of something like that happening,' Hyacinth said slowly. 'But I will check the libraries. I'm sure there will be something in there that can explain it.'

Arla hoped so, too.

CHAPTER 33

For the next few weeks, Arla's life was consumed with training Malarye's army, having Mason teach her to fire arrows in ways she could never have mastered alone, and practising a flying dismount whilst Thara flew with increasing speed.

For once, everything was working out, if she blocked out the fact that she should be figuring out how to unite the kingdoms. She'd overheard one of Mara's advisors reading aloud a letter from another kingdom on the continent begging for more food, more medicine, more building materials as their kingdom fell victim to a wasting sickness no one had managed to identify yet. Mara had refused to send a single healer, insisting that they needed to be here, close, in case Malarye should begin to suffer in the same way as everywhere else.

It had filled Arla with a cold dread. Flambriar wasn't immune to this punishment from the gods, either, so how long until they, too, would begin to suffer?

Hyacinth had filled Arla's evenings with walks through the forest and the town and had two nights ago taken her to the royal box at a theatre built inside an old temple. They had laughed and drunk sweet wine, and Arla knew she would be sorry to leave the princess behind when it came time for her to go home. Which, judging by the progress the army were making, would be soon. She may not have come to Malarye for such a purpose, but at least she now had the promise of an ally that would supply their kingdom with whatever they needed should they have to fight. She ignored the voice in her head that said she might have preferred Malarye's troops over their weapons.

She had heard nothing from Hyacinth about dragonhart magic or what those books in their libraries contained, and Thara had been bound by the fates not to breathe a word of it either. Before, that might have angered Arla, might have felt like a betrayal by the one who was bonded to her very soul, but now she could feel the pain and frustration Thara felt in keeping it from her. Arla found she was beginning to hate the fates increasingly often.

She couldn't dwell on it too much because if she did ... well, she might force her way into those libraries and break Malarye's trust. And for what? It would not be so simple – the answers she sought would not be conveniently lined up in plain view.

So she threw herself into training. Her arrows hit their targets, she managed to jump from Thara's back mid-flight and land without Diath having to patch her back together, and the priests and priestesses improved their swordsmanship daily. It was a deadly combination, but it wasn't going to be enough, was it? There was still too much she didn't know.

She had finished her final dismount of the evening when a priestess approached, a curious smile etched on her face as she made straight for Hyacinth who perched on the outcrop of rocks where Arla had almost broken her spine on that first day. The priestess whispered in the princess's ear and Arla watched a grin breakout across Hyacinth's face.

'There's a court dinner tonight, and my mother would like you to attend.'

~

Arla had expected all the grandeur she had been used to at Castle Grey for a court dinner. There was no long dining table set with approximately eight different forks. In fact, no one sat at all. The hall had been cleared of the desks, and long tables had been placed around the room piled high with bronze platters of food. People stood around the hall, speaking in small groups or eating, and Queen Mara stood at one end of the room in a simple grey dress speaking with the man Arla recognised from the restaurant in the town.

Hyacinth stood beside Arla, their arms close enough to touch as they scanned the room. Hyacinth twisted her hands in front of her, and when not a single person acknowledged the arrival of their princess, Arla couldn't help the burst of irritation that flew through her.

This was nothing like a court dinner. It was ... a simple gathering. Not dissimilar from the evening of the wedding on her second night here, except this time she felt at ease amongst these people. She had been accepted into life in Malarye quickly, and she had come to learn its ways just as fast. So Arla wasn't concerned when Hyacinth left her to go and speak with a group of women Arla had sometimes seen her mingle with.

Good. She needed Hyacinth out of the way tonight. She had come here for one thing and one thing only.

~

The library tunnels were eerily dark without the glow of the priestesses' torches to light them.

Arla had successfully crept out of the court dinner because no one was paying enough attention to her to notice her absence. She waited for the priestesses to leave for the evening. There would be a new, smaller group to watch the texts overnight, but the tunnels would be silent for an hour yet – Arla had learned from Hyacinth that this was a tradition to honour the gods and their ancient texts by giving them an hour of solace.

The air was cool and dry, the scent of old parchment and smoke from where the recently extinguished torches still lingered. Her feet made no sound – an assassin's trick she had spent years perfecting. Her blood positively vibrated with the sneakiness of it all. How she'd missed spying and hiding in places she shouldn't be! The stone steps beneath her feet were worn smooth by the thousands of feet carrying people down into these tunnels to protect the books she could only imagine were inside. Would any of them date back to when the gods themselves walked the earth?

'The gods weren't fond of writing, Dragonhart. Do not be disappointed if you do not find what you seek.'

'The gods didn't seem to be fond of much,' she replied down the bond.

Thara didn't bother to answer, so Arla kept walking, the steps taking her deeper and deeper into the earth until at long last she stood in a long corridor leading to a vast chamber.

The lantern was easy to find and easier to light, the priestesses' habits too easy to observe and imitate on the night Hyacinth had first showed her the entrance to the tunnels.

She kept her steps light and slow. She had come this far without being discovered and she wasn't about to trip and set fire to everything down here. She couldn't afford to be discovered.

When she finally found herself standing in the entrance to the chamber, she lifted the lantern higher, letting soft light wash over the hundreds of books stored on stone shelves. And this place ... she could feel it was magic. Ancient. Like the forest in Flambriar where she had felt it shield her from the rest of the world. This place had been touched by magic, still lived in it, breathed it.

'I wondered how long it would take you to find your way beneath our temples.'

Arla counted Crea's steps until she was close enough that Arla would be able to see her face in the light.

'And I wondered whether you were actually stupid enough to fall right into what I had planned for you.'

The priestess had forgone her pearl vest, the sickly thinness of Crea's frame making her look too breakable in this hidden part of the kingdom. Shock rippled out across the priestess's features, before her face contorted into a frown filled with disgust as she eyed Arla and the chamber of books beyond her. Arla had known the second she'd left the dinner that Crea was following her – in fact, she'd hoped the priestess would follow. Now she might finally get some answers.

'The Queen will have your head for breaching these walls. They are not for the likes of stuck-up little assassins like *you*,' Crea snapped, the veins on her head bulging beneath her thin skin. The woman looked sick, truly.

'Your queen,' Arla mused, beginning to wander through the shelves of books in that vast circular chamber, 'is too scared of war to lay a finger on me. She won't promise to send troops to my aid in a battle that might not even happen, so forgive me, *priestess,* if your threats don't scare me.'

A different woman – and weaker woman – would not have turned her back on Crea and begun to run her fingers over the spines of texts so ancient she thought they might disintegrate beneath her touch. However, for Arla, it was simply too much fun to goad the woman into lashing out. This woman had come for answers, after all.

The swish of a gown across the stone floor of the chamber was the only indication that Crea was following her. 'This is a sacred place.'

Arla laughed wickedly. 'Am I not the most sacred of all?'

There was no warning as Crea unsheathed her *serabti* and threw herself at Arla.

The assassin put the lantern down with such force she was surprised it didn't shatter and unsheathed her own blade to meet Crea's in a deafening clash.

The curve of Crea's blade presented its own challenge, and had Arla not trained with Malarye's army and begun to learn the subtle differences of fighting against it, she may have faltered. As it happened, she'd been working out their technique from the moment she had stepped foot on these shores.

'What's so precious down here that you have to hide it from someone who's gods-blessed, Crea?' Arla taunted, her body moving with the expert fluidity she had developed as a child.

Crea matched her every move, the mask of a religious devotee falling away to reveal a keen swordswoman. Oh, how she'd missed this.

Crea lunged for her, the curved blade snatching the tip of Arla's sword at the last moment, hauling her forwards with the momentum of the swing. Arla ducked and pivoted, avoiding the sharp side of the blade and arcing her own sword high above them.

'You might think you're gods-blessed,' Crea panted,

swinging her blade at Arla's face, 'but you're nothing more than a game the gods invented to fulfil a prophecy told by the fates.'

Cruel *bitch*!

Arla laughed then, her very blood alive with the thrill of the dance. Gods, she'd love nothing more than to drive her blade through the throat of this woman.

'Not a good enough answer. I can stop this at any time, as soon as you agree to give me the answers I'm looking for.'

A thin bead of sweat rolled down Crea's brow, the weight of her robes unthinkably hot with the effort it was taking to match Arla's skill. The assassin's feet moved as though she were waltzing with death itself, a morbid, dazzling skill she had taken pride in the better she got at it. She would have her answers tonight. She wouldn't even have to search for them.

'Mara should never have invited you here,' Crea spat, hissing as the tip of Arla's blade nicked the top of her leg. A game. It was all just a game.

Arla smiled as crimson began to bleed across the sparkling white of the priestess's robes. 'Then that is Mara's mistake.'

She moved like a rainstorm, then.

There was nothing other than a curved blade and a white priestess, a darkened room and the wrath of the gods in Arla's veins. Arla lunged at her like it was an unleashing, a routine of practised skill and deadlier concentration.

Less than a minute.

Less than a minute was all it took for Crea to fall against the wall of the chamber and blink up at her as Arla's blade balanced on the column of her throat.

'Your mistake, Crea,' she said, her voice so quiet in the deafening silence of the chamber, 'was ever thinking you could win against me. You speak so loudly of my reputation and forget that I am all too capable of backing it up. Did you really think I'd allow you to raise a blade against me tonight?'

Panic flared in Crea's eyes as Arla pressed the tip of the blade harder, eliciting a bead of scarlet and a strangled sound from the priestess's throat.

'Please.'

That single word lit a spark in her chest: the need to hurt her; the need to force that blade through her throat; to impale her here in the very place she sought to keep Arla from. She wanted her to bleed, wanted her to hurt and scream and—

'DRAGONHART!'

Thara's voice raced through the bond, jerking her back to herself.

Blood ran in rivulets down Crea's throat and the priestess shook violently beneath the blade.

'Please...'

'Enough,' Arla said, so quietly she didn't think Crea would hear it. She did, though, her prayers turning silent as she squeezed her eyes shut.

Arla removed the blade, swallowing the bile in her throat at how close she had come to losing control again – how it had taken the interference of Thara *again* to drag her out of that deadly spiral. It terrified her.

'Please, I'll tell you what you want to know,' Crea whimpered.

'Good,' Arla said, sheathing her blade. 'Now we're getting somewhere.'

~

Crea led her deeper into the chamber where a desk and two wooden chairs sat hidden at the edge of the room.

'What is it you wish to know?' Crea's voice had lost its hardness, its confidence, its everything. Now she sat across from Arla, her creamy skin stained the colour of rust. There was a piece of Arla that delighted in seeing her undoing of the woman, but mostly she was disgusted by what she'd almost done.

Arla leant back in the chair, arms folded across her chest. She was coming back to herself with every moment she spent in Malarye. Flambriar had knocked her off kilter, had taken her by surprise in the most real sense, and she had felt adrift, like she was floating, for months. Now she was remembering who she was.

'I want you to tell me what I have to do to unite the kingdoms.'

Crea looked at her as though Arla had instructed her to jump off the cliff. Ire flashed through her face quickly before the thin bead of blood sliding down her neck seemed to remind her of the situation and the imbalance of power.

'What makes you think I have any idea?' the priestess said.

Ah, Arla loved when her subjects were not forthcoming. So many games she could play...

'Because you've made it your life's work to study the gods and their ways, have you not? Surely someone as learned as yourself would have insight as to what it is the gods would like me to do, Crea?'

It achieved the desired effect. Crea's muscles tensed as she went to grab Arla over the table, but she clearly thought better of it. Arla raised a brow. She so very loved pressing the parts that hurt the most.

'I have no idea what you're supposed to do. You rescued the mages. It should have been enough.'

It had once been Arla's job to know all the ways a lie

revealed itself on a person's face. Crea's tells were as plain as daylight.

'Don't. Lie. To. Me.'

Something in the priestess's face seemed to change then. Perhaps she finally realised that if she didn't give Arla what she wanted there was no knowing what the assassin would do. Arla herself didn't know, truly. Not given how easily she had lost control of herself recently and became trapped in the shadows in the centre of her chest that only chanted *kill, kill, kill*.

Crea leaned back in her own chair, the action illuminating her face in the lamplight and showing all the sharp angles and sunken cheeks. Had she always looked so ... tired? She twisted her hands in her lap, her eyes faraway, her voice small and insignificant when she finally spoke.

'I never wanted you to come here. The punishment from the gods, the failing of the kingdoms ... I thought it would stay contained to Kastonia and Hadalyn – Flambriar too now, I suppose. I thought the continent would be safe if you didn't come here.'

'The continent has been suffering too, you know it has. I can see how sick you are, Crea. How you're terrified that the wasting sickness that has claimed so many lives across the kingdoms has somehow found you, too.'

Panic erupted across the priestess's face before it melted into something that had ... given up.

'Perhaps. But you being here ... well, I guess it doesn't matter anymore, does it. You fulfilled the second half of the prophecy the moment you stepped foot on these shores. Why do you think I tried so hard to shoot you down before you could land here? The clock has begun ticking and we all live on borrowed time.'

That when the risen takes flight to seek an ally, the clock will begin its duel.

'So, what, by coming here I've set us all on a path to death and destruction anyway? There's no use in trying to unite anything? Don't give me that, Crea. You and I both know you haven't given up.'

'I think,' Crea said, an emotion Arla couldn't place was slowly seeping its way into every line of the priestess's face, 'I think history is repeating itself. Prophecies aren't created without reason. What better justification than to right the wrong that happened a century ago?'

Goosebumps prickled across every inch of Arla's skin, the chamber suddenly colder than it had been a second ago. Crea looked deranged, illuminated as she was by lamplight, her face too knowing.

And yet Arla believed every word that came next.

'You know of Damon, yes?'

She nodded once, a weight settling on her chest at the mention of the last dragonhart. His name was cropping up an awful lot for her liking, and after what Hyacinth had said – that his hunger for power had corrupted him – it couldn't be a coincidence, could it? Elrod was hungry for power too...

Crea continued, looking at Arla through her lashes, a sombreness weighing her down.

'The dragonharts did have power – a magic channelled from the gods, enough to break the world apart. But Damon ... he was the last one for a reason. That power corrupted him. He wanted more and more until he began to turn on the mages too. It sent him mad in the end and he impaled himself on his own sword. It is written that the gods vowed never to allow any future dragonharts to have that sort of magic again lest history repeat itself. They knew you were coming – it has been prophesised for a long time – you were never granted the gift of magic so that you may never succumb to its corruption. The mages are to be protected by the dragonharts, Damon's actions and his obsession with magic went against that.'

'Then something went wrong,' Arla interrupted. 'I know what I felt. It was magic—'

Crea raised a hand. 'If you let me finish speaking, you might get the answers you were happy to almost kill me for.'

Arla bit back a smirk.

'The very magic the gods kept from you is housed within your dragon. Only in the direst of circumstances will that bridge open up to you. That's all I know, I swear it.'

And it wasn't fucking enough.

She wanted *more*.

'Tell me now, Crea,' she said, the softness of her voice giving way to a sharpness that cut the air. 'If you know what I am supposed to do in order to unite the kingdoms, to fulfil this ridiculous prophecy, you will tell me now.'

The woman that erupted before her was not the same person who had surrendered to Arla with a sword at her neck only minutes before.

Crea surged to her feet, sending the wooden chair skittering across the floor. A wildness bit into her face, her eyes wide and unseeing as her hands slammed against the surface of the table.

'You think I don't want you to unite the kingdoms?' she cried. 'You think I want to feel my body fail me? You said it yourself, Arla, I am *sick*, and because of you and your inability to solve a prophecy you were *born* to fulfil, I will likely die before the end of the year. You aren't a protector. You've damned us all.'

Every word was a shard of ice through her chest. Needling. Piercing. And though she felt it all keenly, she knew in her heart that every word Crea spoke was true, she breathed deeply and found that calm place she had spent so many hours disappearing to. Maybe three weeks ago she would have let the words settle upon her, let them bully her into becoming a shadow of herself – the gods knew she'd felt that way since she'd woken up in Flambriar. But now, since she'd come to Malarye, she was remembering who she was, she was remembering the girl she had been made into, and she wouldn't let the words of a dying woman convince her that this was all her fault.

'Believe what you like,' Arla said, rising from her seat, the weight of the sword at her side a reminder of who she was and what she was capable of. 'But if you think I can't appease the gods within eight months, you severely underestimate my reputation.'

She left the priestess slack-jawed and staring after her as she left the chamber, her boots clipping against the floor as she made her way out of the tunnels.

To an observer, it would be the strut of a victor, yet she couldn't help but think she'd lost.

CHAPTER 34

She'd hardly slept. Morning had come too bright and eager, and Thara had been tugging at the bond in the hours she had attempted sleep. It was that call and that call alone that made her rise when the sun did, and trudge slowly down the cliffside to find her dragon resting in the forest.

'Do you intend to ignore me every time you feel like sulking?' Thara's voice echoed in her head.

Arla approached her dragon slowly, lifting a calloused hand against Thara's scales, surprised when the dragon allowed the touch. The bond had certainly grown between them. Arla could no longer fathom what it would feel like not to have Thara's presence in the back of her mind, not to feel connected to something powerful and ancient. She didn't blame Thara anymore for what the fates prohibited her from speaking of, but she felt more lost than ever. If history were to repeat itself, if she truly were to go mad and lose control like Damon had, surely her dragon could do *something*.

'You might not understand the fates and the restrictions they place on my kind, but know that it pains me every time I hear you

question yourself, Dragonhart. There are things I wish to speak of that I would die for you to know...'

The sincerity in Thara's voice, the way her heart hurt at the kindness there...

'Don't kill yourself on my account,' Arla said quietly. 'I don't think I could bear it.'

A huff of laughter pulsed down the bond. *'Know that I would accept the fate, had I not been so determined to see this through with you. I watched the damning of the last dragonhart and the actions that came before it. You may not bear my death, Dragonhart, but know I still mourn theirs. I will not allow it to happen again.'*

There it was. The reassurance she had needed whilst she tossed and turned beneath sheets in the lonely hours of last night. Yes, there were things Thara couldn't tell her, but she had tugged on that bond all night to show Arla that she wasn't alone, that she wouldn't allow her to walk the same path as the one that had come before her.

Gods, Crea really had gotten to her.

'Do not dwell on the possibilities, Dragonhart. It has never done anyone any good.'

She laughed then. A weak sound, but it was there all the same.

'Can we fly?'

A wave of amusement washed through the bond.

'There's more than flying in store for us today.'

~

'You're not bloody serious?' Arla snapped as she dismounted from Thara's back. The dragon hadn't whispered a word of what she had planned for the day as they had practised rolling and diving and twists that had Arla's stomach rising to her throat, but the moment she'd landed in the training ring, Mason had accosted her and told her exactly what it was they would be taking part in today.

'I am indeed. You've improved well enough with that bow that I think it would be a damn shame not to see you combine your skills – the archers too. They're looking forward to it.'

'The gods know why,' she protested, tossing the long sword strapped against her spine ungracefully onto the floor. 'They're going to end up dead – or I will!'

Mason broke into laughter then, and that godsforsaken sound was so contagious she couldn't stop herself from giggling too.

'Trust me,' he said, rubbing a hand across his broad, stubbled jaw, 'you just aim for those targets whilst you're up in the air and you won't kill a single man or woman in this army.'

'You forget I have to concentrate on not falling off a dragon. How is it you expect me not to fall to my death whilst focusing on target practice too?'

'Oh, Arla,' Mason chuckled, 'we've seen you up there twisting and writhing into all sorts of shapes. If anyone can hit a target from the back of a dragon, it's you.'

She was glad of *his* confidence at least. And ... he had called her by her name, something so foreign she often forgot what it sounded like coming from others' lips.

The thought of it hauled a memory back from four months ago, of her bleeding to death whilst Hark said her name over and over. It was the first time he'd ever said it, and she hadn't been strong enough to kiss the very lips from which her name had escaped.

Ugh, the thought of him sat like cold ice in the pit of her stomach. The strain of missing him, of missing his skin, his hands, his tongue, was beginning to show.

She swallowed the lump rising in her throat.

'We will be back with the boy soon. Stop pining! It's not a good look on you.'

She regarded Mason again. She would be a fool to say no to this opportunity. It was important. If she could fire a bow from atop Thara, then it would give them an advantage against whatever came for them. But the archers...

'Do tell me how it benefits your men that they must fire arrows at targets I am weaving between? Your queen has sworn that your troops will not take part in future battles, so what's in it for them?'

Mason, to his credit, didn't flinch beneath the ice in her voice.

'Aye, she did. But there will come a day when we are plunged into war, and the Queen is blind if she cannot see it. This army has watched you train with that dragon, and they've learned skills with a blade they couldn't have mastered without your teaching. There is a respect for you here, Arla. I think that's worth more than the Queen's refusal, no?'

She looked beyond Mason to the dozens of soldiers that had turned up to practice this morning, each of them excited, all of them here because she had something worth sharing. It would be a damned shame to waste it...

She was climbing back onto Thara's back before she could talk herself out of it.

'If you kill me, I'm going to cut all of your throats,' she called out, and enjoyed their varying looks of horror.

Mason only smirked as he handed her the bow and a sheaf of arrows. She bit back her own smile as she strapped the leather arm guards to her wrists.

Before long, the world was awash with arrows.

They rained down around her, each feathered end a different colour as they met the targets she flew by with a thud. Her own bow was heavy in her grip as she struggled to keep her body close to Thara's back as they weaved between targets. Her thighs clenched tightly against the locked plates of scales on the dragon's back were her only grip, her only physical tether, as she nocked another arrow.

She had failed to hit a single target, but she also hadn't killed anyone either, so despite the trembling in her weary arms, she found the determination to keep aiming.

A stray arrow from an archer on the ground whizzed by her, scratching the skin of her cheek and igniting a line of hot stickiness across the flesh. She blinked the pain away. This ... this utter ... madness was what she had been born for.

Her blood sang with the chaos of it. And yet ... she had never felt so calm. This was a job, this was training, she would keep ducking and weaving and sticking close to Thara's body as she fired her own arrows, each one getting closer and closer to the centre of the target with every snap of the bow string.

Her fingers ached and her legs were numb, and then an enormous crack, loud enough to signal that the world was cleaving apart, delivered hailstones and icy cold rain, and still she couldn't shake the smile on her face. This was the sort of skill she had never even dreamed of mastering. Thara was an extension of her body, a living, wild thing beneath her that kept her out of the path of oncoming arrows. Tears of joy streamed down her cheeks, mixing with the blood and reminding her with a painful sting of what would happen if she didn't concentrate.

After almost three hours of arrows and rain and numb fingers, her arrows finally began hitting their marks.

The cheer that came from the ground was so intoxicating she couldn't help the sob that burst free of her throat. She'd done it.

She'd done it, she'd done it, she'd done it!

Thara swooped lower then, bringing her closer to the ground of the training rings where the sodden archers stood cheering, their beaming faces enough to chase away the cold and her various aches and pains. The dragon landed lightly, sighing hot air across the clearing. Only weeks ago, the archers would have been terrified of her, but now they groaned as Thara's delicious heat washed over their soaking bodies. Without it, Arla would not have lasted so long in this weather.

She almost collapsed when she dismounted and her frozen feet hit the floor.

But Hyacinth was there to catch Arla in her surprisingly strong arms as Diath came from nowhere, supporting her too as she tried to stamp some warmth back into her toes.

'That was the most incredible thing I have ever seen!' Hyacinth exclaimed, dragging a woollen blanket around Arla's shoulders.

'Truly, Dragonhart, it was spectacular,' Diath said as their hands hovered over Arla's skin – assessing for injuries, she imagined.

But yes, it had been spectacular. Only a fool would deny it. She had witnessed the falling of coloured arrows around her as she weaved with her dragon through the air, had tasted the elation of it when her arrows finally hit their marks.

She could only imagine what it had looked like from the ground.

The soldiers gathered around her, a cacophony of voices and excitement and—

'The Queen wishes to see you.'

Crea's voice rang out across the training ring like death bells. Everyone turned to look at her, the priestess's face so incredibly pale it was hard to distinguish from her white hooded cloak. It was the first time Arla had seen her since their ... conversation in the library. She looked as though she had given up and invited death right inside that cloak to live with her.

A solemness fell over the soldiers, and she was sure she didn't imagine the tightening of Hyacinth's fingers on the blanket draped around Arla's shoulders.

Her voice was strong when she finally replied. 'Then I had best not keep her waiting.'

~

Thank the gods for the roaring fires in the main hall of the palace.

Climbing back up the cliff had been a lesson in stamina and how not to fucking die from the cold.

The storm had well and truly settled in, and it had taken every last bit of strength to climb the cliff as her frozen body shook. Hyacinth had stayed with the soldiers, clever enough not to attempt the climb until the rain settled. Thara had been all too insistent on flying Arla to the top of the cliff, but the thought of climbing onto the dragon's back and sitting in that position for any longer had been a worse prospect than climbing.

So she wasn't surprised when every person in the hall turned to look at her as she strode through the doors.

Queen Mara was sitting at her usual desk, her eyes widening slightly as she took Arla in. She could only imagine what she looked like. Her hair had come unbraided and lay in a matted knot across her shoulders. She was dripping water *everywhere* and the woollen blanket Hyacinth had given her weighed enough to make a loud slap as she discarded it on the stone floor.

'Goodness, Dragonhart. Come inside and get warm. Someone will bring you something hot to drink,' the Queen ordered, her eyes flitting for half a second to a young man who scurried off quickly to get Arla some hot tea, she hoped.

Her boots squelched as she walked the length of the hall to collapse into the chair opposite the Queen. Mara was as perfect and lovely as usual, her hair shiny and straight and those cunning eyes shone in the light of the fire beside her.

'I do believe congratulations are in order,' the Queen began, leaning back slightly in her chair. 'I watched your display this morning from the top balcony of the palace. "Impressive" is too modest a word.'

Mara was smiling, and not for the first time Arla struggled to work out just what game the Queen was playing. Today, however, she was too elated to let the Queen's games irritate her, and she was content to accept the steaming tea handed to her.

'Mason is the one to thank. I don't think I'd have had the nerve to attempt such a thing.'

Mara blinked lazily. 'And yet you have. A formidable team, you and your dragon.'

'Made even more so by your archers,' Arla said softly, gazing into the tea.

The Queen stopped her right there. 'I will not revise my position, Dragonhart. My troops will not fight in a war, no matter how well you complement one another.'

'Who said there was going to be a war, Your Majesty?'

Mara's gaze seemed to pierce the very depths of Arla's soul. Arla didn't think she was going to answer until the Queen sighed and leant back even further. '*You* did. When you wanted my army to form an alliance with yours. Do not insult us both by denying that there will be conflict. You know as well as I that it is unavoidable.'

At least they agreed on that.

'I didn't call you up here to compliment you on a feat at which you are already well aware you have excelled,' Mara said. Arla's eyes shot up from her tea to meet the Mara's. 'I called you up here to ask why there is blood on the floor of one of my libraries.'

'I'm not sure I know what you mean,' Arla replied.

'That may be true, but I know who you are and what you're capable of. I know what questions you came here to answer. I also know Crea was absent from our morning meeting and has declined my offer of dinner on the excuse of a headache. Do not lie to me, Dragonhart. Tell me why you were in the tunnels last night in the middle of a court dinner.'

There was no anger in the Queen's voice. No malice in her eyes, either. Only a keen curiosity.

Arla leant across the table, lowering her voice so that only the Queen might hear it.

'I came here because I thought a kingdom so devoted to the old religion would be able to tell me how to unite the kingdoms, according to the wishes of the gods. Instead, I have trained an army that will not fight alongside me, leaving my own kingdom without the aid of a dragon should we be attacked. For all I know, my people could be dead, every single one of them. How long would it take the news to reach here? Four days, perhaps? Long enough that there would be no survivors.'

She hadn't allowed herself to contemplate the truth of this idea because there was no room for that way of thinking. She'd squashed the thought every time it rose because of the fear it might sink its claws deep inside and ruin her. But now ... now things were different. She had been away for eight weeks and because she had told Hark and the court not to send a single letter in case they were intercepted, she had no way of knowing if they were alive. And it was slowly killing her.

Mara leant forwards then, the volume of her voice matching Arla's.

'I understand your worry for your people. Please know it was never my intention to drag you away from them to prevent you aiding them. But if you think you might find the answers you seek in my libraries, I am willing to offer you a deal.'

Another deal... Arla had learnt political games as a child. Had witnessed her king manoeuvre foreign rulers as if countries were chessboards. She had contemplated making such a deal with Mara when she'd first set the terms, but ... well this was a clever queen she was dealing with.

No matter. Arla was clever, too.

She had played along so far, had accepted a deal heavily weighted in the queen's favour so that she might earn her trust. Might be able to make a second, more favourable deal, too.

Arla ran her tongue over her teeth. 'I'm listening.'

'I cannot allow you access to those tunnels. Dragonhart or not, only those who have studied in the temples are permitted to enter. But the books inside them may be brought to you here in the palace.'

Now that she could agree to.

'What's in it for you?' Arla probed.

The Queen's face paled slightly, as if what was coming next hurt her. 'Take Hyacinth with you when you leave.'

'WHAT?' The word exploded from Arla's lips before she could stop it, and it drew the attention of a group of courtiers.

Mara dismissed them with a brush of her fingers. 'What do you mean, *take Hyacinth with me?*'

Mara pinched the bridge of her nose between her fingers. Arla would never understand this woman...

'You know as well as I that Hyacinth doesn't have the iron spine needed to rule a country. Perhaps with you, she might develop one. I cannot keep her here, Dragonhart. The people have no respect for her. They see her as the young girl she was when her father—When what happened, happened. But this has to change. I need her to be strong and capable, like you. Her beauty won't help her if she is to inherit my throne. Let her see what it is like to build a kingdom and keep it safe. Take her to Flambriar with you.'

Arla tried to speak but found her tongue wouldn't form words. She lifted a hand and wiped it across her face, not surprised when her fingers came back tinged with red as her cheek stung again.

'You want me to teach your daughter how to rule a kingdom when we are at risk of being crushed?'

Mara blinked rapidly, her eyes desperate and pleading. 'I don't ask this of you lightly, Dragonhart. She is my sole heir. If anything happened to her... But I need her to command people the way I have done – the way you do. I won't let her lose the throne I worked so hard to claim for her.'

It all made sense now. *This* was why Arla had been invited here. Queen Mara had wanted to feel her out; to see if she could be trusted to become Princess Hyacinth's mentor.

The realisation tasted sour on her tongue. She could say no, but she couldn't leave here without answers, and she was tired of not knowing. So where did that leave her?

She wished Hark were here.

'I knew there was deception in your blood the moment I met

you, Your Majesty. I just didn't think it was a trait you'd handed to your daughter, too.'

Mara's eyes widened and she grasped Arla's wrist over the table. It took everything in her not to snap the Queen's fingers for her insolence.

'Please, Dragonhart. Hyacinth did not know. She thought you were coming here to negotiate an ally, that's all. I did not tell her she would be leaving with you. Your friendship is perhaps the only real thing in all of this.'

Arla didn't know if she believed it. But what was the alternative? She had to accept the Queen's terms.

She stood up, resisting the urge to squirm in her wet clothes.

'Don't try to deceive me again, Mara. Queen or not, I won't hesitate to kill you.'

She left the queen gaping as she exited the hall.

Hyacinth, as Arla had predicted, was overjoyed to know she would be travelling to Flambriar when the time came for them to leave.

Thara, as Arla had predicted, was not.

'I am not a mule. I don't remember agreeing to any such arrangement,' Thara growled as she took off from the ground, leaving Arla scrambling to find her grip before she fell at an increasingly quickening pace.

'I didn't expect it either,' Arla called above the noise of the wind. 'But I need this information and the only way I'm going to get it is by taking the princess. And besides, she's ... nice.'

Thara scoffed. *'You and your human heart.'*

Whatever Arla tried to say next was snatched by the wind as Thara dived, aiming straight for the forest floor. Arla jumped with practised precision, rolling the moment her feet made contact with the earth and rising in one swift moment, sword drawn.

The wash of approval that came careening down the bond caused warmth to spread across her cheeks as Diath and Hyacinth stood up and cheered.

'I daresay you don't need my skills anymore, Dragonhart,' Diath said, beaming ear to ear as their eyes glanced over Arla for any injuries.

'You won't be saying that when you're picking arrows out of my back, Diath,' Arla chuckled, already making her way toward the training rings where the archers waited for her. The nerves that had wriggled beneath her skin yesterday had been replaced with a buzzing energy, and now she was eager to take flight and feel the world fall away in a mirage of coloured arrows. If only Hark could see her now...

'Oh, don't say that,' Hyacinth said, laughing and smacking Arla's arm playfully. 'You can't die before I get the chance to see your kingdom.'

CHAPTER 35
HARK

'I don't know why you're so hard on her.' Kase's voice echoed down the hallway of the highest floor of Claret Hall. 'She's young, and the gods know you let her get away with murder. She'll come round.'

Hark sighed, following Kase into the sitting room. Sebastian was already inside, drinking so much of Hark's expensive whiskey that he snatched the bottle from his friend's hand. He had listened to this argument too many times in the weeks since Arla had left.

'She is a *child*,' Seb grumbled, collapsing onto the settee and shooting Kase a look that would have sent anyone else running.

Kase snorted, twisting the rings on her fingers as she stared out of the windows onto the city below. Hark had caught her doing it a lot recently, as if she were constantly searching for something no one else could find. He bet if he stood close enough, he'd find her gaze fixed on the stone building by the river and the man who lay inside it. She was always worse on the days Jack had treatment.

'She's twelve. I was doing a lot worse at her age than disappearing on horseback for a few hours in the afternoon.'

'Just because she isn't seducing her uncle's friends as a leg-up for him in society doesn't mean that what she's doing is safe, Kase.'

A heaviness settled on the room that had Hark stepping forwards, braced to intercept the silver-haired viper that was about to erupt from the corner.

The attack never came, and that meant a wholly different sort of danger.

Kase turned so slowly he feared there was something wrong with her. That's when he saw the pure venom in her swirling blue eyes. She was a sharp sort of beautiful, with angled cheekbones and a narrow nose, every piece of her a perfectly cut line that oozed lethal grace. Where Arla was death's own companion, Kase was its rival. Hark palmed the blade sheathed at his hip.

'I'm not proud of the things I was *forced* into, Sebastian,' she snarled, poison dripping from her tongue, 'but don't forget what I did to my uncle that put me in Larkire's dungeons. I'd be more than happy to show you exactly which parts I cut off first.'

Fucking gods! He didn't have it in him to endure this today.

Seb straightened, his eyes darkening as he eyed Kase, his mouth settling into something cruel. Hark often forgot just how deadly his crew could be. He had, after all, conned them all into working with him in the first place, not because they had fit the mould for the sort of people he wanted as his friends. No, he had wanted them for their skillset. Their violence.

It wasn't often they turned it upon each other.

Seb's lips parted, and though it was rare he ever spoke cruelly – especially to Kase – Hark could see the wound ready to be inflicted. Sebastian didn't back down. Not when it came to Elin or Vivianne.

'Well, forgive me if I would rather my niece didn't follow the same *fucked-up* life you've led.'

The world seemed to stop spinning, and then she was upon him.

Arla had lost control many times – he'd watched them all with too much approval and ... arousal. But Kase? There was nothing to approve in the way she threw herself over the small table by the settee and set upon Sebastian, her fingers clawing at his face whilst he fumbled to draw a blade.

Fucking gods, blood would flow before the night was out!

The pair of them crashed to the floor, grunting and growling, and they wouldn't stop *hitting each other*.

He let it continue until the first bead of blood rolled down Seb's cheek, a consequence of Kase's sharpened nails, but then he marched over and hauled the girl from where she straddled Sebastian.

Attempting to control Kase was like trying to harness a storm. She thrashed and kicked and screamed such vile words at Sebastian that the maids were sure to talk.

What surprised Hark the most, though, was that Seb didn't stop.

He came at them, those usually soft eyes having hardened into something dark and unrelenting. He swung his fists towards Kase's face, and to her credit, she didn't flinch – almost leaned into the hit as if it fuelled her fury.

Hark could understand it. He knew what Kase had been made to do by her uncle. He'd been witness to the long nights after he'd rescued her from Larkire during which she'd stared out of the window in silence and battled hells they had no chance of comprehending.

And Seb ... he hadn't grieved his sister properly, even now. But there was a fierce oath burned into his soul that he would protect those girls. And Elin ... well, Kase was right – she was acting out. She'd taken a liking to Arla and decided she would follow in her footsteps.

He didn't think Arla would approve of the girl 'borrowing' Vetta and disappearing into the mountains each afternoon. Or maybe she would, because it was exactly the sort of thing she'd have done as a child, he imagined. But there was too much risk now, too much danger when those strange soldiers of Elrod's had been appearing in dribs and drabs and took more force than should ever be needed to be killed.

So Hark could understand the anger from both of his friends. What he didn't understand was why they were both so willing to draw each other's blood when up until now nothing had ever turned them against one another.

His slip in concentration cost him and Kase shrugged free of his grip, launching herself at Sebastian with renewed vigour. The glass table shattered beneath them as they landed upon it, the crash so deafening he knew there were only minutes to get this under control before the entirety of Claret Hall arrived in the sitting room and wondered why the courtiers were ready to tear each other's throats out.

He reached for Kase again, only to find himself being shoved roughly out of the way.

Jack had arrived, and he was hauling her back against his chest with far too much ease for someone who could barely walk without aid.

It was the opening Hark needed to grab hold of Sebastian, to wrap his arms around the man and shove him against the far wall of the sitting room.

'Get a fucking grip!' Hark growled, the words clearing that dazed anger on his friend's face.

Sadness leaked across Seb's features then, and realisation of what they'd done as he surveyed the room, his eyes lingering on the shards of glass marked with both his and Kase's blood on the carpet. And then his eyes settled on Kase. To where Jack held her face in his hands, cane forgotten as he whispered to her.

Hark watched the fury melt away, her body going soft against Jack's as he pulled her to him. It dragged a lump up his throat.

To see his friend able to walk – able to separate the fight. And ... to see them together.

Sebastian whistled long and low, dragging a hand through his hair. He'd grown it to his shoulders recently, likely in an attempt to catch the eye of one of the men who worked in the forest. Or perhaps of one of the women who reared goats for them all to eat.

It didn't matter, did it? Because no matter where any of their hearts lay, one thing was clear: with Arla gone, they were tearing themselves and each other apart.

He hadn't been aware of it in the beginning, just how comprehensively she had ingrained herself in this group that she had become the centre of it. But her absence had been a powerful thing that taunted each of them. It sighed in every corridor and danced in every shaft of sunlight. They were falling apart without her.

'What in the gods' names are you all doing?' Jaz's deep voice ruptured the tense silence, each of them turning to face him one by one. He wore dark purple robes, the rings on his fingers gleaming in the light from the sitting room. He clutched a book to his chest – he was *always* clutching a book to his chest nowadays.

'Are any of you going to speak or should I pretend you don't look like you're all on a mission to kill one another?'

'It's nothing,' Seb said, his voice surprisingly steady. 'A misunderstanding.'

Kase's eyes narrowed slightly and Hark didn't miss the way Jack's fingers tightened on her shoulders. The act alone seemed to disarm her, and she relaxed against him.

'A misunderstanding?' Jaz mused, slamming the book down on the wooden table by the door. 'I don't care what it was that drove you to act like dogs, but take your anger elsewhere. What's coming is bigger than us, bigger than whatever *this* is.' He gestured to the space between them. 'There will be no room for *misunderstandings*. You'll need every man and woman working together.'

Lead settled in the pit of Hark's gut. His tongue was heavy in his mouth when he spoke.

'And what would that be?'

Jaz sighed, picking the book back up and clasping it tight in both hands. ''Tis no coincidence that those strange soldiers are appearing in our mountains. You'd better hope your girlfriend finds something to help her in Malarye ... the gods know there's nothing here.'

Silence smothered the group, yet its pressing weight could not drown the bright flame of anger that lurched in Hark's chest. 'Drop these riddles and start fucking talking, Jaz. If she's in danger, I need to know.'

He hadn't let himself think of the fact that they hadn't heard from her and she had not returned. It was just like they'd agreed, of course, but in the darkest hours of night, whether he lay awake in bed or trudged through the mountains looking for Elrod's monstrous soldiers, he'd been unable to prevent his mind from believing Arla Dragonhart to be dead.

Jaz's expression spoke of worry and Hark hated to see it. His deep brown skin was dull and worn with the signs of exhaustion as he spoke.

'Those soldiers we're fighting, they've been here before, back when the last dragonhart was alive. Damon created them using dark magic – forbidden magic. It is said only *his* sword could truly kill them.'

Kase gasped, and the way Seb shifted from one foot to the other beside him expressed the same anxiety rolling through Hark's veins.

'So what now?' Jack asked, his voice strong and clear. The colour was back in his cheeks – at least, for now – and the straightness in his spine bolstered Hark against the information that had him aching to get to Arla. To keep her safe.

'I believe,' Jaz continued, 'that we are seeing the same magic that was here a century ago. Whatever Elrod's done, 'tis just as dark and twisted as what Damon did. If you ask me, he's creating an army of dark soldiers, and only Damon's sword will be enough to stop him.'

'So if we can find the sword and stop Elrod, it will be enough to unite the kingdoms?' Kase's voice held a hope they'd all been missing, perhaps since Arla had left and the letters had begun arriving from their spies, relaying the grinding poverty and sickness spreading through the kingdoms. It was as if a faraway clock had started counting down and they were running out of time.

'Perhaps,' Jaz said with a sigh. 'But knowing the fates, it won't be that simple. I have a feeling there's more to come.'

Unfortunately, Hark agreed.

CHAPTER 36

The next week was filled with training and arrows from sun-up until sundown. At that point, Arla would drag herself back up the cliff to her rooms and begin leafing through the pile of books that had been delivered to her from the libraries.

Hyacinth was there too, every night, bringing cakes and pastries and sweet wine that they chatted and laughed over as they scanned the ancient texts for any mention of the prophecy or how to fix the mess the gods had bestowed on the kingdoms.

By the seventh night, she was ready to throw herself off the side of the cliff.

'Always with the dramatics, Dragonhart.'

'There's nothing here,' she whined, slamming the leather cover shut and choking on the cloud of dust that erupted from it.

'There will be, I'm sure of it,' Hyacinth said softly, reaching across the end of the bed to unravel a scroll sealed with scarlet ribbon.

She didn't know when she fell asleep, only that when she

woke, her room was nothing but inky darkness. Hyacinth had left her sleeping, the books stacked neatly by the desk, and a thick blanket had been laid over her shoulders.

Why was she having to blink back tears?

She fell back asleep dreaming of dragons and swords that were too heavy to carry.

∼

Malarye's army was slowly becoming a formidable force. Arla left each session with new admiration for them – the way they listened to her, the way they wielded swords on the ground and arrows in the air ... it was a sight to behold.

She had improved, too. For the last three days, every arrow she fired had met its mark on targets so far away she had trouble making them out. It lit her chest with an elation she didn't think would ever dim.

Despite her lack of progress with the library books, she felt better than ever. She was still grinning from a particularly spectacular training session in which she had hit the target from so far away she had relied on pure instinct to aim the bow.

Hyacinth was aiding Crea tonight – the priestess was seen about less and less these days and Arla could only suspect her sickness had taken hold with a new vengeance – and the thought of dragging those heavy books onto the bed and painstakingly studying them on her *own* elicited a disgruntled groan.

She forced herself to do so anyway – the kingdoms would fall without it, after all – and before long the hours had slipped away, the small clock in the corner of the room informing her that she had been reading for almost three hours when

Hyacinth's small frame slipped through the door and climbed up onto the bed.

'It's late. You should be in bed,' Arla murmured, not looking up from the book in front of her. Something had drawn her to it, the leather so worn and smooth it felt *alive* beneath her fingers. The dragonhart symbol – a flame inside a heart – had been carved into the leather and she couldn't help but run her fingers over it. She hadn't taken her own brooch off since the moment she had been gifted it by a strange woman in Vorstrum all those months ago.

'So should you,' Hyacinth said, dragging another book onto the bed as she settled against the headboard next to Arla.

'I'm busy. You know I can't stop until I have answers. Crea isn't sick because she happened to catch a wasting sickness. Diath can't heal her so it's not exactly hard to figure out that the gods are responsible, is it?'

She didn't mean to snap – not at Hyacinth who was only ever gentle and kind – but she couldn't keep the bite from her voice. This was serious. She couldn't go home until she knew how to fix this. There was a pull here, a feeling that her answers would be given freely if only she knew where to look.

'Crea has been utterly unbearable, you know. Ever since the court dinner...'

Arla didn't hear what the princess said next because she was so focused on the passage before her, the ink so worn she could barely make out the words. But they were there all the same.

'Shut up, I've found something.'

Hyacinth's incessant chatter ceased immediately.

Arla read the passage to herself again, and again, and again, until she was certain she had committed the words to memory, and she could begin to understand them.

'You're pale. Should I call Diath?' Hyacinth was already making for the door.

'No,' Arla said quietly. 'No, I'm all right. There's something here, and I think it's important.'

'What is it?' Hyacinth climbed back onto the bed, her body warm and soft as she leaned across to see what was laid before them in ink so old the gods must have made it.

'It speaks of Damon,' Arla began. Hyacinth pressed closer, her face solemn in the low light of the lanterns Arla had lit. She could feel Thara there too, waiting, listening through the bond. 'It says he was corrupted by his own greed for magic stronger than his own, but … it wasn't his fault.'

'What do you mean?' Hyacinth asked.

'It wasn't Damon's greed that caused his death. It was a god's.'

Silence stretched between them, an electric thing that had the hairs on the back of her neck standing tall. She cleared her throat before she continued. 'It speaks of the gods, how they worked with the dragons and their harts until … until one god became so hungry for power that he began turning mages against one another.'

Hyacinth had gone utterly still.

'The gods still walked the earth back then, still spoke and lived with the people. That god, in his quest for power, caused a war between mages that nearly wiped out their existence. The dragons and the dragonharts were split between the sides of the war, and it nearly ended the world.'

She was reading quicker now, her eyes jumping over the words and sentences that looped together in handwriting so old she struggled to decipher it.

'The gods eventually defeated him with the aid of the dragons and the magic of the dragonharts, but it left them weak enough that the gods left the earth, leaving only the dragons and their harts behind. The world settled again for hundreds of years until Damon...'

She was shaking, her fingers barely able to turn the pages. Hyacinth hadn't moved an inch, her eyes glued to the book. A lump of ice settled in the pit of her stomach, a warning, maybe, that she wouldn't like what was coming. She had known it the moment she'd picked up the book, the moment she'd seen the dragonhart symbol carved into the leather spine.

'Carry on,' Hyacinth whispered, her voice haunted and shallow. At least the information was new to her, too.

'That fallen god was never killed, only stripped of his power,' Arla explained, her voice hoarse as she scrambled to make sense of it all. 'So when Damon came along and began his life as a dragonhart, so kind and meek, the god saw his chance and corrupted Damon's nature. The greed, the killing of other dragonharts and mages came next, the fallen god acting through Damon's body.'

'It's no wonder it drove him to madness,' Hyacinth said softly, her eyes fixed on a point in the corner of the room, no longer trying to keep pace with Arla's scanning of the text.

'Every now and then, Damon managed to regain control of his mind and understand what he'd done, but he couldn't live with it and killed himself with his own blade. The dragons disappeared not long after that, leaving behind a prophecy from the gods. That one with a heart of flame would unite this world and end the killing of those with magic in their blood.'

The prophecy still elicited the same reaction from her as it always did. Always a flutter in her chest, the overwhelming sense that the world was pressing in on her. And yet the words that followed had her hurling herself into the bathing chamber and heaving into the toilet.

Hyacinth's voice reached her from the bed as the princess muttered the words that had sent Arla vomiting up everything she had consumed that day.

'But not before history will repeat itself.'

∾

The forest floor cut and tore at the bare flesh of her feet as she sprinted through it, her hair loose and streaming behind her, her nightgown tearing on stray branches and thorns. Bile still burned her throat, her eyes sore and streaming as she bolted through the trees, not caring that she was bleeding and couldn't breathe, not caring that she'd left Hyacinth shouting after her as she'd fled the bedroom and its pressing walls.

She had to get out. Had to get out. Had to *get out*.

Because she knew. Had known for a long time now that there was something corrupting her soul. It wasn't that old, familiar slice of wickedness that she had nurtured from the age of nine, it wasn't the violent assassin that lay beneath her skin, ready to be called at a moment's notice. No, because with those things she had always been in control.

As deadly and dangerous and wicked as she was, she had always kept her concentration reserved in that calm, unfeeling place of her mind where she could switch off that violence as quickly as breathing.

But recently...

Those moments where she had descended into violence and bloodshed...

A heaving sob ruptured from her lips as she tripped over a gnarled tree root. Her ankle rolled, but she kept running. Kept fleeing the inevitable because ... because she *knew* that the sharp handwriting in that ancient book was right. History *was* repeating itself. And there was nothing she could do to stop it.

She was snatched from the ground before the next sob spilt through her lips.

And then she was flying.

There wasn't time to scream, and no air to breathe either, because her chest was too tight, and she couldn't stop the heaving panic that had sunk its claws into her when she had understood what would happen: she would become evil and corrupted and make all the wrong choices because of a god who couldn't accept he had been stripped of his status, his privilege and his power.

But through the panic, she looked down, down at the huge claws that had caged her and lifted her from the ground, and she watched the forest bleed into a map of green and brown and grey.

Only then did she manage to get a grip of herself and look up to where Thara soared above her, the underside of her wings such a beautiful shade of olive that Arla had ever seen. She drew a long breath of cool air, finally letting her body fall limp in the dragon's grasp.

'Breathe. Then we shall settle your heart.'

Thara's voice had never sounded so gentle. So ... *motherly*.

Arla didn't attempt to stop the silent tears that spilled down her cheeks as they flew and flew and flew. Only when she could breathe without her chest hitching did Thara finally land on the edge of a cliff sheltered from view of the rest of the queendom. The dragon set Arla down gently, sticking close enough that should Arla fall, Thara would be there to catch her. A shadowy cave opened up before them, a dark hole into which she was all too eager to disappear.

Thara followed her into the mouth of the cave, huffing

gently and sending warm breath over Arla's bare and bleeding skin. It really had been stupid to leave the palace in nothing more than a flimsy nightgown. And she was shaking, every muscle tight and trembling as she made her way deeper into the cave and slumped down to the floor.

For long minutes she hid her face in her hands, knees brought up to her chest – anything to try and hide from the suffocating truth.

Blazing heat and warm light filled the cave, and when Arla lifted her tear-soaked face, she found a fire burning in the centre of the space, wood and torn fabric bundled together to form a fire pit of sorts. She instinctively moved closer, ignoring the throb in the soles of her feet as she shuffled closer to the fire.

Thara rumbled softly, approving, almost.

'Thank you,' Arla murmured, inching as close to the fire as she dared. This fire ... it was hotter, than usual and seemed to burn brighter, seemed to be hypnotising in its collage of colours.

'It is dragonfyre. Don't stare too hard – your human eyes won't bear it.'

Arla tore her eyes away and was surprised to find that she had to blink rapidly before the rest of the cave came back into focus. Thara lurked near her, the dragon's nose close enough to touch.

'Forgive me that I have been unable to share such stories. The way the fates work has long been contested amongst my kind, but their commands are final.'

What was there to say? The one being that could understand her, could feel every emotion, every *thought*, and she was bound not to speak of the things that turned Arla's very world upside down. It ran deeper than betrayal.

'I'll die, then,' she finally choked out. 'I'll die because one of your *gods* is so hungry to rule the world that he will attempt to move through *me*.'

She spat the words, hating the gods and their plans, hating the fates and the prophecies and the sands and stars and everything that had ever plotted against her.

Why her?

'*I had ... suspected, that in those moments where you were not yourself, there was indeed someone moving through you. It is no consolation, Dragonhart, I am sure.*'

'What do you want me to say?' she snapped, flinging her arms out and wincing at the cuts on her skin that stretched with the movement. 'Damon killed himself to stop your god turning him into something evil. The same will happen to me, and there will be no uniting of the kingdoms. You all *failed*, you know! You and the gods and whatever fucking role the fates have!'

She was shouting now, her voice echoing through the chamber as if it would give her strength. She didn't care anyway. She'd shout no matter what.

'You all fucking *failed* to stop whatever god rose above his station. You all claim to be so fucking powerful, and you stopped *nothing*.'

Thara was silent.

And then her voice was there again. Everywhere and nowhere. In Arla's head and in the cave and perhaps throughout the entire kingdom.

'*You believe we have failed you.*'

'Believe?' Arla snarled. 'I *know* you have—'

'*You forget that we have lived for centuries. You don't believe we have learned from our mistakes? Dragonhart, we each vowed not to allow the old wrongs to be repeated. Prophecy or not, we will not allow your mind to fall victim to the fallen one.*'

The fallen one. The god that was going to send her insane and have her kill herself in his pursuit of power.

'How is any of this possible? How is a god *inside me*?'

Thara sighed, heat flooding the cave as the dragon settled beside her.

'He is not inside you, as such. But there is a fragment of him that lives and latches onto any who wields a certain magic. In the war of gods and dragons, we managed to defeat him. But he had been dabbling with dark magic for so long, and magic as an entity ... it does not know how to unexist. A fragment of him – of the darkness he created – has evaded all attempts by the gods to destroy him. He clung to Damon and tried to overtake his mind so that the god might know a body again. He will do the same to you.'

Arla wretched, bile burning the back of her throat.

She wished she could rip off her skin. She wished she could shred her body to ribbons to avoid such a fate.

Her voice was quiet, though, when she managed to form words. 'That's why I've been so angry, isn't it? Why I've not been able to stop myself from being so violent. Only *you* have managed to pull me out of it...'

Thara nudged her elbow and silent tears dripped from the end of Arla's nose at the contact.

'I have seen it happen before. To the one who came before you. The fallen one will send you so far into your emotions that you will lose yourself in them. It is a weakness he has always known how to exploit. It is why I have had to pull you from those fits of emotion. If you wander too far, Dragonhart, you become weak. And when you become weak, he will take control. That's where a shadow of a soul can grow into a god. I will kill you before I let you fall to that.'

The words shouldn't have been so comforting, and yet they were a salve for the fury in her blood. At what was being done to her. To the world.

But the anger was ebbing away, like a tide retreating no matter how desperately she tried to cling to it. Her voice didn't hold the sharpness she wished it did. And she ... she was exhausted.

'And how do you suppose we end this?'

Thara sighed down the bond, inching forward to rest her jaw lightly against Arla's shoulder. The action yanked at something in Arla's chest.

'The fates have not yet revealed that information. I believe the path will become clearer now you are beginning to learn the stories of old. Often it takes the smallest of pulls for a thread to unravel. I don't doubt this path will be similar.'

She didn't think she had the capacity to know any more. For any of it to become any clearer. She still didn't know how she was supposed to unite the kingdoms...

It filled her with incomprehensible fury, the fingers of it latching on and digging beneath the marrow of her bones. Damn the fates for not sharing the path they'd set her on! Arla had thought the secrets Thara had to keep were infuriating, but this ... to keep the fates from the dragon so that Thara could not even guess at what was coming felt entirely cruel. It made her want to burn the world and take the fates out with it.

'Take me back,' Arla said, sniffing, already reaching up for the spikes on Thara's back. 'Please.'

They flew into the night, leaving the flames of the fire roaring like a secret promise in the shrouded safety of the cave.

CHAPTER 37

Hundreds of black-booted feet marched onwards, ice and rock and blood marring the polished leather like an omen of something evil. A wrongness hung in the air, too cloying and heavy as it wafted over everything in sight, corrupting the very earth and turning it grey and rotten with every footfall that passed over it.

Something slithered in her veins, a slimy, wretched thing that called to the darkness spreading over the earth like mould, and she shuddered as that thing within her leaned towards it. Every thought was foggy, like wading through water that was slowly getting deeper, and when there were heartbeats of clarity, she knew she was not entirely herself. There was something other within her, something that had been growing silently. Waiting. Watching. And now with an army of dark, dark magic, the thing in her chest was stirring.

Glittering lights lay in the distance, the mountain borders surrounding the kingdom not enough to halt the leeching darkness as the soldiers bearing Kastonia's crest marched forwards. Arrows rained down upon them, splintering through eyes and chests and torsos.

And not a single man fell.

Blood slid down their bodies, thick and black and oozing – corrupted like everything in sight. She knew then that it was a dark magic, something ancient and forbidden and powerful enough to break and remake worlds.

And it was marching on her kingdom.

She had come here with no body, no sword, and no weapon, nothing other than her consciousness, an awareness that she was witnessing the ushering in of something both new and old at once. There was nothing she could do but scream and beg and curse the fates and the gods forever allowing the creation of something so wrong.

The men didn't pay her one bit of notice. They continued their march, the mass of them spreading out through her mountains, surrounding that sacred kingdom she had only wanted to keep safe.

Something in her heart revolted against the wrongness.

Something in her heart leaned into it, too.

She had no strength here, no way of fighting the threat to her people.

It didn't stop her from trying. She moved through the rows and rows of soldiers as though she were made of mist – a useless thing – but maybe it was better than watching the slaughter about to unfold. Each of them carried heavy swords that no normal man should have been able to lift. But they weren't normal, were they? Because they had been created from something other.

She screamed, she thought, though no one paid her any mind. They were circling the edge of the kingdom now, drawing those long, unstoppable swords ready to storm her home.

She didn't know how she did it, how she managed to get to the front of the army and stand before the soldier who had led them here. There was a wrongness about him, too, a power that oozed off him and stuck in her throat and nose. He would be the one to call this off if only she could convince him. She would have fought him had she been corporeal.

She imagined her fingers reaching towards him, mist as they were, and to her surprise, when she imagined them digging into the armour of his shoulder, he turned to look at her.

Her blood stopped pumping when she saw the face staring back at her was her own.

~

The gasp that ripped Arla from sleep was so violent it made no sound at all.

She had to go. Now.

She stripped the sweat-soaked nightgown from her body, pulling on her leathers as quickly as possible, ignoring the protests of her screaming body as she dragged the material over her cut skin.

She tore through the upper levels of the palace, relying only on instinct and years spent inside royal residencies to guide her to the princess's rooms. The guard stationed outside made no move to stop her as she barrelled through the door, crossing the room in a handful of steps to shake the princess roughly.

Hyacinth woke with swift shock, rearing away from Arla's violent hands as she blinked away the remnants of sleep.

'Arla!'

'We need to leave, now. Flambriar's in trouble.' She began ripping open drawers and dressers, tossing the princess anything that would keep the wind from chilling her skin too dangerously on the way back to Flambriar.

Oh gods...

What if she was too late? What if they were all dead and the kingdom was nothing but ash and rubble and what if, what if, what if—

'*I am here.*'

Thara didn't try to reassure her. Didn't promise they would make it in time. Didn't persuade her it was just a dream.

It was somehow more soothing than if the dragon had tried to assuage her fears.

Hyacinth climbed out of the bed and began dressing, leaving her hair loose around her shoulders as she dragged a cloak around her and clasped it at her throat.

The two women were running before Arla could scrawl a note to the Queen.

'Tell my mother I am safe. I am gone with the Queen of Flambriar,' Hyacinth called back to the guard at the entrance to her rooms, his face frozen in shock as he watched them sprint down the hallway.

Queen of Flambriar.

There would be nothing left of it at all if they didn't hurry.

Thara waited for them, perched on the side of the cliff inside the palace grounds. Arla hauled herself onto the dragon, careful not to stab her with the blades she had strapped to her body so inelegantly that she wondered for half a second if she looked deranged.

Hyacinth faltered then, a frustrated wariness passing across her face as she looked up at the assassin. Arla bit down the nasty retort she wanted to hurl at her friend because she didn't deserve it. Hyacinth had every reason to be nervous, even though Arla was racing against a relentlessly ticking clock to get back to her kingdom.

'You'll be safe, I promise.'

Whether it was the sincerity in Arla's voice or the impatient growl that came from deep within the dragon's belly, Hyacinth reached up a hand to Arla's outstretched one.

There was nothing graceful about the way the princess of Malarye climbed aboard the dragon, and from the way Arla felt Thara tense beneath her she doubted the dragon would tolerate such carelessness again.

'Hold tight,' Arla managed to call out, before Thara beat her wings and they were flying.

Hyacinth threw her arms around Arla's middle, the slightness of the girl already making Arla question her ability to hold onto her for the duration of the journey.

Four days it had taken them to travel here.

'We'll attempt it in one,' Thara said.

It wouldn't be quick enough. If Elrod had truly sent an army to march on her kingdom, they would be too slow to stop it.

History will repeat itself.

Well, the fates certainly had a way of speeding things along.

Hyacinth was silent – was likely in shock, Arla imagined. But she had been brave, and she had not balked when Arla had shaken her awake, demanding their immediate return to Flambriar. She wondered if the princess had ever crossed the borders of Malarye.

'Do you think we'll make it?' She hadn't dared ask the question until they were off the ground and flying over the vast expanse of sea.

'Everything will happen as it is supposed to. I will get us there as quickly as the fates allow.'

Arla fucking *hated* the fates.

The panic was gripping her heart like a vice, the pressure of it threatening to suffocate her. She knew Thara felt her fear because the bond was wide open between them. She could hardly feel the waves of peace Thara tried to send her way. How could she feel anything other than the same dread coursing through Arla's blood? These were Thara's people too, people she had sworn to protect—

'You forget I have fought many a battle, Dragonhart. Nerves are welcome and fear is not an emotion that you can allow to drown you. Remember, you can do anything.'

You can do anything.

The same words her father had said to her when she was little. The same words she had chanted to herself as she crawled through the tunnels beneath Castle Grey to find the dragons all those months ago. Her eyes burned.

'I have to save them...' The words slipped through her lips and were torn away in the wind.

'You will.'

She wondered if it was something the dragon knew or only wanted to believe was true.

Neither made her feel any better.

'I didn't think there would be so much ... space,' Hyacinth announced long after the sun had come up and the sea beneath them had begun to sparkle in its reflections. The princess had stayed silent during the hours of darkness, gripping Arla's middle with enough strength to take down a bear. But after hours of sitting upright and getting used to the way the dragon moved beneath her, Hyacinth had become restless.

It had started with her flexing her fingers and readjusting

the position of her arms around Arla's waist. She had gradually begun to fidget, and Arla had smirked at the ripple of annoyance that came through the bond. It was a testament to how much stronger Arla had got, really. She hadn't felt the urge to move at all yet – a difference so stark from when she had travelled to Malarye the first time – and she couldn't help but feel pleased with the level of fitness aerial training had afforded her. This was the fittest she had been since she was under Cyrus's employ.

'Have you never left Malarye?' Arla called to the princess.

Hyacinth leant in closer so that Arla could feel the princess's breath on the shell of her ear when she spoke.

'Never. My mother kept me close after my father... I was too young to leave before that, anyway.'

Again, curiosity rose in Arla's mind at the mention of the late king. He hadn't been a kind man – she had deduced that, at least. But what harm had he subjected his daughter to? And how had she stayed so soft, so gentle in the face of it?

Thara landed on a small speck of an island long after the stars had dotted the night sky and then disappeared. Arla and the princess slid from her back onto the rocky shore, both women stretching their weary muscles. There was silence as they ate from the meagre provisions Hyacinth had managed to pack into her satchel, and though Arla begged Thara to go and hunt, the dragon declined.

'I spent almost a century asleep, absent of food. This journey will be nothing in comparison.'

'You were asleep then,' Arla shot back through the bond, averting her eyes when Hyacinth looked at her as though she might have done something strange.

'As you should be now.'

Arla sighed as she shuffled closer to where her dragon lay

against the shore. Hyacinth followed, the wariness in her eyes not enough to outweigh the exhaustion there as they huddled against Thara, glad for the shelter she provided against the wind.

The princess fell asleep quickly, and for a while Arla was jealous. If only her mind would allow her the comfort of sleep. Instead, every time she closed her eyes, she pictured Flambriar in flames, her sacred corner of the world reduced to nothing but ash and embers. There was no way they'd make it in time. If what she had seen was true...

She didn't dare think of it.

~

The rest was brief and they were soon back in the sky. Hyacinth gripped Arla's waist, unable to sleep in case she let go.

'When those closest to us are threatened, there is nothing but a longing ache to be with them. Do not seek sleep, Dragonhart. Let it come to you.'

She didn't think it ever would.

'Do you miss your father?' Arla asked out loud, surprised at the strength in her voice when all she felt was a lagging weakness. Arla had met Thara's father once – her first sighting of dragons in Hadalyn. Abredus, the first dragon whom she had ever heard in her mind.

A fleck of emotion pulsed down the bond.

'I have slept beneath the place you call Castle Grey for longer than you could imagine. Leaving my kin behind feels like a constant strain on the bond, always there but manageable with time. I would not change it, if that is what you mean to ask. My place is at your side.'

Arla's throat was tight then, her eyes blurring with the threat of unshed tears.

What had she done to deserve such unwavering loyalty?

'You have shown kindness when this world has demanded you turn hard.'

She wasn't sure which one of them had thought it.

CHAPTER 38
HARK

The soldier standing in front of him looked ready to forego his oath to Flambriar and disappear into the mountains, never to be seen again.

His uniform was ripped, his navy jacket now speckled with grey horse hair as he wiped at a bloodied lip.

This was the fourth man to stand before Hark Stappen this afternoon and recount the events that had happened down in the stables. Six, if you counted the two maids.

'Take the rest of the day off. I'll deal with it,' Hark said with a sigh, dragging a hand through his hair. The soldier bowed curtly before spinning on his booted heel and fleeing the formal sitting room quicker than blinking.

'You can come out, Elin. Those curtains won't hide you forever.'

The speck of a girl slipped out from behind the gauzy curtains, her hair wild, her soft eyes alight with a mischief he had only ever seen in one other person.

A person he missed desperately.

'You know it's wrong to spy on private meetings,' Hark said as he collapsed into a leather armchair.

'It's wrong for them to lie about me. I did nothing wrong.'

Hark couldn't help but snort at the words, so strong, so sure from the girl who was proving to be a real pain in his arse.

'I'd hardly call stealing Arla's horse from the stables and disappearing into the mountains doing nothing wrong, Elin. You know how dangerous it is right now. The soldiers were out looking for you for hours.'

Elin laughed then, a twinkling thing that was so familiar it wrapped a fist around Hark's heart and squeezed.

'They didn't spend hours looking for me,' she said, flopping into the chair opposite him. 'They knew exactly where I was. It was catching me that was the problem.'

Hark chewed the inside of his lip, breathing deeply as he truly looked at Elin for the first time in months. She wasn't as slight as he remembered her. She looked ... strong. Like she had been training. Like she had been wielding a sword.

She looked like Arla Dragonhart.

'Tell me, Elin, how is it you managed to steal Vetta from the stables? Jack tells me she's been extremely temperamental since her owner left the kingdom.'

A smile twisted Elin's pink lips, her eyes widening with ... pride, Hark thought.

'Vetta likes me. She always has. I want to be like Arla and Vetta knows that.'

Gods he really didn't think he could cope with *two* of them.

'Elin, this can't continue. It is *dangerous* now. You could have been killed—'

Hark's words were cut off by Kase barrelling through the doors to the sitting room, her chest heaving with the strain of running.

Hark's stomach dropped. He couldn't cope with another attack. There had been too many. Too much fear, too. He didn't think his soldiers would want to keep fighting an unkillable army.

'Where?' he asked softly, already finding his hand straying to the sword at his hip.

'No,' Kase panted, resting a hand against the door frame. 'Dragon.'

He didn't think as he slammed through the glass doors onto the balcony.

CHAPTER 39

Flambriar was an orange smear on the horizon as Thara finally flew over the mountains separating the kingdom from the sea.

Arla's heart had tripped over and over in her chest at first, her teeth clenched tightly together as they flew ever closer. But her kingdom was not awash in flame, only bathed in the raw colours of sunset.

There was no army raining terror upon her people; there were no arrows or horses or fires scattered through the city. Just Flambriar, steady and solid in the valley she had come to call home.

She exhaled, the panic and fear of what she had dreamt dissipating as they drew nearer to the city. Hyacinth was quiet behind her, and when Arla turned her head to look at the princess, she smothered a smile at the wonder in the girl's eyes.

Flambriar truly was a beautiful place from up here. A landscape of carefully constructed houses of stone and wood, a long winding river with stone bridges arching over it, a remarkable hall with enormous glass windows and chandeliers that reflected the sun, and then there were the people standing on one of the many balconies that wrapped around the hall, the surprise on their faces visible even at this distance.

'Do you know them?' Hyacinth asked cautiously.

Arla didn't stop the grin from splitting her lips then.

'Yes. I know them.'

⁓

Thara landed heavily on the stone balcony, the entire mountain seeming to shudder beneath her talons.

Arla didn't care.

She flung herself off her dragon, ignoring the sharp burst of pain that came from her ankle as she ran towards the one person that had stolen half of her heart.

Hark crushed her to his chest, arms wrapping around her and holding her close, as though she were a treasure too precious to ever let go. She didn't try and stop the tears then, and they dripped silently down her cheeks as Hark held her shaking body upright.

She had missed him more than she ever thought possible. And that aching longing in her chest combined with the dream she'd had...

She hadn't expected him to still be breathing.

'I've missed you,' she squeaked, her voice stolen by the padded leather armour he wore over his chest.

Armour...? What had—

'I missed you too, Dragonhart.'

He tipped her face up to his, his lips a gentle caress against her own, sore where she'd practically chewed through them on her way here.

'It's good to see you, Arla.' She whirled to find Jaz standing in the doorway, his face grim and reflecting none of the gladness she thought he might feel at her return.

If something had happened whilst she was gone...

'I thought I heard someone halting the entire kingdom for the small act of their arrival.'

Sebastian sauntered through the door, a lopsided smirk aimed right at her. She was free of Hark and bounding towards him immediately.

Seb caught her and held her tight, a low laugh rumbling through his chest as Arla held onto her friend tightly.

'Miss me?'

She shoved him back, her own laughter spilling over her lips.

'Never.'

'That's my girl.'

Her eyes filled with useless tears again. This ... this was what she'd come home for. Her family.

Elin was peering at her from the doorway, wide-eyed and wild.

'Hello, Elin.'

The girl smiled before moving to stand beside Seb, her uncle tugging her closer to him. Something was definitely off...

'As much as your arrival deserves a celebration, Dragonhart, we weren't expecting guests.'

Kase's voice cut through the homecoming, her blue eyes piercing Arla from across the balcony. Arla might have thought the girl wanted her dead, had the relief at Arla's return not been written so plainly on Kase's face.

But no one was watching Arla or Kase. Their eyes were fixed on the Princess of Malarye struggling to dismount from the dragon currently occupying the majority of the balcony.

'This,' Arla began, moving to aid Hyacinth in her dismount

before the waves of irritation rolling through the bond led to violence, 'is Hyacinth, Princess of Malarye.'

There was a pulse of silence before Jaz spoke. 'And do tell us why you have betrayed the secrecy of Flambriar's location to a foreign princess, Reinhart.'

Thara growled. It was a warning. The disrespect Jaz hurled Arla's way had been warranted once, but she had discarded her old name in favour of the new, and she expected that choice to be respected. That Jaz should use it now spoke loudly of his displeasure.

'Betrayed?' she said softly, that violent spark waking up in the centre of her chest. 'You think I would betray this kingdom and these people? Think very carefully, Jaz. You forget I am bonded with a dragon.'

'I have always enjoyed your violence,' Thara purred in Arla's mind. *'Perhaps a demonstration?'*

Tempting. Truly.

But before Arla could make him regret his accusations, Hyacinth cleared her throat and stepped forwards.

'I am here because of a deal made between my mother, Queen Mara of Malarye and Queen Arla of Flambriar. It worries me that you think the location of your kingdom is a secret. We have known of its location for months.'

The princess was beautiful in this light. The sunset glowed around her like a personal halo. Arla was almost certain Sebastian had fallen in love just by looking at the woman.

Jaz, however, was silent as Hyacinth continued. 'I'm here as part of a bargain of alliance. Malarye will not march *with* yours, but neither will it march *on* yours, when the inevitable war with Kastonia begins—'

'How dare y—!' Hark stepped towards the princess, an unfamiliar malice in his eyes that Arla had never seen before. But to protect the kingdom he had built ... she knew he'd be entirely capable of wicked things.

She pulled him back before he could touch Hyacinth. Or wring her neck.

'I am here to see your kingdom. Nothing else. The court in Malarye is filled with people who believe I am not strong enough to rule. They'd sooner see me dead than ascend the throne. I am here to learn strength. To learn how to stand before men and make them kneel. There is no better place to learn that than at the side of Arla Dragonhart. In return, there is peace between our kingdoms and your dragonhart has been granted access to our most ancient and sacred texts.'

Arla watched the strength grow in the princess. It was as if leaving Malarye had given her the space to breathe. To feel. To know she was strong in her own way. Despite the unimpressed looks her own court was giving her, Arla couldn't help but smile.

'Don't tell me you made a deal that gets us ... what? A promise not to attack us?' Seb said, incredulous.

But Arla was ready to snap, ready to tear them all to pieces and tell them that they *hadn't been there* and that it was in everyone's best interest that they make an ally out of Malarye.

But then she looked closer at Seb and saw the twinkle in his eyes. The amusement that danced there as he glanced at a scowling Jaz. Kase was smirking too, no matter that she tried to hide it.

Jaz opened his mouth, likely to condemn her or tell her how stupid she'd been.

Hark cut him off before a single sound could be uttered.

'She has full authority to make decisions on behalf of this kingdom. You question her, you question the gods, Jaz.'

She fucking loved Hark Stappen.

Jaz blinked slowly, the frown melting off his face as though it had never been there at all.

'Forgive me, Dragonhart. I mean no offence. You won't forget I was just as cautious when you first arrived here.'

Didn't she know it. Kase had threatened to fight Jaz when he objected to Arla's arrival in Flambriar that night she'd finally woken from her injuries.

She wouldn't allow them all to descend into infighting now, though. Not when the relief that Flambriar was still standing was still flooding her veins.

'Why are you back so soon? Without a letter to warn us, too?' Kase asked. She looked bone-tired. Like she'd been up every night for months. Arla wondered if Jack ... if his injury had worsened since she'd left. He wasn't on the balcony with them either...

'He's fine,' Hark said soothingly, as if her thoughts were his own and he could see the question burning on her tongue as her eyes scanned the balcony. 'He's been with the healer this afternoon. He'll sleep a while yet.'

Arla was certain she heard Kase take a shaky breath.

'Are you going to keep us waiting all night, Dragonhart?' Seb chuckled. 'Not that I'm not glad you're here, but why?'

What could she say? That she'd had a dream so real it had sent her into a blind panic? That she'd expected to arrive here and find their bodies strewn across the kingdom? That there were soldiers in her dream that wouldn't fall no matter how many arrows were fired at them?

She cleared her throat.

'It's complicated. But some of us have flown for days and could quite literally kill someone for a glass of wine, don't you agree, Hyacinth?'

The princess laughed lightly, that meagre strength she had

bolstered slithering inside her again. It would come. Arla would make sure of it.

Seb was striding towards her again, and before she could protest, he crushed her to his chest, planting a kiss on the top of her head that made her eyes water with gratitude for the family she had found.

'Gods, I've missed you,' he said, laughing into her hair.

Something had happened. She was sure of it.

'What's been going on?'

There was a beat of silence, and then Hark replied, 'It's complicated.'

She didn't have it in her to laugh.

'Oh, enough of this,' Kase interjected, ushering them towards the doors and, hopefully, something alcoholic. 'We should be celebrating your return, not sulking.'

They all laughed then, the tension dissolving like a popped balloon.

She watched Hyacinth be swept away by Seb, watched Hark take Jaz to one side, and, she imagined, call him out for speaking to her that way. Kase hooked an arm around Arla, leading her through the glass doors into the familiar comfort of Claret Hall.

'Flambriar's queen, eh?' Kase chuckled, guiding them to the drinks cabinet across the room.

Arla snorted, elbowing the girl lightly.

'Oh shut up.'

CHAPTER 40

There was something to be said for trying to celebrate when her bones were aching with the strain of making a four-day journey in less than two, especially with the darkness of her dream still lingering in her mind.

Arla was too exhausted to enjoy any of the food and wine and they had all ended up in the sitting room almost immediately after the dishes were cleared away, the fire crackling gently beneath the mantlepiece as they chatted amongst themselves.

Jack had joined them during dinner, his face tight with pain. But he buried it somewhere deep and greeted Arla with a warm smile and a hug that had her swallowing around the lump in her throat.

He was walking straighter, less of his weight depending on the cane as he manoeuvred around the table to sit beside Kase. Arla was certain it was the most relaxed Kase had looked in hours when Jack took her hand and whispered something in her ear.

This was the comfort of Flambriar. Of home. Of her court. Each of them splayed over settees around the fire, chatter punctuating the air, a card game rendering Jaz, Hark, and Seb incapable of using inside voices. Hyacinth sat beside Kase and Jack, a steady, polite smile on her face as the two of them quizzed her on how her kingdom functioned and on her reasons for coming to Flambriar.

It was the most content Arla had been in years.

'I am pleased all is well, Dragonhart.'

Arla's chest swelled at the sound of her dragon. Thara had flown so hard and so fast and Arla was grateful.

'Me too.'

The settee shifted beside Arla, and she managed to pull her attention away from the increasingly intense card game to meet the gaze of Elin. The girl had looked half feral when Arla had first arrived, and though her hair had been brushed and she was out of the muddied clothes she'd been in earlier, there was still a fire in her eyes that reminded Arla of herself.

'I hope you've been keeping my horse company whilst I've been gone.'

Something flashed across Elin's face – an emotion Arla couldn't quite place – before she said, 'Whatever they tell you I did, they're lying. Vetta likes me.'

Arla's heart eased slightly at that. Perhaps the strange atmosphere she'd come home to hadn't been something sinister. Perhaps it had just been the misdeeds of a young girl. The gods knew Arla herself had managed to bring the likes of Castle Grey to a standstill when she was thirteen.

'I'm sure you're right. They don't like some of the things I do, either,' Arla said, winking at Elin, whose face split into a grin. Hark joined her a second later.

'I hope you've confessed to Arla how you've terrorised the entire kingdom in her absence?'

Arla was ready to leap to the girl's defence. To argue that

Elin shouldn't have to be placed in a box and taught to be behave just because she was a young girl.

As it happened, she didn't need to, because Hark ruffled the top of Elin's hair and offered a genuine smile. 'You've brought some light to recent weeks, at least.'

Arla's stomach dropped. Something had *definitely* happened whilst she had been away.

'You look ready to fall asleep, sweetheart,' Hark said softly, taking Arla's hand in his.

Arla didn't think her heart could swell any more. Didn't think she had ever experienced this sort of love. It made her stomach twist, her heart flutter, and her throat tighten around all the feelings she would never do justice in describing. She loved him. Desperately.

'Then perhaps we should go to bed,' she said.

Hark exhaled, the dimple in his cheek appearing as he smirked at her. 'I thought you'd never ask.'

There was a quiet luxury to Arla's rooms – the glass ceiling, the stars, the bed large enough to get lost in.

Not that any of it mattered because Hark marched her straight past the doors to her rooms and onwards to his own.

How she had missed this place! Where Arla's own rooms had made her feel freer than she had ever felt in her life, Hark's cocooned her and made her feel safe and secure and hidden. Heavy velvet curtains so dark blue they were almost black were pulled back from the arching windows that spanned the length of the room, the soft glow of lamplight dismissing any lingering tension that she had felt on her flight home. The stone floor was covered with a rug so intricately woven Arla was certain only a mage could have managed it, and the bed was somehow larger than her own. And far too inviting.

Hark removed his hand from the small of her back – the gesture had been so soft and lovely Arla had wondered how they had ever hated each other – and moved across the room to draw the curtains across the windows.

'Leave them,' she said. 'I like to see the stars.'

Hark turned to face her, a wicked grin splitting his lips. 'I hope stars are the last thing on your mind tonight. I've missed the feel of your skin, Dragonhart.'

Her skin flushed at his words. At the promise in them.

'And how much have you missed me?' she taunted, stalking towards him on silent feet. The very air seemed to still between them, her nerves winding tighter with every second.

She didn't stop until she was close enough that her chest brushed his, until she could see the desire and delight in those icy blue eyes.

His lips parted and his hands came to rest on her hips, the feel of his fingertips through her uniform burning phantom flames against her flesh.

'Enough that you won't ever want to leave again.'

There was a heartbeat of tension before whatever was between them snapped, and their lips were crashing together, a million tiny fires setting light along Arla's skin as Hark pressed her against the wall, his hands roaming her hips and thighs as if he would never have the pleasure of doing so again.

She felt him tense a fraction of a second before he pulled back, and something in her pathetic heart stuttered at that.

But Hark wasn't rejecting her. No. His hands were too soft on either side of her face, his forehead now resting against hers as his icy blue eyes tunnelled into hers.

'Are you okay?' he asked softly, his thumb stroking along her cheek.

Arla leaned into the touch, glad to be cocooned in the scent of whiskey and leather and *Hark*.

'I'm fine,' she whispered softly, searching the endless depth of his gaze for something that should indicate she shouldn't be all right at all.

Hark smiled and it made her want to crawl right between his ribs and settle against his heart.

'You would tell me if you needed anything? From me, or from this kingdom?'

'Of course,' she replied, confusion beginning to seep into the edges of her mind, but ... she had longed for this. For many years all she had wished for was someone to ask her if she was okay. If she was struggling in her journey along the dark path she'd been sent on by the fates. And in that simple question – in Hark's ability to see she *needed* someone – she knew that she would never have to walk that path alone ever again. He would always be at her side, ready to take on anything that came for her, just as she would for him.

'I love you,' he said, placing a gentle kiss on her forehead. 'And I want you to be happy here. So anything you need, Arla, it's yours.'

Gods why was her throat so tight?

She summoned a smile to her lips.

'Anything?'

Mischief shone in Hark's eyes, that infuriating smirk she'd known for years beginning to fan out across his face as he purred, 'Anything.'

Before she had a chance to catch her breath, he was lifting her, her legs wrapping around his waist as he carried her to the bed and laid her gently on it. His face hovered inches above hers, the dimple in his cheek bringing a smile to her own lips.

'Perfect,' he murmured, pressing kisses along her neck, collarbone, and shoulder. Her shirt decidedly looser than it was only moments ago. Arla brought her own hands up, one on the back of his neck, the other tangled in the tousled strands of dark hair. She was certain he hadn't cut it in all the time she'd been gone.

He kissed her harder then, a clash of lips and teeth as hands flew and clothes were removed, soft sighs the only sounds in the sanctuary of Hark's room. His hands traced her skin, down her chest, over her stomach, hips, and thighs, never quite where she needed them but electric all the same.

Arla arched her back beneath him, anything to be closer, to feel the sensual assault that came from his skin against hers. Logical thought fled when his fingers found the apex of her thighs, the gasp wrenched from her throat eliciting a rough laugh from his. Perhaps she should have asked what had happened in Flambriar during the time she'd been gone, but honestly, that could wait. Who really cared as long as he was kissing her? Touching her?

'Did you miss me, Dragonhart?' Hark purred in her ear, the sound of his voice drawing ragged breaths from her.

'Yes,' she managed, rocking her hips against him as his fingers moved in masterful precision.

He lifted his head, pinning her with those gods-damned eyes, his gaze burying beneath her skin.

'Show me, then.'

~

Afterwards, when her bones felt soft and her heart full, they lay in darkness, the glowing embers of the fire hypnotic as they lulled her to sleep. Her head lay against Hark's chest, the rhythmic drum of his heartbeat the most reassuring sound in the world. His fingers traced her hipbone idly, and her own ran up and down the length of his arm.

Arla was certain she knew every inch of Hark's body so when her fingers traced a knot of ridged, scarred flesh on the back of his shoulder, she knew with certainty that she'd been right to worry.

She paused her perusal of his skin, sitting upright and flicking the lamp on beside her. Hark tried to move, as if he could prevent the inevitable, the alarm on his face illuminated in the lamplight.

'What—?'

'I wasn't keeping it from you,' he interrupted, reaching out to rest a hand on her shoulder as though it might keep her from attacking him. That ugly, angry thing in her chest was rearing its head again...

'Do not harm him. Regret is a tedious emotion.' Thara's voice in her head did nothing to assuage the annoyance in her blood.

'Tell me. What. Happened?' she growled through her teeth, relishing the wariness that passed through Hark's eyes.

A frustrated noise forced its way through Hark's lips, and for a moment, Arla didn't think he'd speak. She thought he might keep this secret from her after all they'd been through together.

He must have seen the unspoken threat in her eyes because his face softened, the rigidity of his body that had arisen when she'd ran her fingers over the scar melting away.

'There's been ... a problem.'

'What do you mean, *a problem*?' she snapped, rocking forwards in the bed.

'If you'd let me finish,' he barked, the voice of Flambriar's ruler shining through. Arla sat back against the headboard.

'Soldiers have been appearing in the mountains – Elrod's soldiers. We've been killing them before they can get to the city but...'

She knew what was coming before the words arrived. She'd seen it in a dream that had led her to flee Malarye in the middle of the night.

'They don't die. They have the strength of five men. It takes the removal of their heads for them to stay down.'

A shudder ran along Arla's spine, the same dread reflected at her down the bond. Thara, however, was silent.

'It's why I'm back,' Arla whispered, hating the fear that flickered in Hark's icy eyes. 'I dreamt of them. I thought I might find you all—' She swallowed around the lump in her throat and willed away the unshed tears. 'I thought I might find you all dead.'

The tension between them shattered then as Hark pulled her close to him, the solid steadiness of his body a reprieve against an army they could not comprehend. There were things at work here she couldn't hope to conquer, and, judging by her dragon's silence, Thara couldn't either.

They needed an army – greater than the one they were hastily trying to build.

'We'll discuss it tomorrow,' Hark said gently, brushing a blonde curl away from her face. 'Let's not ruin tonight.'

'Okay,' she whispered, already aware of the dreams on the edge of her consciousness that would plague her all night.

They needed an army. And she knew where she might find one.

CHAPTER 41

Flambriar slept as Arla saddled her horse and made her way down the mountain.

The city had grown in her absence. Small cottages made of wood and stone had been constructed by the river, half-built shops squatted around the market square, and what looked to be a new restaurant with blue window frames had cropped up opposite a temple to honour the gods.

All of it sparkled with the remnants of the magic used to build it, like static in the air that Arla had come to associate with the mages. She ran her fingers over the dragonhart brooch on her cloak, finding the quiet sentience of the symbol a balm to the apprehension of what she was about to do.

She had snuck out of Hark's embrace sometime during the night, hastily winding her way through the lower levels of Claret Hall to Noah's office, where she resisted the urge to leaf through the stacks of parchment and letters and instead scrawled a quick note and instructed one of the women working there to send it with a falcon.

Arla had returned to Hark's bed to find him still sleeping,

and, before dawn had fully broken, she was woken by the gentle tapping of a beak against the window.

When she took the scroll tied to the bird's leg and read the two words written in loopy handwriting, she'd wasted no time lacing her boots and sneaking out of Hark's rooms once again.

Hartswood. Sunrise.

Hartswood.

So the place had a name.

'You have felt the draw of magic from those trees, have you not? I told you once it was a sacred place. After whom else should the wood be named if not those it was made to honour?'

Thara was a dark shadow above Arla as she made her way towards the forest, her dragon disappearing in and out of the clouds as if she were part of some game only she was aware of.

'Is she alone?' Arla replied in her head, stomaching the apprehension that grew the closer Vetta carried her to the meeting place.

Thara grumbled softly through the bond. *'For now.'*

Arla hadn't been sure Sylvie would come. Wasn't sure if she'd even acknowledge the letter Arla had sent the Red Blade in the night.

But as Vetta picked her way through the trees to a clearing that smelled of pine needles and earth, a head of auburn hair was clear in the muted light of the Hartswood.

'I wondered how long it would take you to summon me,' the young woman said. 'Your arrival back here spread quickly through our ranks.'

There was a hostility to Sylvie's voice that set Arla's teeth on edge. The strip of red silk tied at her waist was so like the colour of blood that Arla had to blink to be certain of what she was seeing.

'I'll cut to the chase,' Arla began, already twirling a small blade in her hand as she dismounted, her feet making a dull thud against the forest floor. She was sure the trees hummed in response. 'What do you know of the soldiers that have been attacking Flambriar?'

A knowing smirk twisted its way onto Sylvie's face, her cheekbones sharper than before Arla had left. Her eyes were more sunken, too, but the Red Blade's voice was clear when she spoke.

'I know that you'll never beat them. Dark magic is at play, Dragonhart, and not even my mages can hope to fight it.'

Thara growled low and long down the bond, the sound deafening as Arla accepted what she already knew to be true. Indeed, there was dark magic at play, no doubt stemming from Elrod's use of mage blood.

Arla cleared her throat, squaring her shoulders against the news she neither wanted nor knew how to deal with.

'You spoke of wanting freedom for the mages, of being opposed to slavery, and yet you refer to them as *yours*. That's not freedom, Sylvie. It's just another sort of prison.'

'It is *not!*' Sylvie spat, stamping her foot like a petulant child. 'Every single mage in the Red Blades fights against what Elrod did to them. We *will* kill him – and your king too, Arla *Reinhart*. He was complicit in Elrod's schemes too, was he not?'

Cyrus had betrayed nine years of Arla's trust. That betrayal ran so deep she wondered if she would always be trying to outrun it. She'd looked at him like a father, and he had lied to her. He had gone against the treaties, aiding and abetting Elrod in the persecution of mages, in the trading of slaves. That stung like a thousand tiny wasps and yet ... the thought of him being killed filled her with a strange reluctance.

'Is it not enough?' she asked softly. 'Don't you think these people have been through enough without asking them to march on two kings? It is suicide, Sylvie. I won't let you drag Flambriar's people into it.'

A huffed laugh burst from Sylvie. 'You preach freedom, you preach the value having choice, and yet you keep Flambriar's mages so shielded and locked in that you won't risk letting me speak to them. You won't risk the chance that some of them feel as strongly as we do and want to seek revenge on the kings who ruined their lives. Is that not a kind of prison, too?'

'I grow tired of her nonsensical spouting. Kill her and be done with it.'

'Believe me, I'm close.'

'I won't risk these people being sent to their deaths when they have only just been given the chance to live. You will leave my people alone.'

Sylvie laughed again, and this time Arla felt her control slipping away. She was a hypocrite. Sylvie knew it, too. Arla had been so angry that Mara would not lend her Malarye's army in the case of an attack – had been so angry that Mara wanted to keep her people safe and free from war. And yet here Arla was, repeating the same words back to Sylvie that Mara had spoken to Arla. She wouldn't let Flambriar's people march on two kings. She'd been born to protect them, she couldn't ask them to march on two kingdoms ... could she?

'I know why you called me here, Arla. You want my army to fight against those soldiers Elrod sends your way. You think we will protect Flambriar out of the goodness of our hearts. Well, you have that wrong.' The Red Blade's voice settled into something soft and deadly. 'We have no goodness in our hearts. That was beaten out of us by those who wronged us. If you want our help, then you must let me address your people. Give them the choice, Arla. Give them the freedom to choose revenge. You can agree to that, surely? Your kingdom will fall without the numbers needed to kill those who march against it. Don't be stupid enough to deny me, we're on the same side.'

We're on the same side.

They were, weren't they? Only that Arla had come to understand the importance of peace – of keeping her people safe. She'd ask Sylvie's army to come to her aid, but she would not offer hers in return. Selfish. She'd always been so *selfish*.

'You are valuing defending Flambriar over actively attacking two kingdoms. That is not selfish, Dragonhart.' Thara's words settled into Arla's blood and she swallowed thickly.

'But what if Kastonia do come for us? We **will** *need the Red Blades' numbers. The only way we're going to get their help is if I offer Flambriar's army in return.'*

The last kernel of control slipped away from Arla like a feather in the breeze. Sylvie had her right where she wanted her. Flambriar needed Sylvie's help, needed her army of mages to defend their borders. But to risk Flambriar's people deciding they wanted revenge on Elrod ... something violent lurched in her chest at the thought. Her blood screamed at the thought of *any* of her people being in danger. What could she do?

'We don't negotiate with those who try to back us into a corner, Dragonhart. Tell her I will burn her bones to ash for threatening you. We don't need her army. You have a dragon.'

'But what if it's not enough? If they harm you, Thara—'

'I won't allow it.'

It was confidence and bravery, but no one could predict the outcome – or the collateral damage of such a battle.

Perhaps ... perhaps she needed to speak with Hark. Speak

with her court. Maybe the threat of Elrod's soldiers was not as great as her dream suggested. Maybe they didn't need to upend Flambriar and its people and inject fear into a kingdom that had only just begun to know peace.

'I will put it to my court. I may be a dragonhart, but Flambriar is not my kingdom to rule.'

'Isn't it?'

Sylvie looked at her for longer than was comfortable, and it seemed to Arla that a silent decision passed behind the Red Blade's eyes.

Eventually the woman spoke, her voice lined with irritation.

'I will speak to our leader, too. I'm sure he'll be intrigued to know you're at least considering our offer now.'

Arla didn't ask who their leader was. She wouldn't give Sylvie the satisfaction of her curiosity.

'You will leave my people alone until a decision is made. Or you will find my blade at your throat.'

The threat seemed to delight Sylvie, her green eyes sparkling in the dawn light.

'I'll look forward to it.'

~

'Kill her. Our people will not march to their deaths.'

Thara hadn't stopped announcing her dislike for Sylvie for the entire ride back to Claret Hall nor for the twelve sprinted laps of the grounds Arla had forced herself through on her return.

'I don't want them to die, either,' Arla protested, marching through the hallways after she'd completed her run. *'But I won't let the kingdom be invaded because we didn't accept the aid of the Red Blades' army.'*

'Then why have you not told the boy?'

She'd been pondering the same thing. Why *had* she kept it from Hark and their friends? She knew the answer, deep down, but she couldn't admit it to herself because it was selfish. Just like she'd always been.

Maybe she deserved whatever punishment she received when they all inevitably found out that she'd been meeting with strange girls in the forest that threatened her and threatened her people—

'Arla, there you are,' a soft voice called from the open doorway to the sitting room. Arla turned to find Hyacinth, her silk dresses discarded in favour of trousers and a tunic Arla was certain she'd seen Sebastian wear before. 'We've been waiting for you.'

She'd expected there would be a debrief at some stage – had been hoping for one, actually. She followed Hyacinth into the sitting room, biting her lip to stop the smile escaping when her eyes landed on the chaos of the place. There were books and clothes and glasses and a hundred other objects strewn about the room, all of it so thoroughly lived-in that Arla felt some of her earlier tension slide away. She'd missed this. Missed the people, too.

She took the only space available to her: Hark Stappen's lap.

'You smell of dragon,' he murmured into her neck, sending shivers down her spine. She shifted on his lap, dragging a deep breath from him that made her smirk.

'You smell of me,' she said, fighting the swoop in her stomach as she thought of the things they'd done last night. The feel of him against her, inside her—

'Gods fucking spare us,' Kase muttered, tossing a cushion at them. Arla snatched it out of the air without thinking. 'Do you think you two could go for five minutes without making the rest of us want to be sick?'

'And here I was thinking you'd missed me,' Arla shot back as Hark pulled her close against his chest. Gods, she couldn't wait to get out of here and repeat exactly what they'd—

'I think it's best we share all that we know, so we're all on the same page?' Jaz's voice cut through the room like an arrow, and all too quickly solemnity settled on them like lead. It was easy to forget that they'd essentially instigated a war with Kastonia – and possibly Hadalyn, too – by freeing all of the mages Elrod had captured. It was easy to forget that they were being attacked by soldiers that wouldn't die and that the kingdoms were wasting away in sickness and poverty, and she was still somehow supposed to unite it all. It was easy to forget it, hidden away in this frozen valley.

But Jaz was right. They did all need to be on the same page.

And so she told them everything that had happened in Malarye. She told them what she'd learned about Damon and the corruption of an old god and how history was going to repeat itself. And yet she couldn't bring herself to tell them that a resistance group was spying on the kingdom – and that she'd known it for months, too. It had been fear that had stopped her telling them all at first. Fear that everything would change and war would be coming, and she hadn't wanted to deal with any of that. Didn't want to deal with the way she knew it would break her. But then ... well then it was too late to say anything at all. She'd been stupid and selfish, and too much time had passed where she'd kept a secret to protect her own heart. To tell them now ... they'd hate her. Say she didn't trust them as they had blindly trusted her. She didn't want to risk her own mages, but she was willing to risk Sylvie's – and that was pure selfishness. Arla didn't want to look at the expressions on her friends' faces when she told them that. And so she didn't.

Instead, she listened. Listened to how her court – her *friends* – had been fighting waves of a dark army that didn't die. They told her of Damon's sword, too, and that they hoped to prevent disaster by finding it.

If they could find it.

And when everything was laid bare, the severity of it buried beneath her skin and into her blood. Whatever was coming would not be easy. She needed to figure out how to stop it, because one thing was certain: fate didn't deal in coincidences. Her friends had vowed to help her, but the prophecy had spoken of the last dragonhart – of Arla herself. If this was going to end, it was going to have to be *her* who stopped it.

Jack held Kase's hand tightly in his own, Hyacinth and Sebastian were silent, and Hark had gone still behind her. They weren't the ones who frightened her though. It was Jaz. Jaz, who was looking at her like he understood. Like he knew that this came down to her and that whatever was ahead of them was going to try and kill her. Who was she when pitted against the fates, anyway?

CHAPTER 42

Arla knew two things.

Firstly, the library at Claret Hall needed expanding if the piles of books stacked up to waist height around Jaz's desk meant anything. Secondly, and perhaps more importantly, he was keeping something from her.

It had taken all of ten minutes for her to abandon giving Hyacinth a tour of Claret Hall and pass her into the capable hands of Sebastian, who had been all too eager to help. She made a beeline for the library and found Jaz with his head in a book.

'Wondered how long it'd take you,' he said without looking up as she strode across the room.

Arla pulled a chair out opposite him, collapsing into it like the weight of the world was pressing her down. Perhaps it was.

'Tell me.'

Jaz huffed a laugh, a slight glimmer of amusement in his eyes as he sat back in his chair and looked at her. He was silent for a few moments, twisting the gold rings on his fingers as, she imagined, he weighed up whether she was worthy of knowing anything at all.

'What do you know of Damon, Dragonhart?' His voice was low. Deep. Knowing.

Thara was unnaturally quiet on the bond. She was listening. Waiting.

'That the disgraced god acted through him. That he was hungry for power. That he killed himself after causing a war between gods.'

Jaz listened, his gaze on his hands and those gods-damned rings he fiddled with. 'Very good. And what do you know of the magic Damon wielded?'

There was a pulse of *something* from Thara.

'Admittedly not much,' Arla said, bringing her legs up to rest her feet on the table and earning a scalding glance from Jaz. Here, in the library, away from everybody else, he didn't look at her with his usual distrust. This was something deeper. Not distrust but resignation. As if he knew that, ultimately, it all came down to her.

'Damon drew magic from the mages in unnatural ways – forbidden ways. I thought Elrod might not be aware of the method until—'

Understanding dawned on her like a flame catching light. 'Until the unkillable soldiers began attacking Flambriar.'

He nodded slowly, his eyes wide and his gaze fixed on his hands, a grim line making up the structure of his mouth.

'If Elrod has created these soldiers, he's done so using methods not seen since Damon was corrupted. It's dangerous stuff, Arla, forbidden stuff. If he's able to create an army from it, you have no hope of stopping him so long as he has mage blood.'

He had stores and stores of it. She'd seen it, that locked door in Larkire Palace behind which she'd believed were housing the most priceless of jewels.

'He has blood, but exactly how much, I'm not sure. He was taking the mages for maybe four years... How much blood is needed to create an army?'

Jaz frowned, the action igniting a churning feeling in Arla's stomach. 'A lot. If he's replacing the soldiers we cut down, then his supplies will be dwindling.'

That was something, at least.

'Why doesn't he just send the entire army here? Why only a handful at a time?'

Jaz glanced up at her again.

'I don't believe he knows where Flambriar is. I believe these are scouting groups tasked with finding our location and reporting back. We're lucky we're finding and killing them before they can return to Larkire to give our location away, but how can we be certain we've caught them all? Elrod wouldn't send an army out into the cold hostility of these mountains unless he was sure we're here. We have some time, but not much.'

A sinking feeling flowed through Arla's body and still Thara stayed deadly silent on the bond.

'This has gone so far beyond what we thought when Cyrus sent me to the border,' she said quietly, remembering the day he'd told her she would be locating missing supplies. 'The kingdoms were falling because the gods were unhappy with the way Elrod was treating the mages. They're going to continue falling until we stop him, aren't they?'

Resignation lined the soft angles of Jaz's face when he finally met her gaze and held it.

'I'm afraid so. But it's *you* who has to stop it. The fates chose *you*.'

Arla closed her eyes. 'But how?'

'That brooch you wear on your cloak. You haven't taken it off since you were given it. Why?'

It was true. Since a stranger had given Arla that brooch in Vorstrum she had kept it on her, always pinned to her cloak or shirt or tucked away in the pocket of her trousers. Once upon a time, she had hated the sight of the dragonhart symbol. Had believed it all to be nonsense – a resurgence of the old gods and religions she had never believed in.

But there was a sentience in the brooch, she was sure of it. It brought her comfort. She needed only run her fingers across the gold and a semblance of peace would come over her.

And...

'Yes?' Jaz urged.

'I ... I think it saved my life. Twice.'

She didn't *think* anything. She knew it.

'Go on.'

Thara was still disturbingly silent on the bond.

'Back at Larkire, the day I got stabbed, Hark and I were overwhelmed on the battlements. There was no way we could have survived taking on so many soldiers and yet ... something happened when I touched the brooch. It was like a surge of power through my blood, and everyone threatening us dropped dead.'

It had felt like much more than a surge of power. It had felt like the making and breaking of worlds in her blood. As if the stars would bend to her will if she asked them to. It was a pure and ancient power.

'And the second time?' Jaz asked, now scrawling away on a piece of parchment.

'The second time, the priest soldiers of Malarye were trying to kill me.'

Thara grumbled then, and Arla was just glad to feel her presence.

'They were firing arrows, and they hit Thara, and all I could think was that we were going to die ... and then I touched the brooch, and the same thing happened again, only this time a wave rose from the sea and protected us.'

'Interesting,' Jaz affirmed, laying down his quill. 'Do you know what they used to say about the dragonhart symbol, Arla?'

She shook her head.

'They say it helped you communicate with the dragons.'

She *had* heard that. Memories of a campfire and a cold night sleeping on a forest floor by the bloodstone close to the northern border. Hark had told her the very same thing.

'But I communicate with Thara all the time. I don't need the brooch for that, do I?'

Jaz laughed then; a sound Arla had never heard him make before.

'No. As a dragonhart, you do not need a symbol to speak with the creatures the very gods created to protect you. But as a dragonhart, you will need the symbol to access the magic you once had.'

Every part of her went silent. The bond between her and Thara felt suddenly far away, and it made Arla shiver.

Her mouth was dry when she managed to spit out, 'I've never had magic.'

Jaz smirked, leaning back in his chair. 'No. You personally have not. But I told you before you left for Malarye that I believe the dragonharts once did, and I was correct.'

He pulled a book from the floor, the spine cracking as he eased the leather bindings onto the table. It was an old thing, all faded ink and yellowed parchment, but Jaz seemed to read it as if the words were already imprinted on his mind.

'Damon and the Dragonharts before him all had access to their own magic that was strong enough to shatter the skies. But after what happened with Damon and the war that led to his death, the gods intervened and swore no dragonhart should have that sort of power at will. And so, they bound the dragonharts' magic into the symbol we still see today, and through that, they bound it to the very dragons. For a dragonhart to access magic after Damon – for *you* to access the magic in your blood – both your dragon and the symbol must be connected through you. *That* is how the magic has saved your life twice now.'

Her mind spun. Quick. Quicker. Trying to decipher everything Jaz had said. She wanted to deny it, to tell him that he was wrong and that she didn't have the ability to wield magic, let alone anything as strong as he suggested. But ... even as she tried to deny it to herself, she knew it to be true. She'd felt it. Felt the sentience in the brooch, felt the connection between her and Thara as that power had flowed through her and kept her safe.

It was all beginning to make sense now. The dark magic, *her* magic, the symbols...

Her voice was lacking all of its largeness when she spoke.

'You think I can stop Elrod and his soldiers?'

Jaz smiled.

'I think it's a good place to start.'

Arla's hair flew behind her like unspooled ribbon.

The fates chose you.

Perhaps. But truly, the fates could fuck off.

'Were you ever planning on telling me the dragonharts had magic?' Arla called above the wind.

'Why, when you worked it out anyway?'

Arla huffed, ducking before a branch could take off her head. *'Because I've asked you for months, Thara, to help me. You didn't think telling me I could access your magic would help?'*

Thara's voice was oddly flat as she answered through the bond. It only sparked Arla's ire.

'You know as well as I that the fates would have punished me for revealing something so significant. If you would prefer me to share all that I know, Dragonhart, I expect no pity when the fates enact their punishment.'

No. Never. As angry as Arla was, she would never allow Thara to be subjected to whatever punishment would be doled out to her for speaking of forbidden things. No matter if the fate of the world was at stake. The sound of Thara's pain when she'd tried to explain before echoed in Arla's mind like a war drum.

'That's what I thought.'

The dragon beneath her dived and twisted and pulled up from the ground with such speed it made her eyes water. Her muscles ached, the increasingly familiar tightness of her body working together with Thara like they'd done in Malarye.

She had seen Hyacinth pause on one of the balconies at the hall and watch her, the smile on the princess's face clear even from Arla's distance at the training grounds. It was amusing, really, how quickly Hyacinth had settled into Flambriar's court. Only her second afternoon here and yet Arla already noticed a confidence blooming that had been absent in Malarye.

Perhaps Queen Mara's hand was the one that had guided her daughter into a role of pretty subservience.

Flambriar would soon remove that hand. Sebastian

definitely would if the looks between the pair had anything to do with it.

'Will you concentrate? You're making me look bad,' Thara growled through the bond.

As if on instinct, Arla's fingers found the bow string and released it.

She barely had time to see the arrow strike true in the trunk of a pine tree before Thara was spinning again, another target up ahead – a ribbon fluttering at the end of another tree branch. Fluttering. A moving target barely visible at this sort of speed—

'Concentrate.'

The ire in Thara's voice was enough to settle Arla's mind into a place of unwavering calm. That same place she reserved for King's Assassin. She wasn't sure if she truly recognised that girl anymore. She had found the missing pieces of herself in Malarye, but now she was back in Flambriar, it was all melding together into impenetrable armour.

She felt more herself than she ever had.

The whoosh of her arrow flying sounded in her ears, the graze of a feather brushing her cheek as she watched it soar.

And cut straight through that fluttering ribbon.

Arla's feet met the ground with a dull thud as she slid from Thara's back.

'Do not forget how hard you have worked. You disappear inside your own head, sometimes, Arla Dragonhart. Remember who you are.'

Arla snorted, running her fingers lightly over her dragon's scales as she replied, *'I didn't realise you thought of me so fondly.'*

Thara huffed.

'Perhaps I should call you wicked names. It may provoke a reaction other than sarcasm.'

Arla laughed then, the sound escaping her almost lilting as her dragon beat her wings and disappeared into the sky. She was almost out of sight when the words came through the bond.

'Fond is too weak a word, Dragonhart.'

Arla's laughter ceased, replaced with a pressure in her chest that swelled when she thought of the relationship between her and the dragon. There were still so many secrets, still so many things she was sure Thara wasn't allowed to tell her because of the fates. But there was still a bond there that went deeper than anything she'd ever known. A bond that gave her comfort and security and the knowledge she could access a long-forgotten magic if she wished.

'You pout when you're thinking, you know that?' Arla looked up to find Hark leaning against the wall, his hair tousled, the shadow of stubble darkening his jaw. Gods, he made her weak just looking at him.

'I didn't,' she replied, closing the distance between them until the tips of her booted feet met his. She watched the struggle in Hark's eyes, the way he wanted to run his hands all over her.

'Why're you out here? It's going to be dark soon.'

Arla raised a brow, leaning close enough to him that she could smell the cloud of whiskey and leather that accompanied him into any space. 'We fight battles in the dark too, do we not?'

A cloud of concern marred Hark's eyes before his features softened. 'So you think there will be a battle.'

At this point there was no thinking to be done. War was coming, and Kastonia would hunt them until they were all dead.

'For me, at least,' she said softly. And gods, she hated the fear that tightened Hark's features. She wanted to kiss it away, every last speck of it.

'What were you discussing with Jaz?' There was a hardness to Hark's voice, a betrayal of the tight rein he kept on his emotions. If she hadn't known him well enough to recognise that it was because he cared so deeply for her, Arla might have suspected him to be angry at her.

She sighed, shrugging the bow off her back.

'Things, I guess. I should have magic, but I have to use the dragonhart symbol and my dragon, but I haven't tried to do it on purpose, and I don't know if I can. Oh, and Elrod is definitely using dark magic and the gods are angry, and somehow I'm supposed to stop it all.'

Now she said it out loud, the severity of it all seemed to stick in her throat, and she struggled to breathe past it. Her chest was too tight and her skin too hot and had her hair always felt so fucking heavy—

'What are you not telling me?' his voice cut through the panic, and there was ... accusation in his tone. 'You're keeping secrets again, Arla. I know you want to do this by yourself, but you need to tell me what's going on.'

Her first thought was of Sylvie. Gods, she'd been an idiot. She should have told Hark from the very beginning, damn her fragile heart and her worries over what that would have meant. War was coming anyway, and she should have been honest from the start. Instead, she'd lied, and kept secrets, and now it was far too late to say anything at all.

'I don't know what you mean,' she said, tossing her braid over her shoulder and stretching her limbs. Flying was, quite honestly, taxing on the body.

A frustrated sound rushed through Hark's teeth. 'Don't lie.

You're keeping something from me – from us all. I know you want to do this by yourself. I know you want to keep us safe and think the only way of doing so is by not including us in whatever it is you're doing—'

'Enough,' she snapped, her heart thundering as she eyed him. 'You don't understand the weight of this all. You don't understand what it feels like to be the one that everyone is relying on, so forgive me, Stappen, if I want to keep some things to myself lest the entire world judge me for it!'

Idiot. She was a damned idiot. She should have just told him, then. Should have told him about Sylvie, should have admitted that she was *terrified* of what this all meant—

'Pick up your sword,' Hark commanded, pushing off from the wall and drawing his own blade. The words pulled at her memory, the same he had demanded in the clearing by the bloodstone months ago. She had felt entirely lost and useless back then and he had known exactly how to draw her out of it. Now ... now she wasn't lost or useless, she knew exactly who she was, what she was capable of, what she needed to do...

But the thought of it was overwhelming. So heavy. It was like the act of breathing required her to fight a war with her own lungs.

'Pick up your sword, Arla.' Stronger now. More insistent.

She moved as if by instinct, picking up the sword she had placed down before she had mounted Thara. The weight was a familiar comfort, the hilt of the blade rough beneath her palm.

She met Hark's swing in a clash of steel and a roaring in her blood.

They had been made for each other, she was sure of it.

It was like dancing, really. The way they met every sword stroke with ringing steel, the way their feet moved as if they had glimpsed the future and seen what the other was going to do next.

Duelling with Hark was like fighting herself. Impossible and yet so perfectly right. Sweat was slick on her skin beneath her training leathers, and in the fading light of the sun, Hark's face glistened with his own exertion.

Gods, she'd missed this – missed him. Together, they would be damned unstoppable, and she pitied any who stood against them. This synchronicity, this twining of souls, was the sort of thing poets wrote about.

Or perhaps they really had spent too long together and could predict each other's moves like they were sightseers.

When Hark finally dropped his sword, Arla felt significantly better than she had done after leaving Jaz in the library. They would work this out together, piece by piece. Whoever came for Flambriar would be killed, and war would be avoided at all costs.

'Thank you,' she panted. He'd known it would help. He knew her so well.

Hark approached, his hands running down the length of her arms.

'I don't care how many times we need to do this, I will do anything to keep you safe. As long as I'm here, everything will be fine. I know you want to keep things to yourself, and for now, Arla ... for now, that's alright if it makes things easier for you. But don't think for one moment you're alone in this.'

She believed him, she thought.

'I love you,' she whispered.

She heard the emotion in his voice as he placed a kiss on top of her head and pulled her closer.

'I love you too, Dragonhart.'

CHAPTER 43

Drip. Drip. Drip.

The sound seemed to go on for ever and would perhaps continue that way until the unmaking of the world. The woman had watched that drip of water for what had to be weeks now. Watched it drip from the pipe in the cell wall and run across the worn flagstones, wetting the hem of her dress.

Cold had long since fled her bones and left a numbness in its wake. She watched the guard rotation silently. It wasn't as if any of them would talk to her anyway.

She'd tried.

The bruise on her cheekbone was throbbing again. It was cracked, she'd bet on it.

Not that any of her bets had come through just yet.

Hope was a slippery thing. One moment it was there, the next vanished into oblivion. But still, the woman hoped she would come. She was counting on it.

Or maybe not, now. Not after what the king had told her all those weeks ago. Not as she watched him burn every scrap of parchment in *front of her. No ... hope was long gone, disappeared with the friendship that was likely broken now.*

So she steeled her spine against another day locked in this dungeon with only the rats and silent guards for company.

She squeezed the wooden horse in her fist a little tighter.

~

Cold sweat slicked Arla's skin, her heart thumping loudly in her chest.

Just a dream.

It was just a dream.

She couldn't go gallivanting off to every kingdom that appeared in her dreams, not when she'd been proven wrong before.

She was still awaiting the letter from Malarye condemning her for stealing its princess away in the night.

'*Dragonhart?*' Concern laced Thara's voice as Arla tried to slow her breathing. It was just a dream. Her friend was all right – she would have known otherwise. Halos simply wasn't answering her letters because she was scared of being caught.

Not because she was currently residing in Castle Grey's dungeons.

'*I'm all right,*' she replied through the bond.

She knew Thara didn't believe her as she grumbled back.

'*Then go back to sleep.*'

Arla inhaled deeply, glancing at Hark who slept soundly beside her. They'd chosen Arla's rooms tonight, the stars glittering above them through the glass ceiling so perfect and calm and quiet.

Flambriar was still, too, as Arla looked out through the

balcony doors, tiny lights in the distance the only proof that life occupied this valley at all.

'All is well. I watch over them, Dragonhart.'

It was with that promise in her mind that Arla let sleep entice her back into its embrace.

~

There was smoke.

And shouting.

Arla shot upright, the space in the bed beside her empty but still lingering with the warmth of the body that had been there. It was still dark outside, but through the glass there was smoke and the distant flash of fire.

She was lacing her boots before she could clear the sleep from her eyes.

'Thara—'

'I'm here.'

Arla tore through the hall in her nightgown, hair streaming behind her like a golden banner as she bolted towards the sound of the commotion. She barrelled through the doors into the courtyard, eyes wild as she struggled to find the source of the noise.

There.

Up in the mountains there were the shadowy silhouettes of people – and shouting and flames and smoke.

She was running before she could think it through. Up, up, up the mountain, her nightgown tearing as she ran. Thara swooped in above her, the dragon's presence not as reassuring as she'd hoped it would be.

If Elrod had sent those soldiers here...

If her dream had been true...

'Then we will meet it together, Dragonhart.'

As she reached the clearing at the top of the mountain, she thought perhaps the gods had damned them all. Arla had trained for battle all her life. Had spent years perfecting her body and skill and had spent just as long preparing Vetta for it should she ever have to carry her into such chaos.

She hadn't thought it would be like this.

Dozens of Flambriar's soldiers fired flaming arrows across the clearing where bodies hid behind rocks taller than two men. The enemy fired arrows back too, and, somewhere further away, Flambriar's men engaged in a deadly duel with Elrod's soldiers.

Fear clenched a tight fist around Arla's heart. There was no way they could hope to kill them if what she'd seen in her dream was true. There were simply too many. Too many soldiers that couldn't be killed.

There was a tree burning – the source of all the smoke, Arla surmised – a great, towering thing that had likely been around when the gods walked the world.

Arrows flew.

Swords clashed.

And then ... then there was Noah.

Gentle, kind Noah who never complained no matter how many letters Arla asked him to send to Hadalyn. Noah who smiled softly at her no matter how many times she screamed and cursed at the lack of letters she received in return.

And there was an arrow in his chest.

Time slowed then, a heart's worth of shock pulsing through Arla's veins as she watched the man fall to the ground, his hand pressed against his chest in disbelief. He'd come to fight...

Noah, who had likely never once held a sword, had come to defend Flambriar. And now he was dying.

Arla reached for her sword ... and came up empty.

So fucking stupid.

She'd fled the hall in nothing but her night clothes, hadn't thought to pick up a weapon despite the shouting.

'I will burn them all to ash—'

'No!' Arla shot back through the bond to the dragon twisting in the sky above them. *'You might hit our men. It's too dangerous.'*

Thara grunted before an ear-splitting roar erupted in the sky above the mountains.

Time sped up, jolting Arla back into awareness along with the rest of Flambriar's army. There was a deafening call, Flambriar's men surging forwards, their swords drawn. They'd fight for Noah. They'd fight for a kingdom they'd helped to build.

Magic flew then.

It was weak at first, just tendrils of snapping sparks in the faces of those who fought against the mages. But soon enough, there were wisps of it that wrapped around the enemy and pulled, sending them to their knees so Flambriar's men could cut their heads clean off.

'We should have killed the red girl when she first spoke to you with disrespect.'

Every inch of Arla's body turned cold.

The red girl...

It was then she noticed that the arrow protruding out of Noah's chest was decorated with a red ribbon fluttering in the place where there should have been feathers.

Her eyes flew across the scene, taking in the carnage, the bodies on the floor, the girl with auburn hair in a duel with Hark.

There was no time to consider the risk of plunging straight into a battle without a weapon or armour, but Arla ran straight for Sylvie and Hark, averting her eyes from Noah and skipping over the decapitated bodies littering the mountain.

Sylvie was skilled with a sword, Arla would give her that, but neither she nor Hark were prepared for Arla to come flying in from the side and yank Sylvie away.

The girl spun, green eyes wide and blazing as she locked onto Arla.

Arla didn't give her the chance to say a word before she shoved the Red Blade back.

'I fucking *told you* to leave my people alone!' she screamed, anger pulsing through her chest like a wild, ancient thing. 'I TOLD YOU!'

Sylvie was silent for a moment, and it felt to Arla as though the entire mountain stilled their swords and held their breath.

'I didn't attack first!' the girl spat.

That violent thing in Arla reared up, and despite the lack of a weapon it didn't stop her from swinging for Sylvie who ducked with an expert's speed.

'I didn't attack first,' Sylvie repeated, her voice laced with a violent bitterness. 'They attacked *us*. Are we not allowed the right to defend ourselves, Arla?'

There was a rustle of movement, and then Hark was at Arla's shoulder. She turned her head to face him, knowing she would be met with anger and confusion in his eyes.

He didn't disappoint.

'Why does she know your name, Arla?' His voice was hard and full of a threat that teetered over the trust grown between them.

Arla knew her court watched, could see the indecision in Kase's eyes as she made to move towards Hark, and then Arla. What had she done in keeping the Red Blades from them?

'I-I-I...' She was stuttering. Tripping over her tongue as she tried to justify why she had kept this from Hark. 'I was going to tell you, I swear it. But the people were so unsettled. I didn't want to give them another reason to panic—'

Hark stepped towards her, every kernel of his ire simmering beneath his skin.

'You knew there were people watching our kingdom and you kept it from us?'

'No, I-I ... I thought they'd leave. I thought they would go, and we wouldn't have to deal with it.'

She remembered the words her dragon had uttered to her all those weeks ago when she had hidden a bloodied dress from her maids.

Don't forget your lies, Dragonhart. They will fell you when you least expect it.

How ironic that Arla hadn't figured out how to tell the truth even to the one whose soul she was sure was entwined with hers.

Hark was shaking his head, a look in his eyes that Arla hadn't seen for nearly a year. The same look she had made it her personal goal to coax from him at Castle Grey. The look that meant he couldn't trust her as far as he could throw her.

Something in her chest ached at that.

'You'd better start explaining.'

She did her best – Sylvie did too – all while mages gathered around Noah, doing their best, Arla hoped, to keep him alive long enough to get him to a healer. Hark's face betrayed nothing as he listened to the two women speak over the top of one another. How could he possibly believe her?

How could he believe that she had kept the secret of the Red Blades from him because the threat of them building an army to march on Elrod endangered their people too much? That she had kept it from him so he wouldn't worry about that, as well as scouting the mountains every night? That she hadn't told anyone because she was selfish and hadn't wanted to admit things were going to change – that war was coming?

How had he not seen the Red Blades before?

She asked the question, her fingers twitching at her sides as Sylvie answered.

'We were leaving. Just like you told us to. We know a lost cause when we see one, so we decided to go. The forest isn't so gracious a host when you've camped in it for months. This was meant to be our way home across the mountains until your soldiers fucking attacked us.'

This was all Arla's fault.

'Never.'

If she had just taken this to Hark and had Sylvie wait for Flambriar's answer ... well then, this battle, this *arrow* in Noah's chest would never have happened.

'They weren't a threat, Hark. They were leaving—'

The man that erupted from Hark was not the person Arla had come to love.

'You think that makes it any fucking better!' he barked, his hands rising towards her before he thought better of it. The entire mountain was deadly silent.

'You think I wanted to send my men out here to fight when we're up against an army that won't fucking fall? How stupid can you be, Arla? You've been nothing but selfish since you got here and I am so done with these secrets.'

Crack!

The crack drove through her heart.

He was looking at her like he hated her.

Like he couldn't trust her.

The worst part was, she didn't blame him.

She whirled on Sylvie. 'This is *your* fault! If you'd only left when I told you to—'

The Red Blade bared her teeth. '*My* fault? You're supposed to be a dragonhart. You're supposed to protect mages. We have hundreds of them in our ranks, but you put the lives of Flambriar's people over theirs? You don't care about us at all. You care only for your own kingdom and your own people.'

'How dare—!'

'Enough!' Hark snarled, a biting fist wrapping around Arla's arm and yanking her backwards.

'If he doesn't remove his hand from you, he will have no hands at all.'

For once, Arla shared her dragon's sentiment.

'We need their army, Hark. If we have any hope of standing up to what's coming for Flambriar.'

A frustrated sound forced its way through Sylvie's teeth.

'I never agreed to lend you an army. This was about *your* people joining *me*—'

'We need to go, now!' one of the mages shouted from where they crouched around Noah. She hoped the rise and fall of his chest she could see was not her imagination.

Everything was lost to her then. The entire mountain seemed to move around her, dozens of Flambriar's men taking turns carrying Noah down the mountain. The Red Blades shuffled back into their positions, half-hidden behind rocks and shrubs until Arla could only make out the outlines of them in the dark.

Hark released her arm and hurried after his men, before calling back, 'Don't think this is over.'

And then there was only Arla and Sylvie, two unyielding women responsible for the deaths of too many good men tonight.

'I—'

'You don't need to say anything,' Sylvie interrupted.

'The loss of any mage is too much, especially after what we've gone through. Perhaps you were right. Perhaps asking any of them to march on Elrod would be too great a loss. But if you decide one day to let Flambriar's people make that choice, send a falcon to find me.'

The young woman turned then, disappearing into the mountains with her army.

This had all been for nothing, then.

Tonight, the battle that had taken place here, it was all for nothing now that the Red Blades were heading back to wherever it was they came from. And worse, there would be no help from them in defeating Elrod's dark army.

This would be down to Flambriar and Flambriar alone.

CHAPTER 44

'Arla!'

It was the fourth time Kase had called her name since she'd arrived back at Claret Hall, slinking through its hallways as if she could keep herself hidden from the dozens of people rushing past her in the direction of the infirmary. In the direction of Noah.

Arla had done well to avoid that wing of the hall, but Kase had been wandering the hallways too – likely filling Jack in on everything that had happened – and though Arla had tried her best to stick close to the shadows of the walls and avoid the silver-haired woman, Kase's keen eyes had spotted her.

Fine. If Kase also wanted to tell Arla how wicked and selfish she was, it was the least she deserved. Hark had already hurt her with his words, what was one more?

But when Kase caught up to Arla, there wasn't hostility in her eyes, only solemn understanding. And, not for the first time, Arla wondered what had happened in the young woman's past to place that look there.

'He's just angry. He'll calm down soon. He knows you didn't mean to put anyone in danger. We all do.'

Kase's voice brought anguished tears to Arla's eyes. The two women had hated each other not too long ago. But now ... now Kase's loyalty glowed like a flame in Arla's heart. She had been the first to show her support when Reinhart became Dragonhart, and for that Arla thought she might love the girl forever.

'I didn't want Sylvie to convince our people to go to war, Kase. They've spent their lives at the wrong end of Elrod's blade, and they deserve peace.'

'You did the right thing.'

Arla snorted. 'Did I? Should I have kept it a secret? Should I have kept this from you all?'

Kase sighed, her eyes darting down the hallway in the direction of the infirmary and the shouting coming from there. Arla did her best to block the sound out. 'I know you kept it from us so Hark wouldn't worry. But that was your only mistake. We're in this together. We knew running a kingdom wouldn't be easy. We're all here to shoulder its burdens, you know? You aren't King's Assassin anymore. You don't have to keep everything to yourself.'

A single tear slid down Arla's cheek, and she brushed it away quickly. What had she done to deserve this kindness when it was her fault an innocent man lay fighting for his life with an arrow in his chest? But Kase's words ... they were true.

She wasn't King's Assassin anymore, no matter how she longed to cling onto the title. She could admit it now, finally. How she missed that role. How she missed that life even though it had all been a lie.

But that didn't diminish her other feelings, did it? It didn't change the fact that Castle Grey had been home, and she felt as though it had been torn from her. And she'd never got the chance to say goodbye.

'Thank you,' she whispered, swallowing against the onset of more tears. 'I just wanted it all to be okay. I thought if … I thought if Hark knew there was an army on our borders, it would force us into war and I'm not ready for that.' Her voice cracked, the words fighting her throat as she whispered. 'I didn't want us to go to war.'

Kase smiled sadly. 'I'll come and find you once the sun is up. Why don't you go to sleep?'

Arla nodded, breathing deeply as she watched Kase head in the direction of the infirmary. Gods, she hoped Noah was all right. That the arrow had just missed his heart.

She climbed the steps to her rooms, silently hoping the commotion hadn't woken Lilith and Rheia, who slept down the hall. Upon finding the bed sheets crumpled exactly as she'd left them, Arla concluded her maids must still be asleep.

She tried not to think of Hark in that bed with her only hours before. How she had fallen asleep beside him and sworn it was all she wanted to do forever.

But maybe Kase was right. Maybe he would be calmer now, and he would kiss away every worry and regret she had in not having shared the information she'd kept hidden about the Red Blades.

A soft knock on the door tore her out of those spiralling thoughts and for a silly moment she thought it might be Hark until the slight frame of Hyacinth slipped inside the room.

The princess didn't say a word as she approached Arla, and when she wrapped her in a hug that felt so safe, Arla finally let the tears fall. Hyacinth held her steadfastly, stroking her hair and whispering that everything was okay.

When she finally had the strength to stand unsupported, Arla stepped back from her friend and smiled.

'Sorry, it's all a big mess,' she choked out. 'I hoped coming to Flambriar would be pleasant for you.'

Hyacinth laughed. 'Kingdoms are never pleasant, Arla. I learnt that from my mother.'

The princess's eyes held a wisdom that Arla hadn't seen before, as if stepping into Flambriar's mess had provided clarity for Hyacinth. 'People look past my beauty here. Not one person has told me I'm beautiful. It's ... nice.'

'Tell me about Sebastian. You two seem to be getting on well. You've only been here two days.'

Pink spread over Hyacinth's cheeks, a girlish laugh spilling from her.

'Well, he is kind. And handsome.'

Laughter bubbled from Arla then, *proper* laughter. 'I just *knew—*'

A dull knocking turned both their heads to the balcony, where a falcon perched on a chair Arla had left by the doors, something gripped in its beak as it tapped the glass repeatedly.

Arla hurried over, opened one of the doors and allowed the bird to drop the object into the palm of her hand.

Her stomach sank as she turned it over.

'Arla, what is it?' Hyacinth asked, a cloud of peony-scented air surrounding Arla as her friend moved closer and looked at the object in Arla's hand.

She didn't think she could move – certainly couldn't catch her breath as she stared at the wooden horse.

Halos.

'What is it?' Hyacinth asked again.

'Please leave,' Arla said, her body so still she might as well be dead as she tried to figure out what this meant.

None of the conclusions she came to, she liked.

'Arla—'

'Please, Hyacinth,' she urged, trying to keep the bite out of her voice.

The click of the door was the only signal that the princess had left.

∽

Arla paced for what felt like forever with that tiny wooden horse clenched tight in her fist.

Was Halos in trouble? Is that why she'd sent the horse?

What about the twins?

'Do not give way to panic, Dragonhart. Breathe, and then we will deal with what is to come.'

Arla didn't bother with a response. Thara could likely feel her fear anyway. Was this why Halos hadn't been replying to Arla's letters? Because she was in danger?

She could think of no other reason her friend would send this to her. And that dream—

'Noah's dead.'

Her blood stopped pumping.

Arla turned slowly, a rushing sound filling her ears that had her on the verge of collapsing. Hark stood in the doorway, his shirt splattered with crimson, his eyes tired and oddly flat.

'What?' she managed to say, her grip relaxing on the wooden horse so that it clattered to the floor.

Hark made a sound low in his throat, ripping his shirt off over his head and tossing it to the floor before moving to stand by the balcony doors. She could almost feel the ire radiating off him, a warning that she was treading on thin ice just by being close to him.

She stopped herself from reaching for his arm.

'Noah is dead,' he ground out. 'A good man is dead because of you.'

Her chest was too tight. 'I did it to protect us! I thought if I could make them go away before you found out then we wouldn't have to get involved with the Red Blades and they wouldn't spark this war. Hark, I—'

'I don't want to hear it.' He whirled on her and he ... he looked *dangerous*. 'You kept that from me. You kept the fact we had an army camped on our borders a *secret,* and you cost a man his life. You cost multiple men in our army their lives. You are entirely unpredictable and wild, and I should have known it from the very start.'

A roaring opened up in her chest, that violent thing stirring. It was all too easy to let that anger and violence consume her. All too easy to remind Hark Stappen of just who she was. Of just *who* he had decided to get into bed with.

She took a step towards him.

'Was I just an idea you liked, Hark? Something to tame? To bend to your will? Well, I don't know what pretty ideas fill your head, Stappen, but I am not good, or kind, or tameable. I *am* unpredictable, and I always have been. You thought that by bringing me here I would change?'

He exploded then, the chandelier rattling with the force of him.

'Yes! I thought you would fucking change! I thought you would stop being so self-important and realise there's more to life than you and your own agenda!'

A deep calm settled over her, siphoning away the rage that had been ready to fly from her tongue. 'Well, if that's how you feel, then I won't bother you anymore.'

Tension settled thick like curdled milk over the room. Hark's voice was loud in the silence.

'And what the fuck is that supposed to mean?'

'I'm going to Hadalyn.'

A barking laugh erupted from him. 'Like hells you are.'

Thara growled through the bond as Arla spoke.

'If you try and stop me, you will see just how wild I have become.'

'Is that a threat?'

Steel lined her spine as she uttered the words, 'It's a promise.'

Hark's face softened then. And perhaps that was worse than him shouting at her. Than him screaming at her. Than him calling her every wicked name he could conjure up.

Because in that softening, she knew something irreversible had happened. She watched it happen in his eyes, watched him recognise it too. He didn't need to tell her what she already knew. That there was no way the two of them had ever been destined to work. Not like this. Not when they were always at war with one another.

He lifted his hand gently to brush a loose curl from her face.

'I'm sorry,' he whispered. It felt like a punch to the stomach.

Tears came then, unruly and running down her cheeks. Her heart was splintering, surely? There were cracks forming where she had patched it before, and his hand was brushing her cheek, his eyes filled with his father's iciness.

'We had a good run, Reinhart. But I can't do this with you anymore.'

Her heart cleaved entirely.

No.

What about everything they'd wanted?

What about the little house by the river and the hound she would call Treasure and everything they had dreamed together?

Her vision narrowed, her stomach dropping away from her until she was sure she might faint. And she couldn't breathe, couldn't breathe, couldn't breathe—

'I'm sorry, Arla.'

Her voice cracked. 'Hark, no. I'll change, I promise I'll change!'

She'd beg. She'd get on her knees and *beg him* if it meant he wouldn't shatter everything, if it meant he still let her be with him. She'd be whatever he wanted her to be, would bend and break her very framework, so long as he promised he wouldn't leave her. Not like everyone else...

She didn't notice his hands on her. Didn't notice him shoving her into the dressing room until the click of the latch dragged her screaming back into the present.

He'd locked her in.

'No, Hark, no—'

Her breaths came too quickly, her head spinning and spinning, and she couldn't feel her legs or her hands or her face and, and, and—

He'd locked her in.

He'd locked her in.

He'd locked her in, he'd locked her in, he'd locked her in—

Her fists battered the door, the tiny bones breaking as she pounded and pounded. She couldn't do this. Couldn't be locked away. Not whilst she watched a kingdom fall.

Not again.

'No, no, no, no, no...'

She couldn't be in here, couldn't let him throw everything away. She would be *lost* without him.

'Hark, please! Please, I promise I'll change! I'll be what you want me to be! Please don't do this.'

She thought she was screaming, and there was roaring in her head and all around her.

Thara...

She fell, smacking her head hard enough that the dressing room blurred around her. Tears were carving tracks down her cheeks, and her fingers shook where she tried to lift them.

The memories came then, rapid and unrelenting.

The soldiers outside the windows...

The cackle born of nightmares that escaped Elrod's throat...

The image of him neck to toe in blood...

The way her father had tried to fight...

The way her parents had fallen and the way Arla had bitten her own hands to stop herself from screaming at the image of their bodies through the crack in the dresser door...

She couldn't be locked away again, couldn't not fight...

Hark had done this to her.

Hark who had loved her, Hark who had kissed her and touched her skin and promised her he'd fight the world for her. And there had to be a way back to that, surely?

Even if he'd broken every scrap of trust she had by *locking her away*, she deserved it. She deserved it and had broken his trust, and there *had* to be a way back to one another because they'd *promised* they would have that life. They'd sworn that they would get the peace they'd not had the chance to live yet...

'*Dragonhart. Find your way back, Dragonhart.*'

She clung to the bond. Clung to it like her life depended on it. Thara roared outside, and if Arla could just make it out of the dressing room and to a window, she would be free. She'd be able to get away from here and to Hadalyn. To her friend she had been a fool to doubt. She'd been a fool not to go and find her the moment things had settled down in Flambriar.

Because if Halos was hurt...

Well, Arla wouldn't think of that. Not yet. Because all she needed right now was to see her friend, to know she was okay. To know her children were okay.

She held onto that thought, too. Held onto the bond and the thought of her friend. She could do this, she could break her way out of this dressing room. It would be just like in training. Just like when she'd been training for the King's Guard and had had to break her way out of the broom cupboard where they'd locked her in.

You can do anything.

Her father's words.

She stood on shaky legs, clinging to Thara's strength through the bond. She wished for her dragonhart brooch. The one she might be able to use to access the magic Jaz had told her she had.

But she was still wearing her nightgown, and her brooch was currently pinned to her training jacket.

If she could get out of here though ... then she could retrieve her brooch and get away.

'You can do anything, Dragonhart.'

It bolstered her. Gave her the strength to straighten her spine and throw every ounce of strength she had against the door.

It rattled in the frame.

She threw her weight against it again.

Again.

Again.

Again, until a crack splintered the wood.

Again.

The wood bowed against her weight.

Again.

Until that crack splintered further and she could kick a hole straight through.

She held her breath as she managed to climb through the gap into her empty bedroom.

There were voices on the other side of her bedroom door. Lilith. Rheia. Shouting her name.

Hark had locked her away from them, too.

Tears streamed, the salt running over her lips as she tried to swallow the hurt, the betrayal, both his and hers. She had done this... She had broken them and she'd left him no choice but to end it. There had to be a way of saving it, of saving them.

She didn't even believe herself.

It took her mere seconds to unpin the dragonhart brooch from her jacket and secure it to the front of her nightdress. She swiped a bandolier of throwing knives off the chest of drawers. They'd have to do. Just a few more minutes of strength. She could do that. She owed it to herself.

'Thara!'

'I'm here.'

Arla tried the handle to the balcony doors and found them locked.

As if that would stop her.

The glass shattered, a million tiny crystals now decorating the floor as she approached the balcony.

Then her bedroom doors flew open.

Flew open to reveal Hyacinth – gods bless her heart – a wild panic in the princess's eyes as she lunged for Arla.

Only to be held back by Kase.

Arla locked eyes with the woman who had become her

friend. Saw the resignation in her face. Kase dipped her chin, the nod a gift. A release.

Arla would have to thank her for it later – if she ever came back.

She held the gaze of the two women in the doorway before falling backwards off the balcony.

She understood now why Thara had been insistent she practise jumping off the cliff in Malarye because she now fell onto her dragon's back without a second thought, as if it were an action so normal it had been passed down through her blood.

She thought perhaps it had.

Thara swept upwards, her leathery wings beating through the beginnings of a dawn-coloured sky as she let out a roar that rattled the entirety of Claret Hall.

Arla couldn't bring herself to care, wouldn't let herself untangle that knot of hurt lodged in the centre of her chest. She only knew she needed to get out. Needed to be away from Hark who was becoming like his father in ways she knew he would never understand. It had been them both against the world at one point. For one sweet, short moment in time their worlds had revolved around one another. But she had broken his trust and he, it seemed, had been waiting for an excuse to tell her how wild she was.

'Let him. You were never born to be put in a cage.'

A cage. It was exactly what Claret Hall had felt like. Yes, she felt the pull to protect her people. Desperately, she felt it. But she couldn't do that there. Couldn't keep them safe when she was fighting wars within herself.

She'd been meant for more – had been *prophesied* for more – and all Hark cared about was making sure no one hid in the mountains.

Then why did her heart ache so much?

If the kingdoms were to be united, it would be down to her to do it, and she would. Away from Flambriar, she might remember who she was, how she wasn't supposed to act like a queen and abide by rules Hark changed every day. She had felt like herself in Malarye when she wielded a sword or a bow.

No, uniting kingdoms had never been possible whilst she was hidden in the mountains. She needed to be seen. To be felt.

And she'd start to fix everything as soon as she had found Halos – including things with Hark, if there was any salvageable part of them.

'We fly for Hadalyn, I take it?' Thara was a comfort. A certainty. The bond between them running so deep now Arla wasn't sure she'd know how to live without it.

Her voice was surprisingly strong over the wind as she said, 'Yes. We fly for Hadalyn.'

CHAPTER 45

Her heart felt like it might slip between her ribs and disappear into the mountains beneath her. Not that it would have been a problem before – it would have found its way to Hark.

Now she thought it might just shrivel up and die.

She tried not to think too much of it as Thara carried her out of Flambriar Valley. If she thought too hard about Hark and what had happened between them, she might fall victim to the gaping cavern in her chest.

Her heart hadn't escaped. He'd fucking broken it.

So instead she clung to the thought of Halos – of her being alive and well. She hoped she hadn't sent Arla that wooden horse because she was in trouble. Arla's fingers drifted over to the brooch on her nightgown – a stupid flimsy thing; she should have taken the time to get dressed – and something in her chest eased slightly at the wave of warmth that licked her fingers. It felt too similar to Thara's magic in the bond, confirming to her everything Jaz had said.

'Did you know the symbol would grant me magic?' Arla

called out to her dragon. Flambriar was disappearing beneath them now, and soon it would be lost to the mountains. Thara had confirmed she'd known that the dragonharts had once had magic and that Arla herself could access the dragon's. She hadn't said anything about the dragonhart symbol, though.

Thara growled softly, the vibration through her body trembling Arla's bones.

'I did. But you know as well as I the things the fates forbid me to tell you of.'

'Would they kill you? If you told me?' The pain they'd inflicted on Thara before...

Thara was quiet for a moment, though the bond churned restlessly between them.

'In more ways than you could conjure in that wild mind of yours.'

Wild.

Hark had called her that. Her king, too, had said the same. She'd liked it before – had enjoyed knowing people looked at her like she was untameable. Like she was too loud and noticeable. Too much for a girl.

Now she wondered if *wild* was just another word for *failure*.

'Do you think of Elin as wild?' Thara hummed.

'No,' Arla replied down the bond, still marvelling at the way it was possible to communicate with her dragon without having to speak a single word out loud, no matter how many times she did it. *'I think of Elin as alive.'*

'She won't be for long if what is unfolding beneath us has any say, Dragonhart.'

It was the wariness in Thara's tone that had Arla peering over the side of the dragon to the mountain range below before she could untangle the words Thara had uttered.

Her stomach dropped, a rushing, heady panic consuming her as Arla watched a grey mare, almost camouflaged in the rough terrain of the mountain, carry a young girl at a breakneck gallop across ground that was surely going to kill them both.

Elin had come after her.

'Land. Now!' Arla called out, already cursing everyone in Claret Hall for their fucking inability to keep hold of the child. Elin would die if Vetta slipped on this ground.

As if she'd heard the words, Arla's horse whinnied, the sound carrying on the wind to where Thara was descending. There was determination on Elin's face. Even from such a distance, Arla could see the steadfastness in the girl's features. It would be a battle to get her to turn back.

When they were close enough to the ground that she didn't risk shattering her ankles, Arla launched herself from Thara's back, landing on the loose earth of the mountain. They'd made it to flat ground, at least, almost half a mile of it before the mountains began to descend and danger of death really was likely.

Arla stormed towards where Elin had stopped the horse, Vetta's coat slick with sweat, her sides heaving with the strain of the gallop. Arla's heart swelled for the little horse; she knew she would have kept galloping all night had Elin commanded it.

Speaking of, how *had* the girl managed to bond with the mare so well as to ride her?

'Do you know how much trouble you're in?' Arla snapped as she reached the pair of them.

Elin squared her shoulders, a mask of defiance sliding over the young girl's face. 'You forgot your bow. You can't save your friend without it.'

Sure enough, Arla's bow was fastened to Elin's back, the smooth wood gleaming in the morning sun.

'That's beside the point,' Arla said, though she couldn't summon the anger in her voice that had been there moments before. 'You could have died out here. One slipped hoof from Vetta and you're both down. No one would have found you, Elin. Gods, does anyone even know you left?'

Elin raised a brow, and for a fleeting moment, Arla was looking at a reflection of herself. She'd been just as careless of authority at that age, too.

'No, they don't know I'm out here. But you know Vetta won't slip. She's your horse, Arla. I don't think even a dragon could stop her.'

Thara huffed, a sound that was too similar to laughter for Arla's liking. It still softened her voice even further, the worry at seeing the girl out here alone dissipating for every second she stood in the girl's confidence.

'Well, you've delivered my bow. Now you need to go back.'

Challenge lit Elin's eyes, those soft brown eyes dazzled for a second.

Oh gods, they really didn't have time for this argument.

'I want to help. Please let me come with you.'

For a heartbeat she considered it. But that beat passed, and Arla knew there was no way she could put this child in danger, no matter how much Elin wanted to prove herself. Arla made sure to soften her voice as she spoke to the girl, placing her hands on top of where Elin's rested around the reins.

'If you want to help me, you will make sure my kingdom doesn't fall apart whilst I'm gone.'

It was the first time she'd admitted it – that Flambriar belonged to her. But truly, who was there to deny it? Those people were given magic by the very gods she was blessed by. There was no one better to lead Flambriar than Arla Dragonhart, no matter what Hark had to say about it.

Elin looked too small against the might of the mountains,

her tiny face half hidden beneath the fur hood of the cloak she wore.

'I know you didn't mean for anyone to get hurt. I don't want everyone to go to war, either.'

Elin knew too much. Hadn't been kept shielded from the fears of war like Arla had wished for her.

'Neither were you.'

Arla snorted. *'And look how I turned out.'*

'Elin, you must go back. Keep them all in line, until I'm home.'

Her voice was too tiny. 'Will you come back?'

There was a sadness in the girl's eyes. A tale of loss and grief, a hope that she wouldn't have to lose someone else she cared about. Arla squeezed her hands a little tighter.

'I promise you I will come home. I'll bring Halos and her children, too – Vivi will like that, won't she?'

Elin didn't look convinced. 'You'll get hurt,' she whispered.

Arla winked. 'No one hurts me.'

Elin's shoulders sagged and Arla knew then she'd won this fight. The child couldn't come with her, and she knew it.

'Go back. I promise I'll be all right.'

The fight left those beautiful brown eyes, the strength Arla knew the girl carried tucked away safely.

'Okay.'

Vetta nudged Arla gently, a promise, perhaps, that she would carry her rider as safely as she had always carried Arla. She raised a hand and patted the horse gently.

'Go, quick. Before the others realise you've gone.'

A small smile was all Elin offered her before the child kicked the mare into a gallop. Arla had to swallow around the lump in her throat as she watched the navy-blue cloak ride away from her. Gods, she needed to get a grip.

'Do not regret having a heart. Pity those who do not.'

Arla was silent as she remounted her dragon and they launched into the sky.

~

She was airborne for less than two minutes before a blood-curdling scream tore through the mountains.

If Arla's heart had ever stuttered before, it was nothing compared to the way it tripped and tumbled in her chest. Every nerve ending came alive, a sharpness narrowing her senses.

Elin.

Without a second of communication between them, Thara was banking left and twisting in the sky, Arla's legs gripping the sides of the dragon's body like it was second nature now.

Elin was in trouble.

Thara's wings beat beneath her with a ferocity as Arla's eyes scanned the landscape, searching for that gods-damned blue cloak.

All she could see were fucking mountains.

'Can you see anything?'

A pulse of concern through the bond before Thara replied, *'Not yet. But I can feel it.'*

A thick oily thing settled in the pit of Arla's belly. If Thara was able to *feel* something, there was no doubt there was magic involved – dark magic, if Arla had to guess.

Thara soared higher, the mountain range stretching out below them like spilled ink. All Arla could think of was that damned blue cloak. Gods, if anything had happened to Elin, she'd never forgive herself for turning the child back alone—

'There!' Thara growled, an ancient, dark sound filled with a thousand promises that set the hairs on Arla's arms upright.

But sure enough, her dragon was right. There, on a flat piece of land between two peaks, a child clung to the neck of a grey horse as over two dozen black-uniformed soldiers surrounded her.

Bile rose in Arla's throat before she settled her mind back into that calm, unfeeling space. They would all die, then. Every one of them for daring to stop a child. She wouldn't let them touch a hair on Elin's head.

'Take us lower,' she said to her dragon, already nocking an arrow into the bow Elin had brought her. This would all be Arla's fault if the girl was hurt.

Thara obeyed, silently drifting lower through the clouds. They hadn't been spotted yet, Elrod's warriors not clever enough to look up and see their death descending. Arla ground her teeth as the soldiers inched closer to Elin, her unease visible even from this height. Vetta stood like an ox, perhaps aware that her owner was on the way to rescue them. It was a blessing, really. Arla imagined if Elin tried to escape now, they'd cut her head from her shoulders.

'Closer,' Arla instructed through the bond, her fingers itching to let the arrow fly. *'I want to be sure I kill them.'*

Thara growled. *'I will burn them all to ash!'*

'No,' Arla objected, the panic thick in her throat. *'You might hurt Elin.'*

She had no idea how accurate dragon fire was, but judging by the pulses of fury flowing through the bond, she doubted her dragon would keep a check on her flames.

It was as a soldier stepped forwards to grab the reins out of Elin's hands that Arla finally let that arrow fly.

It planted firmly between his eyes.

And then hell erupted.

There was shouting and cursing and two dozen swords

drawn as Arla picked another two soldiers off with arrows. Elin watched, her eyes wide with panic, as soldiers swarmed her.

Arla couldn't protect her from up here. She'd have to be on the ground, swinging a blade she didn't have.

'When has that ever stopped you?'

She threw herself from her dragon's back, landing harshly and ignoring the bite of pain that came with it. Every set of Kastonian eyes turned to face her.

There was a half-second where she thought they might turn and run.

She should have known better.

Instead, Elrod's soldiers squared their shoulders and spread to contain Arla within the circle they currently held Elin in. Arla let them. Didn't try and fight as they forced her closer to Elin.

That was good. She wanted the girl close to her.

'Are we going to stand here all day, or do you need a moment to consider how quickly you'd like me to hand your carcasses back to your king?' she drawled, delighting in the way each of them bristled at her voice.

It purchased her a reaction, at least. One lone soldier stepped forwards, his hair shaved close to his skull, eyes like wicked needles piercing her soul.

'He'll pay us handsomely for *you*, assassin,' he sneered.

Arla slid one of her knives from the bandolier at her waist, twirling it between her fingers with a look of disinterest. She was close to Elin now, could reach out and touch the girl's leg where she sat stock-still atop Vetta. The mare huffed quietly.

'Surprisingly, I'm not for sale,' Arla said, 'so unless you wish to deliver your own heads to His Majesty's feet, I suggest you let the girl go and you turn back to Kastonia.'

The soldiers face remained cold. 'Or what, bitch?'

Arla levelled him with her own cool stare.

'Was I not clear? You will lose your heads.'

As if in confirmation, Thara growled from where she prowled at the edge of the circle of soldiers.

'Don't attack them,' Arla said through the bond. *'Let me get Elin clear first.'*

Just one slip of a bolt from the solid crossbows the soldiers carried, and Elin would die. Arla couldn't sanction that.

The soldier who had stepped forwards laughed then – a hacking, awful sound. Arla watched Elin tense beside her.

'You're in no position to make demands.'

She ignored the voice in her head that was telling her he was right.

'Never.'

But she couldn't hope to fight her way out of this. Not with so many soldiers and no sword. Not with a child to protect.

But maybe she could create a gap long enough for Elin to escape. Long enough for Vetta to carry her home to Flambriar and warn the court.

So Arla didn't hesitate when she threw the knife.

CHAPTER 46

A wet thud echoed through the valley as Arla's knife planted itself firmly in the chest of a Kastonian soldier. She likely had seconds before he got back on his feet.

There would be no time to watch that abomination of nature. The world was erupting around her.

Men came with swords drawn as she gripped a knife tightly in her palm – her very last one because she'd been a stupid fool not to pick up more weapons on her way out of Claret Hall. She dragged it across throats and plunged it into chests.

Vetta kept Elin out of the way, the horse spinning and dodging the ambush as the dark soldiers swarmed Arla. Thara was airborne again, a flash of onyx talons tearing through flesh as the dragon picked off any man who was out of Arla's reach.

Arla was outnumbered in every way that counted, and yet she kept ducking and lunging and kicking. Anything to keep these soldiers down long enough so Elin could escape.

Which, of course, the girl wasn't doing.

The child clung to an arrow she'd packed for Arla, jabbing at any man who came within range of her and Vetta.

Gods, she was going to get herself killed, and it would be all Arla's fault.

'ELIN, GO NOW!' Arla screamed over the din of swords and armour clanging – against what, she didn't know, she only held a tiny knife.

Elin met Arla's eyes across the space, a resolve there that made Arla curse herself for ever encouraging it.

But now was not the time. Not when soldiers she'd already slaughtered were rising to their feet again, that forbidden magic writhing in their veins.

And so Arla kept killing.

And killing.

And killing.

She didn't know how much time had passed. Thara picked off any men she could without harming Arla or Elin, and when the space allowed it, Arla fired arrows at men who wouldn't fall. She thought she might keep fighting forever. Just long enough to get Elin out.

She clung to the thought until the woosh of a thick wooden spike released from a crossbow flew by her cheek, grazing the skin before it tore through the leathery flesh of Thara's wing.

Pain lanced through the bond, swaying Arla on her feet as Thara released a sound so horrific Arla prayed to whatever gods remained she'd never have to hear it again. She had barely a second to turn her head and watch her dragon struggle to stay airborne before the soldiers were on their feet and coming at her again.

Arla sliced with renewed ferocity then, her remaining throwing knife an extension of her hand as she stabbed and cut and hacked at any who came for her.

'Tell me you're okay?' she managed to pant through the bond. There was a beat of silence before Thara replied.

'They will burn for what they have done.'

Good.

Just as soon as Arla managed to get herself and Elin out of the firing line.

Something dark and impatient was clawing inside Arla's chest, demanding to be set free. Demanding to be unleashed. It scared her.

Because deep down ... deep down she knew what it was. Knew that history was repeating itself, and if she gave it an inch of freedom, it would consume her just as it had done Damon.

She didn't have time for vengeful gods today, not when the world around her fell silent and the soldiers stood still.

Thara growled deep in her throat where she hovered in the air above Arla, the sound of her wings so different to usual now her dragon accommodated the hole in her right wing. Arla would kill them all.

'Do not do anything stupid, Dragonhart.'

Arla chanted the words in her head as the soldiers surrounding her parted and revealed a man easily seven feet tall holding a blade just beneath Elin's ribs where she still sat atop Vetta. To her credit, the child didn't whimper, didn't cry as the soldier smirked at Arla.

She'd cut his fucking throat for that.

'Let her go,' she growled through clenched teeth, her assassin's brain already crafting a thousand ways to gut him and leave his innards strewn across the mountain.

The soldier sneered, his face contorting into something of nightmares.

And yet it was nothing compared to the way her entire body trembled as a figure stepped out from behind him, Arla's mouth suddenly too dry as Orson, ambassador for Hadalyn, curled his thin lips at her.

'Oh, how I've waited to get my hands on you.'

∾

Traitor.

It was the first word that came to Arla as Orson crossed the distance towards her. He was as repulsive as ever, his features too rat-like, his demeanour all wrong. *Sadist*, she thought. He'd always bragged about how he'd take great pleasure in hurting her, had threatened to kill King's Assassin more times than she could count. It was why Cyrus had sent him away as ambassador to Kastonia – so that Orson wouldn't kill Arla in her sleep after she had won the title when he was just as skilled as she was.

She'd suspected Orson of treason back when she'd stayed in Larkire Palace all those months ago. Had thought he was a little too close to the king of Kastonia. This just confirmed it; Orson had no loyalty to Hadalyn or its king.

Arla tossed her braid back over her shoulder, steeling herself against the man she'd love nothing more than to kill.

When he was less than five feet away, Arla finally spoke.

'Still so painfully untouched by a woman you can't help but wish to, oh how did you put it? *Get your hands on me*, Orson?'

It got her the reaction she wanted, his face contorting with rage as he held a knife to her throat quicker than blinking. Thara growled in warning, the ground shuddering as the dragon landed behind Arla.

'I'm okay, don't do anything.'
'I grow tired of these orders, Dragonhart.'

This close, Orson smelled sour, his pale green eyes only

adding to the repulsion Arla felt being this close to him. He pressed the blade against her skin harder until a sharp bite signalled her blood must have bloomed along the steel.

'I'm going to take great pleasure in crushing that attitude of yours, *whore*.'

Yes, a sadist indeed.

Arla caught Elin's eye over Orson's shoulders, a silent plea that should the opportunity arise, the girl was to run. To Arla's relief, Elin dipped her chin slightly.

'Shall we get on with it, Orson?' Arla snickered, leaning into the blade and enjoying the way his eyes widened in shock. 'Let the girl go, and we will discuss what it is you want.'

He scoffed, the sound travelling through Arla's skin and setting it alight with goosebumps. She fucking hated him.

'Do you think you're in a position to discuss anything? In case you hadn't noticed, you senseless bitch, I'm seconds away from cutting your throat.'

The snort she let through her nose was clearly the wrong move when Orson said, 'Yarrow, kill the girl.'

There was no hesitation as Yarrow pulled the blade back from Elin's skin, ready to plunge it straight through her ribs.

Arla begged then. 'No, have me. You can have me, just don't harm her, Orson. Don't.'

'You're a fool if you think I will allow them to take you from here.'

'It's me or her. You don't let them hurt Elin. That's an order.'

Arla snapped the bond shut, ignoring the low grumble and the warning of heat on the back of her neck.

Orson raised a brow, stepping back from Arla and removing the blade from her throat. Her blood slid slowly down her neck. 'Orson, please.'

It took everything in her to plead with the man, to show not just a slither of humility but her whole fucking heart. Yarrow, at least, hadn't stabbed Elin ... yet.

'Please,' she whispered, the word slipping from her lips like some vow she was making to him. She thought perhaps she was.

'You'd really trade your life for that of a child, *assassin*?' he was sneering at her with amused curiosity. Arla didn't care. Let him mock her, she could live with his taunting. She wouldn't live with the death of Seb's niece.

She wiped all images of Seb and the rest of Flambriar's court out of her mind. If she thought of them, she might lose control entirely. 'You can have me. I'll come willingly, but you have to let her go.'

'Stay your blade, Yarrow.' Orson's slimy voice carried to the soldier at Elin's side. He sheathed the blade but kept hold of Elin's arm. Gods how were they going to get out of this...

'You don't carry that symbol on your chest for nothing. Use it.'

Of course...

The Dragonhart brooch, the key to the magic in the bond between her and Thara. But she had never wielded it on purpose – had no idea how to...

'Kneel.' The word cut into her like a poisoned blade.

'What?' she half laughed, the sound scratchy in her throat as Orson smirked back at her.

'You heard me, Reinhart. Kneel at my feet and beg me to spare the girl.'

'Don't you dare.'

It went against everything in her. Everything from the cocksure assassin she had grown up to be, right down to the very blood flowing in her veins. She was blessed by the gods, to kneel at the feet of a man was to go against the gods themselves.

And yet she lowered herself to the ground anyway.

Sharp stones cut into her bare knees, the nightgown barely covering her as she knelt at Orson's feet.

They laughed then. Every one of Elrod's soldiers laughed at her, the sound a careful shredding of her dignity.

She didn't care. For Elin she would do this. For Flambriar she would kneel at Orson's feet if it meant only Arla was harmed.

She thought a whimper squeaked from Elin then, the first sign of the girl's undoing.

'Use the magic, Dragonhart. I will not tolerate their mocking for long.'

Orson still laughed as he leered over her. Perfect. Keep him distracted so she could figure out how to access the magic in the bond.

Arla reached her fingers up towards the dragonhart brooch pinned above her left breast. The metal was warm to the touch, that familiar sentience seeming to call to something in her blood. A tugging sensation in her core strengthened, as if her very soul was reaching out to whatever magic lay inside the brooch.

And yet it was still out of reach.

'Reach for it. It will come.' Thara was growing impatient, Arla could hear it in the dragon's voice. Could feel it in the way the ground shook as Thara shifted her weight between her feet. Any moment now, the dragon would snap and kill every man who stood here.

Arla wouldn't allow it whilst Elin was still at risk of having a sword pushed through her ribs.

So she reached in her mind for that old magic. The one she often felt lurking in the bond. The one that watched and waited in her blood, as if it knew one day she might use it. The dragonhart pulsed hotter beneath her fingers, the metal searing hot now as Arla tried to tether it to the bond between her and her dragon. Everything felt too slippery. Like she was grasping at water and watching it trickle through her fingers. The magic was there, waiting, she could feel it.

She just had no idea how in the gods damned hells she was supposed to connect with it.

A sharp kick to her jaw sent her reeling.

Copper coated her tongue, the blood spilling over her lips as Arla tried to breathe through the throbbing in her jaw. Orson glared down at her. 'I don't hear you begging, Reinhart?'

Pride was a fickle thing. Hard to come by, too easy to lose. Arla swallowed it anyway, pressing her body closer to the ground, her very soul screaming at the act.

'Please, Orson. Don't hurt the child.'

A booted foot came to rest harshly on her shoulder, Orson's weight pressing the side of her quickly bruising face into the stone peppered ground.

'You'll come willingly if I spare the girl.'

Not a question. Not a negotiation. A promise that if she didn't comply there would be no stopping him from ordering Elin dead.

There was not a second of hesitation before Arla replied, 'Done.'

A second later and Orson kicked her again, so hard that her body sprawled on the ground, her nightdress rising higher so that the creamy flesh of her thighs was exposed to the dozens of eyes watching.

'I will burn them all.'

'No,' Arla protested. *'Not until she is safe.'*

Orson's lurid voice echoed through the clearing.

'Let the child go. She can deliver the message back to

wherever it is the rest of them are hiding, that we have king's assassin. Her life is dependent on her cooperation.'

Just a fleeting glance to Elin was all Arla was granted before Yarrow released his grip on the girl and her heels were digging into Vetta's side, a clatter of loose stones in their wake as Elin galloped toward Flambriar.

It was a risk, her going alone. Arla could only hope none followed and discovered the whereabouts of Flambriar.

'Now may I boil their insides?'

Arla smiled through her bleeding lips.

'The honour is yours.'

There wasn't time for flames.

Not as three twangs ruptured the air followed by the telltale thud of thick crossbolts penetrating scaled flesh.

The sound that Thara made had Arla retching as those bolts pierced her chest and sides, the pain so blinding it tore through the bond without restraint. Arla gagged again as her dragon roared, fire spewing from her jaws in short bursts, as if the act of breathing was too painful for her.

And then there were hands on Arla's skin. Rough hands that would bruise her as rope was secured around her wrists and ankles. Bile rose in her throat as another bolt was fired at her dragon. This time, it seemed, was the final snapping of the tether of Thara's resilience.

She launched into the air, her wings hardly catching her as she tried to climb higher and higher, her huge body dropping feet at a time before she managed to right herself. Blood rained down upon Arla and the soldiers holding her, scalding hot and too red.

There was no way Thara could help her like this ... not without being killed.

It took every kernel of strength Arla had to whisper the words through the bond.

'Go. Find help. I'll be okay.'

When Thara replied, there was nothing of the strength Arla had come to know in the dragon's voice. That was perhaps the most frightening thing of all.

'I will find you again. Just as you found me.'

Arla was almost certain she heard her own heart break as she watched her dragon fly away, her emerald body disappearing into the grey of the mountains.

She swallowed as Orson gripped her chin, his bony fingers pressing hard into her bones as he hissed, 'We're going to have fun, you and I.'

There was a blunt force to the side of her skull.

And then there was nothing.

CHAPTER 47
HARK

Kase's knuckles colliding with the side of his jaw had sent his head fucking spinning, which for such a slight woman was surprising.

He deserved it, of course. He'd been an insufferable prick. But, gods, Arla had been so stupid, and he hadn't been able to see straight when he'd found out she'd kept the secret of the Red Blades from him. And when he'd watched Noah bleed to death in the fucking living room.

Perhaps locking her away had been the wrong decision, but what she'd said, that she was going to leave and go to Hadalyn...

Well, no matter how angry he was with her, he couldn't stomach the thought of her leaving.

Not that locking her up had helped.

'Are you listening?' Kase snapped in his ear. He turned slowly towards her, dragging his eyes from the direction of the mountains where the other half of his heart had apparently flown off to.

Her balcony doors were still open and rattling in the wind.

'HARK!' Another crack to the side of his head, softer this

time but powerful enough to capture his attention. Kase glared at him with enough ire to go to war with the gods.

'What?' he demanded angrily, raking a hand through his hair.

It was all a fucking mess.

'I said we need to make a plan. Arla's gone to Hadalyn, but she'll be back, you know she will.'

'AND WHAT IF SHE DOESN'T COME BACK?' he roared as the words that had been swirling round his head for the past hour finally burst free.

What if she didn't come back...

He didn't think he knew how to exist without her anymore. He'd gone fucking insane without her whilst she was in Malarye. The thought of her never coming back...

'Hark.' Seb stepped forwards, a solemn look on his usually jovial features. 'I know you regret what happened – we all do. But standing out here wishing she would come back doesn't help anything. We need to calm the people. They know something went on last night and them being scared doesn't help things here.'

'He's right,' Jaz said, stepping out of the shadows of the hall and into the morning sun. Hark hadn't expected Jaz to be down here, not when he'd spent every waking minute in the library trying to find out what it was Arla was supposed to be doing to end this punishment the gods had delivered to the land.

Hark knew he needed to assuage the fears of his people and yet ... he couldn't think past the regret of what he'd done.

To lock her away...

Arla feared small spaces more than anything. She'd been locked away and forced to watch her parents die, and even now could barely breathe whenever she was in confined spaces.

And what Hark had done...

There was no doubt in his heart that she would never, *ever* forgive him.

His fears only increased when a grey mare galloped into the courtyard.

CHAPTER 48

This floating feeling was too familiar. This quiet place where she didn't think or see or feel. It was too easy to stay safe in the oblivion. It was, she recalled with sick amusement, very similar to dying.

Arla's body rocked beneath her – was it perhaps a ship?

No, it wasn't smooth enough for her to be travelling on water. Her eyes fluttered open, a dull ache thudding in her head along with her heart. Her face felt tight, crusted with ... her own blood, probably.

The skin of her wrists and ankles had been rubbed raw, the ropes they'd bound her with so tight that they cut painfully into her. The earth passed her by in a smudge of green and brown, her stomach churning at the speed of the motion. Horseback – it came to her then; she was on horseback.

Slowly she pulled herself upright, wincing at the pounding in her head and the stiffness of her neck from hanging down beside the horse's shoulder. Arla blinked, making out the two guards either side of her, both dressed in the black uniforms of Elrod's dark army.

Gods, what had *happened*?

It came to her suddenly, with startling clarity, and her spine snapped upright as she remembered what had taken place in the mountains. How she'd agreed to hand herself over if it meant Elin could escape.

Arla didn't even know if Orson had been true to his word...

'Whore's awake,' she heard one of the soldiers grumble, and a dozen heads turned to look at her.

Arla committed every face to memory. It was carved as a promise in her heart that she'd hunt each and every one of them down and drag a blade across their throats.

Her blades...

Gone.

She wore nothing but the nightgown in which she'd fled Flambriar, the flimsy fabric torn and bloodstained as they continued on in a rhythmic trot.

She knew without looking at the bruise of a palace on the horizon where they were headed. She swallowed the fear that reared inside her at the sight of it.

But ... perhaps that was better than the other fear currently strangling her. The fear that was enough to induce panic merely at the thought.

The thought that...

She couldn't feel the bond.

Bile rose in her throat. She couldn't feel the bond.

Where Thara had always lurked in Arla's consciousness, there was now a gaping black hole that stretched so far and so wide that Arla wasn't sure she would ever discover the edges of it. She searched her mind, dug as deeply as she could for some inkling that her dragon was there, that she ... that she was still *alive*.

When not so much as a sentient finger tapped along that pathway in her brain, Arla finally accepted her fate.

She was a prisoner and her dragon was dead.

Orson appearing in front of her was nothing in comparison to that sort of dread.

'Finally awake, I see,' he jeered.

She wished for nothing more than to kill him. She reached for the dragonhart brooch just to see if something would aid her.

That too, of course, was gone.

'I'll fucking kill you,' she seethed, her voice croaky and dry.

Orson laughed – a harsh sound that sent spittle flying. 'I look forward to it.'

He turned his horse away from her then, to face the looming iron gates of Larkire. The party halted just outside, and she looked grimly at the King who stood there with a satisfied grin settling onto his roughened face. He looked older than the last time Arla had seen him, as if the corrupt power he was stealing had found a way to drain every speck of life from him.

She was glad.

Arla was dragged off her horse and forced to her knees in front of the King, her blood already spilling from wounds that had reopened during her harsh handling.

'Welcome back, assassin,' the King said, gloating as he lifted her chin with the toe of his boot. She wanted to snap his ankle. 'I've waited a long time to have you on your knees before me.'

Arla's heart sank like a stone.

The things they could do to her here...

Well, it wasn't worth thinking about. She only prayed Elin had made it to Flambriar in time to warn them.

'Get her out of sight before someone sees her. The last thing we need is an uprising in the name of the bitch.'

Orson dragged her off the floor by her bound wrists, his sour scent washing over her and making her wretch. She could fight. She could kick and scream and attract the attention of those Elrod didn't want knowing his business.

But there must have been a hundred soldiers lining these gates – more than she had ever seen before at Larkire Palace. To fight would mean her death.

She wasn't quite ready for that yet.

And so she bowed her head and yielded. She bowed her head and let Orson lead her, bound and bleeding through the front gates of the palace, beneath a stone archway caressed by the flapping folds of a blood-red banner.

And past a silver dragon chained to the ground.

CHAPTER 49
KASE

Elin galloped into the courtyard at Claret Hall with tear-tracked cheeks and the shaft of an arrow clutched tightly in her left fist. Her other hand shook as she untangled it from the horse's mane, her bottom lip trembling as the court turned towards her.

Kase had known the moment Hark had locked Arla away that the damage he had caused was irreparable. What she hadn't expected, however, was that the words that came from Elin's lips would brand that damage with a scar deep enough to mark Hark's soul forever.

Elin spoke, and the thud of Hark's knees hitting the cobbles was probably the worst sound Kase had ever heard.

They've taken Arla.

Her eyes met Seb's. Then Jaz's. Then Jack's, his chin dipping so slightly she might not have seen it had she not been searching for his strength. Everything would change now: the contentment Kase had felt in the months since coming here would be stripped away; her friends would be stripped away because there was no way they could fight this without allies. They'd be dispersed, separated, spread around.

Maybe they wouldn't survive it. But if there was one thing Kase owed Arla Dragonhart, it was her loyalty. Not for the fact she was gods-blessed – though that had been the final piece of the puzzle to solidify Kase's role at Arla's side – but because her heart was in the right place.

It always had been.

Hyacinth stood beside her, another quieter strength that gave Kase the courage to speak out over the noise of Flambriar's leader breaking into pieces in front of her eyes.

'Gather the soldiers.' Every set of eyes in the courtyard panned to her.

'This is war.'

THANK YOU FOR READING
SHADOWHART

IT WOULD MEAN SO MUCH IF YOU COULD LEAVE A REVIEW ON ALL YOUR PREFERRED PLATFORMS AND SOCIAL MEDIA TO HELP SPREAD THE WORD!

YOU CAN ALSO FOLLOW ME ON INSTAGRAM @ABBIEEATONAUTHOR OR TIKTOK @ABBIEEATON FOR ALL THE UPDATES ON MY LATEST WORKS.

DON'T MISS THE EPIC CONCLUSION TO THE DRAGONHART SERIES

COMING WINTER 2026
PRE-ORDER TODAY IN PAPERBACK, EBOOK & AUDIO!

ACKNOWLEDGMENTS

How am I possibly writing another set of acknowledgements? It truly feels like yesterday that *Dragonhart* was released, and I finally got to introduce the world to Arla and Hark after holding them hostage in my brain for so long. *Shadowhart* was a joy to write, but important, too, in showing the selfish, *wild* parts of a girl who desperately wants to be loved. Arla is not a representation of me, though some might disagree, but her struggles *are* relatable, especially when navigating the unknown.

One thing is certain though, this never gets old, and I am eternally grateful to the team who makes this all possible.

Firstly, the biggest THANK YOU to my readers! You guys are the reason I get to keep writing, and you put the biggest smile on my face when I see your posts on social media and the messages you send my way. I hope you enjoy this one too!

To my wonderful agent, Vicki, and the team at High Spot Lit, you're the best, my biggest cheerleaders; I'm so thankful to have such a supportive team in my corner.

To my incredible editor, Jennie Rothwell, thank you for the endless enthusiasm for Arla and Hark. *Shadowhart* would not be the book it is without you. And of course, a huge thank you to Charlotte Ledger and the team at OMC. It takes a village, and you guys make all of my publishing dreams happen – from social media to everything that goes on behind the scenes, I'm constantly in awe of your love and care for my characters. Thank you.

Thank you to my family and my in-laws for always being so excited about anything I get up to publishing-wise – particularly my parents who tell everybody they come across about the book and often have a stack for me to sign for their friends – it never gets old.

To Mick and Linda, who make sure my ponies are in the best of hands when I'm away doing bookish things and are there when I need anything, actually. Thank you endlessly.

Holly, Alicia, Rhiannon – I'm blessed to have the best friends a girl could wish for, thank you for always listening to the endless bookish things I have to say.

To Caitlin, Helen, Sophia, Emily, you make writing a little less solitary, and I am forever thankful to have found the best author friends in the world.

Thank you to Derby Book Festival for making me feel so welcome at my first ever event last year, in particular Scarlett, and Antonia Hodgson, I'm so glad it was both of you I got to sit in-between.

A huge thank you to the booksellers, book bloggers, TikTokers and bookstagrammers! Your enthusiasm and dedication are wonderful, and I am grateful every day for your help in getting books into the hands of readers.

Finally, to my husband, Harry. Thank you for listening to me throw ideas into the ether, for making dinner every night no matter if I'm writing dragons or reading about them. For encouraging every goal I have, no matter how impossible. You remind me every day that I can do anything.

The author and One More Chapter would like to thank everyone who contributed to the publication of this story...

Analytics
Imogen Wolstencroft

Audio
Fionnuala Barrett
Ciara Briggs

Design
Lucy Bennett
Fiona Greenway
Liane Payne
Dean Russell

Digital Sales
Laura Daley
Lydia Grainge
Hannah Lismore

eCommerce
Laura Carpenter
Madeline ODonovan
Charlotte Stevens
Christina Storey
Rachel Ward

Editorial
Rosie Best
Kara Daniel
Charlotte Ledger
Lydia Mason
Jennie Rothwell
Hana Rowlands
Sofia Salazar Studer
Caroline Scott-Bowden
Helen Williams

Harper360
Emily Gerbner
Ariana Juarez
Jean Marie Kelly
Kamrun Nesa
emma sullivan
Sophia Wilhelm

International Sales
Ruth Burrow
Bethan Moore
Colleen Simpson

Inventory
Sarah Callaghan
Kirsty Norman

Marketing & Publicity
Occy Carr
Chloe Cummings
Grace Edwards
Katie Sadler

Operations
Melissa Okusanya
Vanessa Coubrough

Production
Denis Manson
Simon Moore
Francesca Tuzzeo

Rights
Ashton Mucha
Alisah Saghir
Zoe Shine
Aisling Smyth

Trade Marketing
Ben Hurd
Eleanor Slater

The HarperCollins Contracts Team

The HarperCollins Distribution Team

The HarperCollins Finance & Royalties Team

The HarperCollins Legal Team

The HarperCollins Technology Team

UK Sales
Isabel Coburn
Jay Cochrane
Leah Woods

And every other essential link in the chain from delivery drivers to booksellers to librarians and beyond!

One More Chapter is an award-winning global division of HarperCollins.

Subscribe to our newsletter to get our latest eBook deals and stay up to date with all our new releases!

signup.harpercollins.co.uk/join/signup-omc

Meet the team at
www.onemorechapter.com

Follow us!

@onemorechapterhc

Do you write unputdownable fiction?
We love to hear from new voices.
Find out how to submit your novel at
www.onemorechapter.com/submissions